"As a former player in the pressure cooker of big-time college basketball, I congratulate Roy Parker for alerting us in his dramatic book to what could happen if we do not maintain strict supervision and control over college sports and those who play them and run them."
—CONGRESSMAN TOM McMILLEN
Former All-American,
Rhodes Scholar and
NBA Star

THE FINAL FOUR
Roy H. Parker

BART BOOKS
New York, New York

Published by:
Bart Books
155 E. 34th Street
New York, New York 10016

Publisher's Note

Revised, updated, and enlarged from the original hardback version published November 1981 by Baranski Publishing Corporation, Topeka, Kansas.

A Bart Book/published by arrangement with Faction Books

Cover design by Christine S. Meiss

ISBN: 1-55785-022-4

First Bart Books edition: March, 1988

Library of Congress Catalog Card Number: 87-082101

MANUFACTURED IN THE UNITED STATES OF AMERICA

DEDICATION

For my wife, Libby. Neither words nor this dedication can ever express how much you mean to me.

Who thinketh to buy villainy with gold,
shall ever find such faith so bought—so sold.

Shakespeare

* One *

Troy Burton stared at the craggy-faced man seated next to him in the back of the white Cadillac limousine. He couldn't believe what he'd just heard. "Let me get this straight, Mr. Dolci. You want me to *fix* the NCAA championship game?"

"That's right, Mr. Burton. And," Dolci said as he paused to lift a cordovan leather briefcase from the floor, "I'll pay you half now."

Troy watched the short, rotund man place the briefcase between them on the navy blue seat. Like the shock that occurs after a serious accident, the entire scene seemed surreal to him.

"Go ahead, open it," Dolci said.

Troy looked at the briefcase, then at Dolci. Dolci nodded; a slight smile inched across his face.

Suddenly it dawned on Troy. This must be a well-played practical joke. Lee's assistant coaches—they would do something like this. Should he bite or should he end it here? He decided not to play the game.

"Who put you up to this?" Troy asked.

"What?"

"I think I know. Those bastards have gone too far this time. I don't think something like this is funny, Mr. Dolci, or whoever you are." Troy looked forward toward the rear-view mirror and searched the driver's eyes for a hint of bad acting. The driver's expression revealed nothing. "And your driver can head back to the gym now. I've got a lot of work to do. I don't have time to play along with practical jokes. Where's the tape recorder?" Troy asked as he looked around. "They'd just love to hear how big a fool I made of myself."

Dolci smiled as he clicked open the two gold spring locks on the briefcase and lifted the lid. "I don't joke."

Troy looked inside the briefcase: stacks of $100 bills.

Christ!

"Count it," Dolci said.

Stunned, Troy sat immobilized. He tried to regain his composure. Was it real? He picked up one of the stacks, removed the rubber band, and held one of the bills to the window.

"It's very real. Check the serial numbers—they're all different."

As Troy felt the car begin to slow for a stop light, he picked up another stack of bills and thumbed through them.

"It's all there, all $50,000. Count it when you get home."

Collecting his thoughts, Troy put the stack he was holding back in the briefcase. "What makes you think I can fix the championship game? I'm a fund raiser. I'm not a coach or a player. Anyway, we've got to win two more games before we even get to the Final Four."

Dolci reached into the coat pocket of his dark gray suit and pulled out a long black cigar wrapped in gold trimmed cellophane. He removed the wrapper. "I believe your team's gonna make it to the championship game. And I also believe," Dolci said, pausing as he removed a gold lighter from his shirt pocket, "that you're in the best position to set up the fix."

"Why?"

"Because you and Collins are friends, and he's the only player we need to get to."

Troy folded his arms across his chest. "Friends? We play chess together, but I wouldn't say we're best friends or anything like that. It really doesn't matter how well I know him. Ted Collins isn't going to shave points for money in the national basketball championships. He's not that kind of kid."

Dolci lit his cigar. "Oh, I think you underestimate money, Mr. Burton."

Troy smelled the acrid smoke. He hated cigars. "Why would Ted Collins agree to fix a game and risk blowing his chances of being a first-round pro draft choice? Hell, he's gonna make millions if he keeps playing like he is. Why risk a career by screwing up in the championship game?

He'll get a huge bonus just to sign."

Dolci puffed out a large gray cloud of smoke. "A quarter of a million. Cash. No questions. No IRS. And he'll still get to play pro ball. He can play his ass off in the first half, maybe even play five or ten minutes of the second half. Depends on the score. Then all he has to do is fake a pulled muscle—hamstring or something like that. Happens to the best of 'em. The pros will want him. They'll want him bad. He's already a hero. Just think what he'll be by the time he carries the Hornets to the championship game—a goddamned household name."

Troy stared at Dolci, then turned and looked out the window. He didn't recognize the neighborhood they were traveling through. He looked back at Dolci. "You make it sound easy. But it's not. Winning that game, especially for an unknown team like us—I mean, Christ, nobody's ever heard of the University of Charlotte Hornets—has got to be the greatest opportunity any of us have ever had. I don't think any amount of money can replace it. What kind of person could do it. Not me. Not TC. It just isn't worth it."

Dolci's face reddened. "How much?"

"What?"

"What's it gonna take? I underestimated you. I thought I'd made you an irresistible offer. Apparently not. So, what's it gonna be? My next offer is my last. Don't refuse it."

Dolci's tone chilled Troy. "Look, you've got it all wrong—"

"No you've got it wrong, Burton. I'm not playing games. I made you an offer and you refused. That's a mistake. I was led to believe you were smarter. Apparently, my information was wrong."

Troy was frightened. He tried not to show it. Who had given Dolci information? And why? He had to stall. "Look, I don't know who told you about me or what he said, but you kind of caught me off guard. I didn't mean to offend you. It's just that, well, I graduated from this school. We have the opportunity to really make a name for ourselves. I'm sure you can understand that something like this is not easy."

Dolci leaned back against the seat and looked forward.
"That's why I offered you $100,000. Burton, how much do
you make a year? $30,000, maybe $35,000 at best, right?"

Troy just stared at him.

"If you're lucky, you're taking home $25,000 a year after
taxes. It would take you four years to clear $100,000. A
deal like this is a no-brainer. You can't lose."

Troy was silent for a few moments; then he smiled. He
wanted Dolci to believe every word he was about to say.
"You're right. I'd have to be crazy to turn down your offer.
But look, before I take your money, doesn't it make sense
that we should wait 'till we win the East Regional?"

Dolci stabbed his cigar out in the ashtray and turned to
Troy. "Your team's going to make it to the Final Four, and—"

"But what if they don't?" Troy interrupted.

Dolci paused, then rubbed his chin with his right hand.
"Keep the $50,000. We'll do business another time."

Troy looked at the briefcase. Why was Dolci insisting
that he take the money now? Being under Dolci's thumb
for the rest of his life would be hell. He decided to lie. "Look,
this may be my last year at the university. I've been thinking
about making a change. If I do, I'd have nothing to offer
you in the future."

Dolci rested his left elbow on the armrest and tapped his
hand lightly on his left leg while he contemplated what had
been said. He breathed a quick deep breath through his
nose, exhaled, then put his hand on the briefcase and said,
"OK. I'll keep it.

But when the East Regional is over and your team wins,
the deal is on. I suggest you start thinking about how you're
going to handle this with Collins when things heat up. He's
going to be a lot less accessible than he is now. Anthony,"
Dolci said as he looked forward toward the driver, "take us
back to the gym."

Troy wondered where he should go first: the police or
Coach Lee? He'd discuss it with Jenny as soon as he got
home.

Dolci smiled. "A word of caution, Mr. Burton. Don't do
something stupid. I'll guarantee this conversation never

took place. More importantly, if you try something dumb, you'll be looking over your shoulder for the rest of your life, which I assure you will not be a full one.

"If you're smart, and I think you are, you'll take advantage of my offer."

Troy could no longer hold Dolci's stare. He looked away.

* Two *

On the third floor of the Hornets' gym, Troy Burton stopped
at the door that led into the athletic department offices.
He peeked through the floor-length glass window next to
the door to see if any ticket seekers were waiting for him.
He was in no mood to talk. He could think of nothing except
the proposition. And the more he thought about it, the
angrier he got.

He saw Janet Hopson, who doubled as his secretary and
the athletic department receptionist, seated at her desk.
The waiting room that led to each staff member's office
was empty. Gold and black tones predominated and gave
one little doubt about the school colors.

Troy walked in. Except for the sound of a radio playing
easy listening music, the office was quiet. Everybody—the
team, coaches, the assistant athletic director and the sports
information director—had left for Greensboro early that
morning. Troy and Janet remained behind to keep the office
open. He was scheduled to drive to Greensboro tomorrow
afternoon.

Troy bluffed a smile as he passed Janet's desk. "Hi,
Janet—would you hold all my calls, please."

"OK. How was lunch? Is Mr. Dolci going to be our first
sugar daddy?" she asked, using the name fund raisers give
to wealthy donors inclined to donate huge sums to support
a program.

"I'm not sure," Troy said over his shoulder as he unlocked
his office door. He wished he hadn't told her about Dolci's
initial reason for a meeting. Why did he even mention his
name?

"You forgot your messages."

He walked back and took a handful of yellow slips from
her. "Anything important?" he asked.

"No, just more requests for tickets to the regional finals.
I told them we sold out of our allotment yesterday. Guess

they didn't read the paper this morning."

Troy stepped back toward his office, turned and looked at Janet. "Try not to take any more messages. Tell 'em I'm on my way to Greensboro. If we win Thursday and if they're willing to take a chance, they can drive up to Greensboro for the finals on Saturday. The NCAA said a lot of fans from the two losing schools will likely sell their tickets. Besides, I've never heard of any sporting event where people didn't try to scalp tickets outside the gate."

Troy shut the door. As he sat down, he wondered if he should call Jenny at home. He decided to wait. Better to tell her in person. He leafed through the stack of messages, put them in priority order—board members and big donors first—then began dialing. Thoughts about how to handle Dolci would have to be ignored until he got home.

Twilight slowly faded the light-blue Carolina sky as Troy drove home. It was almost dark when he pulled into the driveway of their gray and white clapboard home. He stepped out of his car and smelled the light scent of wood smoke drifting in the crisp March night air. Home fires burning. Spring would soon douse the neighborhood with a new aroma of backyard barbeque, grass clippings and sweet-scented hyacinths, lilacs, daffodils, and breath of spring.

As he walked up the steps to the back door, he wondered how Jenny would take the news. She had been so happy since he'd gone to work for the university. Happy because for the first time in their thirteen years of marriage, he loved his job. Happy because she was now also a part of the university.

Last year she quit her secretarial job to attend his alma mater and work toward a degree in education. He knew Jenny would make a great grammar school teacher. She loved children. And perhaps her students could somehow substitute for the children she could never have.

"Jenny, I'm home," Troy called out as he stepped into the kitchen through the side door. He heard footsteps upstairs, then the jingling sound of dog tags and two muffled barks.

By the time he entered the hall, he saw Drop, their chocolate-brown toy poodle, running toward him. He held out his arms. Drop barked once and leaped straight at him. He caught her in midair, nearly four feet off the ground.

"That was an eight, Drop. Need to work on that takeoff just a bit." Troy grinned as he cradled her in his arms against his chest. He felt Drop's moist tongue lick his neck, then heard Jenny's light footsteps padding down the carpeted stairs.

Jenny bounced around the corner with a bright smile. Her curly auburn hair danced lightly around her face. She looked like a pixie in blue jeans. She kissed him on the lips. "How was your day?"

Gathering his thoughts, he put Drop down. "Let's have a drink and I'll tell you all about it."

"That bad, eh? I thought you were expecting a big day. What happened?" She put her arm around his waist as they walked toward the kitchen.

"You're not gonna believe this. I'm still having trouble believing it myself." He reached under the bar counter that separated the kitchen from the breakfast room for the gin and dry vermouth.

Jenny stopped smiling and sat on an oak-wood bar stool across from him. "Has a player been hurt?"

Standing across from her, Troy leaned forward, placed his hands on the counter. "It's worse. Do you remember that I told you about a man named Frank Dolci who called me and said that he had a lot of money to give away?"

Jenny nodded slowly.

"Well, he didn't mean to the school. He meant to me." Her eyes widened. "You?"

"Right. He wants me to help fix the championship game."

"Fix? You mean—"

"Throw the game. Lose on purpose." Troy stopped leaning on the counter and paced as he recounted the two-hour luncheon in detail. When he had finished, he walked around the bar and sat on the stool beside her. He tossed down the remainder of his double martini and placed the glass down hard on the butcher-block counter.

Jenny stared at him, her eyes fixed, glassy, like those of a rabbit caught in the headlights of an oncoming car.

She reached up and placed her left hand gently on his shoulder. "What are we going to do?" Her tone was soft, supportive.

"I really don't know what to do. The only thing I can think of is that I can't accept."

She nodded.

"My immediate reaction is to go to the police, but just think what that's going to do. The cops could really mess things up, especially if this guy is . . . is . . . in organized crime," Troy said, stopping short of using the word *Mafia*—a weak attempt, to lessen the fear she would feel in hearing that word.

"Do you think he is?"

"Possibly. But it just doesn't make sense. The mob in Charlotte, North Carolina?"

"Does he live here?"

"I don't know. I didn't ask. I've never heard his name mentioned as a big money prospect at any of our board meetings. If he lives here, he keeps a very low profile."

"What about the FBI?"

"I've thought of that. They'd certainly be better than the cops. But no matter what I do, Coach Lee needs to know first. He shouldn't get blind-sided. Just think what will happen if the press gets wind of this. A story like this would be all over the national news. It'd be a three ring circus. And it's just my word against Dolci's."

"Troy, you're not thinking—"

"About going to the press?" he said, finishing the question for her. "The thought had crossed my mind. But that'd be pretty dumb. No, we've got to beat this guy at his own game."

He watched Jenny swivel from side to side on her bar stool, her legs barely touching the foot support. Thinking. Searching. Looking for an answer. Silence. Then the muffled whir of the refrigerator fan and faint hum of the compressor. She looked up at him and said, "Dolci will probably be wrong, won't he? We won't win the regional. We won't make it to the Final Four—will we?"

Troy rested his left elbow on the counter, leaned forward and propped his chin lightly between his thumb and first finger. "Until today, I figured we had a chance, a slim one at that, but a chance. We're on a roll and we're likely to be underestimated.

But he was so confident, I can't help believe that he may be right."

A light seemed to come on in Jenny's eyes. Her voice rose excitedly. "You don't suppose he's fixed it so we'll definitely win?"

"That crossed my mind, but I don't see how it'd be possible. All three of the schools in the regional with us are big time. I can't imagine him getting to players on any one of those teams.

"Think about it. Syracuse? Virginia? Indiana? Not hardly. They've been knocking around the Top 20 too long. They've got history, tradition, and coaches with solid records. And they've got deep benches and really no one dominant player. No franchises, not like Ted Collins. Dolci would have to bribe several players on each team.

"In fact, when you think about it, we're the only team in the East Regional that has a definite first-round draft choice. The press hasn't recognized that yet, but Coach Lee is positive of it. And I'm convinced he's right. If we win these next two games, Collins will get all the recognition he needs to be a first-round NBA draft choice. Dolci believes we're gonna win because of Collins."

Jenny placed her hand on his right thigh. "But why would Dolci come to you now? And why you? Why not go straight to Ted Collins?"

"I know. I'm having trouble with that, too. In one sense, he's trying to insulate himself. If Ted rejects the offer, then Dolci's protected. I'd be the guy on the hook if Ted said anything. But by going through me, not only is he spending more money, he's adding one more person into the mix." Troy shook his head, then added, "I don't know. The big question is where did he get my name? Who gave it to him? Remember that I told you he said something about being led to believe I was smarter? Somebody told him I was the kind of guy that would take a bribe. He was surprised when I didn't jump at the chance."

Jenny frowned for a moment, then her eyes brightened. "So it must be somebody who doesn't know you very well."

Troy swiveled his bar stool toward Jenny, put his right hand on Jenny's left knee, and looked in her eyes. "You're probably right. Needless to say, we've got to be very careful. And until I've discussed this with Coach Lee, I don't want to go to the police or to the FBI. And if we lose either of the next two games, it'll all be over. He can't use me to fix a game we're not playing in, can he?"

She smiled. "It's strange. I never thought I'd feel like I wanted us to lose."

He squeezed her thigh gently. "Well, don't start feeling that way. If we win, I'll go to Coach Lee. We'll find a way to beat this guy, and—"

Drop interrupted him with a short, snappy bark.

They looked down at the kitchen floor where Drop sat with a blue rubber ball in front of her paws.

Jenny got off the stool. "Looks like your little girl wants some attention."

Troy watched her bend over and pick up the ball, her well-rounded rear end tightly wrapped in blue jeans. He saw the outline of her crotch and it stirred him.

Jenny stood up, turned, and handed him the ball. "Go play with Drop while I fix dinner."

He held the ball in his right hand. It was slightly moist with Drop's saliva. As Jenny turned, he moved off the chair and wrapped his arms around her from behind, crossed them across her chest. Fully a foot taller, he seemed to engulf her body with his athletic frame. "I'd rather play with you."

"I had a feeling."

Troy leaned down and began gently kissing her on the nape of her neck. He knew why she'd anticipated his overture. Sex was not only a deeply passionate, unabashed act for them in good times, but was also their salve, a balm that eased tension whenever problems arose.

Jenny wrapped her arms around his and leaned back

against him, her bottom pressed firmly against the top of his thighs and his lower pelvis. "Let's go upstairs."

He tossed the ball from his hand. It bounced toward the corner of the breakfast room. Troy noticed the fluffy toy poodle's reaction out of the corner of his eyes. Drop didn't move. She merely sat, looking up at them with doleful eyes.

After dinner and numerous phone calls from Hornet club members, friends and fans, Troy took the phone off the hook at 10 p.m. to halt any further calls. He stared at the television, but paid no attention to the program that was on. He could not get the bribe off his mind.

When they slipped into bed again, he turned off the light and stared at the ceiling. Sleep came fitfully; he dreamed about being pushed into a well by two men holding guns. Awakened by the sheer terror of his fall down the dark abyss, he sat straight up in the bed. Heart pounding, he looked around and noticed the bathroom light was on. He could hear sounds, the movement of bottles tinkling together in the medicine cabinet.

He rolled out of bed and walked stark naked to the bathroom. "Is something wrong?" he asked as he peeked through the door.

She jumped slightly, nearly spilling the milky pink contents in a teaspoon she held out before her. "You startled me."

"You sick?"

She put the teaspoon to her mouth and swallowed the medicine. "A little nauseous."

"Anything I can do?"

"No, I'll be all right. Go back to bed."

"What time is it?"

"Four o'clock."

Troy looked at her. She looked pale. "Sure you're OK?" She nodded.

He turned and went back to bed. Not because he believed her; he could always tell when she was lying. But she was obviously trying to spare him the additional burden of worrying about her at four in the morning.

She flicked off the bathroom light and slipped into bed beside him. He wondered if they would win tomorrow.

* Three *

Troy Burton watched the final play. The partisan crowd surrounding him in the stands took a collective breath and began to count down in unison, "TEN! NINE! EIGHT! SEVEN! SIX! FIVE! FOUR! . . ."

On the court, Ted "TC" Collins dribbled quickly past a defender on the right baseline and vaulted toward the basket. As he reached the apex of his jump, he crushed the ball through the hoop as though he were stuffing a pillow into a cannon.

The multitude's roar drowned the sound of the final buzzer, but the red lights behind the basket told the story. Jubilant fans poured onto the court and swarmed around the victors. The public address announcer could barely be heard above the din.

"THE FINAL SCORE—THE UNIVERSITY OF CHARLOTTE 95, INDIANA 88. THE MANAGEMENT OF THE GREENSBORO COLISEUM COMPLEX WISHES TO REMIND ALL FANS TO PLEASE DRIVE CAREFULLY."

Troy could not believe it. The upstart Hornets had just defeated the number-one-ranked team in the nation. Champions of the East Regional, they were on their way to the NCAA championships at the Superdome in New Orleans. They were in the elite Final Four. The victory was clearly bittersweet. Now the bribe was on.

He checked for his press pass. As soon as Coach Lee finished the press conference, he would pull him off to the side and tell him they had to talk immediately.

Numerous Hornet fans stood around him congratulating themselves. Several slapped him on the back as they watched the players hoist each other on their shoulders at the front of the goal to cut the net down. The CBS cameras focused on the ritual. Seated in section D of the courtside seats, no more than sixty feet from the south end goal, Troy had a clear view. His thoughts smudged the revelry.

"Troy, we did it! We beat those Big Ten snobs. Number one, my ass. They can take their schedule and shove it. By God we won't schedule any of 'em, even if they beg us."

Troy smiled at Frank Jeffers, the president of the small, boisterous Stinger club, a working group of alumni and avid fans who assisted the University of Charlotte Athletic Foundation in fund raising projects and events.

Another man jovially slapped Troy on the back. He looked familiar, but Troy did not know his name. That was a fairly common occurrence. Troy was the first executive director for the Hornets. Now in his second year at the fund-raising controls, he was blessed with a winner and cursed by a schemer. That clouded his ability to put names, faces and checks together.

He missed Jenny badly. She had not even made it to Greensboro for their semi-final game against Syracuse two days ago and was still at home. Her illness had struck hard. He hoped she was beginning to recover. When he had called her at halftime, she sounded somewhat better.

It all seemed like a blur now. On Thursday the Hornets had taken Syracuse apart in the first game of the East Regional semi-finals. They defeated the sixth-ranked Orangemen by 16 points, 96-80. Many analysts thought it was a fluke. Although the margin surprised Troy, the victory had not.

Walking up the stairs toward the exit sign and passing through the royal blue curtains out into the lobby, Troy turned right, the direction of the press conference area. The aroma of fresh popcorn filled the air as he walked past a concession stand. Fans were filing out of the Coliseum and the lobby was crowded.

Last-minute souvenir hunters gathered around a booth, snapping up Charlotte, Indiana, Virginia, and Syracuse T-shirts, hats, buttons, and pennants. He threaded his way through the crowd.

"Troy."

Feeling a hand tug on his shoulder, he turned and quickly recognized the large gray-haired form of John Windsor, the president of the Athletic Foundation. "John, I looked for you at halftime. Couldn't find you."

"I was wandering around in shock." Windsor smiled through clenched teeth that tightly gripped a meerschaum pipe.

"So was I. A twelve-point lead was a bit unbelievable, even for me. But ye have little faith. Told you we'd whip them." Actually, Troy had not believed his own prediction, but a positive image was the key to his success. He admired the man who had been chosen to lead the Board of Directors.

"I think our money worries are over," Windsor said.

Troy doubted John Windsor had ever been worried. As the president of the Athletic Foundation Board of Directors, Windsor knew the goal was one he could convince the board members was easily attainable—a paltry $250,000, meager compared to the $2 million Windsor had helped raise two years ago for his alma mater, Wake Forest.

Troy had watched Windsor move smoothly through Charlotte's blue-blooded circles. As chief executive officer of First National Bank, the second largest bank in Charlotte, he commanded respect.

"Yeah, we shouldn't have any trouble loosening up their purse strings when they start begging for tickets to the championships," Troy said. He never worried about strategy when he talked to Windsor. The banker knew all the tricks and then some.

"If the Tar Heels beat Texas tomorrow, half of Charlotte is going to be pounding on your door, and mine too," Windsor said.

Troy enjoyed the reprieve, but he needed to cut the conversation short. The CBS announcers finished their live post-game interview; Coach Lee would be on his way to the press room.

Troy glanced at his watch, then grinned. "It'll be interesting, all right. I'll call you Monday. You probably won't be able to get through on our lines."

The two men shook hands as the crowd snaked around them. Before Troy turned away, Windsor stopped him with a question. "Where's Jenny?"

"Home, sick."

"Nothing serious, I hope."

Troy knew Windsor was not playing the"I'm acting like I'm truly concerned, but I'm really not" game. "She's got some kind of stomach virus. I had to beat her over the head to keep her in bed. Even then she wouldn't listen until the doctor told her she was confined to quarters. Thank God for television or she would have been here for sure."

"Give her my best. I want to see her in New Orleans."

Troy nodded, turned down one flight of stairs, and stood on the playing floor level facing the south end goal. A fervent Hornet crowd gathered around Brent Musburger as he interviewed Coach Bill Lee and Ted Collins.

To Troy's left stood two Greensboro policemen checking credentials of those entering the dressing room and press areas. He presented his pass and stepped through the curtains. The conference room was located deep in the lower bowels of the arena. It was a simple, makeshift, curtained space set up during tournament events. Two more police-men guarded its entrance. The spicy scent of hot pastrami mingled with the aroma of freshly brewed coffee. Fuel for the press.

People were still coming in and out. Apparently Indiana's coach, Bobby Knight, had not yet arrived. Troy didn't blame him. The area wolves, many loyal to the Atlantic Coast Conference, would chew hard on the mighty Big Ten coach who had allowed the unknowns from Charlotte to trample on Indiana's masterdom. The loss wasn't Knight's fault. The Hornets had blistered the nets with 62-percent shoot-ing from the floor, including 51 percent from three-point territory and an incredible 92 percent from the charity stripe.

Troy decided to go in and pick a good seat. He wanted to catch Coach Lee as quickly after the press conference as possible.

"Excuse me, sir. May I see your press pass?" The burly policeman spoke with authority at the curtained entrance.

Troy was irritated by the repetitive check, even though

he understood different types of area passes existed. A member of the team's official party, he produced his pass marked NCAA EAST REGIONAL CHAMPIONSHIPS/ WORKING PRESS. Such members were often given credentials to enter virtually any part of the arena.

"Come with me," the officer demanded after looking Troy over carefully.

"What's the problem?"

"There's someone outside who insists he must see you immediately," the burly officer said, directing him away from the press room.

"Who?"

"A Mr. Giannini. He says it's urgent."

Troy tried not to look shocked. Why did they want to see him now? What was so damn urgent? He couldn't resist; otherwise, they'd know he planned to refuse Dolci's offer.

"Where is he?" Troy asked.

"At the loading door back here." The officer began walking toward the rear entrance.

Troy followed.

"Open the elephant door," the burly cop said to another cop standing near the door.

Troy watched as the immense overhead door—aptly named by rowdies who year after year watched circus elephants herded in and out for each performance—began clanking upward. Blasts of cold air streamed through. Dolci's white stretch Cadillac limousine was parked at the crest of the concrete ramp that ran down to the backstage entrance. The waning daylight revealed a driver and one companion seated in the front. The March wind tousled Troy's light brown hair.

He looked at both policemen, who seemed pleased with themselves for finding him. If only he could tell them what Dolci was really all about. Hell, they probably wouldn't believe him. They'd think he was crazy. They said nothing as the Cadillac backed to where they were standing.

The driver remained in the car while another man stepped out from the passenger's side. Troy recognized him immediately. He was the same man who had driven them around while Dolci made his pitch.

"Thank you for finding him for us, gentlemen," Giannini said, smiling. "We appreciate your help."

The policemen walked away. Staring at Giannini's rugged face, Troy's perception changed instantly, like looking at a painting a second time, suddenly realizing what the artist intended. The tall, heavyset man was not the cheap hoodlum he had judged him to be.

Smiling coldly at Burton, Giannini seemed to be reading his mind. For both it was an instant in which complete understanding comes without utterance.

"Step in Mr. Burton, won't you?" It was more a command than an invitation. "Mr. Dolci would like to see you."

"What's so urgent?"

Giannini answered in a clipped, but polite tone. "I don't ask questions. Mr. Dolci said he wanted to see you right away."

Troy stepped into the plush back seat as a gust of wind swirled dust and debris through the opening. Giannini sat up front with the driver, a tall, black-headed man wearing a light-gray wool suit.

Neither man made an attempt at conversation. The car pulled forward out of the access ramp. Troy turned to see the huge door closing as they pulled into a line of traffic departing from the south end of the Coliseum. Moving slowly in the direction of Patterson Street, he felt relieved that he had not been able to execute his plan. Coach Lee still knew nothing, and for the moment, that was probably best.

Troy was in control, but hardly relaxed. The silence of three adults departing from the spectacle reminded him of the losers exiting in like fashion. As daylight quickly faded, headlights of other cars streaming away from the coliseum began appearing like fireflies. They winked on dimly, then grew stronger as darkness descended.

Sensing no immediate danger, Troy was curious as to their destination. He was sure he hadn't given Dolci a reason to mistrust him, unless Dolci read minds.

One thing was certain: he had misjudged Dolci. He had

power. Power far beyond what Troy had ever comprehended. Dolci represented a criminal element that existed in another world, one only talked about, written about or depicted on screen. But North Carolina was one of the last places he ever expected to encounter it.

Troy had regained his composure after the initial surprise of the abrupt invitation. The twinge of fear came from the unknown. Fear, he knew, was good as long as one could deal with it. It kept you from being careless. He had discovered that as a helicopter pilot in Vietnam.

That's where he learned to control his fear. And fear—fear of death—was Dolci's only true weapon. But Troy had faced death many times. It had surrounded him, engulfed him, pushed him into acceptance of its inevitability.

He could always choose death. Freedom—no matter how seemingly limited—was always his.

The vehicle turned south down Interstate 85.

* Four *

Emotionally high, Coach Bill Lee stood on the court beside Brent Musburger in front of the CBS camera. Coach Lee looked dapper in his three-piece gray suit, black and gold tie, and matching handkerchief. Millions were watching the Charlotte coach for the first time. He clutched the net the team had just cut down. Hornet fans clamored around the scene.

Musburger received his verbal cue as the camera's red light blinked on. "Coach Lee, you've been coaching seventeen years and this is your first Division I, post-season tournament. Now, you're on your way to the Final Four. This had to be a great win for you." He tilted the microphone toward Coach Lee.

"It certainly is. We played a great team. To beat the number-one team is something I would have never dreamed possible at the beginning of the season."

Fans pushed in and around them. Many were holding up one finger and whooping, "WE'RE NUMBER ONE! WE'RE NUMBER ONE!" Lee barely heard the next question, but he had anticipated it. After seventeen years he was seldom surprised.

"Your team came out ready to play. They looked surprisingly confident. How'd you prepare them so well?"

"We knew we'd have to contain their big man, Fredricson. Anytime you go against a seven-footer as strong as he is, you have some sleepless nights. We went with a box-and-one and shifted to a collapsing man-to-man as often as we could to keep them off balance. We double-teamed and tried to force their guards to turn the ball over when they tried to penetrate inside and dish-off. Collins did a great job on him in our man-to-man." He knew he'd just baffled half of his audience. The game had some great buzz words.

Any coach in the country worth his salt would have attempted to execute the same plan, Lee thought. But fans believed coaches were magicians when they won and that made his profession a dangerous one. Without the horses you couldn't win. It was that simple. He thanked God for the fine recruiting of his predecessor.

"Were you surprised by your team's first-half performance?"

Shocked was a better word, Lee thought. Brent was being kind. "No, we knew if we played our game we could give them a tough time. We needed that twelve-point lead. Indiana's a second-half team. They pushed us hard with their full-court press. Ted did a great job of getting the ball up the court." Lee smiled. He dreamed up the surprise tactic after studying Hoosier game films. It gave the Hornets a slight edge. A center dribbling the ball up the court was unorthodox as hell. But then, so was Ted Collins.

"We commented on that. When Fredricson picked up his fourth foul, he couldn't press Ted. I'm sure you practiced that," Musburger said.

"A few times."

"Coach, you won't know until tonight which team you'll meet in the semi-finals in the Superdome—Notre Dame or Fort Myers. Any predictions or preferences?"

The pushing and shoving intensified around Coach Lee. Avid Hornet fans, mostly students, closed in hoping to get in camera view.

Lee opted for his politician's speech. "We've seen Notre Dame all year. They're big and quick. As for Fort Myers, they've got some great three-point shooters. Either one will be tough. We're just happy to be going."

Musburger heard the director's brief instruction crackle through his headset. "Coach, we're trying to get Ted Collins over for a word. He's been voted the Chevrolet player-of-the-game for the Hornets. Any comments?"

Lee flashed his winning smile. The CBS camera tightened up on him for a close-up. His graying temples contrasted well with his neatly combed black hair.

"Ted played a near-perfect game. I haven't seen the stats yet, but he might have been 65 percent from the floor. And what did he hit from the line—11 for 13 or something like that?" He knew it was exactly like that. He had a computer-like basketball mind, always aware of pertinent team and individual statistics. Other coaches possessed that skill, but his had been finely honed—and many times it paid off.

"Right, he hit for 41 points."

"Five and a half above his average," Lee added. "Remarkable against Fredricson." He seldom used that word, remarkable. Positive adjectives were jewels saved for special occasions.

"Here's Ted," Musburger said, motioning to Collins. The 6'10" center had difficulty getting through the crowd. Fans bustled around him. Musburger moved a few feet to give the slender, ebony figure room to stand between them.

"Ted, what was the turning point of the game for you?" Musburger asked.

When that big son of a bitch stopped leaning on him, Coach Lee thought.

"When Fredricson picked up his fourth foul early in the second half."

Lee watched the tall center answer. Beads of perspiration glistened on Collins' forehead above a handsome angular face. He spoke in a clear bass voice.

"We've heard reports that you might not want to play pro ball. That's a surprise. What are your plans?"

"I want to win the national championships and graduate. After that, I'll consider it, if I've been drafted. Depends on the team that picks me. I want to be sure I can fit into their system."

It sounded like the prologue of a shrewd bargainer, but Coach Lee knew Collins was sincere. True, they had rehearsed his answer, but Collins really didn't know if he wanted to make basketball a career. The constant pounding his thin, wiry body received during the season had made Collins wonder if he could hold together in the land of giants.

Ignoring fans tugging at his shoulders and slapping him on the back, Lee listened intently to TC's answer. Anticipation and careful instruction paid off again. Collins' stock just rose ten points.

Musburger congratulated both men and moved into his

wrap-up. Lee and Collins headed for the dressing room,
signing autographs on their way.

An ugly thought hit Lee hard. It had been pushed back
into the depths of his subconscious. Now it flooded his
mind like a river overflowing its banks. Stepping into the
dressing room jammed with reporters and players, he tried
to focus his attention on the scene at hand. But the levee
burst and pleasant thoughts drowned.

Damn them, he thought. The one great moment he longed
for was marred by their greed. Just a sport, but everything
had gone absolutely crazy years ago when big business
steamrolled its way into college athletics.

A reporter stuck his notebook in Lee's face and began
popping questions rapid-fire.

"Can't you wait a minute?" Lee glared at the eager
journalist. "What do you think the press conference down
there is for?" he asked, pointing. Silence fell over the
dressing room. His voice boomed, gathering strength like
thunder rolling in from the distance. "I'll answer your
questions in there."

All eyes were fixed on Lee. He realized that he had lost
control with the press once again. Those pushy bastards
were always hounding him, looking for that one hot, contro-
versial story. Making no apology, he turned and walked out
the door.

Lee hated to lose his temper. He knew the reporter would
have the last word.

He decided not to read the article and no one would dare
show it to him. He hated *Sports Weekly*.

Sitting naked on a locker room chair, Ted Collins watched
Coach Lee leave the locker room after barking at the
reporter from *Sports Weekly*. Most of the reporters followed
him. Muffled by the noise of running water, several nervous
laughs echoed off the shower walls. Conversation slowly
resumed. A few reporters remained, pen and pad in hand,
writing feverishly as they gathered around Ted.

He promised himself he would never act like his coach.

Instead, he would carefully weigh each question and politely answer even the most sarcastic ones.

A white towel draped over his thighs did little to hide his genitals. Intent on their stories, they had not taken the hint that he needed some privacy.

Collins knew he impressed reporters. He was an unusual young star. In control and relaxed, he exuded the confidence and poise of an NBA veteran. He did his best to demonstrate he was the team leader.

Chuck Haigler, reporter for the *Charlotte Observer*, sat patiently waiting for Bill Lee to arrive at the press conference. Coach Bobby Knight had been gracious in defeat. Haigler had expected him to breathe fire, but Knight said nothing derogatory about his players or the officiating. He would use the quote from Knight: "They just came out and played their game. We knew they were better than the polls indicated and we didn't take them lightly. We were prepared and played well. Collins played a perfect game against Fredricson. Right now I would say Charlotte is definitely going to be tough in New Orleans. Nobody's going to run over them, that's for sure."

It had been a whirlwind season for Haigler. For the first time since the Hornets' budding program began, the *Observer's* sports editor had decided the huge morning daily would send a reporter to every game, home and away. That was a big assignment considering their traditional coverage of all Atlantic Coast Conference games. When compared to any ACC school's schedule, which generally included Big East and Big Ten powerhouses, the Hornets were romping through the land of unknowns.

Only three teams in their schedule, Haigler reflected, were ranked, and two had fallen from grace late in the season. Charlotte lost two of those three and its other loss came at the hands of a complete unknown that used an unexpected blizzard to its advantage. The Hornets froze on that evening after traveling up a Pennsylvania mountain behind a snowplow. An uncharacteristic fight involving

Collins late in the first half sent the star to the showers. Incensed, the Hornets proceeded to throw away the game.

Haigler was sure that defeat was going to crush Charlotte's chances of gaining an independent berth in the NCAA championships. But the Hornets redeemed themselves in the next-to-last regular season game when they thrashed sixteenth-ranked LSU before a sell-out crowd in the Charlotte Coliseum. The win sufficiently impressed Haigler: the Hornets were solid. He had written: "Cinderella might get a shot at the ball. Whether she will meet the prince, much less steal a kiss, remains to be seen."

Haigler remembered sitting in Coach Lee's private office on that fateful Sunday afternoon when the bids to 64 schools went out. Electricity filled the air when Lee's private office phone rang at 2:04 p.m. with the news that the seven-year-old program was blessed with a royal invitation. No one noticed the rain that day as trumpeters heralded the announcement.

Cinderella rode to the ball on a rocket and Charlotte bubbled. Leafless campus trees stood proudly while wearing a snowy coat of toilet paper, a scene repeated each time she demonstrated her graceful moves. The grounds keepers didn't mind the repetitive cleaning as long as she "kept on dancing."

Haigler was the principal observer reporting on Cinderella. She not only kissed the prince, but also slipped into bed assuming the superior position and 55 million people were going to watch! Haigler amused himself with his overworked analogy. Coach Lee was late as usual.

Bill Lee simply did not care for the *Observer's* treatment of his team's march to glory. He complained bitterly that North Carolina's four ACC schools received far too much attention. In speeches at area civic clubs, he had denounced the *Observer's* staff for sports bias. Little wonder, Lee would always add, since five of the newspaper's staff were journalism graduates from the University of North Carolina. How could they be expected to be objective? He often put that question to his audiences. Their hearts were in Chapel Hill, a school founded in 1795. For the most part, the Tar Heels had been a power in college basketball for over forty years. Numerous post-season appearances, eight visits to the Final Four, including one national championship, made the Tar Heels seem—at least to regional residents—as sure as the changing of autumn leaves.

Haigler knew Lee had a legitimate concern. Charlotte had a budding basketball program and the hometown paper had jumped on the bandwagon a bit late. But why in hell did the coach always blast him about it? True, Haigler was a Chapel Hill graduate, but UNC had an excellent school of journalism. That's what made him such a damn good reporter, he reasoned. And by God, if one thing made him bristle, it was questioning his objectivity.

As he looked over the NCAA pairings, the possibility of a true challenge to his objective standards stared him right in the face. The Tar Heels had placed second in the conference, losing only twice to Virginia: once in the regular season and once in the ACC tournament championship. If they could defeat Texas to win the Midwest Regional championship, they would be headed for the Superdome. If both North Carolina teams won their semi-final games in the Final Four, the Hornets—whom the Tar Heels consistently cold-shouldered when scheduling time rolled around—would be waiting on the hardwood like a motorcycle gang for a rumble.

Lee entered the room and answered questions. He controlled the situation with charming style after first apologizing for his tardiness, a result of the TV interview, he explained. The press found his forthright answers witty and magnetic. Even Haigler loved them.

Clearly, Haigler mused, the Charlotte Hornets would be the sentimental favorites at the Final Four, even if Fort Myers made it past Notre Dame. Fort Myers didn't have a star as charismatic as Ted Collins. No doubt about it, if the Hornets won the national championship, they would rock the nation and solidify their place in college basketball history.

* Five *

Special agent Bert Teague sat at his desk gazing out the window on the sixth floor of the Federal building on Loyola Avenue. The Superdome had become a familiar sight to him over the past sixteen and one-half years. He watched construction begin on August 11, 1971. How could he forget that date? At 7:05 p.m. his wife had given birth to their second child, a seven-pound boy named Bradley Kent.

The massive UFO-shaped dome hovered over six hundred and eighty feet of below-sea-level ground, less than two blocks away from his office. His angled view was obscured somewhat by the concave-shaped Hyatt Regency. Its modern, smoked-glass windows and interlocking steel soared thirty-two stories, contrasting geometrically with the concourse-connected dome that frequently emptied its temporary audience for their bleary-eyed return to the plush confines of their rooms.

Teague picked up the file and began reading again. Frank Dolci and Francesco Mancotta had haunted him over the past six and one-half years. Now, with six months left before retirement, he reluctantly prepared to share the file with the young agent who had transferred in from Kansas City two days ago. Teague hated to leave a task unfinished, but retirement was fast approaching. He would be mustered out of the FBI like a battle-fatigued soldier.

He planned to keep the briefing short. Not wanting to miss the game, he wished he had not agreed to the Saturday luncheon. But much work had gone into choosing his replacement. Even the FBI Director had gotten involved. New Orleans was a tough town with widespread political corruption.

Though young, Don Hardin was a good choice, Teague thought. Hardin had distinguished himself in his five short years with the Bureau by meticulously uncovering a huge automobile theft ring that used Kansas City for its interstate clearing house. He spent three years carefully examining the operation, gathering enough evidence to convict thirty-three of the forty involved. More importantly, his evidence gained an eighteen-year sentence for the brains behind the business, Martin Duval, shrewd owner of Duval's Dress Shops in Kansas City.

"Morning, Bert. I'm ready when you are." The heavy mid-western twang fit Hardin's tanned and rugged appearance like a cowboy on a quarter-horse.

"All settled in?" Teague asked.

"Yeah. Haven't got the view you have, but the office is bigger. I need room to spread around." Looking around the small, plain office, Hardin sat down across from Teague.

Teague could imagine what Hardin was thinking. The Bureau was consistent. No frills. Just some paneling and the necessary office furniture. Even the lifeless artificial plants looked the same in all the offices. Hardin was probably sizing up his office. No doubt he'd move in as soon as Teague retired. An office with a view was a sign of status.

Teague decided to get down to business. "I've been over the DOLMAN Project file. It doesn't give a complete picture, not like you're going to need. After spending six years, I know more than I could ever put on paper."

Teague noticed Hardin's scrutiny. He was probably measuring the discouragement written on Teague's face: tired eyes sunk deep below a weathered, gray brow. If Hardin had learned anything from his three years on the Duval case, it would have been that in long investigations, patience ebbed and enthusiasm oozed away.

Hardin shifted in his chair and smiled. "I'm looking forward to working with you. I've got a lot to learn. Heard I couldn't have picked a better teacher." Pearl white teeth complemented his rugged features.

"You wouldn't think so judging this case," Teague said, wondering if his reputation was that well known outside New Orleans or if Hardin was patronizing an old veteran.

"It's tough to get to the top when they're connected," Hardin said, adding, "I was lucky: Duval had no ties."

"Study the file for a few minutes, then let's go to lunch.

Do cowboys like oysters?" Teague asked.

"Don't know about cowboys, but I sure do."

"I have to look over some other files for a few minutes and then we'll go. You'll have a lot more time during the next few weeks to study the project." Teague wanted Hardin to get the picture through insight. A crash course on a file could lead to false impressions.

Just before Teague closed the door, he watched Hardin open the DOLMAN Project file. As he walked down the hall toward the conference room, he began mentally reviewing what Hardin would learn.

The name DOLMAN Project was derived from the first three letters of each man's surname. Dolci and Mancotta were partners in crime and in legitimate business. Both men were of Sicilian descent and born in New York. They had a clear background in *Cosa Nostra* crime. Teague recalled the literal translation as "Our Thing," and the one used more often by insiders, "this thing of ours." Frank Dolci's father was the notorious Vito Coppola. Coppola had capitalized on prohibition and as *capo* or boss of one of five families then reigning in New York. He escaped the brutal mob wars that ruptured peace between the families. As violence intensified in 1931 during the depths of the Depression, Coppola and Carlos Lucchese, Coppola's *subcapo* or underboss, decided to change headquarters. Their move to New Orleans brought an end to the *Black Hand* extortionist rings operating on the waterfront. Without paying protection to the *Black Hand,* no cargo had moved on or off the docks.

Coppola erased the vicious mob in exchange for political favors. With Huey Long in power, officials looked the other way as Coppola moved slot and pin ball machines into the city, later the entire state. The police payoffs, commonly referred to as ice, helped to entrench Coppola and Lucchese.

During that time Coppola saw a bigger future looming on the horizon: drugs. He set the wheels in motion for his legitimate import/export business to front the operation.

His son, Frank Coppola, graduated from Tulane law school and operated the legitimate businesses: three restaurants, a chain of dry cleaners, and the import/export business. Much of their illegal cash was laundered through them. Young Coppola became close friends with Francesco Mancotta, son of Salvatore Mancotta, Coppola's most trusted *caporegime* or lieutenant. Francesco attended Harvard law school and managed to pass despite his partying and lust for the opposite sex. He became an expert in tax evasion and political tampering. He could shift the balance of votes in an entire Louisiana parish.

The bubble burst in 1962 when the *Cosa Nostra* learned that Joseph Petrilli had broken *omerta*, the code of silence that kept members from exposing the organization's inner secrets. Attorney General Robert Kennedy took extraordinary measures to protect Petrilli. The mob had a $100,000 contract out on him, and only unique measures spared his life. He completed his memoirs—eighteen hundred pages—in various high-security prison cells.

Detailing his involvement as a mob soldier from 1920 to 1960, Petrilli's memory proved letter perfect. Through countless cross-examinations his testimony stood fast. Coppola's New York exploits and move to New Orleans were exposed publicly. Since the mob had a battery of brilliant lawyers, the voice of Petrilli was not strong enough for many convictions. At that time, Coppola was in his late sixties and tired of the constant harassment and public humiliation. Hardly able to move without being under surveillance, he returned to Sicily in 1972, where he died peacefully, the mark of a truly successful *capo*.

Before leaving the country, Coppola had arranged for his son, Frank, to change his name. He became Frank Dolci. The move did not fool the FBI or the press. But with proper payoffs to local enforcement agencies and politicians, word circulated that Coppola's son was only taking charge of his father's legitimate businesses, and the name change was his way of distancing himself from his father's illegal activities.

The ploy worked and the pressure eased. With Francesco Mancotta maneuvering politically to assure continued protection, Dolci proceeded to build his empire. As a result,

Dolci offered his counselor an equal partnership. They expanded their territory under the new arrangement.

It was then that the synergistic relationship assumed its present form. Dolci masterminded a multimillion dollar drug-smuggling operation that blossomed during the sixties and seventies. And in the first half of the eighties it exploded with the rise in popularity of cocaine.

The flower children had ushered in the drug revolution in the sixties. Later giving up long hair and protest marches, the drug cultists settled into the middle and upper class mainstream. Their methods of anesthetizing their brains had changed. To many, alcohol was no longer the drug of choice. Marijuana and cocaine were greatly in demand. Doctors, lawyers, businessmen, teachers, white collar workers, blue collar workers, teens and pre-teens were getting high. The percentage of users mushroomed like a nuclear explosion.

A new generation of politicians smoked joints and snorted coke in the confines of their homes, patiently waiting for enough political power to topple the stiff penalties being handed out to users. Organizations surfaced to lobby for repeal of marijuana laws. Several states gave up the fight altogether. The user was no longer in danger of facing felony charges for possession of small amounts. Alaska led the way by legalizing the growing of marijuana for personal use, providing a home-grown remedy for cabin fever.

Frank Dolci capitalized on the government's paraquat-spraying program that began in the seventies. Uncle Sam's efforts in Mexico strengthened the drug business instead of eroding it. When Mexican officials agreed to the multimillion dollar eradication program, Colombian growers boosted the market with their far more potent weed. In the mid to late-seventies, Colombian fields bloomed abundantly. Later, in the early eighties when the drug of choice became cocaine, Dolci shifted with the tide. The government had made it much more difficult to ship the huge bulk that marijuana required.

To meet market demand, the mob bosses poured in huge sums of money to finance the smuggling of millions of tons of marijuana in the sixties and seventies, and several hundred thousand pounds of cocaine into the United States in the '80s, primarily from Colombia. The Drug Enforcement Agency estimated their operation to be the largest of its type.

Choosing Florida and North Carolina for his bases of operation, Dolci built million dollar homes on Captiva Island, Florida, and Lake Norman, North Carolina. Captiva was located within miles of Cape Coral, barely an hour from the Everglades, excellent drop-off spots for drugs. Enormous profits far exceeded losses that resulted from occasional seizures by local authorities, the Coast Guard, and the Drug Enforcement Agency.

Located midway up the eastern coast, North Carolina afforded other ports for Dolci's mother ships, which steamed around Florida and up the East Coast feeding the supply route. His Lake Norman home was only twenty minutes from Charlotte, the third largest trucking center in America. It provided a myriad of methods to smuggle the drug inland, not the least of which was Charlotte/Douglas International Airport.

Ranked as the twenty-third largest airport in the nation and the thirty-fourth largest in the world, Charlotte's busy airport boarded over six million passengers a year. It was a perfect destination where "mules"—the name given to drug runners—could easily disappear.

Dolci's underworld connections solidified the entire operation and territorial fighting was uncommon. Small-time dealers were allowed to operate until they affected the profits. When that happened, Dolci either arranged for their sudden disappearance or anonymously tipped off the authorities. Small busts kept officials happy and reassured the public that President Reagan's drug war was effective. And occasionally, some of Dolci's larger shipments fell into the authorities' hands.

Mancotta remained in New Orleans, cleverly operating in a state racked with political corruption. With political protection, the legitimate businesses used to launder untold sums of money had grown into an oil-importing firm, a fast-food fried chicken chain, and over one hundred company-owned dry cleaners spread across the Southeast.

Both men were highly respected civic leaders in their communities and their generous donations to various charities brought respect and numerous favors in return. The press wrote glowing articles about their philanthropy.

To achieve even more diversification, Dolci and Mancotta started a bookmaking operation in 1968 in Las Vegas, an open territory for the *Cosa Nostra*. It grew by feeding on citizens' insatiable desire to bet on sports. Careful not to infringe on other syndicate territories, their meticulous planning provided another source of income. They used the additional funds to propel politically ambitious friends into positions of importance. One friend even became governor of the state. In return, the grateful politicians shielded them from scrutiny wherever they could exercise influence.

Even the IRS was unable to wrestle the empire to the ground. Funds that could not be explained were circulated underground and the excess poured into cooperating banks, both in and out of the country, under false names. Remaining unchecked, the power base continued to grow rapidly into an intricate, layered web. Penetration seldom got past the first layer before the legal system ensnared itself and the proceedings became ludicrous.

Standing in the break room, Teague swept away further thoughts about the DOLMAN file and looked at his watch. It was time to go to lunch. By now, Hardin had probably read enough. He walked back down the hall and stepped back into his office.

Hardin looked up, "This is incredible. Hard to believe."

"Exactly," Teague said. He had heard that same comment several times before. "That's what makes it so damn insidious. Nobody believes it."

"I see what you mean. I'm reading it, yet I can't believe they could have gotten this powerful without being exposed. They sound like they're indestructible." Hardin reached into his shirt pocket and pulled out a cigarette.

Teague walked around behind his desk and sat in his

chair. "They might be."

"Where did you get all this information?" Hardin asked, lighting his cigarette.

"From just about every source imaginable. The DEA and the CIA contributed heavily. The Justice Department set up a strike force four years ago when they realized no one agency could handle the case by themselves."

"I can understand the DEA's involvement. Why the CIA?"

"Political corruption, both here and in Colombia. Dolci and Mancotta like the cards neatly stacked," Teague said in a matter-of-fact tone.

"With all this information, why haven't we been able to jail them?" Hardin asked, shifting uneasily in his chair.

"Not one shred of solid evidence. Everything's circumstantial, and not enough of that. Nothing to substantiate it. Our best source was a soldier, Thomas Reina, who started talking after we nailed him on a murder charge." Teague leaned over the desk and flipped the file to the appropriate page.

"One of Dolci's men?" Hardin asked.

"No, an outsider from the Valachi family in Chicago. He'd become friends with Angelo Tummenelo, one of Dolci's soldiers, and wanted to move to Florida. His bad health was aggravated by the cold climate." Teague remembered the incident with both amusement and dismay.

Peering at the file, Hardin asked, "When did the mob start transfers?"

"They didn't. Tummenelo took it on his own to offer Reina a way into Dolci's organization. For a soldier that was a damn bold move. Apparently, he reasoned that if Reina executed a contract for him, then he could convince Dolci that Reina was trustworthy." Teague stood up and put on his coat. It concealed his snub-nosed .38-caliber Smith and Wesson revolver snapped into a black-leather shoulder holster. Teague felt he was in pretty good condition for a man who had put a lot of miles on his fifty-four-year-old body.

"Backfired," Hardin said.

"On both of them. Reina botched the hit. When we caught him, Tummenelo disappeared. Not a trace."

"Dead," Hardin said, closing the file.

"No doubt. In exchange for protection in prison and a lesser sentence, Reina told us everything he'd heard through channels. We didn't realize he could only give us second-hand information. Some of the names he gave us were new. Unfortunately, he died of a heart attack one week after he started talking—probably scared to death. Whatever else he knew went to the grave." Teague looked disgusted as he stood at the door.

Hardin took the hint and rose from his chair. "That's what bothers me about this job. You get a big break, then something happens to screw it up. I was awfully naive when I finished law school—thought justice always prevailed in the end. After five years with the Bureau, I know how stupid that was. And what I just read confirms it."

Teague was pleased with the intensity he saw on Hardin's face. "Bring the file and we'll lock it in the vault. This office has been broken into twice in the past three years."

They locked up the file, took the elevator down, and headed toward the parking lot. Teague unlocked the late-model white Chevrolet. Both men were quiet, engrossed in thought.

After Teague started the car, Hardin spoke. "You know the Duval case, my Kansas City bust, was bantamweight in comparison to this case. I got impatient with it in just a couple of years. I can imagine what it's been like for you, following those two guys for six years, knowing that every day innocent people were victims of the system."

Teague turned onto Canal Street from Poydras. "You know, you sound just like me after I'd been with the Bureau four or five years. But it didn't take much longer before I realized I couldn't change things, so I decided to just do the best I could."

Hardin acknowledged with a half nod.

Teague wondered if Hardin's silence signaled thoughts about possible incompetent handling of the DOLMAN Project. Never mind, he thought, Hardin didn't seem like a second guesser. Even if he was, he would learn soon enough. The DOLMAN Project would wake him up at nights: questioning, seething, feeling helpless.

It was not time yet, Teague reminded himself as he made a U-turn at the end of Canal Street and turned right on Chartres. The informant. He could make the difference. He might not. It was too early to tell. Hardin was sharp, Teague mused, but he had worked too long to let a rookie make a mistake and screw things up. Young Hardin would have to know soon enough, but not yet.

Teague parked the car and they walked toward Bourbon Street. The charm of the Vieux Carre livened Teague's spirits. He smelled the smothered aroma of steamed meat and fresh chili sauce as they passed a street vendor selling hot dogs. Cool March air gusted through the historic inner city. Teague gave his brief tour-guide explanation of the preservation of New Orleans' heart and soul, and ended with the statement that native New Orleaneans regarded as accurate: "The city that care forgot."

"What a perfect description," Hardin said as they stepped up to the oyster bar inside Felix's.

Teague looked at him. "And what an easy place for the kind of people we just discussed to prosper in. Anything you want—it's right here. And if it isn't, don't worry, it'll soon be. New Orleans has a way of attracting it all."

* Six *

Seated in the plush Polynesian-style home, Troy looked at the full moon through a floor-to-ceiling, convex, plate glass window. Moonlight silhouetted the tall trees lining the cove and sent silver-yellow beams bouncing off the dark water. He loved Lake Norman's variety. Over five hundred miles of shoreline and a vast array of finger-like coves jutted in all directions from its huge main body.

He was tense. Only three hours ago he had been swept away from the frenzied scene of victory. He did not like the nature of his "invitation." For what purpose? Over and over again he tried to think of any clue he might have given them to mistrust him. Only Jenny knew that he planned to tip Coach Lee. Could Dolci possibly have known that? Maybe the timing was a mere coincidence.

"Good evening, Mr. Burton."

The deep, graveled voice of Dolci was immediately recognizable. Troy stood to meet the short, squat man.

"You enjoyed the game?" Dolci asked.

A tall male servant entered the room with a tray of hors d'oeuvres and the bourbon and water Troy had previously ordered. The servant set the drink on the table and presented the hors d'oeuvres.

Troy picked a large stuffed mushroom and two barbecued fantail shrimp. He decided on a direct answer to Dolci's question. "I like to win. But I didn't enjoy the game."

Dolci arched his brow as he sipped a cocktail garnished with a large slice of pineapple that rested neatly on the rim of the glass.

Troy understood the silent question. "You gave me little choice but to accept your offer to fix the game." He started to eat his shrimp.

Dolci set his cocktail on the glass-top bamboo table. He leaned back in a large wicker chair and lit a cigar. His studied approach to the answer made Troy uneasy.

"Mr. Burton, we're both intelligent people. I appreciate your candor. I can communicate with you on that level. What I can't do is read your mind. If my initial offer offended you, you should have told me so. Instead you told me you would handle things if and when you won. Now, it sounds like you're not so sure. If not, then let's put our cards on the table. I'm a reasonable man." Dolci picked his drink back up and puffed on his cigar. The same acrid odor which filled the car in their first meeting now filled the room.

Troy knew he was being conned. He decided to probe. "I appreciate your open mind. But before we discuss alternatives, would you mind telling me why I was dragged here right after the game?"

"You weren't forced to come. You could have refused. You're free to leave at any time; just tell me and you may go."

"I was stopped at the press conference by a cop and told Mr. Giannini had to see me immediately. What was the big rush?"

"We've got plans to make. I don't like wasting time. There's no harm in getting right down to business now, is there?" Dolci signaled to the servant who stood patiently several feet away. "Freshen Mr. Burton's drink."

The servant took Troy's glass, turned and left the room.

Troy watched the servant leave the room. "Of course not. But next time you want to meet, I'd like a little more notice. It bruises my ego when people think they own me."

"And I suppose the $100,000 we offered hurt your pride, also."

"Yes, as a matter of fact it did," Troy said, deciding on an answer that would surprise Dolci. This whole thing is absurd, Troy thought. Why not push it to the extreme?

Dolci leaned back in his chair and folded his arms. He seemed surprised and amused at the answer. "I asked you this once before, Burton—how much more? Consider your answer carefully."

The servant returned and served Troy his second cocktail of the evening, a Manhattan on the rocks. He picked up the near-empty silver hors d'oeuvres tray, added Dolci's empty glass, and left the room.

Troy used the interruption to his advantage. He needed time to weigh his answer. Not wanting to allow the dizzying surrealistic scene to dominate his emotions, he reminded himself he was not dreaming.

"Mr. Dolci, I think you're missing the point. I can't go to Ted Collins and tell him to fake an injury, not for any amount. As I said before, I don't think Ted would even consider such an offer. He's a good kid, a damn good player who fought his way to the top."

Troy wanted to add the question about the necessity of Charlotte being favored. You can't shave points if you're not favored. Besides, how could Dolci be so sure that Charlotte would even get to the championship game? He would save both questions for later.

"You think he'll refuse $250,000 in cash? Don't kid yourself." Dolci leaned forward and pointed at Troy with his cigar. "Just who the hell are you to make decisions for a black kid that hasn't got a pot to piss in? Your naivete is second only to your stupidity, Burton."

Sensing the danger signal that Dolci's heated response radiated, Troy called upon his diplomatic skills to ease the tension. "Look, I've met you only once before in my life. We go to a restaurant, then for a ride, and the next thing I know I'm staring at $50,000 in a briefcase. And you ask me to fix a game, not just any game, the national championships. Can't you see why I'm reluctant to get involved?"

"Do you think this is a game of marbles where you can just pick up and say you don't feel like playing anymore?" Dolci asked. "You misjudge me. I thought you were an intelligent man. Apparently, I misjudged you. You're lucky you haven't done something really stupid yet. Be thankful that I anticipated a problem. Were you going to sound off to somebody at that press conference?" Dolci stood up, walked over to the window and looked out as he waited for an answer.

"Of course not," Troy said. It was finally beginning to sink in: he was in another league, one that he had read about but never really believed existed.

Dolci turned around and snapped, "You'd better wake

up." He hesitated, then softened his tone as he continued. "In our meeting I felt you understood and I thought we had a deal. Perhaps I'm also at fault. I overestimated you. I was sure you had sense enough to realize that when I offered to put $100,000 in your pocket and you didn't say no, I expected you to perform the service requested. Failure to do so is deadly serious."

Dolci's emphasis on the word "deadly" sent a chill through Troy's spine. He'd been in tougher situations in Vietnam, but there he been trained and combat-ready. Here he felt like an empty-headed schoolboy who failed to study for an exam. He had no excuse.

Feeling that Dolci would allow one blunder, he seized the opportunity to accept a wrist slap and buy more time. He vowed not to make any more asinine mistakes. Dolci's offer was impossible to refuse now. Acceptance would allow him time to sort out possible alternatives.

"I understand. I accept your offer." Troy looked directly into Dolci's dark brown eyes and held contact until Dolci broke first and glanced up at the ceiling. If anything can betray a lie, Troy thought, it's failure to maintain eye contact.

"You said that once before, remember? Don't step on your dick again—I'll cut it off," Dolci said as he sat down in a wicker chair.

Troy stared at Dolci. He thought about how easily he could take him apart. Not more than five and a half feet tall, he looked like a fat, ugly Napoleon. The chair swallowed his pudgy body.

Troy finished his drink. "I won't make any more mistakes. I learn fast once I understand the rules. Would I be presumptuous to point out some flaws in your plan?"

"Yes, but that's not out of character for you now, is it?" Dolci smiled, revealing a chipped front tooth.

"No, I guess it isn't," Troy said, laughing lightly. He continued. "What I mean is that basketball is how I make my living. True, I'm not a coach, but I am around one of the best in the business. His expertise has to rub off.

"I listen a lot to Coach Lee's philosophy and watch

practices throughout the season. When I see him studying films or working out plays on the blackboard in his office, I ask questions. Depending on his mood, he usually answers them."

Dolci knew all of this and interrupted, "Get to the point."

"Excuse me for rambling. I just want you to know that as executive director at a small school like Charlotte, I have somewhat of an unusual situation. My contact with the coach is much more frequent than it would be if I were the fund raiser at a larger university.

"Lee wears two hats—athletic director and head basketball coach. I report directly to him. He's the man who hired me; he's the man who can fire me.

"With all that in mind, let me ask you this question one more time. Why did you pick me to act as a go-between with Collins instead of approaching him directly? I know you said it was because we're friends, but adding another person seems more risky, certainly more expensive."

Dolci tamped his cigar, spilling cinders into a silver ashtray. "I didn't just pick your name out of the Hornet program, if that's what you're asking. You and Collins are good friends. Someone approaching him off the street might not be trusted."

True enough, Troy thought, but his friendship with Collins was not common knowledge. Only those in the athletic family at the university knew it existed. He and Collins never frequented public places together. They played some friendly chess games in Collins' dorm and complained about Coach Lee's moodiness. No big deal. But how did Dolci learn about their friendship? That question kept coming back to haunt him. He had to find out who tipped Dolci off.

Could he press Dolci for that answer? Obviously not. He decided to appear satisfied with Dolci's answer, although he wasn't. "OK, that makes sense. Let me ask you something else. How can you be so sure we'll make it to the championship? We've still got one more team to beat in the semifinals, yet you were positive two games ago we'd be there."

Dolci looked smug. "Let's call it a well-planned educated guess."

Troy knew there was more to it than that. Dolci was hiding something. He decided to ask for another prediction. "Who's going to win tonight, Notre Dame or Fort Myers?"

"The Chargers."

"What? The Irish are favored by seven."

"The Chargers will win." Dolci smirked.

Goddamn, has he fixed that game? Troy wondered. Dolci's arrogance permeated the room. Ego. He faced it everyday. Dolci was a member of that quintessential species of self-anointed kings.

Troy shifted in the cushioned bamboo chair and said, "I don't bet on basketball—it ruins the game for me. The sport is more than the number of points on the board at the final buzzer. It's execution, ability, creativity, and luck."

"Care for another drink while we watch the Chargers win?" Dolci motioned to the servant who had unobtrusively entered the room.

"I really need to get back to the hotel." Troy's tone was half-hearted. He did not want to miss the contest. He could watch for signs of a fix. Having the advantage of a pre-game suspicion, he felt sure he could detect point-shaving. He could also size up Fort Myers. He had watched the Irish on television three times during the season. But he had not seen the Chargers since last year, when they burst onto the scene by advancing to the Mideast Regional championship, falling to Marquette on a last-second jump shot.

"I'll pass on the drink and stay for the game."

"Fine. How about dinner?" Dolci asked.

"That sounds good to me."

Dolci turned to the servant. "Serve us in the recreation room."

Troy followed Dolci through the room into a passage that branched out in five directions. He was fascinated by the cluster of round, cedar-sided structures, connected by a large hallway that spanned over a huge garage. Closed-circuit television cameras were trained on the garage entrance. Access could be gained only through an elevator controlled by a guard from a remote area. The home was a fortress among the tall pines, maples, and oaks covering the peninsula. Obviously, Dolci considered privacy and security important.

They entered another of the six congruent structures. Fine wood-grain paneling, light-colored and heavily etched, set the tone for the windowless room. Indirect lighting revealed a billiard table on the left and a standard pool table on the right. Tiffany lamps hung over the tables from the twelve-foot ceiling. A stone fireplace rose right in the middle of the room. A black metal flue hovered over it, the fire visible from all sides.

Dolci directed Troy to a grouping of gold and brown upholstered chairs, a brown leather recliner, and a semi-circular gold sofa. Dolci sat in the recliner. A large-screen television projector, including a video recorder, rested ten feet away from a six-foot screen mounted on the wall.

"The game will be on in just a few minutes," Dolci said, pressing a remote control switch that activated the television.

Troy sat on the sofa and propped his feet on a brown leather ottoman. The comfort of the surroundings was disarming. The alcohol coursing through his veins tranquilized him.

"Your home is unique."

Dolci nodded. He turned the volume up and seemed engrossed in the pre-game chatter of the CBS commentators. Troy waited for a commercial.

"Did you design it yourself?"

"Design what?"

"This house."

"No." Dolci opened a gold cigar box that rested next to a large Stiffel lamp on a round oak table. Looking at Troy, he offered a cigar with a questioning gesture. Troy waved a polite no thank you.

"I gave an architect the general idea and he came up with this. We made a few changes. Nothing major."

"The windows?" Troy asked.

"What?"

"Why aren't there any windows in this particular room?"

Dolci swiveled his chair toward the television screen. "I

find them distracting sometimes."

"May I ask what you do for a living?" Troy asked right before tip-off.

"What?"

"What's your occupation?"

"Let's say I'm an investor," Dolci responded. "Are you interested in this goddamn game or not?"

Troy sort of enjoyed needling Dolci. It was a ploy he used frequently just to yank a person's security blanket away. His forthright, inquisitive nature, or style, as some people called it, got him into trouble occasionally. Knowing that most people liked to talk about themselves, he generally walked a fine line between being either a downright nosy bastard or a skillful interviewer with a knack for coaxing people to lower their guard. Deciding to settle back and refrain from further questions, he turned his attention to the game.

Notre Dame pulled out to an early lead. The Chargers looked tight. But in the closing minutes of the first half, they shook their early jitters and slashed the Irish's twelve-point lead to three at the half.

Throughout the first half both men had looked on dispassionately, not uttering a word, eating their dinner: cornish hens, wild rice, and a spicy stuffing. Troy had enjoyed three glasses of a dry chablis.

At halftime Dolci turned and asked, "Would you care for some coke?"

"No thanks. The wine's fine."

Dolci smiled. "That's not what I was referring to. Cocaine, Mr. Burton, not the soft drink."

Troy attempted to conceal his surprise. "No thanks. I never touch the stuff. I've seen it take too many good people down."

"Well, that's very admirable, but since you smoke marijuana, I thought you might enjoy some fine cocaine." Dolci set his wine glass on the table. "Excuse me for a moment, won't you?"

Stunned, Troy watched Dolci leave the room. How in the hell did he know that? he wondered, trying to clear his mind of the dulling effects the wine produced.

Dolci had just played a black ace. If there was one personal
secret that Troy closely guarded, it was the fact that he
smoked marijuana in the privacy of his home. It was a habit
he'd picked up soon after he got back from Vietnam. It took
the edge off the adjustment.

Besides Jenny, only four people knew he smoked, and
they were his most trusted friends: Russ and Shelly Stinson,
and Donnie and Linda Powers.

They would never talk, Troy thought. They were his
suppliers, hardly big-time pushers. They all knew of the
social dangers exposure would create, especially for Troy.
So how did Dolci get his information? Had he been followed? No. Even if he had been, Dolci's man would have
had difficulty finding out. Troy never left his home carrying
pot.

He was really paranoid about smoking grass. And his
paranoia was aggravated by his high profile in North
Carolina's largest city. In the past two years he had spoken
to over seventy-five different civic clubs throughout the
Charlotte community and surrounding areas and appeared
on television during halftime of two games that were televised by the city's leading station, WBTV, the CBS network
affiliate. Because those games were against ranked opponents and the Hornets were gathering strength in the
ACC-dominated territory, the audience was very large, over
a half million.

Troy radiated enthusiasm for the basketball program.
There were still many who doubted the young team could
compete against big-name opponents. ACC televised games
had bombarded the Charlotte airwaves for nearly thirty
years. Children grew up convinced that the Atlantic Coast
Conference was the best basketball in the United States.
And they had some justification for believing that. Yet,
historically, post-season tournament play indicated the Big
Ten was superior.

Troy's speeches were designed to sway Charlotteans to
support two allegiances: the university that they graduated
from—which was often an ACC school—and the university

that represented the community they lived and worked in.

The approach worked quite effectively until Bill Lee lowered the hatchet, severing any chance for a harmonious relationship to develop between the University of Charlotte and the ACC. One Sunday morning on the Charlotte coach's show, Lee ripped ACC coaches for what he termed, "a conspiracy to prevent the rise of some natural rivalries in order to stymie Charlotte's efforts to gain national recognition."

Though the show had a small following, word of his accusations spread across the state when the *Charlotte Observer* reported Lee's complaints the next day in a front page story. From that point, battle lines were drawn and Troy's job toughened despite the Hornets' march to the top.

Deep in thought, Troy did not hear Dolci's question. As the pudgy man sat down and reclined in his chair, Troy realized that something had been said.

"Excuse me. What did you say? I didn't hear you."

Dolci answered as he bit off the end of another cigar. "I said you must have one hell of a bladder. Don't you ever need to piss?"

"As a matter of fact I do. Where is it?"

Troy returned just in time to see the second half tip-off. He wanted to question Dolci further, but not during the game.

Fort Myers grabbed the opening tap and quickly cut the margin to one point with a slam dunk from Jeffries, the 6'10" black senior from Harlem. Troy was impressed with the Chargers. They played a hard-hitting, run-and-gun game, launching aerial bombs from just about anywhere on their offensive court, often from three-point territory. They forced Notre Dame out of its zone defense.

As far as Troy could tell, there was no fix. The Chargers were simply dominating with incredible accuracy from the floor. Hitting the open man with regularity, they jumped out to a ten-point lead early in the second half.

With less than five minutes to go, the Irish started a frenzied rally. But the Charger coach, Patrick McLaughlin, recognized his team was sagging and signaled a time-out.

Whatever McLaughlin said to his players worked. They came back on the court and played inspired basketball, trading shots with the Irish, winning the game by five points.

There was no fix: Troy was sure of that. He looked closely at the statistics that flashed on the screen. The readout was a new feature added by CBS to give fans a complete display of individual and team statistics. It also compared each team's game averages with its regular season statistics. Everything indicated the Irish had performed up to par, matching and sometimes bettering their previous performances. But the figure that spelled their defeat was the sizzling shooting of the put-it-up-from-anywhere Chargers. They scorched the net with 70-percent accuracy from the floor in the second half. Their 21 turnovers to the Irish's 11 were the only reason the final margin was close.

The CBS commentators announced an interview with the University of Florida at Fort Myers coach. Troy watched Dolci adjust the controls on his Mitsubishi recorder. Why would Dolci tape an interview? Troy could understand recording the game and even the statistics. But why the interview? The question passed quickly through his mind: too many other thoughts vied for control. Without attempting conjecture, the reflection vanished like a ripple from a single drop of rain falling on a pond.

Coach McLaughlin spoke with authority. He had an interesting accent—a deep, resonant, Irish brogue tinged with a slight southern accent. He praised the performance of both teams.

Troy could not help but think that the coach was politicking for the Notre Dame job, a coaching spot that rested on the top rung of the ladder with 15 or 20 other prestige universities around the nation. Not that Troy thought the position would be vacated anytime soon. Digger Phelps had performed exceedingly well throughout his coaching career. But fickle fans required consistent winning in a heavyweight billet. Few coaches ever stayed long enough to endear themselves so solidly that they could withstand a three or four-season slump. And a slump to a perennial power was the failure to make a good showing in the NCAA tournament. Coach Phelps had accomplished that.

Dolci clicked off the television and turned to Troy. "Thought you knew basketball, didn't you? Looks like you underrated the little school from Florida."

Troy poured himself a glass of water. "Well, it was the first time I had gotten to see them play this year. I believed the seven-point line like everybody else. They played a weak schedule, nothing like Notre Dame's."

"That's the same mistake people make every day. They take the line for gospel. If the underdog wins, it's an upset. Bullshit. The line is determined by the bettor. Forecasting basketball games is sheer sentiment for 90 percent of the shmucks across the country. They don't study the teams and they're swayed by their emotions."

Troy sat forward. Where had he heard that before? The scene flashed quickly through his mind. Once, on the road with Bill Lee late at night as they returned from an unproductive recruiting trip—Lee sometimes had Troy drive for him on the longer journeys—the conversation turned to gambling. Lee made it clear that he abhorred the practice of betting on the outcome of a game. Then, he proceeded to point out how stupid the average bettor could be by failing to study the intricacies of the game: every man-to-man match-up and possible alternate combinations; patterns, plays, and various defenses deployed; overall strengths and weaknesses of the teams, including size, speed and quickness; and individual strengths and weaknesses, including ball-handling ability, shooting range, shot selection, and tendencies to favor right or left movement. To Lee, forecasting the outcome was a science.

Dolci sipped more wine and said, "There is so much to consider before an accurate forecast can be made. And what about the intangibles? Desire, confidence, emotion, game-day routine, just to name a few. The average bettor can't investigate all those things. He has to rely on the syndicated experts who report how they arrived at their final prediction. But even those guys fuck up. They're spread too thin. Hell, they're lucky to be right 65 percent of the time.

"It's the power of the pen. Some jerk gets pretty good at making predictions and has a flair for doing it. Suddenly, everybody listens to him, except the few that do better homework.

"It's tough to tout a line. If you're well known, sometimes you get fed bullshit information. That doesn't happen a lot, mind you, but it does happen. And that will blow a prediction 180 degrees off course," Dolci said.

Taking a deep breath, he continued. "But see, that's when reputation saves the guy's ass. Why, it was an 'upset' of course. That's a bunch of crap." Dolci pointed at Troy with his cigar.

"You mean you think it's possible to predict the outcome of a game all the time?" Troy asked.

"Certainly not. But if you study your ass off and get the proper information—the kind the majority of the jerks out there don't have a prayer of learning—you can be accurate 80 percent of the time."

Troy found that hard to believe, but Dolci sounded convincing. And the craggy-faced Italian was obviously in a better position to know more about betting than he did.

"Remember, the people who determine the line seldom tout the winner. Bookies covering bets play the percentages just like the house does in Vegas. If you ride long enough with the odds, you've got to come out a winner. Numbers don't lie; people do."

Troy squinted at Dolci.

Like an instructor taking his cue from a troubled student, Dolci leaned forward in his chair and clarified his statement. "It goes back to what I said earlier. The press and the oddsmakers need information from the coach's mouth, right?"

"OK," Troy said, beginning to anticipate what might follow.

"So, they look right at the two coaches involved and start asking questions. Many times a coach gives it to 'em straight and answers to the best of his ability. But there are some coaches that don't really know the answers; some that do and won't answer; and others who know, but have a good reason to lie. Those are the ones that try to set up the game to their advantage by psyching the opponent out.

"Maybe you've got a kid with a bruised knee, but you know he'll be ready to play when the time comes. So you let the word get out that the kid is doubtful. You can't do that too often or somebody will figure out what you're up to. Timing is essential. You tell the press only what you want them to hear and do it carefully. They get wise to these little games and hate to be used," Dolci said as he put his cigar out. Smoke hung lazily in the air fogging the scene.

Troy wondered what Dolci was leading to. Reading between the lines gave him several clues. Yet, a question remained, looming in the back of his mind. Early in the evening it had raised its ugly head and he had ignored it. He decided to ask and watch Dolci's reaction carefully.

It hissed out like a torpedo. "Is Coach Lee involved in this?"

Dolci responded quickly without flinching. "No. If he was, I wouldn't be using you."

Troy leaned back. The answer made sense. Lee wasn't the kind of coach who would allow a man like Dolci to pull the strings. And if Dolci had made such a contact, he damn sure wouldn't need Ted Collins to shave points. The coach could handle that matter all by himself.

"You're right. I just wanted to know who all the players in this venture were. Is anybody else in the athletic department involved?"

Dolci's eyes hardened. "This is the last question I'm answering and the answer is no. I'm damn tired of your questions. I want to remind you that I call the shots. You just do what you're told." Dolci stood and walked over to the fireplace, turning his back on Troy.

"I'm—"

Dolci turned around. "Shut your damn mouth and wait until I finish. I don't want to hear another goddamn word out of you. I'll talk; you listen."

Troy wanted to kill him. He knew he could, but he knew he'd never get out alive.

"It's time for you to leave. But before you do, I want to

get something through that thick skull of yours. You're a dead man if you make another mistake. Go to the cops and it's simply my word against yours. You've got nothing to hang your hat on. And should you be so fucking stupid to do something like that, I'll make you look like a fool.

"I think that grass is affecting your brain. What the hell do you think the public would think?" Dolci paused to emphasize the point. He wasn't waiting for an answer; none was required.

"You're out of your league. Don't misjudge me. Do as you're told. In the future, answer any questions that are asked by me or any of my men. Make damn sure you tell the truth. And don't try anything cute like going to the press. There are libel laws, you stupid bastard. You think they're going to risk a suit? You would end up looking like you took your dick out in public and pissed on the street."

Troy did not even consider refuting that argument. All he wanted to do was to get out, away from Dolci. He was afraid of losing his temper, like the time he exploded in Nam. A man could just take so much.

Dolci continued. "You've got nothing, absolutely nothing on me. Don't forget that. If you start poking around and sticking your nose where it doesn't belong, you'll end up at the bottom of that lake out there. Now get the fuck out of my sight. The car is waiting for you. The next time I see you, you'd better have the deal with Collins set. We'll make the payoff in New Orleans," Dolci said, pointing to the door.

As Troy turned left through the doorway, he almost bumped into the tall servant, who held a .357-magnum pistol down by his side. The sinister looking barrel was long, and a silencer extended its malevolence.

Troy tensed. It was the first time he had ever seen the ominous muffler and had always regarded it as a Hollywood prop.

The man motioned with the weapon to continue walking. Stepping onto the elevator, Troy noticed his palms were sweating. It didn't bother him—he'd sweated a lot more in Nam the day he was shot down.

As he walked to the vehicle, he glanced at the man behind

the wheel. He was the same driver he had had previously. Troy sat in the back. Giannini was not there, only the driver.

Dolci would not have him killed, Troy reasoned as the driver shifted into reverse and backed out of the garage. Not tonight, anyway.

* Seven *

Jenny Burton leaned on the dresser to regain her balance. Her illness had been compounded by a night of worried sleeplessness. Where is he? She asked herself again and again. As she reached out for the glass of crushed ice, tears began to roll down her baby-soft cheeks. She sipped slowly, hoping she would be able to hold down some fluid this time.

She looked at the clock: 2:35 a.m. Having phoned the Albert Pick Motel at least ten times since the game ended Saturday afternoon, she had begun to believe the worst: Troy had to be in trouble or he would have called.

What happened? She had no idea. Lindsey Ellis, the sports information director for the University of Charlotte, told her over the phone that he had not seen Troy since the beginning of the game. Lindsey's room was right down the hall from her husband's. Ellis had said Troy had not attended the press conference. The staff wanted to know where he was, too. Coach Lee had canceled a staff meeting because Troy could not be located.

Ellis had offered Jenny a plausible explanation. "Troy's probably out somewhere celebrating with some of the Foundation members. He just forgot to check in with you. Don't worry; he'll be all right. Maybe a little drunk, but he'll drag back to the hotel soon."

She walked over to the bed and eased under the covers. Feeling the cold nose of Drop, she embraced the furry animal, caressing it lovingly. Their only "child," Troy bought the fluffy "Chocolate Drop," his name for the chocolate-brown female poodle, the day after they had received the news Jenny could not bear children. Jenny remembered how hard the news had hit them both.

Even when sick, she suffered little moodiness. Her faith. Yes, it was her faith that enabled her to get through tough times like the one she faced now. She believed firmly in the Lord God Almighty. Even on the day she received the news that she would remain childless, her faith was never shaken. Let God's will be done, she had thought to herself.

Tonight she was truly being tested; of that she was sure. She was determined to remain strong in facing the most difficult situation she and Troy had encountered in the thirty-three years of her life.

The nausea returned. It was time for another suppository, she thought. Only a 50 milligram dose of WANS NO. 2 had been effective in quelling her spasmodic vomiting. The last dose had lost its efficacy.

Waves of queasiness returned. She looked on the nightstand at the bottle containing the medication. She was determined not to use another dose. The concentrated barbiturate always put her to sleep for several hours. Slumber would be welcomed any other time but now.

Turning the bedside light off, Jenny rose dizzily and slowly walked to the window. Standing to the right side, she parted the curtains and peeked out. The car was still parked at the end of the cul-de-sac only one hundred yards away from their two-story home.

The silhouetted figure seated on the driver's side was still clearly visible. The bright, full, March moon radiated shadowed light through tall pines lining the street. She saw a light flicker inside the car—a match struck to light a cigarette. The dim kindling failed to illuminate the features of the figure's face, but she knew by the silhouetted outline the form was a man.

Jenny barely made it to the bathroom before she began retching. The yellow bile-like substance was bitter. Her stomach was empty. Her tiny body was racked by the heaving. She leaned on the bathroom sink. God give me strength and keep Troy safe, she prayed to herself.

Unsteadily, she walked back to bed and lay down. Drop licked Jenny's ear, as if the animal understood her poor condition. She began sobbing quietly.

Who was that man in the car? She had wondered all night. Could it be one of Dolci's men? Jenny reached under Troy's pillow and felt the cold steel of his nine-shot .22-caliber High Standard revolver, a small source of security.

Twice that night she had started to call the police. She stopped, realizing that she might endanger Troy's life by alerting the authorities. If one of Dolci's men was hauled off to jail for questioning, Dolci might retaliate.

According to Lindsey, Troy had not been seen after the game. Yet Troy had told her he would talk to Coach Lee immediately after the press conference, then call her. Something had gone wrong. Jenny knew that as well as she knew her husband's personality. He never forgot a promise, and once he said he was going to do something, he always followed through.

She loved him with all of her heart. Tears wet her pillow. "God, please keep him safe," she prayed out loud. She began reciting the Twenty-third Psalm.

The pungent odor of marijuana filled the motor home and the celebrators had finally quieted. Exulting in the fruits of victory as they had for every game that season, Donnie Powers and Russ Stinson continued to pass the gargoyle-shaped handmade pipe between them. Their wives had fallen asleep, draped over the disappearing sofa bed that was only partially pulled out from the wall.

"What time is it?" Powers asked, as he exhaled a heavy cloud of smoke into the cool, uncirculated air of the motor home.

Looking bleary-eyed at his watch, Stinson replied, "Three o'clock."

"Wonder where he is?" Powers asked, scratching his full black beard.

"Damned if I know," Stinson said.

Rising from the swivel chair, Powers walked to the front of the motor home and peered through the windshield. The parking lot of the Albert Pick Motel was well lit and jammed with vehicles. A brisk March wind moved debris and confetti along the ground. The Greyhound bus, painted Hornet gold and black, sat motionless 60 feet away, void of occupants.

Powers rubbed his red, congested eyes. "I still don't see

his car."

"Some friend he is." Stinson scratched his thinning scalp. His light brown hair bounced back into its frizzy afro style as he moved his fingers around his head. "We invite him for a drink and a couple of puffs, and the bastard doesn't even show."

Powers turned and looked at his brother-in-law. As he walked back, he picked up a bottle of Crown Royal. The tone in Stinson's voice was not harsh, Powers thought. It sounded as if he were more concerned about Burton than angry.

Powers was worried. It was not at all like Troy Burton to promise to attend one of their revelries after a game and then not make an appearance.

"How about another drink?" Powers held the half-empty bottle up in a toasting gesture.

"Hell, yeah." Stinson raised his empty glass.

Looking at both women, Powers said, "They can't handle it. Two of a kind—no hang time."

"That's the trouble with marrying sisters. They tend to stick together like two peas in a pod," Stinson said, referring to their wives' relationship.

"We should have thought of that before we arranged that stupid double wedding," Powers said, hoping to elicit some response from Linda or Shelly. Neither stirred.

After mixing the whisky with Sprite and crushed ice, Powers handed Stinson his glass as the liquid spilled over the brim, spotting the gold carpet.

"Whoa! You know, you're not worth a damn as a bartender," Stinson said as he blotted the soggy spots with a black and gold cocktail napkin. "Well, what do you think?"

"About what?" Powers slumped in his chair and sipped his drink.

"The tickets. Think we can swing four of them from our buddy Troy?" Stinson tossed the wet napkin in the direction of a trash basket.

"I told you six damn times, I don't know."

"Why not? We're like that," Stinson said, holding his first three fingers up pressed tightly together.

"That doesn't mean a fucking thing."

Powers' wife, Linda, mumbled, "Quit using that nasty language." She kept her eyes closed.

Pleased that he had finally aroused her, Powers said, "This is family. Don't jump on my ass for using that word. What would you like me to say?—'That doesn't mean an intercoursing thing?'" Pointing to Linda while looking at Russ, he continued, "Don't let her kid you; she loves that word. She's like a rabbit."

"If that's true, I take it back about them being two peas in a pod," Stinson said, chuckling. He looked at his wife, Shelly, who was fast asleep.

Linda rolled over and pulled her husband's leather coat over her head. "Shut up," she murmured half-heartedly.

Powers looked at his well-shaped wife curled in the fetal position. It accentuated her firm, well-rounded bottom. Powers' sexual awareness was momentarily awakened. He reached over and rubbed her leg.

Linda said softly, "Hope Troy can get us those tickets." Exhausted from the excitement and the revelry that followed the Hornets' glorious victory over Indiana, she drifted off to sleep.

Powers understood his wife's concern. Charlotte was her alma mater, too. In fact, all four occupants of the motor home were graduates of the University of Charlotte.

"Forget her and think about the angles, will you?" Stinson kicked his foot in the air to gain Powers' attention.

Powers swiveled in his chair uneasily. Their friendship with Burton should not be tested in this manner. "Man, I told you I really don't know if he can get us tickets. He told me he would try like hell—something about the Superdome being bigger than any place the double A has ever used for the championships. He thinks the ticket allotment should be at least twice the two thousand they usually have for each of the four teams. Troy has an obligation to see that the Athletic Foundation raises at least $250,000 this year. If he doesn't, he'll be looking for another job, and—"

Stinson interrupted. "Bullshit. We'll make at least three hundred grand by going to the Final Four, win or lose. Don't you read the paper?"

"That's different. Troy said they're going to use every dime of that for the new athletic offices. They'll still be a quarter of a million short for that little project. The $250,000 they're trying to raise is just to meet this year's budget."

Stinson thought for a minute as Powers' explanation filtered through his drugged brain. Then, speaking confidently, he said, "He'll raise it, no sweat. Look at all the mother-fuckers who are jumpin' on the bandwagon. We couldn't fill an eleven thousand-seat coliseum two months ago, and now those high society bastards are pouring out of the woodwork like cockroaches after cake."

"Exactly, and our measly little hundred bucks that we had to practically borrow to give to the Foundation this year isn't going to carry a whole lot of weight," Powers said, thinking about all the bills he had accumulated since he married less than a year ago, only two years after graduating from the University of Charlotte.

A wry grin inched across Stinson's face. "Hell, man, we just got out of school. Can we help it if it took us eight years to finish?"

Laughing, Powers replied, "We had a damn good time, didn't we?"

"Right, brother," Stinson said, slapping Powers' outstretched palms-up hands.

"If we could swing a grand each to join the Gold Hornet club, I know we'd get tickets," Powers said. Seeing a way to gently bring up the subject, he coupled the thought. "I know where we can get the bread. What do you think? Will your connection come through next week?"

Stinson said, "Don't know—he's over on the coast right now. The ship's due in sometime soon. They don't exactly print schedules, you know."

Powers laughed. "Really. I thought they might. Then they could send a couple to the DEA so the narcs would know when to be there to help unload."

Shelly Stinson turned over on her stomach. "Donnie, would you shut up. We're trying to sleep."

"Well, look who's awake. Sleeping beauty has graced us with her presence." Powers reached over and slapped his blond-headed sister-in-law on her bottom.

"Leave me alone," Shelly said with little malice in her voice.

Powers slapped her again. "Go back to sleep or wake up and party with us."

Stinson watched the antics between his wife and Powers, but his mind was not on the playful scene. He was concerned about the connection. He would be risking a lot when he accepted the fifty-pound shipment of marijuana. It was his first connection with big-time smugglers. The whole affair made him nervous. He never had planned to get involved until Powers had asked him to cultivate the contact.

Stinson was content with his Boogie Beverage Company, a convenience store and tobacco shop, which in reality was a head shop. Business was booming. The tobacco shop in the back of the store was grossing over $5,000 per month. Peddling paraphernalia in the guise of tobacco pipes and products to eager drug cultists was a profitable venture. Coupled with $25,000 per month in beer and wine sales, the entire operation provided a steady middle-class income. Drug paraphernalia was generally marked up 100 percent, a profit far in excess of beer and wine. He had to hold those prices down in order to compete with the grocery stores that surrounded him.

He knew that prices were not the only reason people frequented his store. Although the west side of Charlotte was generally populated by the tougher elements of society—and he was a college graduate in accounting—his personality drew repeat business. Always friendly and plainly dressed in jeans, T-shirt, tennis shoes, full beard and afro hairstyle, he liked the west side lifestyle.

So did his best friend, Donnie Powers. When he and Donnie married the Owens sisters right out of college, they sealed their friendship in a true family. Powers bought a failing lounge less than a mile from the picturesque Char-

lotte campus. He turned the lounge's failure into success
with sound business practice—he, too, had an accounting
degree. Like Stinson, Powers did not fit the role of a numbers
cruncher. They looked like brothers.

Powers changed the name of the lounge to the Hornets'
Nest, and began catering to the college crowd. He dropped
draft beer prices and relied on volume. The first six months
the business suffered from under-capitalization, but volume
rose steadily, and soon the Hornets' Nest became a popular
hangout for Charlotte students.

Stinson still did not know where his brother-in-law had
obtained the down payment for the lounge. Powers told him
not to ask questions—he would learn when the time was
right. That answer had shaken Stinson. Until that point,
both men had shared secrets during their twelve-year friendship: their sex adventures, disappointments, achievements,
plans and expectations.

Now, in the wee hours of the morning—despite the shared
gaiety of the victory—Stinson was worried. Powers was
hiding something from him.

When Powers had asked him to make solid contact with
a drug dealer, who was one step on the ladder above their
normal supplier, Stinson had been surprised. Sure, they
could make a lot of money, but there was a hell of a risk
involved. Powers was asking him to make a giant leap. That
meant serious association with organized crime.

Where had the money for the lounge come from?

Troy Burton stepped out of his Chevrolet Beretta in the
Albert Pick Motor Inn parking lot. A blast of cold night
air met him squarely in the face. Deep in thought, he barely
noticed the sub-freezing temperature. He walked slowly
around the vehicle, examining all sides.

The ride back from Dolci's home in the limousine had
been somber. The only surprise was that his courtesy car,
the Beretta, had been removed from the Greensboro Coliseum parking lot. Dolci's driver had driven him directly to
the Greensboro/High Point/Winston-Salem Regional Air-

port. The driver had simply handed Troy a parking receipt
and pointed to the long-term lot.

No damage, Troy thought, as he turned and walked toward
the front entrance of the motor inn. Bitter cold quickened
his pace. Large, black, steel gaslights lining the front of the
white stucco, square-columned, two-story inn, reminded
him of the New Orleans-French Renaissance-style architecture that lured tourists to visit the "Crescent City." Four
days from now, he would return to the home of all his teenage
years. The irony of the whole situation struck him: for an
apparent winner, he had a trunk full of skeletons to fly back.

As he walked back into the warm, red-carpeted lobby, his
thoughts returned to Frank Dolci. Why had he arranged
for the car to be moved to the airport? The airport was
only one mile away from the motor inn.

The answer dawned on him as he reached the front desk.
Had Dolci decided to kill him, the airport parking lot would
have been an excellent place for his car to be discovered.
Dolci would probably have arranged a baffling disappearance. Troy smiled at the thought: Dolci knew he'd figure
out what movement of the car meant. Another attempt at
intimidation. It won't work, Frank. I've been shot at before,
you son of a bitch, Troy thought to himself.

"Yes, sir. May I help you?" asked the young, red-headed,
female front-desk clerk.

"Yes. Do I have any messages? I'm Troy Burton."

"Room 202?"

"Right. How'd you know?" He had never seen the pretty
night clerk before. If he had, he would not have
forgotten.

"You've had more messages than Coach Lee." She turned
to the message boxes that lined the wall behind her.

"You're kidding," said Troy, somewhat amused.

"You must handle the tickets for the Hornets." She handed
him a thick stack of messages and a plain white envelope
marked "Troy Burton, Confidential."

He recognized the handwriting. It was Bill Lee's small,
bold printing. He could guess the message. No doubt—Lee
had been looking for him.

"Did I guess right?" the clerk asked politely.

"Hmmm?" muttered Troy, deep in thought.

"Do you handle the tickets?"

"Not completely, but I'm the one who determines who gets them and where they sit. How did you know?"

"I used to work in the Wolfpack ticket office. We were bombarded with calls when we went to the national championships in '74. What a year!"

"You worked for North Carolina State? How long?"

"Five years."

"Why did you quit?"

"I wasn't going anywhere. The job got to be a drag after the glamour wore off." Running her fingers through her long hair, she smiled at him and asked, "What's your position, ticket manager?"

"No. We're not that big yet. I'm the executive director of the Athletic Foundation. I handle lots of different things. Guess you could say I'm the chief cook, bottle washer, and head waiter all rolled into one." Troy smiled for the first time in twelve hours. The conversation was a good diversion.

Eyeing the thick stack of messages he clenched in his right hand, she said, "Looks like it's going to get worse."

"Sure is." He leaned on the counter, closing the distance between them. He detected the faint, delicate odor of her perfume. The scent was familiar: Chanel No. 5. Jenny sometimes wore it.

Moving closer to him, she said, "Your team surprised everybody. You're in the big time now. Pretty exciting, isn't it?"

Reflecting on what she'd said about her own brief bask in the spotlight, he reasoned she probably really knew what he was supposed to be feeling. Friends, relatives, complete strangers, probably all called her and begged for tickets. It was an instant when the world seemed to turn its head in your direction. A moment when perspective drowns in ego.

Glancing down at his watch, he said, "I'm not sure it has registered with me yet. Damn, it's four thirty. I'd better get some sleep."

"Well, if I don't see you again, good luck."

"Thanks. I'll be back here for a fund-raising conference this summer. Maybe I'll see you then."

"I'll look forward to seeing your NCAA championship watch."

Smiling, Troy turned and walked toward the winding, red-carpeted staircase that led to the second floor. She certainly was pretty, he mused, and tempting, but there was only one Jenny.

Inside his suite, he settled onto the dark brown sofa and clicked on a brass lamp that rested next to the telephone. He began leafing through his messages. Several were from Jenny. God, how could he have forgotten?

He'd promised to phone her immediately after his meeting with Coach Lee. Dolci's unexpected invitation was reason enough not to call then, but why had he completely forgotten? No phones. That was it. There were none in Dolci's home—at least the sections that he had been in, anyway. Another Dolci riddle. Obviously, the man had a reason for everything he did. Perhaps the phones were located in one of the other structures that he hadn't visited. After all, Troy mused as he dialed long distance, he had only been in three.

"Hello." Jenny's voice sounded weak.

Troy said softly, "Honey, I'm sorry I didn't call."

"I've been worried sick. Where are you? What happened?" Her voice cracked.

She probably hadn't slept at all. He tried to calm her. "Everything will be all right. I'll explain when I get home tomorrow afternoon."

"Tomorrow? I thought you were coming home today."

"That's right, I forgot. It's Sunday morning."

"What time will you be home?" She could not wait to see him. His voice almost made her forget her nausea.

"I hope by two o'clock. You sound weak. Are you OK?"

"I've been vomiting all night. I couldn't sleep. Troy, you didn't go to the press conference, did you?"

"No. How did you know?"

"I got worried and called Lindsey. He said he hadn't seen you. What's going on?"

"I don't want to discuss it on the phone, OK?"

She paused, then began softly, almost whispering, "There is a man parked at the end of the street. He's been there all night. I noticed him when I let Drop out to go potty. I didn't think much about it at first, but he's still there. He's been watching our house. I'm sure of that."

Another piece of the puzzle, Troy thought. Fear and anger congealed. It was one thing for Dolci to pose a threat to him, but quite another to threaten Jenny. "Did you call the police?"

"No."

He knew that her lack of action had been appropriate. Dolci would not harm her at this point. He was probably using her as a trump card. It had to be a scare tactic, a pure show of power.

Another thought struck Troy. The man outside might be listening to their phone conversation.

The long pause was too much for Jenny. She broke the silence as she sat up, propping her head against the green velvet-tufted headboard. "Should I have called them?"

"No. You did the right thing. Don't worry. No one's going to hurt you."

"OK." She sounded somewhat relieved.

He decided to change the subject. "Have you taken your medicine?"

"No. It makes me too sleepy. I didn't want to sleep while that man was out there. Besides, all I could think about was you."

"Take the medicine. You need to get some rest."

"But what about the man out there. I can't sleep knowing he's—"

"Look and see if he's gone now."

He heard her put the phone down on the nightstand. It did not surprise him when she returned to the phone and told him the car was gone.

"Good. Please try and get some sleep. You need the rest. I know you don't want to miss the trip to New Orleans."

"Don't worry. I'm going no matter what."

"I'll see you in a few hours. You know how much I love you."

"And you know how much I love you. Please, honey, drive carefully," Jenny said softly.

After hanging up, he undressed and tossed his clothes on the left side of the double bed. He knew his preparation would be in vain. Charged with the events of the past eighteen hours, he focused on the details rolling past his mind's eye: like film in a projector. Forward, reverse, search, critique, edit, all in rapid succession.

No sleep tonight, he realized as he slipped naked between crisp, fresh, white sheets. There would be no solution to the problem tonight.

He reached over and picked up the stack of messages. He arranged them in order of importance. Then, he opened the white envelope marked confidential. The message read: "Where have you been? Your job is to raise funds and handle PR. See me at 7:00 a.m. sharp, Sunday morning. Bring a damn good excuse." Coach Lee's signature was scrawled across the bottom.

* Eight *

As dawn broke, a rose-pink sky greeted the new day. Wispy cirrus clouds faintly suggested a high pressure system was gliding in from the northwest. The light gray, bulletproof plexiglas that circled the round structure, one of six clustered together on a Lake Norman cove, provided a panoramic view of the morning scene.

Frank Dolci sat across from Francesco Mancotta at a round, glass-top breakfast table that rested on a bamboo pedestal. Dolci read the sports section of the *Charlotte Observer* while his partner studied the business section. Steam disappeared lazily as it rose from large, white, china coffee cups.

Breaking the silence as he neatly folded his paper, Francesco Mancotta said, "You know, I think I enjoy this home more than your Captiva Island retreat."

"Even in the winter?" Dolci lowered the paper and glanced at the sun as it peeked over tall trees which lined the cove several hundred yards behind his partner. Although the scene repeated itself throughout the year, it never failed to inspire him.

"I think so," Mancotta said. He turned to view the source of light that beamed through the floor-to-ceiling encircling window.

Dolci said, "It's beautiful, but cold. Captiva's probably seventy degrees by now. I don't like cold weather." Dolci was glad he would soon be returning to his million-dollar island retreat in Florida. He'd noticed that cold weather bothered him more since he'd had his heart attack.

The handsome, black-haired Italian considered Dolci's evaluation for a moment. Then, after sipping coffee, he replied, "No, I think it's more than that. I like warm weather, too. But this place is so peaceful and it changes with the seasons. Captiva remains the same year-round."

"You're right about it changing all right. Peaceful? Have

you ever been here on Saturday or Sunday during the summer?"

"No. Come to think of it, I haven't."

"That would alter your perspective. Ski boats race up and down this cove like it was a drag strip. I stay away from here on weekends and holidays."

Mancotta dabbed his black mustache with a linen napkin. "I didn't realize that. You can't find privacy anymore. There's no place to escape to."

"Especially if you want to live near water," Dolci added.

Dolci smelled the aroma of fried bacon before the servant crossed the room. He watched him set a platter of food on the center of the table, refill their coffee cups, turn crisply, and leave the room.

Dolci selected three fried eggs, two pieces of crisp, thick bacon, and a large slice of salty country ham. He watched Mancotta eye the generous serving with amusement. His partner was in excellent condition for a man fifty-five years old and watched his diet carefully. Dolci didn't care. He believed in living life to the fullest. One of his greatest pleasures was richly prepared food.

"Aren't you hungry?"

"Not really. I'll try a little of that ham on a biscuit, but that's all. You know I seldom eat breakfast."

Dolci decided to tease him. "Thought you were worried about your cholesterol. You're always giving me hell."

"But I'm not the one who had a heart attack. You know I can't get North Carolina country ham in New Orleans."

"I bought a whole one for you to take home."

"Thanks."

Dolci stabbed a large piece of ham with his fork. He decided to get down to business. There was no need to repeat the conversation he'd had with Burton last night. Mancotta had heard their entire conversation through a hidden intercom that could eavesdrop on any one of the five structures. It was centrally located in a large study, with a legal library that Dolci had stocked for Mancotta's benefit. Dolci swallowed the ham, then asked, "Well, what do you think about Burton?"

"You scared the hell out of him. But he's got a lot of balls. You might have to cut them off before it's all over."

"Do you think he suspects the coach is involved?"

"I doubt it. You gave him a good reason not to."

Dolci picked up a crisp slice of thick bacon. "He was right though, you know. Lee is in a hell of a lot better position to fix the game."

Mancotta searched the pocket of his black satin robe with his right hand. "I know. That still bothers me. I don't like letting that goddamn coach sway our instincts about how a fix should be handled."

"He made some good points. But remember, he'll be with us for years. We'll jeopardize his career if we have him throw the game with coaching mistakes. People will ask a lot of questions. He's right when he says he's under a microscope. And there's no way in hell that he could go to the Collins kid and tell him to fake an injury in the second half. Think of the risks involved."

Mancotta looked at the breast pocket of Dolci's gold robe. "Frank, you have my pen."

"I picked it up. You left it in the study." Dolci handed him the pen.

Mancotta began writing on a slip of white paper. "Let's take a look at this as it stands now. You say we've got several options. I want to get them straight in my mind." He scrawled the names of two teams on the right side of the paper: Charlotte vs Fort Myers. "They're in for sure," he said, pointing to the paper.

"Right."

"Fortunately, both of those teams are in our pocket." Mancotta added four names to the list: UNC vs Texas; UCLA vs Marquette. "These four aren't."

"Unfortunately, there are many teams that will remain in the top twenty forever, and we will never have the opportunity to control them. There is a definite dividing line in college basketball between the 'haves' and the 'have nots.' We couldn't offer the coach of any one of those four teams enough to consider working with us. It would be too risky. To those men, pride and institutional values would likely outweigh any financial gain or physical threat we could present. Outraged public opinion and exposure are our biggest problems. As long as it's our word against an unknown coach's, we have little to worry about." Dolci lifted his coffee cup and eyed Mancotta over the brim.

"I agree, but why don't you try to pocket the referees?"

Dolci replaced his cup heavily on the saucer; an audible click resulted. "That's been tried before—it didn't work."

Mancotta tapped his pen on the glass tabletop. "Maybe it was handled improperly."

Dolci speared another slice of country ham. "Those fucking officials have a built-in honesty ethic. It's been drilled into them. I think it's far too dangerous to approach them. Besides, we would have to bribe a lot of them. We wouldn't know which two are handling the championship game until a few hours before it starts. Keep in mind that the refs picked to handle the Final Four are the cream of the crop. They take that shit seriously. Another thing— instant replays would make their calls smell like dead fish. No, this is the best way. I was sure of that four years ago when I picked out five coaches of unknown stature with unheard-of teams."

"Well, you know I haven't had as much faith in this plan from the beginning as you do," Mancotta said. "But I guess I have to agree. I just don't like this Burton character. He strikes me as an independent bastard."

"I'll think about that," Dolci said. "Perhaps I can arrange to shake him up enough to make him think twice before he does something stupid. But I think I've got it pretty well covered. If he still decides to go to somebody for help, it'll be Coach Lee."

"I think you're probably right. Wasn't that what Lee thought, too?"

"Exactly. According to him, Burton's so damn loyal, he'll run to the coach to keep things quiet. If he talks to the police, he knows the lid will blow off, and his precious alma mater will be smudged in their moment of glory." Dolci liked his psychological assessment of the situation, but a nagging thought lingered, and he thought Mancotta might point out the flaw.

"I still think you've taken too big a risk here. I don't know why you didn't let Anthony go straight to the Collins kid. Why have a middle man?"

Although Dolci had anticipated it, the question stung. He began to eat again. With his mouth full, he had time to think. He wanted to consider his answer to Mancotta's question carefully. He knew that Burton had not acted as predicted. When he had discussed it with Lee, the coach had insisted that Burton would leap at the chance to be the middle man; yet he had not.

Dolci was concerned about that response. He smacked his lips and swallowed. "I think Lee was right in his analysis of the situation. Burton's a bit impetuous, and sometimes fails to get all the facts before jumping in and swimming. I think he misjudged the temperature of the water. He's almost too candid for his own good.

"You heard what his answer was when I asked him if he planned to speak out at the press conference. He said, 'Of course not.' I did that on purpose. I didn't want to let him know that we knew he was planning to talk to Coach Lee, but I wanted him to sense that we didn't trust him either. It wouldn't have been good if he had gone to Coach Lee. No way could we let Burton know the coach is on the—"

"You're not answering my question," Mancotta interrupted.

Dolci was irritated. "I'm getting to it. We used Burton because Lee is not sure how Collins will react. Burton's his friend and has the best chance of persuading him. After all, there's $100,000 in it for him if he does.

"I gave Burton a hell of a lot of reasons to keep his mouth shut. That tip from Lee about Burton's pot smoking was a damn good one. You should have seen the expression on his face when I laid that on him." Dolci motioned to the servant who had just entered the room.

He pointed at the empty, white, china coffee pot. "More coffee."

"Yes, sir." The tall, black-haired servant stacked the soiled breakfast plates on a silver serving tray along with the coffee pot, and left, balancing the tray on his fingertips above his right shoulder.

"I just don't understand why you're handling this matter in person." Mancotta reached in his pocket and pulled out a fine Havana cigar. He handed it to Dolci. "I brought you this from New Orleans."

Dolci smelled the fat cigar and smiled. Mancotta was right—he was taking a hell of a risk. He wasn't exactly sure why, either. Possibly it was that it had been years since he'd gotten involved in something that made him feel alive again, part of the action. He clipped off the end of the cigar with a silver clipper. "Thanks," he said as he lit the cigar. "I don't like running that risk either. But remember, neither man has ever met you. They don't even know you exist. There's no risk for you."

"So far, that's true. But why didn't we assign this project to one of the soldiers?"

"We've been over that five times before. You're beating a dead horse." Dolci recalled his initial insistence on handling the entire setup with the five different coaches. He realized then he would be exposing himself in a fashion he had never dared before. His reasoning had been simple: most coaches are egocentric. They always want to deal with the top man. Since he had a legitimate cover as a shrewd, wealthy businessman, it made sense for him to make the contacts personally. And Mancotta seemed convinced the scheme was too dangerous.

So Dolci had decided to handle the thing himself. Unwise, maybe, but after his brush with death, it gave him the feeling he needed. He had to feel his adrenaline flow again. After all, he wondered, how much longer did he really have to live?

And so far, his plan was working perfectly. He remembered making contact with the coaches about four years ago. Each of the five coaches he picked was located in a different area of the country. When Dolci had expressed a personal interest in their careers, they all paid close attention. Few struggling coaches could reject a possible friendship with a multimillionaire sugar daddy.

At first, Dolci had offered assistance in recruiting. Nothing illegal in the beginning: just some high-paying summer jobs for the players, a practice already widely accepted by the majority of coaches. As long as the student-athlete was not being paid more than any other student would be for the same work—and he was qualified to do the task—the NCAA considered the summer job to be legal. Yet, in some cases, summer employment was used as an inducement for a recruit to sign the National Letter of Intent.

That provided Dolci the perfect "in" with his selected coaches. With his help, they cleverly skirted the NCAA rules, and provided incentives to young recruits, resulting in favorable final decisions. Some highly sought-after high school stars signed on the dotted line. And the rationalization used to justify such practices generally followed the line that, "Everybody else is cheating in some form or another, so why shouldn't we stretch the rules just a bit."

Later, Dolci pushed things to the limit. He helped some of his coaches falsify transcripts. In some cases, he even bribed junior college officials to produce records that showed students had attended their school, when in fact, the players had never even been inside the campus door. That practice enabled some of the coaches to pluck "playground pros" out of Harlem and other ghettos throughout the country. Many hadn't even graduated from high school.

After that came cash inducements—cars, clothes, and just about anything a player would request if he were playing up to his potential. Their athletes were professionals in an amateur sport. And when a student started flunking out, Dolci came to the rescue with funds to bribe professors to pass the player.

If caught, such flagrant violations would bring immediate punitive action from the NCAA in the form of probation. Then a team—and perhaps all inter-collegiate teams fielded by that university—would no longer be eligible to participate in post-season tournaments or appear on televised games for a specified number of years. Probation was intended to serve as a deterrent, an agreed-upon punishment that all member universities feared.

Those were the risks inherent in cheating. A few coaches

looked for loopholes, testing the water. Once they got their feet wet, they often plunged in deeper.

Dolci and Mancotta learned the ins and outs of college basketball in Las Vegas. Their bookmaking operation provided numerous insights. After careful deliberation, Dolci had then presented his long-term plan to Mancotta.

By helping selected coaches land "blue chippers," they could expect return favors. Such favors would come in three different sizes, ranging from small to excruciating: providing inside information, shaving points, and deliberately throwing a game. The latter, a true sacrifice, was never discussed with any of the coaches. But Dolci knew that the time would come when betting lines dictated a loss.

Such control provided their bookmaking operation with a definite edge. Gambling always favored the "house" anyway. The plan would tilt the scales heavily in their favor.

When he realized that his voice had reflected irritation with Mancotta's redundant questioning, Dolci decided to break the silence. He would humor his partner. "Francesco, I'm sorry. I interrupted you long ago. We haven't completed our discussion about our various options." He pointed to the slip of paper Mancotta had begun scrawling on.

"Please forgive me," Mancotta responded, "for plodding along here. I realize you understand the options far better than I do. You're the expert in this field, so the exercise is really my pedantry."

Dolci smiled at Mancotta's use of the word pedantry. Long ago, he had pointed out that his partner should have been a science professor, and he labeled him a "pedant." And Mancotta had replied, "Yes, and you would probably never pass my course."

Mancotta stared at the paper he had written on. "You anticipate that North Carolina will defeat Texas and UCLA will defeat Marquette. Therefore, those two teams will play each other in the semi-finals."

"That's right." Dolci nodded at the servant who had entered the room with a fresh pot of coffee. He refilled their cups and left the room.

Mancotta continued. "And you believe that North Carolina will defeat UCLA?"

Dolci nodded before sipping the steaming brew of coffee and chicory.

"You plan to have Fort Myers lose the game against Charlotte in the semi-finals," Mancotta said, assuming an affirmative answer. "But assuming all of this is correct, what leads you to believe that Patrick McLaughlin will consent to throwing the game? He's a proud Irishman. I'm sure he's like any other coach who dreams of winning the national championship."

The question had nagged Dolci for several days. Mancotta had a point and he knew it. The answer was clear. "He must cooperate, or we'll take matters into our own hands."

Mancotta frowned, nodded slowly, and exhaled. "One thing I'm still not real clear on is how you expect Charlotte to be favored over North Carolina with a large enough margin that shaving points is possible?"

"I'm not sure it is. Our bookies tell me that public sentiment will lean toward them. However, they probably won't be favored to win."

Mancotta interrupted, "Then we have the wrong team in our pocket."

"No, my friend, we have the right team. Let me show you." Dolci took the pen and paper from Mancotta. "Suppose the line is Charlotte plus 4." He wrote: UC = plus 4 vs UNC. "We can have some of our bookies give Charlotte plus 7 or 8. Easy action, right? Those sentimental bastards that love underdogs are going to see Charlotte as an emotional favorite. After Charlotte thrashes Fort Myers, they are going to think that the Hornets have a shot at it. And if we don't pull in the reins, they might just beat Carolina. We've got to arrange a loss big enough to beat the spread."

"That makes sense," said Mancotta.

"So, everybody wants a piece of the soft action that we're handing out. They grab Charlotte plus 7. We cover the seemingly foolish bet. Then Charlotte loses by 10 or 12. We win millions." Dolci smiled.

"Wait a minute," Mancotta said, now somewhat puzzled. "Just a few minutes ago you said that Lee was right. He would be under a microscope and you couldn't afford to lose him."

"He'll cooperate. In fact, he's cooperated more than any of the others. If Collins fakes an injury and stays on the bench for the whole second half, North Carolina will blow them off the court.

"I've simply been humoring Lee with the point-shaving idea, and the pro coaching position that I promised him. He thinks I can fix it so he can still try to win, just shave a few points. I don't think that's the way it can happen. Not that way at all. But he'll go along no matter what. We've given him money and could expose him as a cheater."

Mancotta thought for a minute. After weighing the consequences of various options, he said, "Suppose we make some arrangements with some of the other people in Vegas."

"What kind of arrangements?"

"We push for Charlotte to be slightly favored over Carolina. If we get the line close, we can really look like we're giving easy action with Charlotte plus 4."

"I don't know. I'm not sure we have enough bookies in our ranks to exert that kind of influence. Remember, the press does more to sway opinion than anybody else. Besides, we don't want the word to spread to all the syndicates."

"I know. But what about the 'Oddsmaker?' He owes me a favor."

Dolci had considered this his best and most plausible option. Bobby Nevada, prominently known as the "Oddsmaker," wrote a weekly syndicated column for 179 major newspapers across the country and predicted outcomes of important sports events. Many bettors stuck closely to his line. He had a good track record in predicting the outcome of basketball games. He could certainly sway public opinion. Dolci was pleased he had maneuvered Mancotta into making the suggestion.

"I think that should be our first option. Nevada owes you one on that fight fix. He knew the debt would come due someday. There's no better time than now."

Puffing on his cigar thoughtfully, Dolci paused, then continued. "I don't think he'll get Charlotte in a position to be favored enough so Lee can just shave a few points. They'll have to lose all right. But with Nevada swaying some opinion for us, Lee can at least go for a respectable loss. Who's going to blame him if his star gets hurt?" Dolci smiled.

He was pleased with his psychology. He had maneuvered Mancotta right into the plan without making the suggestion himself. Bobby Nevada was not indebted to him, only Mancotta, who had arranged a championship fight fix that shook the boxing world: a returning, over-the-hill underdog had managed to regain his title by knocking off the heavy-weight champion of the world. Mancotta had tipped Nevada in advance, and the "Oddsmaker" successfully predicted the outcome, seemingly against all odds. Dolci had not been involved in that scheme.

"I get the feeling you had this in mind all along," Mancotta said. "But don't worry. I'll take care of the details with Nevada. You handle the rest. Looks like Charlotte needs to trounce Fort Myers in the semi-finals. Let's hope McLaughlin has enough sense to see it your way."

"He'd better, or I'll make sure that he never coaches again."

"Frank, I'm not sure this scheme is worth that kind of risk."

"You worry too much."

Mancotta nodded. "What about that shipment you've got scheduled out of Colombia? There's three and a half million I've got invested in my half of the deal."

"It's all taken care of," Dolci said confidently. He hoped he was right.

* Nine *

Troy Burton was exhausted. Looking in the mirror one last time before he left the room, he saw telltale signs of insomnia etched on his face like a road map: puffy pouches under red, sore eyes, and wrinkled pale cheeks.

He checked his watch: five minutes to seven. He would be a few minutes early. Better early than late when Lee is involved, he thought as he stepped outside and turned to his left. Lee's room was just a few steps down the hall, room 208, the Albert Pick, Jr. suite. The door opened just before he started to knock.

Helen, Bill Lee's wife, was startled. "Troy, you scared me. What are you doing up so early?"

"Bill wanted to see me at seven." Troy admired her. For a woman in her mid-forties, she had an attractive figure, and in spite of being a coach's wife, she had few worry lines. Her face was smooth, youthful, framed by dark blond hair, shoulder-length and neatly coiffed.

"Well, I was just on my way to breakfast. You two can chat alone." She stepped outside the door.

"By the way, congratulations." He hugged her.

"Thank you. It sure was a big one." Pointing to the room, she whispered, "Go in there and cheer him up. I think he's already worried about the next game. I'm just happy we're going." She smiled.

"Me, too." He squeezed her hand affectionately.

Helen turned and walked down the hall. Troy fully expected that Jenny would look just as becoming when she was forty-five. Both women had that radiant, effervescent animation.

"Come in, Troy." Bill Lee stood holding the door open.

"Thanks," Troy said, noting Lee's serious tone. It was the first time he had been in the expensive suite. As he walked through the large foyer with mirrors, a small table, and two padded straight-back chairs, he noticed the teakwood floor immediately—his leather heels clicked sharply.

"Have a seat," Lee said, pointing to a flowered gold, black, and burnt orange couch.

Troy sank deep into the soft cushions. He was surprised by the oriental decor. The New Orleans flavor that the outside of the inn suggested had given him little reason to expect the inn's most expensive suite would be decorated in such fashion.

"Like a drink?" Bill Lee stepped behind a dark-stained wet-bar.

"Yes, thanks." Troy knew Lee meant orange juice, no vodka. The coach was a strict Southern Baptist, a teetotaler.

Lee handed him a tall glass of orange juice and sat on the opposite end of the sofa. "I trust you brought a good reason for disappearing last night. Let's have it."

Troy knew Lee was not going to accept his answer, but it was the best he had to offer. After sipping some juice, he plunged ahead. "Coach, I'm sorry, but I simply can't tell you where I was last night or who I was with. It's very personal."

Lee's eyes widened, his eyebrows arched. "I'm afraid that's not a satisfactory answer. In fact, it clouds the issue even more. You're here for a purpose. You know how important it is for you to stay in touch with me when you travel with the team. How many times have we discussed that?"

"Several."

"You're not being paid $33,000 a year to have a good time after the games, disappearing when the mood strikes you." Lee rose from the sofa. He walked over to the bar and picked up a dark brown pipe and a gold, plastic, tobacco pouch. He dipped the pipe in and scooped a bowl full of tobacco.

Troy watched him carefully, looking for a sign, a hint of any sort. Was Lee involved with Dolci? He hated to think that was possible. His suspicion was vague. Something he could not put his finger on tugged at his conscience.

Lee lit his pipe. "Troy, we may never get this far again." His tone was serious, fatherly. "Do you have any idea how lucky we are to be in the Final Four?"

Troy exhaled. "I know we've been lucky. But it's been more skill than luck."

"Not really," Lee said. He poured another glass of orange juice and returned to the couch. "I've been in this business for seventeen years. In coaching, you learn a great deal about people. You find players that don't give a damn about anything but themselves. Ego trippers. Oh, how they love the spotlight. And they usually crumble under pressure. They're losers in more ways than one.

"None of our kids are like that. And as a team they just happen to have jelled. Their chemistry's right. They can take the heat, too. When nobody believed in them and the press acted like they were a bunch of ragtag yardbirds, they did their talking on the court. Amazing how long it takes to change a skeptic into a believer, isn't it? It's a helluva lot of hard work, faith, and luck.

"Troy, you're important to our program. We all have to pull together. More so now than ever. People are depending on you to handle the tickets and fund-raising. Do it professionally, and we can raise that $250,000 and more. This opportunity may never come again for you or me or the University."

Lee paused. He looked at Troy and held his eyes as if to drive his next point home. "And above all else, don't sacrifice your integrity. That's something you've always demonstrated; it's the reason I picked you for the job. You're honest and you're loyal. Our supporters recognize that. You set a good example for them. Don't screw it up by doing something stupid."

The coach's speech was well received. The tugging thought that Lee might be involved let go.

"I appreciate that, Bill. I really had no control over what happened last night. I wasn't goofing off."

"OK, I'll accept that. And I won't press you about the matter any further."

Troy finished his juice. "Thank you. I'm sorry I screwed up your staff meeting."

"How did you know that I had planned one last night?"

"Jenny told me. She was worried about me and called

Lindsey. He told her."

"I hope you gave her a better explanation than you did me." Lee stopped himself. "Sorry, I didn't mean to bring it up again."

"That's OK," Troy said, smudging his glass with oily fingerprints.

Lee asked about Jenny's health. Troy appreciated his interest and explained how tough the intestinal flu had been on her. "I had to practically tie her down to keep her home."

Lee laughed. "She's really a fan, isn't she? I hope the win cheered her up. You think she'll be able to make it to New Orleans?"

"Absolutely. Even if we have to bring her doctor with us."

Lee smiled broadly, took his pipe from his mouth and pointed the stem at Troy. "I bet he wouldn't even charge you for *that* house call. Just hand him two tickets and he'll pack his bags."

Lee knew Troy's doctor had graduated from medical school at the University of North Carolina. Although he was a Tar Heel, he also contributed to the Hornets' Athletic Foundation. Troy had collared him with his "support two allegiances" theme.

"I think he'll qualify for two tickets anyway, but I bet we can move him up to Gold Hornet status."

"What club's he in now?" Lee asked, rolling his blue eyes as if searching his memory for the answer.

"He's a Big Hornet—gives $250 a year." Troy placed his smeared glass on the table. "I think a lot of folks are going to up their ante."

"Everybody loves a winner. Jumping on the old band-wagon is a familiar trait of sports fans," Lee said.

Both men had discussed that aspect of fund-raising before Troy accepted the job. Bill Lee had fought hard to have the new position of executive director approved. It had not been easy. Two years ago the university athletic coffers were stretched very thin. The most the foundation had raised before was $75,000. The hiring of a full-time fund-raiser had worked. Troy had quickly doubled gift giving in his first year at the controls. His methods of organization and salesmanship had complemented a fine twenty-game-win season. Although no tournament invitation was extended, the Charlotte community had excitedly anticipated their current success. All five starters had been expected to return and the schedule had been beefed up to include three "name" teams.

Lee stood up, glanced at his watch, and said, "It's 7:30. Our meeting starts at 8:00. Have you had breakfast yet?"

"No," Troy replied as he rose from the sofa.

"Good. John Windsor said he would be having breakfast about now. He wants to talk with you about tickets. I've got a few things to do to get ready for our staff meeting. Why don't you go on down and chat with him."

"OK." Deep in thought, Troy turned and left the room. He wondered if his decision not to tell the coach or the police about Dolci was a wise one. He knew, however, that once he revealed the plot to anyone, he would lose control of the situation. He wanted to consider all the ramifications before he jumped to conclusions. Maybe somebody else in the staff was guilty?

After Coach Lee had concluded his discussion with Troy, he walked over to a closet behind the wet-bar. Opening the white doors, he picked up his black leather briefcase and returned to the sofa.

Carefully unlocking it with a silver key, he searched in a pocket and retrieved a small, brown, leather booklet. Using a tiny gold key, he unlocked his secret diary.

He had been writing in it for several years. He only made entries when he felt compelled to do so. As an additional security measure, he wrote in a code he had devised. If the diary were discovered, he was sure no one would understand it.

He twisted his gold Cross ball-point pen to the ball-out position and decided on his entry. Neatly printing, he wrote: "Sunday, AM, day after ERC. The wolves have captured the hare. He's trapped and searching for escape. Question the hunters' decision."

He heard a clicking noise at the door: the sound of a key penetrating its mated lock. He quickly closed the diary and returned it to the inside of his briefcase. He was sure his wife was returning from breakfast; he did not want her to discover the private record. Even she had no idea that the diary existed. And he thanked God that she didn't.

* Ten *

Lindsey Ellis sat at a small circular table working feverishly. Statistical sheets were strewn about the room in an order only he understood. The work that had to be accomplished in the next week was staggering. It overshadowed the excitement the young SID—sports information director—was experiencing in anticipation of his first trip to a national championship. Ellis did not have to pinch himself to awaken to the reality of the situation. The NCAA had already done it for him.

At two o'clock this Sunday morning, he received a sleep-interrupting phone call from Bob Conway, director of information for the NCAA. "Where are the stats for yesterday's game?" Conway asked politely.

Ellis jumped out of bed immediately. He had forgotten the assignment completely. Mistakes were not a normal part of his repertoire. After apologizing to Conway, he began updating all the year-to-date information, adding in the statistics from the victory over Indiana.

The information was now completed, but Ellis could not rest. The press kit would have to be updated and ready for immediate distribution. He had already been forewarned by Conway that the media would descend upon him like vultures on a newly discovered carcass. The University of Charlotte was virtually unknown, and the mystique behind its sudden emergence into basketball prominence would have to be unveiled.

Helping the press obtain all the necessary background facts was the role of the SID. Ellis had longed for the opportunity to serve his alma mater in such a capacity, but he had never dreamed, when he accepted the position five years ago, that he would find himself in the national spotlight.

He eased back in his chair and looked around his hotel room. Boxes of press guides and other assorted information were stacked in piles along the walls. He handed them out to the press like after-dinner mints. Sometimes the news he provided was used, but generally it gained only a cursory reading. A sports information director always knows that a good reporter hunts the unusual. Looking for angles and related human-interest stories is a sports reporter's primary goal.

Ellis provided facts and figures for analysis of the team's success, but most journalists wanted quite a bit more. Some dug for dirt. The SID had to be handy with a vacuum cleaner.

Because of the sudden emergence of the unknown team from Charlotte, Ellis knew his job was clearly going to be more taxing than that of a sports information director for one of the perennial powers like UCLA, UNC, Texas or Marquette. The nation's press was already well in tune with those schools' powerful programs. Their players were well known, their dominant stature understandable. And they had big budgets and large staffs to get the word out.

Ellis thought for a moment about his counterpart at UFFM. Was he going through the same thing? Probably not. The Chargers from Florida had already been to the NCAA tournament last year. They had been defeated in a close game with Marquette. Since that game had been televised nationwide, UFFM had gained a great deal of recognition. No, Ellis mused, UFFM would not be the mystery team the Hornets would.

He checked his watch: 7:47 a.m. The staff meeting with Bill Lee would begin in thirteen minutes. He decided it was time to stop working and finish dressing. As he rose from his chair, his legs cramped. Tension and sleepless nights had assailed his athletic body. As always, the first place that suffered was his legs. He had dodged surgery for nine years after a high school football injury ruined his chance for a scholarship. Until that moment, he had been a promising defensive halfback and was sought after by several recruiters. Normal disappointment did not prevail; Ellis was stoic. His rock-steady character did not allow room for bitterness.

He framed his best memories and decided to attend his

hometown college, the University of Charlotte. At that time, the budding Charlotte campus did not even have a gym, and sports were a twinkling in the chancellor's eye. Football was out of the question—too expensive. Plans were formed to develop a major college athletic program with basketball as the primary sport.

College basketball was adored in North Carolina. With four very potent ACC schools located in the heart of the state, the richness of the sport had captured the fans' devotion.

After graduation over a decade ago, Ellis had been offered the first full-time SID slot. He understood from the beginning that his job was going to be tough. The team he was promoting was unknown, untested, and almost laughable when compared to Duke, Wake Forest, North Carolina, and North Carolina State. Those schools had tradition, the aura that surrounds a university only after years have melted countless coats of paint and breathed generations of memories into hallowed halls of repetition.

Ellis dressed, foregoing a suit and tie in favor of a comfortable pair of jeans and a gold pullover sweater. While combing his light blond hair, he looked carefully for signs of fatigue. None was present. His adrenaline was flowing—the electric high of finally experiencing the dream of his career. Exhaustion would have to wait until the tournament was over.

He heard the phone ring. The same beckoning that jangled his nerves throughout last evening was back to interrupt his privacy. He did not mind talking to people. The only problem was the questions were always the same; only the voices were different. He felt like the lone survivor of a plane crash.

"Lindsey Ellis," he answered, hoping that the party on the other line might realize he had the wrong person.

"Morning, Lindsey. This is Chuck. Hope I didn't wake you up," said Haigler politely.

"No, of course you didn't. How in the hell are you?" He liked Chuck Haigler, the *Charlotte Observer* reporter who covered the Hornets.

"Still recovering from the shock. Slapped myself this

morning to make sure I wasn't dreaming."

"What can I do for you, Chuck?"

"I need a couple of hours with Ted Collins. Can you clear it with coach Lee?" Haigler asked.

Ellis knew the request was a mere formality. Haigler had a right to anticipate approval. "Sure, I've got a staff meeting with him in a few minutes; I'll ask him. What have you got in mind?"

"Want to feature him in an article on Friday. Sort of a follow-up on that story we did on him last year. Expand it a little more."

"Sounds good. I'll get back to you with the details of where and when. Ted's going to be pretty busy these next few days," Ellis said. He had already received calls from all over the country requesting interviews. Suddenly, Collins was becoming a nationwide folk hero.

"Thanks," said Haigler, pausing momentarily. "You wouldn't happen to know where Troy is?"

"No, and you're not the only one looking for him either," Ellis said. "Did you try to call him this morning?"

"Yeah, just a few minutes ago. I tried to reach him several times last night. We were supposed to go to dinner together."

"Maybe he's already gone to breakfast," Ellis said. He wondered what would cause Burton to forget a dinner with Haigler. They were friends. Not close, but nevertheless, it was not at all like him to forget a dinner meeting.

"Well, when you see him, tell him to call me. He stood me up—we were supposed to go to Flannagin's."

"I'll tell him. Hope he's at the meeting." Ellis had already decided not to explain that Burton's absence had forced the postponement of last night's staff conference.

"One other thing."

"What's that?" Ellis asked.

"I understand there's going to be a big reception for the team at the Civic Center. Do you know any of the details?" Haigler asked.

"Yeah. It's being promoted by WBTV. Heard they're expecting a pretty big crowd."

"What time?"

"Two thirty."

"OK. I'm going to be leaving in a few minutes. I'll check with Clawson to see if he wants me to cover it," Haigler said, referring to Dave Clawson, the *Observer's* sports editor. "Haven't been able to reach him this morning. Maybe he's assigned it to somebody else."

"See you back in Charlotte." Ellis hung up and checked his watch. It was almost eight o'clock. He grabbed his notebook and hurried out the door. Bill Lee always expected staff members to be punctual.

Troy Burton pulled a brown straight-back chair into the athletic staff's circle between Lindsey Ellis and Bo Evans. "Sorry I'm late. I got tied up with John Windsor. He thinks we're going to pick up a lot of new Gold Hornet members. Most of them just want the privilege of getting tickets to New Orleans. That's a fair trade—we get a $1,000 donation; they get two tickets."

The entire executive staff of the Athletic Department was present. Bill Lee sat on one end of the couch and used the coffee table to spread his notes. Lane Gilliam, the assistant athletic director, sat on the other end of the couch. A medium-sized box rested between them on the middle cushion.

Earl Ward sat in a rocking chair and he asked casually, "Coach, did you get that note I put in your message box about Bobby Furlough?"

"Yes, I did. I hope he changes his mind," Lee said. He peered at his notes again.

The only other person that understood the full meaning of the brief exchange between Ward and Lee would be Bo Evans, Troy reflected. As assistant basketball coaches, Evans and Ward shared duties in recruiting and mapping strategy. They were Bill Lee's right-hand men.

Troy had made it his business to ask questions and keep abreast of what was going on with recruiting. They didn't tell him everything, but they had talked about Bobby Furlough. He was a promising young recruit from New

Jersey. All three coaches had visited him and were confident he would sign the National Letter of Intent. Most Division I teams honored the document as a legal contract that obligated a student-athlete to play at least a year for that university. After that, if the athlete chose to transfer to another school that honored the letter, he would have to sit out a year. The waiting period was intended to discourage impulsive young athletes from transferring from one university to another when they became unhappy. But in recent years, transfers were becoming a major problem. The deterrent was not strong enough.

Ward, the stylish black assistant coach, had jotted a short note to Bill Lee about the results of his phone contact with the slender black recruit. The "kid," a term coaches used when referring to recruits, had announced that he had been contacted by Notre Dame and planned to make a visit to the Irish campus. He had told Ward that he would probably sign in April if they made an offer.

This morning as they met, passing through the hall on the way to breakfast, Ward had confided that he was puzzled by that news. The recruit had watched Charlotte's impressive victory over the number-one team in the nation. When Ward called him to get his reaction right after the game, the recruit dropped his bombshell about Notre Dame.

Earl Ward would not give up, however. When Bill Lee hired him right before hiring Bo Evans, Troy knew that the former personnel counselor was going to make a fine recruiter. He was sincere, straightforward, and intelligent. Lee had recognized those qualities over fourteen years ago when he recruited Ward to play basketball at a private Georgia college, Lee's first coaching slot.

"Don't tell me the kid's getting cold feet," Evans said to Ward.

Stroking his mustache with his right thumb and forefinger, Ward merely nodded, a sign that he preferred not to discuss the matter in front of the rest of the staff.

Recruiting was a touchy subject, particularly with Bill Lee. The three coaches had agreed long ago that the less said to other people about recruits the better. The kids were fickle, and any talk about who the coaches had on the hook, or who they thought they had on the hook, could serve no useful purpose. If a recruit signed, coach Lee would have Ellis put out a carefully worded press release at the proper time, not necessarily immediately, since the announcement could sometimes scare off another prospect.

Like most other recruiters, Ward and Evans faced a tough assignment. Getting into the back of a young man's brain and figuring out what made him tick was the key to building a solid team. One wrong player could dissolve the psychological glue that held the team together. Bill Lee called it "the right chemistry." Regardless of talent, a team had to have it to perform successfully.

Lee looked up from his notes. "All right, gentlemen, I think we're about ready to start. Let's discuss tickets first. There's going to be a mad scramble for them. We'd better have our act together. We need to present a picture of fairness to the public.

"Troy, I expect you to coordinate with Lane in handling them. Be damn sure you two guys can account for every last one of them. Keep a list; make sure it's accurate."

"Do you want to know individual seat assignments?" Troy asked.

"Yes, that wouldn't hurt. You never know what may come up. We may need to find somebody on short notice and not want to announce it to the rest of the world," Lee said, alluding to the Superdome's paging system.

Turning to Gilliam and tapping his pen on the brown box that rested between them on the center sofa cushion, Lee asked, "Are these the tickets?"

"Yes," the assistant athletic director answered.

Gilliam had received the tickets from the host university ticket coordinator at Wake Forest. At all tournament sites, the NCAA chose a member university to coordinate with them in handling the various details required to raise and lower the curtain. Fans seldom ever realized just how many details were included in that process. Those involved behind the scenes, especially those participating on a host university's volunteer staff, quickly discovered the intricate tasks required an enormous amount of hard work. Ticket sales, press conferences, practice schedules, television and radio coordination, cocktail parties, game program production, concession sales, lodging, and transportation required skillful planning and preparation. With numerous sites involved throughout the nation, NCAA administrators had to work all year preparing for their showcase event.

Lee stopped studying his notes and broke the long silence. "Let's talk about ticket sales and priority. How many and to what groups?"

"How many did we get, Lane, two thousand?" Ellis asked.

"Right."

"Bill, I think we're going to have to give the students at least half of that allotment," Ellis said.

Troy was glad he didn't have Ellis's job. As sports information director, Ellis often found himself in a position of having to defend various policies the athletic department set. The most difficult for him to deal with were those involving students and tickets. He cringed whenever various student representatives descended upon his office. They seldom came to compliment him on the fine job he was doing.

"That's going to make things awfully tough on us," Troy said, referring to the Athletic Foundation.

"I know, but the students are what this is all about," Ellis replied.

"True. But without the contributors, the students would have nothing to cheer about." Troy had argued that point with Ellis numerous times. He agreed the students were very important. Yet the financing of collegiate sports— particularly in states like North Carolina—was a very tenuous situation.

No taxes were funneled into the state's higher educational system to support intercollegiate sports. The universities had to rely on three avenues for revenue: gate receipts, student fees, and donations. Gate receipts only related to spectator sports and were entirely dependent on success. People came to see winners. In Charlotte the problem was compounded by the fans' desire to see not only a winner, but also first-rate competition. The ACC's domination on television and radio tended to spoil them. And the new NBA team in Charlotte was stiff competition indeed.

Financial problems had doubled for all universities in the nation when the government enforced Title IX of the Civil Rights Act in the late 1970s. Equal, proportionate scholarships for women put many programs immediately in the red, particularly when basketball and football were not excluded from the head count. Suddenly, female athletes burst into the locker rooms of campuses throughout the nation, requiring huge sums of capital. Athletic directors were forced to make cuts in order to equalize spending. Their only other choice was to raise more money.

At the University of Charlotte, that responsibility weighed heavily on Troy's shoulders. Since the key to fund-raising rested in what Troy termed "social exposure of privilege, directly translated through team success," he pushed hard to see that all donors were given special privileges whenever possible.

He had translated his theory into a computer program developed to objectively assign point values to each foundation member. They received points on a sliding scale in four categories: funds given in the current year, number of consecutive years as a donor, total amount given since becoming a member, and an added point if the contributor was an alumnus.

The computer tallied the points and assigned priority numbers from one on up to the last foundation member. It was his method of converting dollars and longevity to privileges for season-ticket seat assignments, post-season tournament tickets, and rights to attend special functions.

Realizing the problems at hand, Troy said, "Coach, we are going to have a number of members who aren't going to get to go to the game. I agree students are important. I just want you to be aware that some folks are going to be upset. We'll have to explain our policy carefully."

"I know. We're going to catch it from all sides. There's no way we can sell tickets to everybody who wants to go."

Troy smiled. "That could be a double-edged sword. Some folks are going to threaten to withdraw support, but if we handle it right, we might find them increasing their donations."

Every staff member understood. Supply and demand in fund-raising operated essentially the same way it did in the world's economy.

"What about the chancellor? Has anybody spoken with him or Dr. DeWitt?" Lee asked.

No one spoke. Troy and Ellis shook their heads.

"Well, I think he's going to ask for a good number of tickets. The legislature is in session this year, and we've got several proposals up for approval—about fifteen million dollars in new classrooms. He's going to want to do a lot of politicking. You can bet on that." Lee looked at Troy and Ellis.

"What if the Tar Heels beat Texas? Won't they be likely to take care of some of those folks, too?" Ellis asked.

Lee smiled wryly. "Probably. But they have enough pull already to get whatever they need—half of the House graduated from Chapel Hill."

Troy knew Lee's exaggeration was his method of making a point. The University of North Carolina had prestige, tradition, and above all, people in high places.

"Coach, I don't think they have anything pending this year," Lane Gilliam said. "Besides they're going to have a tough time handling all their contributors. You can bet they won't be giving their students one thousand tickets."

"No, they sure won't," Troy said. He recalled a controversy that flared up when the Tar Heels went to the championships at the Omni in Atlanta in 1977. Because the location had been within less than a day's drive, the mad rush for tickets had been bitter. That year the newspaper reported the Tar Heels allocated about a hundred tickets for students, not counting the pep band. Such decisions looked callous on the surface, but in reality they weren't, Troy thought. Without contributors the program would fade into oblivion. College athletics had become big business; tough, sound management decisions had to be made.

"Lindsey, I think you and Troy should schedule a meeting with the chancellor as soon as you get in Monday morning and find out what he needs. Be tactful. He understands our problem probably better than we do. What it comes right down to is whatever he has to have, he gets. He's the man. Don't forget—if it hadn't been for his foresight, none of us would be sitting here right now." Lee looked around the room. Everyone agreed.

Troy was surprised. Not by the coach's candor—that was normal. But he never heard the coach make such a positive comment about any administrator before. And there had been times when Lee harshly criticized the vice chancellor for development, Dr. Art Goldman. From that point on, Troy had the impression Lee thought all administrators were blind and uninformed about the value of athletics. Again the coach continued to confound him.

Lee was not an easy man to gauge. Even after two years of working closely together, Troy still continued to observe new and various personality traits bubbling to the surface. Lee was highly intelligent, intense, opinionated, sincere, dedicated, angry, candid, audacious, humble, and some-times retiring.

In short, he was an enigma. But the more Troy witnessed of the multifaceted personality, the more he came to admire him. As Troy had originally thought, Lee was clearly the best person with whom to discuss Dolci's proposition. It would drop an unbelievably heavy burden on his shoulders, but he might see a solution.

"When do you want to put tickets on sale for the students?" Lee looked at Ellis, then Gilliam.

It was Ellis's additional administrative duty to see that tickets were distributed to students. Late in the season, though, his job as SID escalated so much he had asked for Lane Gilliam to assist him. Gilliam hated handling tickets: balancing the books worried him.

"I suggest we start as soon as possible after we talk to the chancellor," Gilliam said. "And I think we should be the only people to handle these tickets." He patted the box.

"Absolutely!" Lee said.

Troy said, "Coach, I've heard those tickets will be worth about $800 apiece on the street. A lot of students are going to be tempted to sell them. That's something else to consider before we go handing out half our allotment to them."

"Good point. See what I mean about being caught between a rock and a hard place?" Lee asked, shaking his head.

Lee held up a note. "OK. While we're on that subject, I received a phone message from Major Thames last night while we were out to dinner. All it said was there was some problem with students and tickets. Anybody know what he wants?"

"Yeah, he called me, too," Ellis said, lighting a cigarette. "Students have started camping outside the gym. They're lined up at the ticket office."

"Already? Hell, we couldn't give away tickets last year." Bo Evans sat up in his chair. "Oh, how they love it when you're in the big time." He crossed his legs and chewed on a slim cigar he had taken from his pocket and not yet kindled. The handsome former UCLA basketball star—he had later warmed the bench in the NBA because an arrogant coach gave up on him prematurely—was considered to be Lee's heir apparent.

Lee shook his head. "We need to solve that problem immediately. I hate to see them standing out in the cold. Can't we let them inside or make some other arrangements?"

Ellis puffed on his cigarette and looked out of the corner of his eye at Lee. "Thames did last night, but he said the line is going to be too big tonight, and since there are faculty offices inside the gym, he can't take the chance of having people in there with nobody to keep an eye on them. I'm not sure there is a whole lot we can do until we get back today, but I've got an idea of how we can solve the problem for tonight."

Lee smiled. "I figured you would come up with something, Lindsey."

Bo Evans winked conspiratorially at Lee and said, "Right, Coach. Lindsey sure doesn't like having those students on his back." Turning to Ellis and holding his unlit cigar between his thumb and first two fingers, tapping imaginary ashes in the air, Evans added, "I believe you'd rather wrestle a gator than mess with those students."

Everybody laughed except Ellis. Then a smile crept across his face and became a grin.

"OK. Handle the details, Lindsey," said Lee, turning to Gilliam. "Lane, give him a hand—he's covered up to his ass in press releases."

Gilliam groaned. Troy knew what he was thinking. Gilliam was on the hook again. Oh, how he despised selling tickets to students. No doubt he was going to push for hiring a full-time ticket manager when budgets were being prepared in the next few months. Gilliam was right—tickets shouldn't be the an assistant athletic director's responsibility. It wasn't the SID's job, either.

Troy knew all of that could mean trouble for him. If worse came to worse, they might try to pawn the job off on him. They would probably use the reasoning that he was the most logical choice. After all, Troy mused, he had to make the decisions as to who got them and who sat where; so why not give him the entire job? Troy shuddered at the thought.

"OK. What about travel arrangements?" Lee asked.

"I spoke to Bob Conway late last night," Ellis said. "He's got us staying at the Marriott. It's downtown at the foot of Canal Street. He said it has a great view of the city and the river. Told me it was either there or the Fairmont. I said it didn't matter to me. I don't know the difference between the two. I've never been to New Orleans."

"There's a lot of difference," Troy said. "I was raised in New Orleans. The Marriott is a fine hotel, but it's modern. It doesn't have the charm or the history the Fairmont has. The Fairmont's the old refurbished Roosevelt Hotel on University Place. It's closer to the Superdome. I think we'd be better off there." He looked at the staff for reactions. No one seemed to have feelings one way or the other. But to him, it was important. The Fairmont was New Orleans.

"What's the closest hotel to the Superdome?" Gilliam

asked.

Troy said, "The Hyatt Regency is part of the whole complex; it has a walkway that connects with the arena."

Ellis lit another cigarette. "That's where the NCAA will be set up. All the press will be staying there, and I'll need to stay there."

"I don't want us there. That's also where the NABC will be holding their meeting this year. It'll be a madhouse," Lee said.

"What's the NABC?" Troy asked.

Evans leaned back in his chair. "The National Association of Basketball Coaches. They meet every year during the tournament."

Troy decided to build a stronger case. "The Marriott is right on the edge of the French Quarter. The Fairmont is on the other side of Canal Street and several blocks up from the river."

Lee turned to Ellis. "The further away the better. I know the players are going to find Bourbon Street, but I'd rather not stick it right under their noses. Call Conway back, Lindsey, and see if you can get him to put us in at the Fairmont. If he hasn't already scheduled another team to go there, I doubt you'll have any problem getting it switched."

Lee glanced at his notes. "Lindsey, have you talked to Cathy at Travel Unlimited?"

Ellis crushed his cigarette in an ashtray. "Yes. She's already working on the details."

"When did you tell her to schedule us out?"

"Early Thursday."

"Damn, I wish we could make it Wednesday to give the kids an extra day to settle in," Lee said, thinking out loud to no one in particular.

Ellis said, "The NCAA has chartered a bus for us. It'll be waiting for us at the airport. They're also going to provide us with five courtesy cars. Think we'll need more?"

"No. That should be plenty," Lee answered, checking his watch. He looked at Earl Ward and asked, "How about the kids' studies? They've already missed a lot of classes. Any problems there?"

Ward leaned forward in his rocking chair. "Just the usual things, Coach. Some of them are having trouble getting their instructors to cooperate. Can you believe it? They don't want to postpone some of their tests. I called some of 'em to ask them to give our players a break. Some would; some wouldn't. You know how some of 'em feel about jocks."

Lee frowned. "Crap. These kids are putting the University on the map, and we've still got problems with some of the faculty. What do you want to bet the ones who are giving us the most trouble have tenure?"

Ward nodded.

"Hell, I'm not going to get on that subject," Lee said. "Stay on top of it, Earl. Let me know who you've got problems with and I'll speak with the chancellor."

Troy knew Coach Lee took pride in his record of prodding his players to complete their educations. In seventeen years of coaching, only two had failed to graduate: one died in a tragic automobile accident; the other simply could not make the grades.

Lee picked up his pipe. "Got anything planned for the Foundation members, Troy?"

"Nothing yet, Coach. We've spent a lot of money for parties at the other sites. Howard called me last week to warn me we were way over budget."

"How much?"

"About six thousand."

Lee whistled. "Well, give it some thought. I'll leave it up to you."

Troy was relieved. Their performance thus far in the tournament would prompt a lot of contributions; more entertainment would probably be a waste.

"Coach, it sure would help if we could get that Furlough kid down to the finals," Ward said, fairly sure there would be no way they could arrange it.

Gilliam spoke up. "That's strictly a no-no. It's against NCAA rules to provide tickets to a recruit when you are appearing in a post-season tournament. It's considered an unfair advantage."

Gilliam knew the NCAA rules by heart and everyone on the staff relied on him. It was probably the most important part of his job as assistant athletic director. Whenever a question arose as to the legality of a specific situation, Lee called Gilliam in and asked for the pertinent rule and possible interpretations.

Gilliam did a superb job. It was not an easy task. The NCAA had a very large manual that detailed all its various governing laws. The complexity of some questions concerning the legality of various practices could confound some of the best legal minds in the country. Yet he had managed to keep Charlotte in compliance.

As far as Troy knew, the Hornets had never knowingly committed a violation. If they had, he preferred not to know about it.

"There's no rule that says we can't give tickets to the kid's coach, is there?" Ward asked Gilliam.

Gilliam looked at Ward. "No, I suppose you're right technically. But that would be a violation of the spirit of the law, and if discovered, you can bet a full investigation into all of our practices would begin."

"And that is absolutely something we don't want," Lee interjected firmly. "So, consider the issue closed. No tickets for the kid or his coach. We have a good record, and as far as I know we haven't done anything illegal, but those investigators have a way of turning the tables on you. I don't care how clean a university tries to be. An NCAA investigator will come in looking for certain violations, and walk out with a completely different set of charges none of us even knew about. I doubt there is a university in this country that hasn't violated some rule inadvertently."

Earl Ward nodded agreement and glanced at Bo Evans. Evans winked and smiled. Troy caught the drift. It had been Evans' suggestion to ask about tickets for recruits via the high school coach. Ward had been sent to the wall by his buddy, but that evened the score. Evans had covered for him once when they were both out on a recruiting trip. Ward had failed to scout a player because he had stayed in bed too long with one of his "honeys." He had girls scattered all over the country. His black book was as thick as a telephone directory.

Troy surveyed the room and its occupants. Was there an inside source? Dolci had gained his foothold through knowledge that was sound, and it seemed impossible to the executive director that all of it could have been obtained without some help.

He had known everyone in his athletic family for two years. He trusted them. The uniqueness of their positions gave them all a feeling of pride and a sense of unity through goal-oriented purposefulness. Why would anyone here betray that loyalty?

He struggled to push the thought from his mind. He simply could not imagine there being a traitor in the group, particularly now that he had determined Lee was not involved. The coach's words still rung in his ears: "Don't sacrifice your integrity."

Perhaps there was no traitor. Dolci had enough power to gain any type of information. The nagging question of Troy's quiet friendship with Ted Collins—as discovered by Dolci—might be explained in another way. If he had been carefully followed, then he would have been seen with the player.

Oblivious to the conversation at hand, he moved closer to the edge of certainty. Decisions involved logical deductions, but his final determination would include more than rationality. It would require faith.

He decided to make his first leap—no one in the room had betrayed the athletic program. He would not raise that question again unless something knocked him off the new cliff he now balanced on. Decision made, he turned his attention back to the meeting.

Lee looked at Ellis and asked, "What time did you have the bus scheduled to leave today?"

"Eleven o'clock."

"Well, I received a call from Harold Billings late last night," Lee said, rolling his eyes.

"Who's that?" asked Ward. He did not follow local politics at all.

Troy said, "He's the mayor pro tem."

"Yes, and he's going to stand in for the mayor at the Civic Center welcome home when we get back to Charlotte this afternoon." Lee said. "Too bad the mayor is in Europe." He paused, then added sarcastically, "I thanked him; said we would be proud to have him there."

He considered the mayor pro tem to be another late bandwagon rider. Troy disliked that same "way to go, guys, you're my team" baloney as much as Lee did.

Lee said almost under his breath, "I hope it doesn't turn our kids' heads too much. Guess at this point there's not a whole lot we can do to stop that from happening. They're celebrities now."

Lee paused, then closed his notebook and looked up. "OK, I think that about covers it. We'll stop for lunch on the way back. Anybody have any questions?"

"Yeah, Bill," Ellis said. "Haigler called me this morning and asked for permission to interview Ted. He wants to do a feature story on him."

"I thought he already did a story."

"Yes, but he wants to expand on it. He thinks the readers will show a lot more interest this time."

"All right," Lee turned to Evans. "I think we need to talk to Ted first. Let's have Haigler get with him Tuesday evening."

Ellis was slightly surprised by Lee's caution. The coach had never worried about Collins being interviewed before.

The meeting was adjourned. Ellis and Troy walked out together.

"How's Jenny?" Ellis asked.

"Still pretty sick."

"Think she'll be all right to go to New Orleans?"

"Hope so. If not, she'll probably go anyway."

"Same way with Nancy. I think she's already packed her bags," Ellis said, referring to his wife.

Troy stopped at his hotel room and opened the door. "See you later."

While packing his clothes in the hotel room, Troy thought about the decision he'd made. It felt good, but the next one would be tougher. He would have to do something soon—time was running out. Dolci would be expecting positive results.

His thoughts were interrupted by a knock at the door. Stepping around his suitcase and walking to the door, he wondered who would be visiting him so early.

"Burton, you son of a bitch, where in the hell have you been?" Donnie Powers asked. Standing next to him was Russ Stinson.

Smiling broadly, putting his hand to his head in an "Oh! I forgot!" gesture, Troy said, "I'm sorry. Everything went wrong last night. You know I wouldn't miss one of our celebrations. Come on in."

Stepping inside, both men headed for a place to recline. Stinson reached the bed first and collapsed. Powers detoured to the couch and flopped on it.

Troy stared at them. "Looks like my absence didn't kill the party."

Stinson moaned. "We drank a couple for you, Troy-boy."

Troy moved over to a chair. "Sounds like you had more than a couple. That smoke that's coming out of your ears smells a little like 'wacky-tabacky.' "

Stinson said, "Man, you know we don't do that crap. Why, we're upstanding Charlotte alums."

"Where the hell were you last night?" Powers asked.

"I got tied up on some important business."

"What kind of important business?" Stinson asked, turning to Powers. "Donnie, what could be more important than being with your two best friends?"

"Don't know, man," Powers answered, rubbing sleep from his eyes. He looked at Troy and said wryly, "We know where we stand now. We're the low-life. You've got to look after the big money boys first. Then, if you have time, you'll speak to us as you ride by headed to the glory road."

Troy grinned. They always kidded about their friendship—generally this same routine. He believed it was only half in jest. It was their way of reminding him not to let the limelight go to his head. They knew he liked all the attention; through their kidding they were continually bringing him down to earth. He was sure they would remain friends long after his streaking star burned out.

He decided to take advantage of Powers' barb—Stinson's question was better left unanswered. One lie usually led to two. "What did you two think about the game?"

Stinson said, "See there, man? He's trying to change the subject on us again; doesn't want to tell us why he couldn't make it to our peon party. That's all right, we understand. You were probably off fucking some girl's brains out last night, taking advantage of Jenny being sick, and you don't want your best friends to know about it, right?" Stinson laughed loudly and rolled on his side.

"Right," Troy answered. "Greatest little piece in town; gives great head, too."

Powers chuckled. "You liar. You haven't had a piece of strange since you've been married." Turning to Stinson, he added, "Rosy palm is the only strange he's been getting."

All three men laughed. Troy enjoyed their company—it gave him a chance to unwind. They might be able to do more for him than provide comic relief. Both had small "street connections." Maybe they would know something about Frank Dolci. If not, perhaps they could check around. He decided to feel them out later.

"You two guys are screwing up," Troy said.

"How so?" Stinson asked.

Troy rolled his eyes toward the ceiling and scratched his head. "Well, I'm assuming you might just be wondering about tickets to the Final Four."

"No man. We're not worried about tickets. We've got a connection," Stinson said.

"Oh! Really? And who might that be?" Troy asked.

"We're good friends with the guy who decides who gets what," Powers said confidently.

"You sure? I thought I heard someone say he was an s.o.b.," Troy said, trying not to smile.

"Russ, did you hear me say something like that?" Powers asked.

"No, man. You'd never say anything like that."

"And I don't recall hearing you say something like that," Powers said, turning to Troy. "I think you must have heard wrong. I mean we are real tight with this guy; we'd never call him a . . . what was it you said?"

"A son of a bitch," Troy interjected, no longer able to hide his smile.

Powers said, "What terrible language to use when you're talking about your buddy."

"I agree," Stinson said, adding, "I know we'd never say something like that about our best friend, Troy Burton."

Troy feigned a serious expression. "Yes, it doesn't pay to piss off best friends who hold the keys to paradise."

Powers asked, "Can you handle it for us? Can you get us four tickets?"

Troy decided to bait his trap. "Four tickets! Damn! You don't ask for much, do you? I'm going to have to stretch to get you two."

Powers and Stinson were silent for a moment. They scratched their beards and looked back and forth at each other, conspiring mentally.

Powers spoke first. "OK, that's fine. Hell, who needs wives in New Orleans anyway."

Troy laughed. They had turned the tables on him, as usual. "You sorry bastards. I keep forgetting how you guys like to play around. I should have realized that you wouldn't look out for those two sweet ladies you're married to." He knew that was really not the case, though at times they could act like they didn't care.

"Seriously, can you get us tickets?" Stinson asked.

Troy arched his eyebrows. "Four of them?"

"Right," Powers said.

"I think that could be arranged."

Both men let out a yell and slapped each other's hands.

"Wait a minute. Before you get too excited, there's a string attached."

They stopped clowning.

Powers said, "OK, we knew you would lay catch-22 on us. We've already decided to join the Gold Hornet club."

"That's great. But that's not what I was going to ask you,"

Troy said, his tone intent, serious.

Stinson smiled. "Put the old foot right between your choppers, didn't you, Donnie?"

"I sure did," Powers said sheepishly, turning to Burton. "Well, what is it? I feel like a puppet danglin' on a string." Powers held out his arms limply, miming a marionette.

"First, I need you both to agree to two things. One, you need to promise me that you won't tell anyone that I asked. And two, you won't try to find out why I'm asking." He stared at them and saw curious expressions.

Powers spoke first. "OK, you've got it."

"Right," Stinson said firmly.

"Good. I want you to check with some of your sources and find out what you can about a man named Frank Dolci." Troy searched their eyes, looking for a glimmer of recognition.

Powers looked down at the carpet. Stinson stared ahead, a quizzical expression on his face. No one spoke.

Troy broke the silence. "Well, do either of you know who he is? I get the feeling the name may have rung a bell. If you can't tell me what you know, that's OK. I'll understand."

Stinson looked at Powers. "I've never heard of him, have you?"

"No," Powers looked at Troy. "But we can check around."

Troy couldn't put his finger on exactly why he sensed a lie had been spoken, nor could he tell which man was lying, but the feeling was strong, almost pervasive. It scared him. Somebody knew something he needed to know, but was not talking. Then again, he could be wrong. Maybe he was being paranoid.

Troy leaned forward in his chair. "Look, I'm sorry to put you both on the spot, but it's very important that I find out as much about Frank Dolci as I can and soon."

"Can you tell us where he lives?" Stinson asked.

"On Lake Norman in that Polynesian-style clustered home that we've skied by before."

Both men recalled the estate. They pointed it out to everyone who went water skiing with them.

Stinson had been blessed with a generous mother. She had purchased a beautiful summer cottage on Lake Norman two years after selling the farm property she inherited from her father. Her son, Russ, helped her with the details. As a result, she bought him a boat and gave him the keys to the cottage.

During the summer, Stinson traveled up to Lake Norman every weekend he was not working at the Boogie Beverage Company. Powers and his wife always came. But so had Troy and Jenny, on occasion at first, then with more frequency.

On those long, peaceful Saturdays and Sundays, their friendship blossomed. Troy loved the water and was a good skier. All three couples looked forward to the summer, when the harried pace of life was suspended and sunsets signaled the relaxation response. Beer and hamburgers, water and suntan lotion—fond summer memories. A distant cry from Vietnam. They all shared different nightmares of the same place. That had been the additional bond.

"So, that's who lives there," Powers said.

"So far as I know, it's Frank Dolci," Troy affirmed.

"What's he do for a living?" Stinson asked. "To own a place like that, you've got to be rich."

Troy shrugged. "That's why I'm asking. I don't know what he does. I'm not sure if his line of work is listed in the yellow pages, if you catch my drift. That's why I want both of you to check it out. Ask your connections. Be careful, though."

Stinson looked at Powers, then at Troy. "OK. I don't know how much we can find out, but we'll give it our best shot. I wish you could tell us why you need to know. That might help. I mean, we don't know what it is you're looking for."

"I just need to know about him, particularly where he gets his money."

Powers said, "All right, we'll do our best."

Troy stood and shook their hands. The feeling that someone knew more than he was telling still remained.

* Eleven *

Noonday sun mellowed the balmy March Sunday in New Orleans. Most of Bert Teague's neighbors were already working in their yards tidying landscapes. Warm weather had hastened the shedding of the short winter coat the city wore only briefly each season. Teague checked the temperature on his garage thermometer: seventy-five degrees. Late March brought longer days, warmer nights. The average normal temperature of sixty-two degrees would jump a full seven degrees higher in April, seven more in May. By then it would be hot and humid.

Teague loved this time of year. He hated the bitter wet cold that often swept into the city in December, January, and February. Although March could offer some of the same, it generally spread warmth, awakening the Crescent City occupants to outdoor activity.

Smiling to himself at the thought of just how quickly the weather could change in New Orleans, he wondered what his replacement would think about his new home. Yesterday, they were wearing coats; today, T-shirts and shorts would be the uniform of the day.

Teague felt a tugging at his jeans. Small hands, those of his youngest child, Anne Marie, required attention. "Daddy, can I help you?" she asked.

Looking down at his beautiful black-haired child, into her big brown eyes, Teague said, "Hi, honey, how about raking for me?"

"OK."

Annie, now seven, had been a late surprise for Teague and his wife, Maria, who was forty-three when she discovered she was pregnant with their third child. They walked around the side of the garage into the back yard. Stopping at a circular bed of gardenias, Teague began weeding and cultivating the ground with a hoe while the child looked on.

"Rake the weeds and leaves I throw out on the grass,

Annie."

The youngster nodded and began working slowly, sweeping each piece into a pile.

Teague's mind wandered as he worked his way in and around the flower and shrub bed, preparing it for annuals. They provided early spring color for his favorite backdrop of shrubs. The fragrant gardenia scent wafted about on hot summer nights; at times like that, he loved to pamper himself with a homemade mint julep.

It would not be long before he would be free from the boundaries of his job at the FBI. He wondered if that would mark the beginning of the end. Many men retired at great cost—lives melting into endless days of nothingness. Stripped of purpose and direction, they simply grew bored to death.

At fifty-five, he did not want to let that happen. He would use the time carefully, not squander it. His gardening, hunting, and fishing would fill the days when he became tired of reading.

Overall, he had a good record with the FBI. But the final note had begun to sour. The discord was Frank Dolci and Francesco Mancotta. He blamed himself for the failure to jail both men.

For six years he had followed their paths of crime and had looked on helplessly while their power grew. True, he was not alone; many others were involved in the project. But thus far, the specially appointed strike force had been impotent.

He hated to leave the Bureau without personally seeing to it that two of the strongest bosses remaining in the *Cosa Nostra* were sent to prison for life. Every time he turned around, they were involved in new, unique schemes, crippling legitimate enterprises and institutions.

Unlike their counterparts in the north, Dolci and Mancotta had eluded prosecution that toppled numerous crime bosses in the mid-eighties. Their partnership had been clever. By avoiding membership in the northern coalition of crime bosses, Dolci and Mancotta had managed to carve out a niche that was difficult to penetrate.

Charges had been brought against them several times. But clever legal maneuvering had kept them free. What has happened to the judicial system? Teague asked himself. Prosecutors and law enforcement officers shook their heads each time the sharks swam off with the bait, spitting back straightened hooks. Grinning, displaying row upon row of razor sharp teeth, they disappeared into the ink-black waters of the night, only to return again and feed at will.

It was a pattern Teague knew only too well. He wanted to slice through red tape and deal with organized crime on its own terms. But then cries of police brutality would rain down, and the press would carry the banner. The press represented another species of fish to Teague, piranha. Their frenzied feeding on a hot story generally left only a skeleton exposed, ugly, stripped.

Distorted perspective had caused him to lose the biggest sharks he had ever tried to land—Mancotta and Dolci. When Thomas Reina started to sing, the piranha circled and ripped his flesh. That alerted the sharks and they quickly devoured the evidence, swallowing Angelo Tummenelo before he could corroborate Reina's story.

The fear that splashed on the informant drowned him. Reina's heart attack came with the frenzied feeding. Restraint had obviously not been included in the curricula of journalism schools, Teague mused.

"Bert, will you be much longer? Do you want me to start lunch?" Teague's wife, Maria, asked from the kitchen window.

"Yes, honey. I'll only be another few minutes. What time is it?" He wiped beads of perspiration from his graying temples, then leaned on the hoe with both hands. He noticed Anne Marie mimicking his stance with the rake, holding it one-third of the way up the handle.

"One thirty," his wife called out, after checking the kitchen clock.

"Fine. Don't let me forget about those basketball games."

"How could I? That's the third time you've reminded me today. Since when did you become such a big basketball fan?"

He chuckled and shook his head. She knew him well. Basketball was not one of his favorite sports. But his interest in the college game had been ignited.

This afternoon and tonight he would watch the Midwest and West Regional Championships with more than mild interest. If Dolci and Mancotta can become ardent fans, he thought, so can I.

The black and gold bus rolled smoothly off the exit ramp of Interstate 77. A green and white sign marked the direction to downtown Charlotte. Heading east on Trade Street, the driver suddenly began slowing the bus.

Seated with his wife in the front seat of the ten-year-old Greyhound bus, Bill Lee looked up and saw two blue and white Charlotte police cars, lights flashing. They were stopped and one of the police officers signaled for the Hornets' bus to pull over.

As the officer walked up to the bus, the driver opened the door. The policeman stepped up the stairs inside the bus and recognized Coach Lee.

"What's the problem, officer?" Lee said.

"Nothing's wrong, Coach, except we've got a madhouse down there." The policeman pointed in the direction of the Charlotte Civic Center.

"What do you mean?"

"Coach, I've never seen anything like it. There must be over ten thousand people down there waiting for you and the team. You're going to need an escort and a lot of help with security. We don't want your players getting mobbed before the championships."

Lee looked at the policeman, then back at his players, who were listening attentively. Turning back to the policeman, he said, "Everybody loves a winner. I wonder where they were during the season."

Troy Burton stood behind the policeman. He had followed the bus in his car and had stopped to see what the problem was. "That's incredible. How many people did you say?" he asked the policeman.

Before he could answer, Lee said, "A lot!"

Evans, Ward, and Ellis walked to the front of the bus. Lane Gilliam, who had been riding with Troy, joined in.

"What do you want us to do?" Lee asked.

"Follow us and we'll escort everyone through the entrance. Have everybody stay close; don't stop to talk to anyone in the crowd. We'll get all of you to the stage."

"Sounds good," said Lee.

The policeman turned and walked back to his patrol car. Burton and Gilliam returned to the car shaking their heads.

The procession moved forward slowly, police sirens blaring, blue lights flashing. Conversation picked up on the bus slowly, muted by surprise and anticipation of the impending reception.

After crossing Tryon Street, the players began pointing. Crowds of people surrounded the huge white Civic Center, and cars—some still spilling out frenzied passengers—were jammed all over the six lane street. People pointed and yelled as the bus came into view behind police cars. A sea of black and gold clothing, placards, banners, ribbons, hats, and balloons splashed the white backdrop. The sun shone brightly, warming the scene.

As the occupants departed the bus through a human corridor of policemen and campus security guards, the crowd began chanting, "WE'RE NUMBER ONE! WE'RE NUMBER ONE!"

Burton and Gilliam stepped out of the car and two policemen escorted them into the line. The crowd pressed tightly, slapping players on the back, wanting to touch the hometown heroes.

As the official party mounted the stage, roars of approval echoed throughout the huge chamber. City officials were already on stage. Live television news camera crews from three of Charlotte's television stations beamed the scene into over one million homes.

When Troy mounted the stage in his gold jacket, he felt as if he had entered a dream world. Looking over the bodies that pressed forward against the stage, he recognized many supporters. His flooded ego temporarily pushed Dolci's proposition from his mind.

Mayor pro tem Harold Billings stepped to the microphone and addressed the crowd. Charlotte city council members sat, listening jealously. Here was a chance to be seen and heard by a joyful constituency.

Troy leaned over to Gilliam. "Look at Billings. He hasn't given us a dime and now he's acting like he was here all along. Politicians are a pain in the ass."

Gilliam chuckled and said, "Where were all these people when we played in the coliseum? We only sold it out once."

Smiling at the crowd, Troy shook his head. "Looks like the bandwagon's overflowing, doesn't it?"

"Yes, I'd say it's pretty full," Gilliam responded.

The ceremony lasted over half an hour. The politicians presented plaques and city proclamations announcing this date as "Hornets' Day," and a band struck up the tune "Way Down Yonder in New Orleans."

Near the end of the delirious reception, an AP reporter nudged Troy. "You're the executive director of the Athletic Foundation, aren't you?"

"Yes, that's right."

"Did you graduate from the University of Charlotte?"

Troy nodded and tried to listen to the reporter's questions with one ear, the speeches with the other.

"Could you tell me what this means to you?"

"It's fantastic. It means that we have finally arrived in the eyes of the fans."

The reporter scribbled the quote and asked, "What do you think this will do for the Foundation?"

"I hope that everybody here will be emotionally charged enough to send in donations to keep our team strong and competitive. It takes a lot of money to support a big-time athletic program."

"What about tickets? Will you be in charge of them?"

"Only in directing who in the Foundation gets them."

"Do I take that to mean that the general public won't be getting any?"

Troy smiled. "Unfortunately, I'm afraid there won't be enough to go around for the people who have closely supported the program or for even a tenth of our students. We've got to take care of them first. Believe me, I wish we had a lot more tickets so we could sell them to the public. We could use the support at the games.

"But since the vast majority of these fans won't be able to attend, we know they'll be watching on television along with the rest of the nation. They'll still be with us in spirit."

Despite the fact that bandwagon support was evident, Troy knew better than to point it out. After all, the Hornet phenomenon was even surprising to him. The team had only begun proving to people near the end of the season that it was a legitimate national power. Perhaps the new fans deserved the benefit of the doubt. It was not that bad to jump on the old bandwagon late as long as you stayed for the remainder of the ride, detours included.

The reporter left Troy and began quizzing others on stage. When the fanfare was over, the players and coaches were mobbed by autograph seekers. Even Troy was asked by children and adults to sign his name. He felt strange doing so, and every time he attempted to explain that he was just the executive director—not somebody important enough to be included in the ritual—they still insisted he sign on whatever it was they held out to him: miniature black and gold basketballs, balloons, T-shirts, scraps of paper, leg and arm casts, and just about anything else available.

He finally broke free when the crowd began to dwindle. He wanted to get home to Jenny, where peace and quiet would soothe his nerves. He phoned her before he left Greensboro with the team. She sounded much better.

* Twelve *

The private Jet Commander gently touched down on runway 23 at Page Field in Fort Myers. As the aircraft rolled to a stop, Frank Dolci awakened and peered out of the window. Light, puffy, cottontail clouds dotted an azure sky.

After the pilot opened the hatch, Dolci stood for a moment to let the warm salt air rejuvenate him. This was the place to be in the winter, he thought.

"What's the temperature, Tony?" Dolci asked the dark-haired pilot.

"Seventy-eight degrees, sir."

"Perfect." Dolci stepped down the plane's short steps.

Winter was a foreigner in southwestern Florida. On Captiva—the enchanting island where Dolci's two and a half million dollar winter home sat snugly entrenched on the beach less than a half mile from Blind Pass—the average normal high in March was a pleasant 76.5 degrees, and the average normal low dipped at night to a cool 59.8. Even in the dead of winter, daytime and nighttime temperatures averaged 72.0 and 55.5, respectively.

Dolci looked forward to peeling off his cardigan suit and changing into his favorite shorts, the cutoffs with the worn back pocket. He longed to rub his toes in the sun-baked sand at his private Gulf-front home.

However, before he could unwind, his first order of business would have to be completed. He always preferred to clear the cobwebs of impending chores before relaxing. He would not allow problems to spoil his paradise.

His chauffeur, a tall, muscular man in his late thirties, opened the door of the Mercedes sedan. "We're glad you're back, Mr. Dolci."

"Thank you, Robert. I'm glad to be back. Any problems while I was away?"

"No, sir. Except Sanibel and Captiva are packed with tourists as usual."

Dolci frowned as he sat in the back seat. He hated the transition which had taken place since the building of the causeway. It spanned three miles of open water and permanently landlocked the islands of Sanibel and Captiva. When the causeway was completed in 1963, growth began on the barrier islands and took a heavy toll on the previously unspoiled beauty.

Dolci remembered November of 1974 when he and other outraged islanders voted to make Sanibel an independent city. Wresting the island away from the control of most of Lee County commissioners saved it from hungry developers who were chopping away its tropical jungles. Had that not happened, the entire paradise would have been crushed in a wave of uncontrolled development; spoiled forever, much like Fort Myers Beach, a hodgepodge of hotels, restaurants, houses, bars, and businesses.

Captiva was not included in the new incorporation plan because the slender five mile long island that stretched into the Gulf of Mexico beyond Sanibel—bridged at Blind Pass—needed Lee County funds to stem the erosion that carried away an estimated 265,000 yards of sand each year. Since the tiny island had a maximum width of less than a half mile, the islanders were forced to rely on help from the very people who threatened to bury it with buildings.

The drive north on Fowler Street was brief. He arrived in the heart of Fort Myers in less than ten minutes. He checked his watch. He was fifteen minutes early.

"No need to bring my bags, Robert. I won't be staying aboard," Dolci said as he stepped out of the sedan.

"Fine sir. Shall I wait?"

"No. Pick us up at Punta Rassa in four hours. We should be docked by then." Dolci turned and walked down the concrete pier toward his yacht.

The Fort Myers yacht basin was crowded with boats, all sizes and shapes. Dolci's 48-foot cabin cruiser was moored at a temporary berth. The basin was not its permanent shelter, as Dolci preferred the privacy of a smaller and more convenient dock closer to the islands.

Two men stood at the gangplank. He recognized his

captain, John Tortocci, and his bodyguard, Joe Buona.

"Good afternoon, Mr. Dolci. Looks like we picked an excellent day for cruising." The captain extended a warm handshake.

"Yes, John. Let's hope our meeting won't spoil the day." Dolci turned to his heavyset bodyguard. "Joe, my friend, you look like you've been into the pasta while I was away." He jabbed at Buona's distended belly with one finger.

"My only weakness," Buona replied with a smile.

"Take her out, Captain." Dolci said as he boarded the vessel.

"Aye, sir."

The sleek cruiser slipped out of the harbor into the main channel of the Caloosahatchee River. The captain steered the vessel toward the mouth of the river which emptied into the Gulf of Mexico approximately thirteen miles away. Dolci stepped onto the flying bridge and removed his jacket. The sun-sparkled water reflected rays of silver light. A five knot breeze quartering off the starboard bow gently billowed colored sails on sailboats slicing through the water.

Noisy speedboats darted about; they frequently interrupted the classic silence of the sailboats. Dolci spied a bikinied skier slaloming a hundred and fifty yards off the port bow. Peering through binoculars, he admired her shapely figure until she failed to maintain balance in a difficult turn. Her body cartwheeled and disappeared in a heavy spray of water, skipping twice across the water like a jagged stone. The ski boat circled back quickly to pick her up. The busy river was no place for a marooned swimmer.

The cruiser moved forward under twin engine diesel power at a leisurely five knot pace. Dolci's thoughts turned away from the scenic cruise past riverfront houses and a few towering condominiums. His meeting with Coach Patrick McLaughlin was less than half an hour away.

Dolci was ill at ease. He doubted the fiery-tempered Irishman would obey his order. If he did, Dolci would have to question the coach's sincerity. He wondered if a McLaughlin lie would be detectable.

As Shell Island came into view two points off the port

bow, the captain asked, "Where is the rendezvous, sir?"

"Approximately one-half mile south of the Siesta Keys."

"Aye, sir." The captain pushed the throttles forward and the cruiser picked up speed to approximately ten knots.

Dolci searched the horizon for the familiar blue and yellow mainsail of McLaughlin's twenty-eight foot sloop. He focused his binoculars on the red mangrove trees lining the nearby keys, and swept south from starboard to port. After a few minutes, the familiar sails became clearly visible as the sloop swung north, tacking before a gentle breeze. The white hull glistened in blue-shaded waters. The sea was relatively calm with one- to two-foot gentle, rolling swells.

Dolci pointed and the captain saw the sloop. Fishing boats plodded in and around San Carlos Bay; some headed to sea through Punta Rassa Pass, others into the apparently protective waters of Pine Island Sound. During storms the sound could boil like a cauldron. Many an unwary sailor had drowned.

They closed the distance rapidly and came alongside the coach's sloop as McLaughlin lowered the already reefed mainsail. Their pace slowed to a crawl. Buona cast a line attached to a monkey fist over the bow of the sloop. McLaughlin went forward, captured the line, and fastened it to a cleat. Buona lowered several plastic covered styrofoam bumpers to soften the impact of the sailing vessel as it nudged the cabin cruiser.

The coach hauled his huge frame up the accommodation ladder. Dolci greeted him and they disappeared inside the large mahogany cabin.

"Good to see you again, Frank. I trust you enjoyed the game," McLaughlin said in a southern accented Irish brogue.

"I certainly did. Your boys looked sharp." Dolci poured the coach a shot of fine Irish whiskey.

McLaughlin lifted his glass in a toasting gesture. "Aye, that they did. That they did." He swallowed the whiskey.

Dolci refilled the shot glass. "What do you think about the Charlotte Hornets?"

"They're good—especially their center, Collins. If he keeps playing like that, he'll go high in the first round of the draft." McLaughlin downed his second drink as quickly as he had the first.

"Can you beat them?"

"I think we've got a good shot at it." He watched Dolci refill his glass. "Have any dark beer to wash this down with?"

"Right here in the reefer," Dolci said as he walked to the shipboard refrigerator.

He tossed the can smoothly to the coach, who caught it gingerly, attempting not to shake the contents. "You've still got good hands, Patrick. Not letting old age creep up on you, are you?"

"Hell, no. Glad I'm still involved in basketball—keeps me feeling young. But the players that come out of high school today are bigger, quicker, and stronger than in my era. They would run me off the court."

"Patrick, I've never known you to be a modest man. Holy Cross will never forget you, and you know it," Dolci said, reflecting on the coach's college career.

McLaughlin had played the forward position with a flare for penetrating to the basket. He was an All-America candidate in the days when college basketball was still in its infancy: the national championships barely drew front page attention. Even if he had been on a team that made it to the finals, it's unlikely that his name would have appeared in the headlines.

In those days, McLaughlin was a shy and retiring kid who had been raised in Brooklyn, New York. Avoiding fights by the sheer presence of his size, he seldom got into trouble.

The army changed all that. As an infantryman in Korea, he saw a lot of action. A valiant fighter, he was highly decorated for a daring rescue of a fellow soldier on the battleground of the celebrated "Pork Chop Hill."

When he returned home, he taught and coached at a high school in Brooklyn. His fiery temper and ability to squelch any student fights earned him a reputation as a man to be dealt with carefully.

When he worked his way into the college ranks as an assistant coach, it became apparent his fortes were discipline and recruiting. He recruited for an unknown Division I college and quickly learned his only chance to compete with major colleges required signing borderline "head cases," young men who were immature and self-serving. They had to be cajoled into making sacrifices.

He had an effective way of handling his tougher problem players. If they performed properly and followed instructions, they received privileges. If they failed to acquiesce, he ran them ragged with brutal laps and quickness drills.

Other coaches adopted similar techniques, but McLaughlin's unique method of meting out punishment set him apart. He participated in the laps and drills. Having honed his body with endurance tests, the coach was in finer condition than any player on the squad. He was capable of running a marathon. He could run a player into the ground.

His players called the after practice punishment "the meat grinder." But because he never asked them to perform a task he himself would not do, he was revered as a fair and just man. To them, he was both a father and a brother.

Most of the players on his squad came from Northern ghettos. It was that circumstance which led him to accept assistance from Dolci. Few of the players could afford to return home for the holidays and McLaughlin hated to see them have to stay on campus. Though he knew it was against NCAA regulations, he provided cash for his players to travel home at Christmas.

Occasionally, when he discovered a wayward star on a ghetto playground, he cut through UFFM's entrance requirements. He managed to get his prospect enrolled by falsifying high school transcripts. Dolci had assisted in that enterprise twice.

McLaughlin had told Dolci on several occasions that those particular players would never rise from the ghetto unless their raw talents could be developed. The fact that they hadn't graduated from high school was a "technicality" he circumvented when he judged the risk worth taking. Most of his "playground pros" made it through college with a maximum amount of pushing from behind and help from "cooperative" professors.

Dolci watched McLaughlin down the beer and sensed the coach was beginning to relax from the effects of the alcohol. The Irishman's temper could be doused somewhat, but not completely.

"I suppose you're wondering why I asked you to meet me today?"

"That has crossed my mind. I get the feeling this is not just a social visit."

"That's right. I have a very important favor to ask you."

"If it is within my power, you know I'll help you."

"It's not quite that easy. It is within your power, but maybe not in your personality." Dolci looked into McLaughlin's eyes.

"What do you mean?"

"I want you to lose the semi-final game against Charlotte."

"What?" McLaughlin asked as if he wasn't sure he had heard the statement correctly.

"You can't win the game against Charlotte, Patrick. I need you to make sure that **you** lose by at least five points."

"Are you crazy?" said McLaughlin, raising his voice and starting to stand up.

"Sit down!" Dolci said firmly. "Listen to me. I don't like it any more than you do. But that's the way it has got to be."

"Lose the game? For Christ's sake, what for? I mean, I always thought the reason you were helping me was to see that we made it to the championships. Now, here we are knocking at the door and you're telling me to lay down. I don't understand." McLaughlin said, pausing, shifting in his chair. "You've given me money for the players, right?"

Dolci nodded.

"You've helped me get a couple of 'em into school, and you've bailed one or two out of trouble with your influence. But Frank, tell me, will you? Why do you want me to throw in the towel after we've come this far?" McLaughlin rubbed his temples with his fingers.

"Have I ever asked you for anything?" Dolci rose from

his chair and walked to the refrigerator.

"No, but—"

"Damnit, there are no fucking buts about it," Dolci said loudly.

The coach looked confused. He had not anticipated the request and was puzzled. McLaughlin had never seen Dolci angry.

"I am just having trouble understanding why. I mean, if it's a bet that's involved, why not wait until the championship game?"

"Don't question me, coach. Just answer yes or no whether you will do what I ask." Dolci poured himself a glass of wine and started to refill McLaughlin's shot glass.

The Irishman put his hand over the glass. "No thanks, I've had enough."

At that moment Dolci made his decision. He was the conductor. The coach was a failing pupil. Silent dissonant notes played an ominous strain.

After a long pause the Irishman answered. "I'll have to think about it. You're asking me to throw away a lifetime dream, and you're not giving me a reason. I think that's a bit unreasonable."

Dolci understood that the answer was a put-off no. It pained him. He truly liked the coach, but business was business. He could have offered money, but he had a good reason for not doing so. It was an unreliable stimulus. If the coach failed to perform, he might be under the mistaken impression that by returning the bribe later, he would be absolved. A last-minute emotional decision to win the game might result. No, Dolci thought, this had to be a loyalty decision, and no explanation would be possible or wise. He decided to relieve the pressure and allow the Irishman to relax.

"OK, I can accept that. Can you give me your answer by Tuesday?"

McLaughlin smiled. "Sure. Can we meet someplace else? I'm real busy and it takes an awful lot of time to sail out here."

"That will be fine. I'll have Joe give you a call to set it up," Dolci said, sipping wine.

Both men stood and walked back to the fantail. Dolci shook the coach's hand firmly. McLaughlin turned and boarded his sailboat.

As Dolci's captain slowly eased forward on the throttles, the sloop and yacht parted company. McLaughlin hoisted the sail. An increasing seven-knot breeze filled the sheet quickly; it billowed out with an audible pop. He shifted the helm and the mainsail luffed briefly. The sun was low on the horizon. Orange marmalade clouds dotted the sky behind the mast.

As the cabin cruiser moved away at a brisk eighteen-knot pace, Dolci watched the sloop fade in the distance. It would have been easy to have arranged an accident at sea, Dolci mused. A drowning would have been undetectable, but not appropriate. It would take the coach out of the picture all right; yet, a different strategy was required.

"Joe," Dolci said to Buona.

"Yes, sir."

"Get on the ship-to-shore and patch a message to Mr. Mancotta in New Orleans. Tell him, 'Urgent business meeting. Suggest you come immediately.'"

* Thirteen *

Jenny Burton looked out of the upstairs bedroom window again. The driveway was still empty. She knew Troy should be home any minute. The reception for the Hornets at the Civic Center had interrupted the Sunday matinee movie on WBTV.

She felt tired and weak, but the impending return of her husband buoyed her spirits. The nausea had finally subsided. Some hot tea and a baked potato had settled her stomach and provided the first solid nourishment she had been able to hold down in several days.

She heard Drop barking loudly downstairs. Peering through the curtained window, she saw the familiar vehicle and Troy. He lifted his suitcase out of the trunk.

Racing downstairs, she almost fell and had to grab onto the handrail before she reached the final step. In her excitement she had forgotten just how weak she really was. She regained her composure, walked to the door, and opened it. He was fumbling for his keys.

"Jenny, what are you doing up?" He hugged and kissed her.

"I'm feeling much better." Her eyes glistened with tears of joy. Thank God he is home, she thought. The fear that had permeated the depths of her soul last night when she had been unable to contact him lingered. The experience would not soon be forgotten.

"You look pale, Honey. Go lie down in the den and I'll take my suitcase upstairs."

"OK. But hurry up, I want to hear what happened. I've been dying for you to get home."

Troy walked upstairs and put his suitcase on the bed. He noticed Drop sitting at his feet, patiently waiting to be recognized.

"Drop, I'm sorry." He reached down and picked up the

soft, furry animal with both hands. As he cradled the fluffy, living bundle in the crook of his left arm, she lay on her back, paws pointed toward the ceiling, supremely confident her master would not drop her. She licked the underside of his chin.

"Have you missed me, Drop?" Troy asked, knowing the answer and almost expecting a reply.

After several minutes of affectionate greeting, he put her on the bed. She pawed at his hands as he opened the suitcase.

"How about unpacking for me, Drop? I've got to go spend some time with Mommy." He patted his surrogate child on the head.

She spied one of his socks in the suitcase, leaped in, snatched it up in her mouth, twisted around, and looked up at him defiantly. She knew exactly how to steal clothing and heart simultaneously.

"That's a girl. Be sure and fold it before you put it in the drawer. On second thought, I think that one's dirty. Take it to Mommy so she can wash it," he said, chuckling.

Drop cocked her head as if attempting to understand what her master had just said.

He decided on simpler instructions. "Take it to Mommy."

She leaped off the bed with the sock in her mouth. He watched her disappear through the door and heard her pad down the steps. He loved the obedient affection the animal displayed. Drop was obviously an intelligent dog, and Troy knew that his father—a veterinarian who died several years ago—would have been proud to see some of the new tricks she had learned.

He decided to delay his unpacking so he could be with Jenny. He took off his coat and tie and walked downstairs.

"Look who got one of your socks," Jenny said, pointing at Drop.

"I know. I told her to bring it to you so you could wash it."

Jenny giggled and curled her feet up under her warm, green robe. She patted the sofa. "Sit down and tell me what happened."

The phone rang. She rolled her eyes and said, "That thing's been ringing since yesterday. After the game you started getting calls from people I've never even heard of."

"Wanting tickets, I suppose." Troy got up to answer the phone.

The caller was Martin Tomlinson, a former fellow worker with Troy at IBM. The conversation was brief and Troy was polite but firm. No, he told Tomlinson, he doubted seriously he could get him tickets to the championships.

"Now, where were we?" Troy asked.

"You'd better take it off the hook," Jenny said, adding, "The calls come in waves."

Before he could respond, the phone rang.

Jenny frowned. "See what I mean?"

Troy answered. The caller was a former classmate in college. He had not heard from the man in over five years and barely remembered his name. The call went much the same as the previous one. Troy hung up and found himself both irritated and amused that people were attempting to pry tickets from him, using past acquaintance as a lever. It surprised him they could be so bold as to think the past familiarity they had not cared to cultivate until this very moment would influence him.

He looked at the phone and decided to take the receiver off the hook. Then he sat by Jenny and put his arm around her. "OK, that ought to take care of it."

Jenny nestled close.

They talked for an hour. He detailed his experience with Frank Dolci and told her about his meeting with Bill Lee. She listened intently and stopped him with only a few questions. Troy had an excellent memory; his vivid descriptions of the events fascinated her.

"Well, what do you think?" he asked.

She rested her head on his shoulder. "I don't know. He scares me. Why don't you go to the police?"

"We've been over that before. I'm glad now that I didn't go to anyone. He has obviously had us under surveillance; I think our phone has been tapped. Frank Dolci is a powerful man. I'm almost certain now that he's a boss in organized crime."

"You said that before. I just have trouble believing the Mafia is operating here in Charlotte."

"I know it's hard to believe, but who ever said crime recognized boundaries? Think about it—when people think that the South doesn't have organized crime, that makes it easier for crime to go unnoticed."

Troy kept flashing back to Vietnam. He remembered what it felt like when he flew his first serious combat mission. Facing death for the first time in a mindless war, his immediate reaction had been fear and confusion. Why? Why should men kill each other? What was it worth? Nothing. Absolutely nothing.

How an individual handled that unique pressure situation could never be fully explained, he mused. To some it was a time of strength, an exhilarating experience much like conquering a treacherous mountain. To others, it was a moment of dread, when fear froze the heart and movement was paralyzed. And to the majority in between, the experience was one of coping to the best of one's ability.

He believed he understood the psychological aspects of his new situation. He pictured himself flying over the middle of a battlefield with .50-caliber machine guns trained on his UH1B helicopter, a Huey gun ship. Though no shots had yet been fired, he knew that the decisions he made would ultimately determine his fate.

"It's absurd, isn't it?" he said.

Jenny nodded.

Troy knew she understood the dilemma. But her strength pulsed from a different philosophy than his. While he believed he was totally in charge of his destiny, she believed in Divine intervention. She always prayed to God that He would provide an answer.

"We have to have faith that things will work out for the better. You have to do what your conscience tells you." She squeezed his hand.

"My conscience tells me that I am damned if I do and damned if I don't. I would like to go to the police, but look what happened in Greensboro. Two cops escorted me out of the Coliseum into that goon's hands. Dolci made a point of telling me that he held all the cards. What if I go to the police and they ride in like a herd of elephants?

"Sure, that might stop him," he said, answering his own question, "but a man like that won't rest until I am silenced."

"What about me?"

"Since you've never seen him, I doubt he considers you a threat. We would still have to live the rest of our lives looking over our shoulders."

"What about the FBI?" she asked.

"They might handle things better than the police, and I doubt that Dolci has any of them in his pocket, but the same problem arises in the end. We are still going to be left with our pants down."

"You look good with your pants down," Jenny said.

He leaned over and nibbled on her ear. "You look a lot better."

When Troy finally turned the television on, it was halftime. Texas was leading North Carolina by three points. He settled down to watch the Midwest Regional Championships. The game provided few surprises. Texas ran up and down the court attempting to set a blistering pace, while North Carolina showed a patient and patterned offense.

With less than four minutes to go in the game, North Carolina grabbed the lead on a well-executed three-point play, a perfect pick and roll, a lay-up shot, and a foul committed by the Texas center. The successful conversion gave the Tar Heels a two-point lead. Texas lost its next possession to a zone trap that forced a freshman guard to throw away a pass.

From that point on, Dean Smith's players gained confidence and began hitting three-point shots from just about anywhere. Texas was forced to play catch-up near the end. They deliberately fouled in an attempt to regain possession immediately, hoping for the miss on the front end of a one-and-one foul-line opportunity. But the Tar Heels never missed and their lead lengthened. The final score was

UNC-91, Texas-77. North Carolina became the third team to enter the Final Four.

There was no fix. Troy was sure of that. The super powers were not likely to be vulnerable to an offer from Dolci. Their perennial strength tended to shield them from illegal overtures. Deep in well-paid personnel and wealthy from bountiful gate receipts and rich athletic foundations, the larger universities would be a dangerous maze to attempt to penetrate.

As he waited for the next game to begin, he munched on crackers and cheese, and sipped a California chablis. The West Regional Championships featured two powerful teams, Marquette and UCLA. The Bruins—playing in their own Pauley Pavilion—had a home-court advantage.

The game looked like it would be a runaway affair in the first ten minutes as the Warriors got off to a cold start. But near the end of the half, they clawed back to within six points of UCLA.

The Bruins demonstrated quickness and their height advantage was winning the battle on both the offensive and defensive boards. Marquette's tenacious defense kept them in the game. They forced twelve turnovers and only committed five. When their three-point shooting heated up, they came back to within four points at the half, 47-43.

The second half featured Marquette's superb outside shooting; the Warriors took the lead. Several slam dunks punctuated UCLA's bid, and with six minutes to go the Bruins regained the lead by a mere point, 87-86. The lead seesawed. With thirty seconds left, UCLA had the ball and was one point down, 95-94.

The Bruins' coach called a time-out and diagramed a play on a chalkboard. The Warriors settled into a tight 2-3 zone, careful not to foul while still exerting solid pressure. As the seconds ticked off the clock, it became apparent that UCLA would be forced to take an outside shot. With eight seconds left, the Bruins' point guard found himself open at the top of the key. He fired up a shot that caught the back of the rim and bounced high in the air. The unusual carom forced every player who crashed the boards to leap prematurely. The Bruins' superior height advantage paid off. Their seven-foot center managed to tap the ball in with both feet still on the ground.

The Warriors called time-out with three seconds remaining on the clock. Their only option would be a desperation shot after a long in-bounds pass. UCLA foiled that plan by stealing the ball as it floated down ten feet from the basket.

The fourth team had emerged and the match-ups were entered in the record books. It would be Charlotte versus Fort Myers and North Carolina versus UCLA in the semifinals. They were the final four teams remaining from the sixty-four team field that began vying for the national championships two weeks ago.

Jenny sat quietly, uninvolved with the spectacle that had passed. Then she remembered she had forgotten to let Drop outside. It was nearly time to go to bed.

"Troy, I forgot to let little one outside."

Engrossed in the game statistics that flashed across the screen, Troy did not respond. He analyzed the various categories to detect the strengths and weaknesses of the victors. He wondered if Dean Smith had watched the game. The wily coach would be quick to spot any chinks in UCLA's armor.

After the analysis and commentary, Troy got up to turn off the television set. He was tired and ready to retire for the evening. Jenny had gone to the back door and he could hear her calling Drop. Since their backyard had been fenced in a year ago, the chore of watching the fur ball meander about looking for just the right spot had been simplified. Before, Jenny had constantly worried that the animal might wander off, get hit by a car, or tangle with one of the larger dogs that roamed the neighborhood.

"Troy, come here," she called.

Troy walked to the back door and asked, "What's the problem? Drop taking her good sweet time again?"

"I can't see her. She must be back in the corner."

The left rear corner of the yard was the only place where floodlights did not illuminate the yard. The cold night was inky black. Clouds had swept in and blanketed the moonlight. He grabbed the flashlight he kept near the door and called Drop's name in a stern voice. Unless the animal was in the middle of voiding, she would respond immediately. There was no movement or sound.

Troy stepped out on the porch and shined the light into the darkened corner. The batteries were weak; the thin beam did little to aid his vision. The cold raised goose bumps on his bare arms. Wearing only a T-shirt, the bottoms of his blue pajamas, and leather slippers, he bounded down the steps forgetting the cold. A mental alarm had gone off in his head; his chest tightened.

Jenny stepped out on the porch and called Drop's name.

Troy turned quickly while continuing to walk toward the corner and said over his shoulder, "Get inside, Jenny. You've been sick and you'll catch pneumonia." He continued walking.

Jenny remained standing on the porch.

A tall oak tree stood dormant at the fenced-in corner. As he walked around the huge trunk of the tree, his flashlight caught the form of the animal laying still on the ground. His heart leapt into his throat. He jerked the diffused light back to the form and moved quickly.

Drop whimpered faintly. He kneeled down, shining the light closer. He saw her glazed eyes open and stare up at him. She was on her back. At once the entire picture flashed through like a gruesome nightmare.

Drop's head was bleeding: her chocolate ears had been completely severed. They lay on either side of her body in ritualistic fashion. Her abdomen had been split open from her sternum to her vulva. Blood flowed from severed capillaries and veins. Viscera were exposed in a bloody mass.

"Oh, God!" Troy said in a pained, tearful voice.

He quickly placed the flashlight on the ground and removed his T-shirt to cover the grotesque wound. "Hang on, Drop," he said softly.

"Troy! What's the matter? Where are you?" Jenny called loudly. She walked toward the scene.

Troy recognized that her voice was close. "Stay back," he yelled. He wrapped Drop's abdomen with his white T-shirt, and it quickly stained crimson. He knew that the tiny animal could not withstand the huge loss of blood. His experience in treating severe injuries—he had helped his father at the animal hospital during the summer vacations of his school years—had trained him to act swiftly.

Just then he heard Jenny's footsteps.

"For God's sake stay back!" he yelled. He kept his right palm over the covered wound and lifted the animal to his bare chest with his left hand. He had to get Drop inside to the warmth. She was deep in shock.

Jenny reached her husband as he stood up. Seeing him cradle the animal in his arms she cried, "Oh my God! What happened? Is she all right? Oh please, please, don't let her die." She tried to keep up as he ran into the light toward the back door.

His mind raced. He wanted to put as much distance between him and his wife as he could. He did not want her final memory of their beloved animal to be burned indelibly with horror.

"Troy!" she called. "Answer me! Is she alive?"

As he bounded up the steps of the back porch, he answered, "Barely. Please stay away." He plunged inside, ran into the bathroom, flipped the light on with one hand, and locked the door.

Jenny followed him, sobbing pitifully. Troy heard her slump against the locked entrance.

Why? Troy asked himself. Why? Rage seeped into his veins. Hatred boiled. Never before in his life had he ever felt such anger.

He wanted to get his gun. He'd take care of the bastard that did this. But he couldn't leave Drop. He had to try to save her.

He yanked two towels off a cabinet shelf and gently wrapped Drop in them to provide warmth. His only hope was to get the animal to the emergency veterinarian clinic ten miles away. He had to try.

"Jenny, get my keys and wallet," he called through the closed door.

She responded immediately. He heard her run upstairs.

Troy held the animal close to him. Drop was still conscious, but barely breathing. The fury that built inside Troy would have to be vented. There was no doubt in his mind that Dolci was responsible. The tactic was clearly intended to frighten him. But why? After all, he had agreed to comply with Dolci's request. Troy vowed revenge. Dolci would burn.

Drop shuddered and a weak, audible cry escaped. It was her final exhalation. The tiny animal died with her eyes open.

"No, Drop, don't die," Troy said softly as he removed the towels, attempting to massage her heart back to life with quick short pushes on her chest. He stopped and felt for the heart beat. There was none. He dropped to the floor in total despair, holding the bloody animal high on his chest. Tears rolled down his cheeks. He cradled Drop in his arms and rocked back and forth continuously. Blood smeared his cheeks. He did not hear Jenny knocking at the door.

"Troy, please let me in."

Her request broke through his consciousness and he responded. He gently wrapped the body with towels. Resignation that Drop was lost forever slowly gained a foothold.

Apparently having understood the meaning of his lack of response, he heard her slump to the floor. He unlatched the door and opened it. She could not stand. She pulled her body inside with her hands, her robe sliding across the floor. Her tears splashed on the tile.

Troy moved closer to her as he held Drop's lifeless body in his arms. Jenny reached out to touch the shrouded form. He put his right arm around her.

He wanted to get up and look for the bastard who did this, but he knew his search would be futile. Whoever it was had obviously left immediately. There had been no cars parked on the cul-de-sac.

For more than an hour, he sat on the floor with Jenny, mourning.

* Fourteen *

Bert Teague sat at his desk and sipped a cup of coffee as he reviewed his Monday morning mail. Flyers and directives from Bureau headquarters in Washington and various requests for information from other agents across the country were stacked neatly in a black plastic tray marked "In."

"Good morning, Mr. Teague." The middle-aged secretary smiled, stepped into his office, and handed him a teletyped message. "It just came in over the scrambler."

"Thank you, Martha."

The message was marked confidential. Teague unfolded it and read: "Maintained surveillance on subject as requested. Interest in the game intensified. B-77 spent several hours at D-32 base on Sat. night. D-32 departed on private jet late Sun. a.m.; flight plan revealed dest. Fort Myers, Fl. M-26 left Sun. p.m. on commercial flight Eastern 221, dest. New Orleans. Advise action requested."

Teague spoke to his secretary on the telephone intercom. He requested the file on B-77. She responded quickly, and in less than two minutes he was immersed in the file on Troy David Burton.

Teague thought that it might be possible to bring Hardin in and discuss the new aspects of the case in a few more days, but not now. Timing was important. He did not want to reveal his plan to a newcomer before he completed his evaluation of the situation at hand. He realized he had taken liberties with regard to the safety of private citizens, but saw no other way. He hoped his instincts would prove to be right. If not, he might end up retiring in disgrace.

Francesco Mancotta enjoyed the scenic ride across the toll causeway to Sanibel and Captiva islands. The leisurely 25 miles-per-hour speed limit had been imposed to keep the heavy traffic from vibrating the bridge into further deterioration. It afforded him time to enjoy the cloudless blue sky. The reflection of the sun's rays flickered silver on light blue-gray choppy waves.

He thought this would be a nice place to start the week if it weren't for the fact that the business he was going to have to discuss with his partner would be rather unpleasant. He hoped they could arrive at a decision within a reasonable length of time. He wanted a few moments of peace and quiet before he returned to New Orleans, where several pressing business matters would fill the rest of his week.

There were advantages to the agreement both men made several years ago, he mused. The primary one, of course, was absolute secrecy. By always making major decisions and plans in person, they avoided the dangers involved with other forms of communication. Nothing was more reliable than in-person discussion in a private place. It allowed them freedom to explore all possibilities without fear of being overheard by the authorities.

The disadvantage of such a rigid policy was that each man found himself traveling a great deal more than he would have if the procedure were not in force. Not that either man reported to anyone other than himself. For that was certainly not the case. They were conscientious, however, and the work schedules they imposed on themselves were restrictive. They seldom found time for unnecessary trips. Today was definitely one of their more important meetings.

Dolci's driver chauffeured Mancotta down Periwinkle Way. The traffic was heavy and sluggish. Mancotta peered out of the window at the various shopping centers they passed along the route. Overhanging, luxuriant, tropical growth gave the road a tunneled appearance.

Shoppers roamed about in shorts and colorful T-shirt. The shopping center motif that prevailed was Tahitian— dark-stained, exposed wood bleached by the sun, and wooden shingles. The entire island of Sanibel had an enchanting atmosphere.

After turning onto the Sanibel-Captiva road and bypassing the Tarpon Bay Road intersection where traffic was bottle-necked, their pace quickened. As they crossed the bridge on Blind Pass, Mancotta looked to his left and saw Turner Beach. Numerous beachcombers were scouring the site looking for seashells. Here was one of the three best shelling locations in the entire world. Jeffreys Bay in Africa and the Sulu Islands in the southwest Pacific were the only spots that rivaled it. Mancotta had listened with interest as Dolci described his visits to those locations to appraise them for himself. Dolci argued that in years past Turner Beach had the finest shelling in the world. That was before the huge influx of tourists began clamoring over the beach taking live shells by the handful instead of carefully returning them to the sea and keeping only one specimen.

Mancotta admired the beautiful collection his partner had encased in a thick, clear, plastic resin on a custom made, oval, dining room table. But when Dolci began spouting off the names of the various specimens, Mancotta became bored with his partner's surprising passion for shells. To him, dissecting nature's art was a tedious exercise. The shells were unusual and pleasing to look at, but what they were called and how they functioned as part of the sea kingdom was of little interest.

Less than a half mile after they crossed the bridge at Blind Pass, the vehicle slowed and turned onto the private road that wound its way through the dense foliage which grew on Captiva Island. The multimillion-dollar home was completely hidden from the road. A barbed wire fence surrounded the twenty-acre estate. The home looked like a giant beach house. A dark wood exterior gave the three-story structure a rustic appearance. Mancotta looked forward to swimming in the private pool that overlooked the Gulf of Mexico.

Dolci stepped outside to greet his partner. "Welcome, Francesco. I trust your plane ride was comfortable."

Mancotta smiled. "Yes, it was very smooth. I had barely unpacked in New Orleans yesterday when I got your message."

Dolci disapproved of Mancotta's penchant for riding on commercial airlines. It was one subject they never could agree on. Dolci insisted his private jet was safer than flying commercially. Mancotta argued that private planes—no matter how expensive they might be—sustained far more accidents.

"Al will take your bags up to your room. Why don't you slip on your bathing suit and meet me at the pool." Dolci was already clad in a bright red swimsuit, yellow knit shirt, and sandals.

"Sounds good to me."

Dolci was in the pool when his partner plunged in. The warm water—heated by the winter sun that climbed overhead—eased tense muscles. The Olympic-size pool was surrounded by a thin screen that kept insects from troubling swimmers. Thin, white, wooden beams cast a shadow on the pool area. Numerous hanging baskets and large potted plants yielded a sweet, clean odor. Bluebird and red-heart hibiscus, yellow buttercup, japonica, and jasmine were just a few of the flowering shrubs that graced the river-rock patio surrounding the pool. Various palms and fruit-bearing trees provided a barrier along the outside of the screened-in area. But the view of the Gulf and the waterfront beach was unobstructed.

Mancotta exercised vigorously, swimming consecutive laps at a very quick pace. Dolci paddled about slowly with an even-paced breast stroke. Thirty minutes later the two men sat side by side at the pool's edge; their feet dangled in the water. A servant brought them two tall drinks— planter's punch garnished with pineapple and orange slices.

"Frank, sometimes I think we should both retire. We have so much to be thankful for, and certainly enough money to live comfortably for the rest of our lives."

"Retire? You've got to be kidding." Dolci laughed loudly. "We would die of sheer boredom." He slapped his partner on the back.

"I doubt that. We have too many hobbies to keep us busy."

"What hobbies are you referring to, my friend? The only hobbies you have are collecting women and racehorses."

Mancotta laughed. "I suppose you're right. They're enough to keep me busy. But you do have a lot of hobbies," Mancotta said, recalling Dolci's various outside interests.

He gardened and fished, and collected shells, coins, and stamps.

"Yes that's true. I like to keep busy. But you are a born leader and you will die a leader. I doubt you will ever enjoy life unless you are working."

Mancotta looked at Dolci and saw lines of sincerity etched on his face. Dolci had always been the driving force in their partnership. His desire for power was insatiable. Mancotta did not have his partner's zest for pursuing risky quests. He knew that one day he would back away from one of Dolci's more grandiose schemes. He hoped that day would never come, and perhaps it would not. Dolci would probably die before him, succumbing to age and poor health habits.

He decided to change the subject. "How is our friend, McLaughlin?"

Dolci shook his head. "Not thinking clearly, I'm afraid. Our meeting yesterday proved that he has too many doubts. After all I've done for him, he hesitates to accept my request."

"Ego?"

"Yes, just as I predicted. He doesn't want to give up the idea that he can win the national championship." Dolci stood and walked over to a white cane lounge chair. Beside it stood a short parson's table. A small wooden box of cigars rested on top of one corner. He dried himself with a towel and reached for a cigar.

Mancotta followed him and chose an orange from a bowl of fruit. He sat in a cane chair across from Dolci and drip-dried in the sun. After thinking over Dolci's assessment, he asked, "Have you thought of an acceptable course of action?"

Dolci puffed on his cigar. "Not acceptable, but operable. Unfortunately, our coach does not give us very many options. We're going to have to remove him from the picture."

Mancotta did not like that alternative. It was risky and he never enjoyed ordering the removal of someone who had previously performed satisfactorily. This was another reason why he considered retirement drawing near. Too many dangerous moves were surfacing from what had initially

started out as an elaborate but fairly safe plan to bolster
their bookmaking business.

"You see no other way?"

"No. And we can't stop here after we've come this far."

"But will his removal ensure Charlotte's victory?"

"That is a very good question. I've thought a great deal
about it. We have to destroy his career in a very special way.
He commands a great deal of respect from his players. If
he falls sentimentally, then those players will have something special to play for. We don't want them taking the
court with a 'win one for the coach' attitude."

Mancotta nodded his head in agreement. "I assume you
have worked out a plan?"

"Yes. The results will be quite different from that plane
crash three years ago."

Mancotta recalled the incident. An uncooperative new
basketball coach threatened to go to the authorities when
one of Dolci's soldiers offered to bribe a recruit to attend
the university. The coach reacted indignantly and when the
soldier confessed what he had done, Dolci erased both men.
The soldier drowned at sea in a boating accident; the coach
was killed in a plane that crashed into the Gulf after running
out of fuel. By using a clever timing device, carbon monoxide
had been released into the cabin one-half hour after the
plane ascended. The aircraft flew on automatic pilot while
radar controllers and scrambled Air Force jet pilots looked
on helplessly. Dolci had taken the extraordinary action
when he learned that the soldier had boldly mentioned his
name to the coach.

Dolci described his McLaughlin plan in detail. Mancotta
was surprised by the clever details. Such a plan would
probably never have occurred to him. Dolci was boldly
creative.

"What do you think?" Dolci asked.

"It sounds like you have it pretty well thought out. I can
offer no better method. It seems you have little
alternative."

"Fine. I'll see that Tortiglia is instructed immediately."

Mancotta nodded and stood. He was hot and wanted to

cool off in the pool. Another question came to mind before
he dove in. "Did Giannini find our friend Burton in an
acceptable mood?" he asked, referring to the results of an
order to continue to bug Burton's house to see if the
conversation between the executive director and his wife
demonstrated willingness to go along with the bribe.

"No, I'm afraid not. He indicated Burton was wavering;
so, I told him to frighten them. He said he had the perfect
idea; it involved their dog."

Mancotta paused for a moment, then said, "Burton
worries me, Frank. He isn't acting predictably."

"I know. I told Giannini to keep a close eye on him. After
he's done what we need him to do and the game is over, I
think we'd better have him eliminated."

* Fifteen *

Troy and Jenny Burton stood solemnly over the freshly dug grave in the corner of their backyard. The noonday sun shone brightly and the tree they stood under cast a shadow on the grave site. Troy placed his arm around Jenny and she softly prayed. Tears rolled down their cheeks. Jenny's voice cracked several times during her prayer.

Emotionally drained, the couple turned and left the horror of the previous evening temporarily under the tree. It would back up to them at various moments throughout the rest of their lives, sneaking in at unexpected moments—times when joy would return to their lives and times when depression grabbed them from behind. The joy of the memory of Drop would always be darkened by the scene of the brutal murder.

Troy drove Jenny to his uncle's house close to town. He took a circuitous route and eyed his rearview mirror all the time to make sure he was not followed. His uncle's wife, Karen, would look after her until the evening, when Troy would pick her up. They made the arrangement under the guise that Jenny was still weak from the flu, and the sudden death of Drop had added to her poor health. They explained that Drop had apparently died from a heart attack.

Troy had phoned the office and told them he would be late because he had to take Jenny to the doctor. As he drove to work, he thought about how stupid he had been in not having anticipated that Dolci could have placed listening devices in the house. Since Dolci had made his first approach, it was obvious he must have had them under close surveillance. That had to be how he managed to know precisely when to intervene before the press conference.

"Asshole!" Troy said loudly as he slammed his fist against the steering wheel at a stoplight.

The afternoon passed in a flurry of confusion. When he arrived at the university, he had already received over one hundred calls from Foundation members and others requesting tickets to the championships. Had it not been for the valuable assistance he received from members of the Stinger club, he would have been buried in the landslide of requests. Three members stayed with him the entire day and followed his instructions closely.

He and Lindsey Ellis attended a conference with Chancellor Hollings and his executive staff. The chancellor fully understood the squeeze on tickets, and he attempted to minimize his ticket requirements as best he could. Unfortunately, he had also been inundated with requests from patrons, politicians, and friends. Everyone was putting pressure on him. As a result, Chancellor Hollings found he needed two hundred and fifty tickets.

As Troy suspected, the staff also agreed that the students should receive exactly one half of the two-thousand-seat allotment. By the time everyone had stripped away the requirements for tickets, Troy was left with only seven hundred tickets for Foundation members. With over a thousand members, he could have filled requests for at least fifteen hundred tickets. He set the limit at two for each qualifying Foundation member. He bent his rule for some of the larger donors who had given at least one thousand dollars a year for three consecutive years or more. If requested, he provided four tickets to individuals who fell in that category.

As a result, only three hundred and fourteen members would go to the championships. No public tickets would go on sale. The value of being a substantial donor came into sharp focus. The price of Hornet basketball had just tripled.

As Troy set the criteria and arrived at the priority number that served as a cutoff point, a line of members waited outside his office door and in the hall to see if they qualified for tickets. Most had come because they had been unable to get through the Athletic Department's jammed telephone lines. He felt like he had become at once the most popular and the most hated man in Charlotte. Those who qualified for tickets under his sophisticated priority system loved him. The rest, who learned first-hand or through announcements on television and radio that all tickets had been spoken for, cursed him. Explanations of where tickets went and how the system worked were given a great deal of attention. Troy was interviewed over the phone by Chuck Haigler.

Money was the prime mover. The University of Charlotte Athletic Foundation moved ever closer to its $250,000 goal that day. Thirty-one new Gold Hornet club members and two new courtesy car dealers surfaced as a result of prodding from John Windsor and Troy. The minimum donation that had to come from the pocket of a new prospect to gain the right to purchase two tickets was one thousand dollars. That information was not publicized, but by merely being passed on quietly in telephone conversations, the coffers quickly swelled. Troy had never seen anything like it. Fortunately, he had held back enough tickets to take care of the new segment.

He was exhausted when the day ended; the activity had temporarily distracted his attention from the Dolci problem. He collapsed into his courtesy car and drove to pick up Jenny.

On his way, he thought about Dolci. He was going to nail him.

* Sixteen *

A small, flat bottom, aluminum skiff—powered by an electric trolling motor—glided noiselessly along the water. Dominick Tortiglia sat quietly on the seat in the bow of the boat. He pointed dead ahead, a signal for the man in the stern to continue toward the canal.

Tortiglia watched carefully as the boat slowly entered the manmade thirty-five foot deep canal located between Riverside and Nautilus Drive at the edge of the Caloosahatchee River. The numerous interlocking waterways of Cape Coral provided hundreds of waterfront home sites backyard access to the Gulf of Mexico through the Caloosahatchee.

He was glad moonlight had been subdued by clouds; only porch and pier lights along the waterway reflected softly off the water. Few people were awake—it was almost fifteen minutes past midnight. The small boat passed unnoticed after traveling approximately one-third of a mile past Mikado, Malibu, and Mayfair Courts—short blocks which also had channels providing deep water access.

At Malaluka Court the boat turned in the one-quarter mile long canal. As it slowly moved north, Tortiglia pointed at the house. The man in the stern guided the craft to a berthing place along the concrete seawall next to a small wooden pier. Dressed in black, Tortiglia felt nearly invisible as he climbed out onto the pier. The boat reversed, turned, and headed back out of the passage.

Tortiglia disappeared quickly into the shadows at the back of the house. He crouched low between the screened lanai and a tall Royal palm tree. He was certain no one had seen him.

A light was on in the interior of the house. Having memorized the floor plan, he believed the illumination emanated from the center of the house, where the study was located.

Crouching low, staying in the shadows, he moved to the

screen door of the lanai. It was unlocked and he entered
quickly. It was a cool evening and only one bedroom window
remained open. Through it, he heard the muffled sounds
of soft mood music.

The sliding glass door that allowed access to the house
was locked. Taking out a large screwdriver from his back
pocket, he kneeled down and wedged the tool under the
bottom corner below the door latch. He applied downward
force using the raised concrete door sill as a fulcrum. The
glass door moved up approximately one-half inch—enough
to release the catch on the lock as he pushed back with his
right hand. No obstruction had been placed on the track;
it slid open silently.

He entered the dark living room and relocked the door.
He walked softly to the hall and toward the source of light.
He had guessed correctly: the light came from the study.
He heard the faint sound of rustling paper. His quarry was
awake and apparently at work in the study. He removed his
gun—concealed underneath his black nylon windbreaker—
from his shoulder holster.

When he appeared at the door abruptly, Coach Patrick
McLaughlin looked up at him, startled, speechless. Tortiglia
pointed a large caliber pistol directly at his head.

"What the—"

"Don't move. If you make another sound, I'll kill you," he
said firmly as he stepped into the room.

McLaughlin froze.

"Stand up," Tortiglia ordered.

McLaughlin stood and the man looked closely at the
coach's attire, pants and a T-shirt.

"Put on socks, shoes, and a shirt." He waved his gun
toward the door.

"What for? Where are we going?" McLaughlin asked as
he moved around his desk toward the door.

"I told you to be quiet. Just do as you're told."

"OK, take it easy. I'll have to get my things from the
bedroom." He walked slowly down the hall.

Tortiglia followed. He knew no one else was in the house.
McLaughlin was a confirmed bachelor and earlier surveil-

lance revealed he had no visitors that evening. Keeping his captive quiet was Tortiglia's method of control.

He asked for the coach's keys and his wallet. After checking for cash, he handed it back to him without removing any. McLaughlin looked at him quizzically. Then a light seemed to go on in his eyes. Undoubtedly, he had realized this was no robbery.

Tortiglia led the coach through the entire house turning some lights on and the study light and radio off. Then he instructed McLaughlin to go to the garage through the indoor entrance. He opened the trunk of the coach's late model Cadillac Seville. "Get in."

"I'll suffocate."

"No you won't. Now get the fuck in or I'll blow you away."

The Irishman climbed inside, having to tuck his long legs up to fit. Tortiglia closed the trunk lid, walked around to the driver's side of the car and got in. He searched the glove compartment and found the small remote control box that opened the garage door with the press of a button.

He smiled as he started the engine. Everything was going like clockwork. He was a pro. The best. That's why Dolci always used him instead of those other fuckheads who couldn't snatch a puppy from a litter.

As he left the garage, he pressed the button a second time and the door closed. No one was outside; the neighbors were apparently asleep.

His route took him down El Dorado Parkway onto Del Prado Boulevard to Cape Coral Parkway and over the Cape Coral Bridge across the Caloosahatchee to Fort Myers. He turned right on McGregor Boulevard and accelerated. When the road forked, he veered left on Route 865. Crossing the bridge to Estero Island, he slowed and watched his rearview mirror carefully. At Fort Myers Beach he drove cautiously. The beach road was patrolled heavily. He could ill-afford to be stopped by the police.

After he turned right into a private drive and parked under the blue house on stilts, he breathed easier. He knocked on the door four times.

An attractive young woman in a red satin robe opened

the door and asked, "You have him?"

"Yes. Turn off that goddamn porch light." He knew her name, Virginia Clavell, but he had already told her no names were to be used. She knew him by one of his aliases, Danny Greene, but that wouldn't matter either.

Tortiglia opened the trunk of the car and told McLaughlin to get out. He forced the coach up the stairs and inside. Pushing him into a bedroom at gun point, he said, "I've lined up a real nice lady for you."

McLaughlin looked at the blond woman sitting on a chair beside the bed.

"Take off your clothes," Tortiglia instructed.

"What the hell is this all about?" McLaughlin asked.

"You're going to get the best screwing you ever had in your life," Tortiglia replied.

"Sure, and I suppose you went to all this trouble just to see that I could have a good time," McLaughlin said sarcastically.

"Right," Tortiglia said, motioning with his pistol. "Now, take your fucking clothes off."

Virginia Clavell sat with her legs crossed in a relaxed pose. She smiled at the coach, then slowly stood and removed her robe. She wore a short, sheer, red negligee and her large breasts were plainly visible. Tortiglia stared at her blond pubic hair—proof that the long, golden blond hair on her head had obviously not come from a bottle. She was a great looking woman. He admired her tanned and silky smooth skin and believed her reputation as a "high class hooker" was well deserved—worth every bit of the five hundred a night she charged.

She walked over to McLaughlin as he slowly removed his shirt. "Let me help you with that," she said, reaching out.

"No thanks, I can do it myself." He pushed her hands away. Throwing his shirt on the floor, he looked at Tortiglia and said, "Where's the camera? I mean that is what you have in mind, isn't it?"

"Don't worry about it. Just relax and enjoy yourself."

"This is ridiculous. How the hell do you expect me to get it up under these circumstances? Why don't we cut the crap and you just take me to your boss? He is Frank Dolci, isn't he?"

Remaining silent, Tortiglia walked over, stuck the pistol right on the coach's lips, and pulled back the hammer. "Say one more word and you're brains will be splattered all over this room."

McLaughlin's eyes widened. The business end of the barrel of the .357 magnum pressed his lips against his teeth. He moved his head back enough to speak. "OK, OK, just take it easy with that thing, will you?"

Pulling the pistol away, but still aiming it at McLaughlin's head, Tortiglia said, "Get on with it. Just pretend like I'm not here. Enjoy yourself."

The coach started removing the remainder of his clothes.

"Come here, honey," Clavell said, patting the side of the bed next to where she was sitting. She pulled her negligee off over her head, dropped it on the floor, and began rubbing McLaughlin's hairy chest and flat stomach.

Tortiglia could see it in her eyes. She would have preferred having McLaughlin for a partner alone, but she had been paid handsomely to perform sex while Tortiglia remained in the room. Although he had sent her many a wealthy "John" and had never asked her for a pimp fee or sex, he knew she didn't like him.

This was the first unusual request he had ever made, and she had leaped at the money he offered her—five thousand dollars. "Sounds fair to me," she had said when he had told her how much.

She had no idea who Tortiglia's boss was. However, after hearing the coach speculate that it was a man named Dolci, she realized McLaughlin may have guessed correctly.

The coach pulled down his shorts and sat on the edge of the bed. She began fondling him, careful not to scratch him with her long fingernails.

Tortiglia sat on a chair and watched. He had never thought of himself as a voyeur, but the scene was beginning to arouse him. He considered himself a ladies' man: handsome in a rugged way, cool, tough, rich and generous. And even when they became a pain in the ass, he simply walked away. Roughing up women wasn't his style. Unless, of course, it was business.

McLaughlin did not respond. The hooker looked up at him and said, "Let's see what you think about this, baby."

She leaned over and began sucking him. Tortiglia could feel himself stir. Watching the scene and hearing the sound of her full-throated motion excited him far more than he'd anticipated. No matter what the coach was thinking, sooner or latter he'd get a hard-on, Tortiglia thought. Being raped by a woman as beautiful as her was impossible to ignore.

"What's the problem? Can't you get it up for the little lady?" Tortiglia asked.

"I'm not used to having an audience," McLaughlin answered.

"Forget about me. I'm just here to see you don't hurt her. Have a good time. If I was you, I'd fuck her brains out. Look at her. How can you resist?"

"That's easy. You're sitting over their holding a gun on me."

"The only way I'm gonna shoot you is if you don't fuck this chick. So you'd better start concentrating."

Mclaughlin looked down at her, apparently resigned that he was going to have to cooperate.

Tortiglia enjoyed watching. She was a true pro. No way could McLaughlin ignore her. The instructions had been explicit: Tortiglia had to make sure McLaughlin came inside her. That was the tough part. He knew McLaughlin would have trouble getting a hard-on, much less coming. But orders were orders.

Finally, he could see that McLaughlin was responding. Tortiglia could understand why. Like Willie Nelson, an actor in *The Electric Horseman*, had said in the movie, Clavell could "suck the chrome off a trailer hitch."

When McLaughlin became fully aroused, she pulled him on top of her and wrapped her legs around his upper thighs. She said, "I want you." Then she reached down and guided him in.

Tortiglia got up and walked to the closet. He opened the door, removed a camera case, then unbuckled it. A mere formality.

McLaughlin heard him and turned to see the camera. He appeared somewhat relieved to see it—pictures of a rape were unlikely. Tortiglia knew the coach now believed he was simply going to be blackmailed.

"Turn around and pay attention to the little lady." Tortiglia held the pistol in one hand, the camera in the other.

McLaughlin obeyed and tried to position his head away from the camera. Tortiglia didn't care. All he wanted was for that bastard to come.

He waited and watched as Clavell arched her hips and wrapped her legs around McLaughlin. She moaned. A fake moan, Tortiglia knew, but moaning and feigned pleasure almost always made a man shoot-off quicker. The tricks of the trade, he reflected.

By now McLaughlin seemed to have lost himself. He was beginning to pump in and out. She was good alright. Apparently, she liked her work.

It was just like in all those pornflicks Tortiglia kept at home. Only one difference: he was on the set and the climax was going to be something he enjoyed even more than usual. He suddenly noticed he was hard against his pants. This really had turned him on. He had to regain control.

Finally, he saw McLaughlin begin to increase his pace. No doubt the coach was getting ready. Clavell arched her back and cried out. "Yes, yes. I can feel you, baby. Good! That's it. Shoot!"

That was Tortiglia's signal. He hoped the bitch really could feel the coach coming like she said she would be able to.

It was time. As Tortiglia raised the camera and began clicking shots, McLaughlin buried his face in the pillow beside her head. Perfect, Tortiglia thought, just as planned. He moved forward toward them on the left side of the bed.

She saw what was about to happen a split second before Tortiglia struck. In one smooth, quick motion, he reached underneath his jacket, removed a long pair of stainless steel scissors, and plunged them into the coach's back. She was stunned by the unexpected turn of events.

McLaughlin's body jerked as the eight-inch, closed blades of the razor sharp scissors penetrated the right side of his spine below the scapula. He let out an anguished cry and jerked in pain.

Clavell screamed. Tortiglia left the scissors in the coach's back, dropped his pistol, and grabbed her around the throat. She looked at him in terror and fought for her life—scratching, clawing.

The crinkling sound of the cartilaginous structure of her larynx mingled with choking, guttural noises—her death knell. She struggled less tenaciously and clawed weakly at his face and arms. Her face turned livid; her eyes bulged. Her body went limp as she lost consciousness. He maintained pressure for another minute to ensure death.

McLaughlin had rolled off of her body and on his side, helpless and unable to move further. He fought for life-giving air. Paling, then turning blue, he gasped—hungry for that which the body was incapable of providing. Massive internal bleeding filled his chest. A final, convulsive shudder signaled his death.

Tortiglia sat on the edge of the bed breathing heavily from the struggle and tension of his double murder. He felt the sticky wetness in his pants. This was the first time that had ever happened. It bothered him.

He stood and tried to clear his thoughts. The instructions he received from Dolci had been precise, explicit. Although he wanted to leave the scene immediately, he could not. If he left out one detail, his career as a paid assassin would end. He took pride in his work and considered himself a highly skilled technician. These were his twenty-second and twenty-third victims. He had been paid handsomely.

As he looked around the scene, he recalled his instructions. He picked up the camera and case and placed them by the door. He wiped off the scissors' handles without removing them from the coach's back; blood trickled from the wound. He took the naked woman's right hand, placed her fingers around the handle, and squeezed tight to mimic a grip. Carefully removing her hand, he repositioned her body and moved McLaughlin's corpse closer to hers. Taking one hand at a time, he raked the coach's face and arms with her long fingernails.

Satisfied he had staged the scene properly, he looked at the handle on the closet door and wiped it off with his handkerchief: it was the only place he had touched that would show his fingerprints. Perfect, he thought, as he picked up his pistol and holstered it.

His black sweater had been ripped at the collar; he checked in the mirror to make sure it was a tear and no pieces were missing. Blood flowed slowly from his right cheek where she had scratched him. He blotted it with his handkerchief.

He looked around and remembered another important detail. He walked over to the nightstand beside the bed and opened the drawer. Grabbing her arm, he stretched it out to make sure it would reach, then replaced it by her side.

He placed the camera inside the case and stood at the door surveying the scene. Carefully, he went over all the details in his mind. The clothes on the floor reminded him of one last detail: he still had McLaughlin's keys. He placed them inside the coach's pants pocket.

The job completed, he picked up the camera case, walked out, and pulled the door shut with his two fingers shielded by his handkerchief. Outside, as he passed McLaughlin's car, he wiped the door handle and remembered previously wiping the steering column clean. He walked down the private drive out to the street.

Headlights blinked on as a vehicle moved forward to pick him up. Without speaking to the driver, he sat in the front seat. The car disappeared into the early morning darkness.

* Seventeen *

Chuck Haigler sat at his desk on the fourth floor of the *Charlotte Observer*'s five story office complex in downtown Charlotte. He stared in frustration at his empty notebook. All morning he had been attempting to make contact with the Chargers' coach to ask questions about the semifinal game against the Hornets. He had a story to write for the Wednesday morning edition and without some good quotes from McLaughlin, he figured he might as well go fishing. The excitement that infected all of Charlotte screamed for the vacuum of knowledge about the Florida team to be filled. It was his job to fill that void with first-hand information.

He picked up the phone and dialed the number again. As it rang, he tapped his pencil nervously on the desk.

"Charger Athletics," the woman answered.

"Coach McLaughlin, please."

"I'm sorry, sir, he's not in. May I take a message?"

"Do you know where I can reach him? This is very important."

"I'm sorry, sir. He was due in early this morning, and he hasn't come in yet. Is this Mr. Haigler?"

"Yes. I'm sorry to keep bothering you, but I've got a deadline. I was afraid he might have overlooked my message."

"I marked it urgent, Mr. Haigler. I promise I'll make sure he gets it. He's received quite a few other calls so far this morning; so, I can't promise when he'll get back to you."

"All right. Thank you for your help," Haigler said, hanging up the phone. Where in the hell is he? he wondered. He had already attempted to reach him at his home in Cape Coral, and there had been no answer.

The phone rang and he grabbed it quickly. "Sports, Chuck Haigler."

"Morning, Chuck."

He recognized the voice—it belonged to Lindsey Ellis. "How are you, Lindsey?"

"I don't know. I haven't had time to check."

Haigler knew the feeling. "What can I do for you?"

"It's what I can do for you, Chucky-boy. I called to let you know that your interview with TC is cleared. He's over at the dorm right now. Give him a call to set up a time."

"Great. At least something's going right."

"What?"

"Sorry, don't mean to be crying on your shoulder. It's just that I'm having a hell of a time reaching UFFM's coach."

"That doesn't surprise me," Ellis said. "If it's anything like it is here, the poor man's probably losing his mind. Bill's phone hasn't stopped ringing. Shit, for that matter, neither has mine. That's why I thought I'd better call you. Wasn't sure if you could get through to me."

"Thanks. What time are they practicing today?"

"Two thirty, but practice is closed."

"Putting in a secret weapon, eh?"

"I guess. Bill made a point of telling me that absolutely no one would be allowed in, including the staff."

"OK. I hadn't planned on coming anyway," Haigler said. "I'll give Ted a call right now."

"Good. He should still be there—I just talked to him."

After hanging up, Haigler phoned Ted Collins. The player answered the phone. After exchanging pleasantries, Haigler suggested a time for the evening interview. "Seven thirty OK?"

"Yeah, that's fine with me," Collins answered.

"In your dorm?"

"Sure, but a lot of people have been hanging around here," Collins said.

"Hmmmm . . . tell you what. Let me pick you up and take you someplace for dinner."

"OK. I'll wait for you here," said Collins.

As Haigler hung up the phone, he saw Joe Meeks, the *Observer*'s daily sports columnist, rushing into the sports editor's office. Curious, he watched both men begin conversing excitedly as they stood at the computer terminal screen.

The exchange between the two men through the glass front partition of the office told him something big was breaking. Stuart Ingram, the editor, got up and walked to the door.

Ingram waved at Haigler. "Chuck! Come here!"

"What's up?" Haigler asked as he closed the door behind him.

Meeks handed Haigler the teletype copy. "This just came in over the wire."

Haigler read the Associated Press message: "Patrick A. McLaughlin, the University of Florida at Fort Myers head basketball coach, was murdered early this morning. At 10:55 a.m. E.S.T., Fort Myers police were called to investigate two murders at a private home on Estero Island (Fort Myers Beach, Florida). McLaughlin was positively identified. Police are withholding the name of the female victim, pending notification of next of kin. Exact details are not available. However, sources close to the investigation indicate male victim stabbed, and female victim apparently strangled. The Chargers are scheduled to play in the NCAA Final Four in New Orleans this coming Saturday against the University of Charlotte in the semifinal game at 2:00 p.m. C.S.T."

"Jesus! When's the next plane to Fort Myers?" Haigler asked.

"Now wait a minute, Chuck. You've got a job to do here," Ingram said. "If anybody goes, it's got to be Joe."

Ingram's statement let the air out of Haigler's sails. He started to speak.

Ingram held up his hand, palm out, like a school crossing guard. "There isn't a guy here who wouldn't give his right arm to cover that story. But I need you here. You've got that feature to do on Collins."

"What about that one on UFFM for tomorrow?" Haigler asked.

Ingram thought for a moment, then said, "Dig up all you can on the team. Find out what kind of relationship the players had with the coach. Try to figure out how this will affect the game Saturday."

"How am I going to do that without going down there?"

Haigler asked.

Ingram shifted forward in his chair. "Call the assistant coaches and the SID. In the meantime, Joe will catch the first plane to Fort Myers. Find out all you can before he gets down there. He'll call you when he arrives. You might be able to give him a good place to start. I want you both working on the story."

Haigler didn't like the compromise move, but he had to accept it. And there was no doubt that Joe Meeks was more experienced in dealing with this type of story. He had previously been a reporter on the city desk.

"Wonder what the NCAA is going to do. Think they'll cancel the games?" Meeks asked.

"I doubt it," Ingram said, turning to Haigler. "Check it out. If you have trouble getting through, don't worry—we'll probably get a statement from them over the wire."

Haigler rose from his chair. "OK, let's go, Joe."

"Right," the bald-headed reporter said, smiling at Ingram.

Haigler knew he had been thrown the short bone. That was all right, though. It was certainly better than nothing. His work schedule had just doubled. Already scores of questions streamed through his mind. He would not be the only one asking those questions. By now he imagined that reporters from all over the country were preparing their assault on Fort Myers.

He had studied the history of the national basketball championships. Never before had a coach been murdered during the event. This was headline news all right.

Troy Burton scanned his computer priority listing and marked off two more names with a black felt-tip pen. He had only ten more tickets left and dreaded deciding which five members would receive them. He had about seven hundred names left in front of him.

That reminded him of Powers and Stinson. He had been sure they would have been the first to pick up their tickets, yet he still had not heard from them since their discussion

Sunday morning.

He believed he had to be fair to all concerned in deciding who would receive tickets. He had tried to reward the best Foundation members—those who gave money consistently and those who worked hard for the program. The priority system he had designed measured the former. The latter was a category for which he had to rely on both his and Frank Jeffers' judgment.

Jeffers, the president of the hard-working Stinger club, supplied information that had been extremely helpful in determining which members of the group's one hundred families worked the hardest to help the Hornet program throughout the season. They hawked Hornet souvenirs at every home game and sold season tickets at the beginning of the school year. Since some of the Stinger members also donated substantially to the Athletic Foundation, Troy was able to include them with the moneyed group. Eight members had qualified for tickets in that category. In addition, he decided that twenty-three hard workers from the club should receive tickets—despite the fact that they did not qualify on the regular priority system. He admired their spirit, as did Coach Lee.

Considering all the facts, he had to make his final decisions. About fifty people still lingered outside of his office, and he was seeing them one at a time. If they had a high enough priority number, he would allow them to purchase two tickets. The telephone intercom rang, interrupting his thoughts.

"Yes?"

"A Mr. Powers is here to see you. He says it's very important. I told him he'd have to wait with the others, but he insisted that I tell you he was here," Janet Hopson said, sounding somewhat irritated.

"Send him in."

"But what about—"

"I know, Janet—it won't look good, but I have to see him. See if you can't sneak him back here."

Troy heard her sigh, a click, a dial tone. Despite all the jubilant celebration going on all over campus, nerves were wearing thin in the athletic department. The crush of phone calls, reporters, and ticket seekers had flattened daily routine.

Powers entered. Troy shook his hand. "I wondered where you were. As a matter of fact, I was just thinking about you."

"I know, man. We've been swarmed at the Hornet's Nest. Business is buzzing."

"Cute. Sounds like you might be too busy to go to New Orleans," Troy said wryly.

"Not *that* busy. If you've got tickets, we're going."

"Right here." Troy held up four long, glossy tickets.

"Thanks, I appreciate that. Our wives are going to love you. I'll pay you for them before I leave, but that's not the only reason I'm here."

"You have some information?"

"Yes, but Russ doesn't know a thing about it, and I don't want you to tell him I told you anything. He's completely in the dark, and for reasons I can't tell you, I want it to stay that way."

"No problem. I won't say a word."

Powers looked Troy squarely in the eyes. "That's another thing. You can't tell a soul where you got this information."

Troy nodded slowly.

Leaning forward in his chair, speaking softly, Powers said, "The man you asked about owns a number of legitimate businesses across the Southeast. He's a multimillionaire. He's also involved in the drug business in a big way, and I don't mean pharmacies.

"He's a very dangerous man. He's a boss in organized crime. He can have people rubbed out with the snap of his fingers."

Troy remained silent. Two weeks ago that same information would have fallen on deaf ears. The Mafia was an element in society that he considered foreign, like aliens from another planet. His awakening to the reality had been nightmarish.

Powers leaned back in his chair. "What's important is that you understand that this man has power; anybody that

fucks with him is gonna get hurt. Now, I don't know why
you asked me to find something out about him; you made
me promise not to ask. But I can guess that you've either
had contact with him, or you're thinking about asking him
for a donation. Steer clear and you'll be OK."

"How do you know all this?" Troy asked. He regretted
not investigating Dolci sooner. He felt like a complete fool
and blamed himself for the death of Drop.

"Don't ask me how or why I know. I like you and we're
good friends, but I can't tell you," Powers said seriously.

Troy nodded. He wondered how Powers had become privy
to such information. Was it Powers' involvement with
drugs? That had to be it.

"Thanks for the information, Donnie. You have my word.
I won't tell anyone."

Powers paid for the tickets and left quietly.

The information had been helpful. Troy had discussed
the alternatives with Jenny last night on their way home.
A partial decision was made. Troy felt he had no other
choice but to go to the FBI.

Included in that decision was their agreement that first
he should consider revealing Dolci's proposition to Bill Lee
in strict confidence. Obviously, the coach would have to
become involved in some way; perhaps he could be helpful
in providing some clear thinking. Troy recalled Lee's words
and had quoted them to Jenny: "Don't sacrifice your
integrity."

There was a knock at the door. Troy looked up and saw
Lindsey Ellis. The sports information director entered.

"Have you had your radio on?" Ellis asked as he sat down.

"No. Why?"

"I just heard a bulletin you're not going to believe."

"Try me."

"Patrick McLaughlin has been murdered."

"What?" Troy's pulse quickened.

"Police found him and a woman dead in a house at Fort
Myers Beach. He was stabbed and she was strangled."

Shocked, Troy stared at Ellis. But it did not take him
long to recover and make a quick connection. What had

Powers just said? *He can have people rubbed out with the snap of his fingers*. So, this is how we make it to the finals, he thought. "Does Bill know?"

"I just told him," Ellis answered.

Without saying another word, Troy got up and walked out of the office.

"Where are you going?" Ellis asked, just before Burton disappeared.

Troy did not reply. He walked to Coach Lee's door and entered without knocking.

* Eighteen *

Bert Teague looked at the terse teletype bulletin that had just been delivered to him. Holding the phone between his shoulder and his left ear, he drummed his pen impatiently on his desk with his right thumb and forefinger. When Harry Murtagh, special agent in the Tampa field office finally answered, Teague's voice boomed loudly through the long-distance telephone connection. "Goddamnit, Harry, I thought you people were keeping an eye on McLaughlin."

Murtagh said coolly, "Listen, Bert, I think you are jumping to conclusions. You don't know what happened. You can't expect our resident agent in Fort Myers to spend all his time on one case. Florida's a damn busy place. We're stretched awful thin down here, you know."

Attempting to check his anger and frustration, Teague took a deep breath. Murtagh was right. After all, it had been merely a gut feeling that prompted Teague to request surveillance.

"I'm sorry, Harry. This case has just got me on edge. Is Hall at the scene?" Teague asked, referring to Tim Hall, the resident agent in Fort Myers.

"He called me and said he was on his way about an hour ago."

"What were the investigating team's preliminary findings?"

Murtagh described the murder scene, recalling every detail local authorities had given him over the phone. The consensus was that the woman apparently stabbed McLaughlin with a pair of scissors as he was strangling her.

"Do they know anything about her at all?"

"Yes. Her name's Virginia Clavell. She's from New York and has been living in Fort Myers for five years. She's been arrested for prostitution twice. Word is that she was a high-class whore and pandered only to the wealthy."

"That doesn't make sense, Harry. Why would a guy in

McLaughlin's position pay for sex?"

"Maybe he had her before and she was blackmailing him," Murtagh said.

"So, he goes in, screws her, and chokes her to death," Teague said sarcastically.

"Does sound crazy, doesn't it? But that's one of their initial theories."

"I don't buy it one damn bit. They don't know what we know. How good are they in forensic pathology down there?"

"That's in our favor. Florida's got one of the best systems in the country. Dr. Vaughn is the examiner in Lee County. He's got a lot of experience."

"Have you talked to him?"

"No. He was at the scene, though. I left a message for him to call me."

Teague leaned back in his chair. "Good. I suppose they're a little bit curious why we are sticking our noses in. I'd better stay out of the picture. We don't want it leaking to the press that agents from all over are taking an interest. I'm counting on you, Harry."

"I'll do everything I can. Hall's a good man, Bert. If there's anything to be found that will reveal a setup, he'll find it."

"All right. When you talked to him, did he indicate whether he had ever seen my suspect with McLaughlin?"

"No, but he admitted that he couldn't follow him everywhere, and his informants said they never saw a thing."

"All two of 'em, right?" Teague laughed sardonically, reflecting on his inside joke. Since Congress passed the Freedom of Information act in the late '70s, the FBI's list of informants had plummeted from six thousand to less than twenty-eight hundred. It was like tying one arm behind a swimmer's back and asking him to swim the English Channel.

"I'm afraid so," Murtagh said. "Our friends in Disneyland might wake up some day."

Teague sighed. "It'll be too late by then. But that's a whole different subject. I'm getting too old to worry about it.

"When you hear from Hall, please ask him to call me. If

I'm not here, tell him to leave a number and I'll get back to him. I might be taking a little trip." Remembering his new partner, Teague added, "Damn, I almost forgot. We've got a new man down here. Name's Hardin. He's my replacement. Tell Hall to talk to him if I'm not here. I'll fill Hardin in, OK?"

"No problem. Listen, Bert, don't let this get to you. You did all you could under the circumstances. I'm sorry if you feel like we dropped the ball. There was just no way we could see it coming."

"I know. It's nobody's fault. It's the system, and the guys on the other side know it."

After hanging up, Teague called his secretary and asked her to make reservations on the next available flight to Charlotte. He called Hardin and briefed him on everything, including his informant. He decided it was time to begin turning the screws.

"Coach, I've got to talk to you right now," Troy said as he shut the door behind him. Normally, he would never have entered so brusquely, but he was too upset to care how Lee reacted. He was somewhat surprised by the coach's calm response.

"Sit down, Troy. You look upset."

"I sure am. We've got a big problem. I don't know who to turn to, but since it involves the team and the championships—not to mention the murder of Coach McLaughlin—I've got to tell you what's happening. Maybe you can help," Troy said all in one breath. The strain had been almost too much. His nerves quickened his speech pattern; his palms were sweating.

Lee said, "I hope I can. This sounds serious. Suppose you tell me about it."

"Will you keep this in strict confidence?" Troy asked.

Lee puffed on his pipe. "Certainly."

Troy began recounting everything that had happened from the beginning: the offer in Dolci's limousine, the trip to Lake Norman, Dolci's bribe, the death of Drop, and his suspicion that Dolci had McLaughlin murdered.

As he told his story, Lee sat quietly and listened dispassionately. His unruffled demeanor did not match Troy's expectations. Several times he anticipated the coach would stop him for further explanation or appear surprised. That never happened. Only once did he notice that Lee's hands shook slightly when he refilled his pipe with tobacco.

After finishing his story with speculation about why McLaughlin was murdered, there was a long silence. Lee was apparently deliberating. Troy felt very uneasy. He was positive the coach knew something; that thought frightened him.

"Troy, I want you to listen to me and listen carefully," Lee said as he leaned forward in his chair. "I don't want you to breathe a word of this to anyone. I want you to see me immediately after practice this afternoon."

"Coach, excuse me for saying this, but there is something wrong here. You are taking this much too calmly. You know something, don't you?"

"Yes, I do. I know a great deal, and don't think for one minute that I'm not as scared as you are. I just hide it a little bit better. We're in a hell of a mess, but we've got to keep calm, OK?"

Troy nodded his head and sighed heavily. His mind shifted into overdrive. Prompted by Lee's disclosure, questions sprang up like puddles in a thunderstorm. He probed. "How long have you known about this? Why haven't you talked to me about it before now?"

"I've known for quite a while. I'll explain everything to you tonight." Lee paused, obviously seeing that Troy didn't like the answer. "I know this is all hard to understand. I don't blame you for being concerned about my role. But you have got to trust me. Trust the instincts that told you to see me. Do your best to continue as if nothing happened. I'll see you after practice."

Lee rose from his chair and shook Troy's hand firmly.

Troy nodded and left. All he had was a gut feeling that his decision to talk to Lee had been correct. Exactly what Lee knew and how he was involved, puzzled him though.

He felt relieved that he had not told the coach about his plans to go to the FBI. It was the only card he had not played. If Lee was involved with Dolci, he could play his trump card—provided he had time to do so.

He left the office complex to look for a pay phone. Anybody in the department could pick up on his line; he couldn't take that chance. If something went wrong, Jenny would need to be in a position to play his last card.

* Nineteen *

The news of Coach McLaughlin's death spread swiftly. It rocked the sports world and Fort Myers was in shock. Haigler had talked to several people at the palm-tree-lined campus located on College Parkway. One woman cried the entire time he interviewed her. He wanted to capture the essence of the aftermath. Even if he could not be there, he was determined to develop a sharp picture of a campus dealt a severe blow in the midst of celebration.

Haigler enjoyed delving into people's lives. His ears often told him more than his eyes did. He believed a good reporter had to be a perceptive listener.

When anyone asked him what made him tick, his answer was simple: "People." He was fascinated by humanity, and his pet theory was that sports was a representation of life. Sports drew out the best and worst man had to offer.

After several hours, Haigler was finally able to reach one of the assistant coaches with the Chargers, Tim Sherwood. The young coach was badly shaken.

"Coach, I'm very sorry to bother you at a time like this. I've been trying all day to gather some information on your team for our readers in North and South Carolina. I never dreamed something like this would happen. Do you mind answering a few questions for me?"

"Mr. Haigler, right now I'd rather not. Can you call me back tomorrow and give me a chance to collect my thoughts? I just got finished talking with the police, and I really have some pressing matters here."

"Listen, I know how you feel. I won't keep you long—just a couple of quick questions."

Sherwood sighed. "OK."

"Thanks. Can you tell me what kind of relationship Coach McLaughlin had with the players?"

"They loved him. He was a father and a friend to all of them and a helluva fine coach."

"What kind of effect do you think this will have on them?"

"It's going to make Saturday's game awfully tough to play. We lost somebody we were all very close to. Hell, we don't even understand what happened."

"I wanted to ask you about that," Haigler said as he scribbled some notes. "What's being said down there?"

"Well, it depends on what station you listen to. Some are speculating that Pat started strangling her, and then she stabbed him. Others are just describing the scene and leaving it up to your imagination."

"What do you think?"

"There is no way in hell he killed her. I've known him for ten years, and I can tell you he was just not capable of something like that."

"Have they released her name yet?"

"Yes, it's Virginia Clavell."

"Did you know her?"

"No, and I never heard Pat mention her name, either."

"Who was she?"

"Look, Mr. Haigler, I've really got to be going. We've called a meeting with the players."

Haigler sensed the coach was avoiding the question. He decided to push gently. "Coach, this thing is going to be turned upside down by everybody. Now, surely there must be something out about this woman. Wouldn't you rather tell me about her than let me hear it from another source?"

Sherwood remained silent for a moment, then said, "OK. The word is she was a prostitute. But damnit, I want you to know that Pat would never have been involved with a woman like that. He's just not that kind of guy. You can quote me on that."

"Thank you. I fully intend to." Few things in life surprised Haigler. People did strange things. But the more he heard about the facts behind the case, the more perplexed he became. Two and two were not adding to four. Why would a coach get involved in a situation like that during a week when he stood smack in the middle of the national spotlight? It did not make sense.

He had another question for Sherwood. "Did he have a

girlfriend?"

"Several. Believe me, if you saw them you'd see why none of this makes any sense. I'm telling you, he didn't need to go out and pay for sex."

"Could you tell me who they were?"

"I could, but I'm not. That's not fair to those women. You'll have to ask somebody else," said Sherwood.

"It's going to get out. What does it matter whether you tell me or I find out from somebody else?"

"It matters to me," Sherwood said firmly.

"OK. Let me ask you one last question. Who will take over as head coach?"

"The administration just informed me a few minutes ago that I have been appointed acting head coach. Alan Tyler will remain as my assistant. Now, if you'll excuse me, I've got to get to the meeting." Without waiting for a reply, Sherwood hung up.

Haigler stared at his notes. The biggest issue now was exactly how McLaughlin and the woman were found dead. What did the scene look like when the police arrived, and what were their findings? He knew those questions would have to be answered by Meeks when he arrived in Fort Myers in another hour and a half.

In the meantime, he decided to contact Bill Lee and determine what his reaction was. He picked up the phone and dialed the Hornets' office. The receptionist told him Lee was already on the court with the team practicing. He asked for Lindsey Ellis.

"Sports Information, Lindsey Ellis."

"Lindsey, this is Chuck. Have you heard about the coach at UFFM?"

"Sure did. It's hard to believe."

"Yeah. Did you talk to Coach Lee about it?"

"Briefly."

"Well, that's why I was calling. I wanted to get his reaction."

"He's at practice now, Chuck."

"I know. What did he say when you talked to him?"

"Not a lot. He just sat there. I think it shocked him just

like it did all of us."

"Did he know him?" Haigler asked.

"Not very well. He met him last year at the annual NABC meeting. Said he seemed like a real nice guy."

"That's what everybody says. Is that all he said?"

"Yeah. Like I said, he was shocked. It's got everybody around here pretty upset. We know how we'd feel if it happened to us."

"Is that tie-line press conference still on for tomorrow?" Haigler asked, referring to a phone hookup with all four coaches. Some local and regional reporters close to each of the four participating coaches would visit their offices, and simultaneously, through speaker phones, they would be able to hold a joint press conference.

"As far as I know, it's still on. Wonder which one of UFFM's assistants will get the nod?" Ellis asked.

"Tim Sherwood—I just spoke to him. He's convinced that McLaughlin didn't kill that woman."

"Who was she? The radio reports haven't indicated."

"Her name was Virginia Clavell. She was a prostitute."

"Are you kidding?"

"No. Sherwood didn't want to tell me that, but I told him it was going to surface anyway. He seemed quite sure that McLaughlin didn't know her and had little reason to shack up with her."

"Smell something rotten?" Ellis asked.

Haigler paused. "Maybe. Meeks is on his way down there. Reporters from the television networks are probably crawling all over the place. Some of what we've got will be old news tomorrow."

"Yeah, but maybe they'll blow it. Then you can straighten us all out." Ellis laughed.

"Right," Haigler said, chuckling. "Would you have Coach Lee call me when practice is over? I need to get some quotes from him on this."

"No problem. I doubt he can give you much more than I told you, though. He just didn't know the man. By the way, did you get in touch with Ted?"

"Yeah. We've got our meeting scheduled for seven thirty."

"Good. Anything else I can do for you?"

"No. Appreciate your help, though. I'll see you tomorrow."

After Haigler hung up, he decided to try to reach UFFM's sports information director again. There was not a lot more he could do. He was running into a blind alley. Maybe the SID would open a door for him. Then Meeks could take over from there.

The story was getting bigger with each new fact, and more mysterious.

Coach Lee was in the officials' dressing room, talking with Ted Collins in private. Collins was the finest athlete Lee had ever had the pleasure of coaching. The young man's ability had been strengthened by his desire. In high school he showed little promise. At Charlotte his skills sharpened quickly when Lee put in a system that centered around his position in the middle. The previous coach—the man who recruited Collins—used a hard hitting run-and-gun style. Lee's patterned and patient offense replaced it effectively.

"Ted, I called you in here to chat a moment about the interview with Haigler tonight. Have you heard about the death of Coach McLaughlin?"

"Yeah," Collins said, seated on a steel gray folding chair, legs stretched out before him, leaning forward, his huge hands engulfing a basketball.

Lee sat on another chair next to the player. "Well, that's what I wanted to discuss. I've got a feeling you'll get several questions from Haigler about that."

"What sort of questions?" Collins asked.

Lee sensed Collins was uneasy. The discussions he had alone with Collins were sometimes difficult. He often tried to dig inside his head, attempting to penetrate the coach/player barrier.

"Well, for one thing, he'll ask you how you think Coach McLaughlin's death will affect the game. What do you think?"

"I don't know. It might make our chances a little better,

I guess."

"No, TC, you were right with what you first said—you don't know. It might. Then again, it might not. Their players could really be up for the game or they could be down. It's hard to say. I don't think we should comment one way or the other. Leave the speculation up to the reporters. That's their job, not ours."

Collins looked at Lee. "What difference does it make?"

"It might not make any. But should we reduce the importance of the game or the toughness of the competition because their coach is dead?"

"So, what do you want me to say?" Collins asked.

Lee sighed heavily. He was not getting through. "Ted, I've told you before, I'm not trying to put words in your mouth. I want you to say what you think. I guess it's just that I've had more experience with the press than you have, and I know how they can twist things around sometimes. I just hate to see you make the same mistakes I have. I've gotten into trouble with the press when I've said what I honestly felt, instead of thinking first how it would come across in the paper." He tapped his temple with his first finger and added, "All I'm asking you to do is to think."

"Coach, have I ever said anything wrong to the press before?"

"No, you haven't. But let's face it, you haven't been interviewed that many times before."

"What about all those times after the games?" Collins asked.

"I'm not saying you're inexperienced, but those kinds of questions dealt with game situations. What I'm telling you is the questions are going to get tougher. We're under a microscope now. You're the team leader, and you definitely have a shot at being picked in the first round by the pros. The scouts are very high on you."

"I'm not sure I want to play pro ball."

"We've talked about that before. Whatever decision you make is fine with me. But keep your options open. Once you close the door, it's too late.

"Look, Ted, I know we've had our differences in the past,

and sometimes you've wanted to throw in the towel. But you didn't. You stuck with it. You're not a quitter. Now we've got a shot at the biggest prize in all of college basketball. We made it here because we believed in ourselves and felt we had something to prove. It's not over yet. I'm counting on you to give it your best shot, and I know you will.

"Which brings me back to my original point. Let me ask you a question and think about it a minute before you answer. Suppose something happened to me and I wasn't around to coach in the championships. Do you think you could win without me?"

Ted smiled broadly and bounced the basketball a couple of times. He did not answer, but Lee did not have to be a mind reader to guess what his answer was.

Lee laughed and said, "I put you on the spot, didn't I? You don't have to answer that. I'll answer it for you. You could win without me. There's no doubt in my mind about that. Sure, I've done some things that have won us some games, but let's face it—I don't execute the plans, nor make the shots, or shoot the free throws. Players do. That's why I think it would be unfair to anyone to cheapen our game against Fort Myers. They've learned McLaughlin's system. Hell, they've played over thirty games this year under him. They know what to expect."

Collins nodded. "You're right. Guess I hadn't thought about it that way."

"Good. I think you already know what the bottom line is. We can't get lax. We've got to practice with the same intensity that we have for every game this season. We can't look ahead or they'll beat us. This is a once-in-a-lifetime opportunity. Let's give it our best shot.

"I could say that same thing to some of the other players and it might go in one ear and out the other. If they see you're taking it seriously, they might pay more attention," Lee said. He watched Collins closely. He was confident his message had been understood.

"OK, let's go practice."

Both men stood and Lee asked casually, "Incidentally, have you talked to Troy lately?" He watched Collins' eyes carefully.

"No, why?"

"It's not that important. I know you two are friends, and I thought he might be pressing you on the pro ball decision. You know how important fund-raising is to him. He's probably already counting on you for a big donation," Lee said, grinning. Ted had not lied. He was confident of that.

Collins shrugged and chuckled at the same time.

The team slopped through practice for the first half hour. Every player except Collins had a lackadaisical attitude. Lee yelled at them to no avail. Finally, he called them to center court.

"Gentlemen, you people look like you're getting ready to play the women's team. And you know what? I think they could beat you. If you think the game against the Chargers Saturday is going to be a cakewalk because they lost their coach, you're making a big mistake.

"I've got news for you. They can damn sure beat us without him. They've got a lot of talent, and I'm warning you, we'll never make it to the championship game if you don't wake up and get serious. Now, quit playing grab-ass basketball."

Lee blew the whistle and practice resumed. The players did not respond immediately. But as practice progressed, each player began to notice Collins' intensity. Just as Lee had planned, Collins' leadership-by-example began to pay dividends. Near the end of the workout, all players began working hard. Lee's psychology worked to perfection.

If only he could have handled Dolci like he did the players, he mused. Then maybe he wouldn't be in this mess. The meeting with Troy was going to be tricky and dangerous. One wrong move, he could end up like McLaughlin.

* Twenty *

Frank Dolci smiled as he walked along the quarter-mile trail in the waning sunlight. The plan to handle McLaughlin had come off without a hitch.

His passion for the serene walking trail was born the first time he set foot on the sandy soil with his wife, Annette. Her yearning for peace and quiet had infected him.

Since she had gone to Sicily to visit relatives, Dolci had returned almost daily to his favorite spot without the pleasure of her company. Having left over a month ago, she was still not scheduled to come home for three more weeks. He thought of her as he walked along one of their favorite trails.

He enjoyed the J.N. "Ding" Darling National Wildlife Refuge. Named after political cartoonist, conservationist, and Pulitzer prize winner Jay Norwood Darling (nicknamed "Ding"), the refuge spanned over forty-seven hundred acres on Sanibel Island.

Darling's interest in conservation had frequently surfaced in his cartoons. For nearly two years, he had served as chief of the U.S. Bureau of Biological Survey, which later became the U.S. Fish and Wildlife Service. Darling played a major role in the development of numerous wildlife refuges across the country. During the years he had wintered on Captiva Island, he helped establish the refuge on Sanibel known as the Bailey Tract.

Today, Dolci was not alone. Several tourists walked quietly ahead of him, occasionally stopping and pointing at various sights. He lagged behind them, walking slowly, aimlessly recalling pleasant thoughts, particularly recollections of past walks in the refuge with Annette.

The tart, aromatic bouquet of key limes reminded him of the time they had picked up a basketful of the small, round, yellow fruit that was scattered along the ground and carried them home to make key lime pie, a Florida dessert-lover's delight. The citrus trees were a remnant of an abandoned grove planted in the late '20s.

Gnarled tree limbs overhung the thick jungle walking trail, casting intricate shadowed patterns on the ground. Dolci's thoughts were interrupted by the squeamish yelp of one of the tourists. By the way the woman swatted at her face, he guessed she had run into the web of a golden orb spider.

That had happened to him many times. He recalled the first time he was ensnared in the sticky substance. Annette pointed out a particularly beautiful orchid, and as he walked closer—enthralled by its beauty—he plunged right through the trap. He admired the spider's ability to surprise its victim.

The cabbage palms along the way sheltered beautiful night-blooming cereus. Pineapple air plants, ferns, vines, bushes and cacti all provided an enchanting wonderland, undisturbed and growing wild. Dolci's concerns about the death of McLaughlin—its consequences and possible repercussions—faded into oblivion.

As he came to the end of the trail, he walked faster. He decided to continue his respite at his favorite vantage point. He saw his driver waiting patiently by the car. He stepped in and told him to proceed to the observation tower. Today, there were many visitors in the park. Traffic was heavy and their pace was slow.

It irritated him. If he had just had the power years ago to stop the construction of the causeway that connected the islands to the mainland, his paradise would not have been invaded. Fortunately, the island had been partially saved. Thanks to the foresight of some of his fellow islanders, nearly one-half of Sanibel would remain unscathed by bulldozers.

Dolci knew his love for conservation seemed contradictory to his lifestyle. He remembered when Mancotta once told him so and an infrequent argument had resulted.

"How can you build a place like this and speak of conservation, Frank?" Mancotta had asked.

"You see this acreage? We have gone to great pains to

preserve it in its natural state," Dolci replied.

"And what about this sprawling house and the swimming pool? Are you going to tell me nothing grew here?"

"Of course not. But what I will tell you is this. We took great pains to see that for every tree cut down, three more would be planted. And you may be interested to know we removed a Melaleuca and an Australian pine. Both trees are invaders and are known to cause damage to the environment."

"Christ, Frank, how can trees be more harmful to the environment than the monstrosity you built here?"

Irritated by his partner's lack of knowledge, Dolci launched into a discussion about the havoc the trees wreaked. He explained the Melaleuca was deliberately brought into the Everglades to vegetate the swamp with a wood-producing tree. Only later did experts realize the wood characteristics were unsuitable for practical application. The tree's enormous capacity to survive drought, flood, and fire enabled it to virtually take over Cypress heads and tree islands, which forced native animal populations out of their natural habitat.

In another failed attempt to improve on nature's plan, the Australian pine had been imported to manage erosion. Furry in appearance with its dense long needles and soaring height at maturity, the foreign pine tree had an intricate root system formidable enough to accomplish the job it was imported for, Dolci had explained to Mancotta. But the carpet of fallen needles the tree shed stopped smaller plants from growing beneath it, which eventually increased the possibility for beach erosion. In addition, the pine had supplanted natural coastal habitat for nesting birds and sea turtles.

"OK, so you cut down two lousy goddamn trees and replaced them with a multimillion dollar structure and some pretty fruit trees. I still don't see how you can get on your high horse about conservation. The only thing that makes you different from the developers down the road is they're putting up multiple structures for more people to visit the island. They take up a little bit more space. You just want to have this little island for yourself. Don't bullshit me with your big-hearted efforts at conservation."

Dolci had then stormed down to the beach, enraged by Mancotta's piercing analysis. He had wanted to kill his partner. Mancotta had truly insulted him.

Minutes later on the beach, he stumbled across a rare orange and brown lion's paw; he began to cool off. He was delighted to find a perfect specimen for his collection. A mid-afternoon storm had apparently washed the single-valve shell ashore. The lion's paw had a moderately deep-water habitat which made it an uncommon find for anyone other than a sponge diver. Vowing never to discuss conservation with Mancotta again, Dolci left his anger on the beach and carried his prize back to the house.

Frank Dolci knew he was guilty of rationalizing. It didn't bother him. Neither did his brutality to his fellow man. Long ago he categorized himself as a "selective predator." He reasoned his behavior was entirely justifiable through the laws of nature. He concluded he never killed without purpose. By donating huge sums to preservation foundations, he believed his conservation efforts atoned for his violence.

The chauffeur stopped close to the observation tower. Several cars were parked along the side of the road, idling, lingering long enough for a good view of the swampy area. A group of people descended the tower, got in their cars and slowly pulled away.

Binoculars in hand, Dolci had only a short walk up the tower steps. He planned to observe the beautiful white ibis. The birds nested in the mangroves during March and April in colonies of hundreds of pairs. With an average wing span of slightly more than two feet, they presented an intriguing display as they returned to their platforms of twigs and leaves. Mated pairs were unable to recognize one another, which compelled a returning bird to perform an appeasing ritual to avoid being attacked as an intruder. Dolci watched the behavior repeated numerous times.

He spotted several roseatte spoonbills feeding. The large birds strained fish and crustaceans from the water with their flattened bills. Located on the leading edge of their white wings at the humerus bone, their distinctive scarlet marking blended with their bright yellow and scarlet tail. It reminded him of a painted glider he flew in his childhood.

Night herons swooped about searching for their evening meals. Dolci focused on the mangrove tree branches looking for tiny, greenish-brown crabs. It was difficult to spot them. Their color provided a perfect camouflage, matching the bark of the trees they skittered along. The herons feasted on the crustaceans, and sometimes the sound of a cracking shell could be distinguished from the muted noises of marsh life.

As Dolci started back to his car, he saw two brown marsh rabbits hop across the dusty road, undoubtedly on their evening meal rummage for tasty clover and grasses. A large brown pelican soared on the dusky horizon looking like a compact version of the dinosaur-age pterodactyl.

He had not spotted an alligator this trip, which was somewhat unusual. Normally, the reptiles patrolled the water silently for prey, like submarines on torpedo runs. He admired the creature, a killer and survivor with both power and grace. The gator made no apologies—it simply functioned.

As he rode home, he felt relaxed and at peace with himself. The pressures of the day had dissipated. He decided not to watch the evening news. Instead, after his dinner he would swim for awhile, take a walk on the beach, and turn in early. In two more days he would leave his paradise and fly to New Orleans. His four-year plan would soon come to fruition.

* Twenty-one *

"Bert Teague?" asked the sharp looking man in a black pin-striped suit.

"Yes," Teague answered.

"I'm Martin Ronson. Welcome to Charlotte," the FBI agent said as he shook Teague's hand. "Baggage claim is downstairs at the end of this concourse. I've made reservations for you at the Radisson Plaza Hotel. It's right in the center of downtown, or uptown as some Chamber of Commerce members prefer to call it."

Teague smiled. "Thanks."

While they waited for his suitcase, both men chatted casually about the weather and the city. Neither would discuss the case in public. They waited until they stepped into Ronson's white Ford in the short-term parking lot.

"Any problem with surveillance other than the one you said occurred on Sunday night?" Teague asked.

"No. I'm sorry that happened. It was totally unexpected."

"I understand. But we can't afford any more surprises. Not after what happened to McLaughlin. Did Hardin call?"

"Yes. He said Hall phoned him right after you left. He suggested you call him after you check in, and he'll fill you in."

"OK. What about our informant? Did you talk to him?"

"Yes. Everything is set. So far, it's going just like you predicted."

Teague sighed and stared out of the window. "Not hardly. I damn sure didn't count on McLaughlin's death. Our friends are getting harder to predict, but they're also getting careless. All over a stupid game. What's surprising is they don't need that money. They just get their kicks pushing chess pieces around the board."

Ronson paid the parking attendant and headed toward Billy Graham Parkway. Teague liked the rolling, forested terrain of Charlotte, and the streets were in far better condition than those in New Orleans.

"Do you think we'll ever get Dolci's partner to surface?" Ronson asked as he turned left off the parkway onto Morris Field Drive.

"I don't know. He's like a fox. I have a feeling he smells trouble in the wind."

"Got any ideas how you can smoke him out?" Ronson asked.

"Not really. That's what this is all about tonight."

When they arrived at the modern smoked-glass and interlocking-steel office and hotel complex, they ceased conversation. Teague checked in and they proceeded to the eighth floor.

Inside the room Teague headed straight for the phone and dialed Hardin in New Orleans.

"Hello, Bert. Did you have a smooth flight?" Hardin asked.

"Yes. What did Hall say?"

"Everything looked real neat, almost too perfect," Hardin answered.

"Then he agrees it might have been staged?"

"Yes," Hardin said. "He still hadn't talked to the medical examiner, though. He thinks we might get some clues from him to confirm that suspicion."

"Did he say when he might have those answers?"

"No, but he suggested you call him as soon as possible."

"All right. Anything else?" Teague asked.

"No. Let me give you a number where you can reach him."

Teague jotted down the information and hung up. Ronson sat quietly in a chair.

"Hall still hasn't gotten together with the medical examiner. Sounds like he has his thumb—" Teague stopped himself. He did not want to step on anybody's toes; however, as far as he was concerned, Hall was incompetent.

Ronson nodded. "I think I know what you were going to say. I've talked to him before. He moves awfully slow. Why don't you call Murtagh? Maybe he's got something."

"I believe I will," Teague said, picking up the phone.

The receptionist in the Tampa office put Teague straight through.

"Harry, this is Bert. Have you heard anything?"

"Yes. I just got off the line with the medical examiner. Everything looked like you'd expect, except for two things."

Teague leaned forward in his chair hoping the findings would be enough to hang his hat on. "I hope they're significant."

"I think so. Vaughn said he found the wound in McLaughlin's back to be almost too deep and too damn lucky. From her position, he doubted she could have inflicted it," said Murtagh.

"But it's questionable?"

"Yes, but the second thing is a lot better. She was scratched deeply on the back of her neck. McLaughlin's fingernails were trimmed very short, right down to the quick. Dr. Vaughn couldn't even get a scraping from them. And judging from the marks left on her neck, he said the person who killed her appeared to have smaller hands than the coach."

"That's what I was looking for. Anything else?"

"Yes. Hall called me and said he listened to the police question the maid. She was the one who discovered the bodies. After she calmed down, she told them Miss Clavell didn't own a pair of scissors like the murder weapon. She said she did all the sewing for Miss Clavell. The scissors were the type tailors use to cut cloth. From the position Clavell's body was in, it looked like she had to have grabbed the scissors from a drawer in the nightstand next to her bed. The maid says she cleaned the table and opened the drawer to put a book away yesterday. There were no scissors. She's positive of that," Murtagh said.

Teague thought for a moment. "That's a little shaky. I doubt it would convince a jury. The woman could have had the scissors and moved them to the drawer when she worked at night. Whores occasionally run into some pretty rough customers. She may have expected trouble."

"You're right. What Vaughn has come up with is pretty solid, though, except for one thing," Murtagh said.

"What's that?"

"The coach apparently had sex with her. There was a semen match, at least as semen matches go. They're not definitive you know."

"True. But all that tells us is that they did have sex. That would bother a jury, not me. I know how clever our man is. The real problem is—and you know it as well as I do—our chances of catching a hired killer without positive I.D. from a witness are very slim. And even if we did nail him, he'd probably never talk.

"That's not saying we can't use this information. Maybe we can blow a little smoke of our own. Did you talk to Hall about maintaining a low profile?"

"It was too late, Bert. The press had already spotted him."

"Damn. What did he tell them?"

"He put them off, told them he was there to see if he could be of any assistance to the local authorities."

"Good," Teague said, thinking that was the only thing Hall had done right on the case so far. "Listen, Harry, I think we really need to hang loose for awhile. I hope you agree. I don't want to scare our suspects off right now. We've come too far."

"That makes sense. You've been a lot closer to the case than we have. We'll follow your lead."

"Thanks. Did Hall have any suspects in mind? Does he know of any hit men in that area?"

"I'm afraid not. His sources are pretty dry right now. He's checking around, though. I'll tell him to do it quietly. Then, I'll wait to hear from you. If you want to blow smoke, just let me know."

"Thanks, Harry. Let me give you my number. Call me if anything further develops." Teague gave Murtagh the necessary information.

After hanging up, Teague explained everything Murtagh had found out to Ronson. Then they discussed plans for the evening. It was unusual for an FBI agent to travel out of his territory, but the circumstances for Teague's presence in Charlotte dictated the departure from standard procedure. And it was time for him to turn the screws.

* * *

Troy Burton sat in his office. He looked at his watch: 6:35 p.m. The team was still practicing and he was on edge. He wanted to get the meeting with Lee under way.

Searching for his pen, he shuffled through the papers—a flood of letters and donations—on his desk. He wanted to write a note to his secretary giving instructions on the next day's work. His mind kept shifting back to his conversation with Jenny.

When he had told her over the phone about his conversation with Lee, she reacted predictably. She was adamant about calling the FBI. If he did not call them, she would. He tried to convince her to wait until his meeting with Lee was over, but she would not listen. In the end he tentatively agreed with her point of view, but asked for a compromise and she agreed. He would call her after talking with Coach Lee. If she did not hear from him by 10 p.m., she could call the FBI.

He called it a compromise; she called it a putoff. She was very upset and was convinced Lee's mysterious meeting was dangerous. Those same doubts had begun to gnaw at him.

He had not told her everything. The snub-nosed, .38-caliber pistol he concealed in his coat pocket was evidence of that. If she knew what he had in mind, she would be horrified.

Yesterday, he had taken the weapon from his uncle's gun collection. With so many guns, he doubted it would be missed anytime soon. At his insistence, she was carrying their .25-caliber Beretta in her purse. The gun he had taken had more knockdown power and with its shorter barrel was easier to hide.

Troy generally tried to suppress any tendency he had toward violence. His experience in Vietnam—the memories, the night sweats, the body count—all had driven him to a desire to avoid destructiveness.

An internal justice scale balanced in his mind. The death of Drop had tipped that scale badly. Troy intended to even it. If the meeting with Lee held a surprise, he would counter with one of his own.

He walked to the bathroom to check his appearance one more time. If he left his coat unbuttoned, the gun was not visible. But if they frisked him, it would be easily found. He decided on a better hiding place and slipped the pistol under his belt next to his spine. His suit coat covered the protruding handle easily. It would be difficult to detect.

As he walked out of the bathroom, he saw Bill Lee coming up the stairs. The hall was empty.

"I'll be with you in five minutes. Got to make a phone call first. Go ahead and lock up," Lee said.

"I thought we were meeting in your office."

"No, we're going out. Let's take my car. Warm it up and I'll meet you out there," Lee said, tossing the keys to Troy.

Troy pictured Lee's car exploding as he turned the ignition key. "That's all right. I'll wait for you. I've got a few things I can work on for tomorrow."

Lee shrugged. "Fine. I'll see you in a couple of minutes."

Troy stepped back into his office and noticed none of the phone lines was lit. Lee was apparently using his private phone. Time passed slowly and he kept glancing at his watch. Five minutes became ten and ten slipped to fifteen. After nearly twenty minutes, he heard Lee open his door.

"Let's go," Lee said, standing in the doorway. "Sorry I took so long."

"Coach, where we going?"

"To the Hornets' Nest."

"It's pretty noisy there. Why can't we just talk here?"

"Troy, relax. All your questions will be answered in a few minutes."

It was dark when they stepped outside in the cool air. March had been colder than normal, but the erratic weather was beginning to break toward spring. Only a few cars remained in the parking lot. Troy noticed a figure seated in a vehicle not far from them and sensed they were being watched.

As they walked toward Lee's shiny black and gold Lincoln

Continental—a courtesy car provided by a Charlotte Lincoln/Mercury dealer—Lee said, "You drive."

As he left the parking deck and drove toward the highway, he noticed a car behind them. Looking more closely in the rearview mirror, he wondered if they were being followed.

Lee pulled down the visor, looked in the vanity mirror for a moment, then said, "Take a left here."

"The Hornets' Nest is that way," Troy said, pointing to the right.

"I know, I want you to drive to the Gold Skillet. I think we're being followed," Lee said.

"By who?"

"Your guess is as good as mine."

Pulling onto the highway, Troy glanced at Lee, then checked the rearview mirror. The car was still several hundred yards behind them. When they came to the restaurant, Lee directed him to turn into the parking lot. The suspicious driver continued on, turned on a dirt road a hundred yards away, and parked. A small line of people stood outside waiting to get into the restaurant.

"It's crowded here. Whoever is following us will think we decided not to stand in line. Let's drive on to the Hornets' Nest," said Lee.

"Coach, what the hell is going on?" Troy asked.

"I told you, you'll have your answers soon enough."

When they pulled into the Hornets' Nest parking lot, the car following them drove past, turned around at the first break in the median, and parked across the highway. After watching for a moment, they went inside.

Donnie Powers greeted them. "Troy, Coach, good to see you."

Customers turned their heads and stared at Lee.

"Let's go," Lee said to Powers.

Puzzled, Troy followed both men as they walked past wooden tables filled with boisterous beer drinkers shouting to be heard above the raucous rock-and-roll of the juke box. Several people stopped Lee and shook his hand.

Troy leaned over to Powers. "Where are we going?"

"To my van out back so we can get away from your

company out there," Powers said, pointing.

Troy was dumbfounded. What was Powers' part in all of this?

Lee broke free from his admirers. All three walked briskly out of the back door and climbed into Powers' blue Dodge van.

"Keep your heads down," Powers said as he started the engine.

Lee slid down in the front seat and Troy did the same in the back. Powers drove out and made several turns.

"OK, you can get up now. We're not being followed," Powers said.

"Would one of you please explain what this is all about?" Troy asked.

Powers glanced at Troy in the rearview mirror as he turned south onto I-85 and said over his shoulder, "I think you're in for a big surprise."

"I don't like surprises."

Lee lit his pipe. "We're going to see someone we can all trust."

Troy sat back as they rode down the interstate. Nothing made sense. As questions rolled over in his mind, he stared out the window. Mystified, he searched for answers. None came.

When Powers exited off I-85 at the I-77 interchange, Troy tensed. Unless Powers took the approaching left fork that looped back south on I-77, they would be headed toward Lake Norman. That would force him to make some quick decisions.

The ten seconds it took to confirm the direction seemed interminable. At the last moment Powers steered into the left lane and looped back south. They were driving toward downtown Charlotte. Although he had absolutely no idea where they were going, it would not be Lake Norman.

Powers took the downtown exit and continued east on Trade Street. When they crossed Tryon Street, he pulled into the Radisson Plaza Hotel entrance and parked.

* * *

They stood in front of room 824 after Powers knocked
on the door. A silver-haired man opened it. "Come in,
gentlemen."

Troy had no idea who he was. He hesitated before walking
in behind Powers and Lee.

"Mr. Burton, my name is Bert Teague, special agent, FBI."

* Twenty-two *

"Like Italian food?" Haigler asked as he drove toward the campus exit.

"Not really," Collins said.

"Where would you like to eat?"

Collins shrugged. "McDonald's."

Haigler glanced at him and laughed. "Ted, the dinner's on my expense account. The paper can afford a little bit more than burgers and fries."

"I just like their burgers," Collins said.

"Well, that's OK with me, but I had a little quieter place in mind."

"McDonald's is quiet when they're not busy."

Collins was obviously in the mood for a Big Mac and would not be easily swayed. "OK. Which one's closest?" Haigler asked. He seldom ate at fast-food restaurants.

"The one on North Tryon Street."

"Right."

When they arrived, Haigler listened to the player's order: three Big Macs, two large fries, a large coke, and a cherry pie. He wondered what the bill would have been if they had gone to a steak house.

While they ate in the back booth, Haigler asked, "How'd practice go today?"

"Rough."

"Working you hard, eh?"

Mouth full, Collins merely nodded.

Haigler decided to wait until they finished their meal. Hopefully, Collins would loosen up and talk more. He had been quiet during their ride, which was somewhat unusual. He seemed tense and Haigler wondered why. The young man was normally a great deal more animated.

During their meal several children walked up to the table and asked for Collins' autograph. He signed his name and talked to the kids quietly. It was obvious he didn't mind the interruptions. Parents smiled at his genuine display of interest and walked away happy that their wide-eyed children had the opportunity to meet the hometown star.

"You really like children, don't you?" Haigler asked.

"Yeah."

Haigler removed a small notebook and pen from his shirt pocket and began writing. "Any plans for marriage in the near future?"

"No. I haven't even got a steady lady."

"Ted, I spoke with your high school coach yesterday and he said you weren't very good when you played for him. Could you tell me a little bit about that?"

"He's right. I didn't get to start until my senior year. He used to yell at me a lot, told me I'd never be any good. I worked real hard in the summer to show him I could play—practiced late at nights. I just liked the game and I wanted to go to college. Scholarship was the only way, you know. We were poor."

"Are you the oldest in your family?"

"Now I am. My older brother was killed in a wreck along with my parents."

Haigler recalled his conversation with Collins' high school coach. The wreck had been tragic. Collins' parents and his older brother were killed when their car had careened down the side of a mountain after skidding off an icy winter road four years ago. It left their other four children homeless. They became wards of the state. It was an old story by now. Haigler decided to stick to basketball.

"What about pro ball, Ted? You've said you're not sure about it. Why?"

"I don't know. I came here so I could learn to teach in elementary school. I really didn't think much about pro ball. Some things are more important than shoving a ball through a hoop. A lot of kids want to grow up and be big stars. They dream about fancy cars and fast women. What are they going to do when they don't make it?"

"True, but if you could make it, why would you turn your back on it?"

"I'm not sure I will. I just want to make sure I'm doing

the right thing. I like to play the game for fun. Playing for money is a lot different. But if I play pro ball, naturally it'll be for the big money. We need it.

"Then I could support my three brothers and my sister. I hate seeing them stuck in an orphanage."

Haigler nodded. "Coach Lee didn't recruit you, but you seem to fit into his system real well. Do you think his style of coaching has made the difference in the team's improvement?"

"That's hard to say. He teaches a different kind of game. We used to play a lot of run-and-gun. We play a lot more deliberately now, and it works real good. But look at our record before Coach Lee came. We were winning then, too. The teams we played weren't tough, though. I think we've all improved. The team has come together more. Coach Lee calls it the right 'chemistry.' I'm not sure what it is or how you would describe it, but whatever's happened is good, real good. We think we can beat anybody in the country."

Still scribbling the quote, Haigler nodded.

Collins turned sideways in the booth, leaned back against the wall, and stretched his long legs across the yellow plastic bench-seat. "I guess we all feel like we have something to prove. Nobody gave us a chance to get into the tournament. Now, we're going to the championships. It's strange. All of us were overlooked by a lot of recruiters and suddenly everybody's looking around and asking, 'Where did those guys come from?' The experts aren't always right. Some people give up on themselves too quick. Somebody tells them they're no good, so they just quit. You've got to hang in there and believe in yourself."

"What do you think about UFFM's coach being killed?" Haigler asked.

"What can I say? I was surprised. I hate to see something like that happen to anybody."

"How do you think it will affect the team?" Haigler asked.

"We won't get overconfident. We're not going to ease up just because their coach died."

"No, Ted, that's not what I meant. How do you think it'll affect *them*?"

"I don't know."

His answer was quickly accepted. In fact, Haigler had not considered it to be an important point. He was simply curious how Collins would interpret the effects of the bizarre event. The assistant coach at UFFM had already made it clear McLaughlin's death was devastating, which Haigler thought was obvious.

The last time he interviewed Collins, he concentrated more on what his life on campus was like. He followed him to class and through a typical daily schedule. The routine of attending class, then practice, and returning to the dorm to study, revealed the athlete's life was filled with constant activity. A player missed a great many of his classes during the season, and Haigler zeroed in on that scholastic disadvantage. To offset that problem, most instructors cooperated and made special allowances. Some other students— usually those not athletically inclined—complained bitterly about such practices.

They continued to discuss the forthcoming spectacle. Collins was unaffected by all the attention he was receiving. He kept his role in perspective and appeared to have both feet firmly planted on the ground.

"One last question, Ted. If you win Saturday, the possibility exists that you'll meet the Tar Heels in the championship game on Monday night. How do you feel about that?"

"I think we'd better take one game at a time. Let's wait and see what happens Saturday."

Haigler thought he was hearing Coach Lee's words come out of Collins' mouth. It reminded him Lee hadn't returned his call. That irritated him. He still wanted to talk to Lee about McLaughlin's death.

* Twenty-three *

Troy Burton felt like he had walked into a movie an hour late. He sat quietly and waited for the FBI agent to explain the part he had missed.

The man who introduced himself as Bert Teague sat in a chair. "Mr. Burton, we're pleased with your decision to come forward and discuss the situation you find yourself in. I'm sure you're wondering just exactly how everyone in this room fits into the picture."

Troy nodded and looked at Lee and Powers. The other agent, Martin Ronson, sat quietly in a chair with his feet propped on the bed. His shoulder holster was plainly visible.

Teague sat in a chair across from Troy. "I work out of the New Orleans office. For the past six years I've been working on a special case with a federal prosecutor's strike force. Two men that are heavily involved in organized crime—one of them you know, Frank Dolci, and another that you may not—are the targets of our investigation. I won't go into all the details of their alleged activities. That would take more time than we have and I'm not sure it would be prudent to involve you in things that don't concern you.

"First, I need to ask you to do something very important. I need your word that whatever we discuss in this room will go no further. If you talked, it could endanger your life as well as the lives of many others."

Burton stared at Teague for a moment. Then, choosing his words carefully, said, "You have my word. I'm glad I'm not alone in this anymore."

Teague said, "I want to caution you that you're far from being out of danger. This thing is really just now heating up, and I can't guarantee you anything like complete safety. I wish I could, but that's not realistic. If you cooperate, you might find yourself in a very tight situation. You can back out if you like. The problem is things have already gone too far, and I think you would find that you're better off working with us. The man you are dealing with won't allow you a moment's peace because you're too dangerous to him."

Troy nodded. "It's my wife I'm worried about. I can take care of myself."

Teague got up from his chair, walked over to the dresser, and poured a cup of water. "You're right. She's in danger, too. But don't underestimate your situation. You can't protect yourself against a man like Dolci. That's what we're here for. And if this thing ever gets to court, you and your wife will have to be closely guarded. That's before the trial. Later, you may have to be relocated and have your identities changed for protection. Unfortunately, you don't have many options."

"I don't like what you're suggesting," Troy said, pausing. "But for now, what choice do I have? Let's get on with it. My wife and I will cooperate. We have a score to settle with Mr. Dolci."

"I'm afraid I know what you're referring to. I'm very sorry that happened." Teague's voice sounded sincere.

"You mean you know they killed my dog?"

"Yes. We've had your house under surveillance for several weeks now. This may be very difficult to understand, so please try and hear me out. Mr. Ronson was a block away when it happened. Whoever came, did so through the woods behind your neighbor's house. Because of the poor light that evening—especially where the killer trapped your dog—Agent Ronson didn't see anything until you walked outside. By that time it was too late. We have your house wired, so he was able to piece things together from your conversation with your wife."

Troy had a feeling Teague was not telling the whole story. Even if they had seen the killer, they probably would not have acted. It would have exposed their surveillance team.

The whole idea that Troy had been kept in the dark made him furious. He could feel the blood rushing to his head. "Wait a minute. You mean to tell me that you people have known all along what has been happening, and you didn't come to me? Goddamn! What are we—puppets on a string? If I'd known all this in advance, I would have been more cautious."

Teague nodded his head empathetically. "I realize that. Please let me try to explain why we handled it this way. I'm not saying we are blameless, but we did have our reasons."

"I don't give a damn what your reasons were. You took a chance with my life and my wife's. And I lost my dog. She was like a child to us," Troy said, standing, pacing.

"Mr. Burton, we handled the situation as best we could. You see," Teague paused, "we couldn't be sure how you were going to handle the bribe attempt. Coach Lee was convinced that you wouldn't accept it. In fact, he's the one who involved you in the first place."

"What?" Troy said. He looked at Bill Lee and stared right through him.

"Mr. Burton, don't be upset with him. He involved you at our instruction. Let me explain why," Teague said.

"Please do," Troy said, sitting. He crossed his legs, folded his arms and looked back at Teague.

"Coach Lee has been an informant for nearly three years. Ever since Dolci approached him, he's been working with us. We've been able to gather a lot of evidence because of his help—"

Troy interrupted. "Well for Christ's sake, why haven't you used it?"

Teague raised his left hand, palm out. He held the cup of water in his right hand and gestured in a sweep that nearly made the contents slosh over the top. "Please let me finish. Cool down a little bit and save your criticism until after you've had a chance to evaluate everything. I know how you feel. But at least give me the benefit of the doubt for now."

Troy said sarcastically, "Sure, I'll give you the benefit of the doubt, just like you people gave me when you dragged me into this. Go right ahead."

Teague took a deep breath and continued quietly. "Coach Lee wasn't exactly sure what Dolci was looking for when he was first approached, but the inferences were strong. That's when he came to Agent Ronson here and told him about the meetings. Martin had been watching Dolci for over two years. At that time we weren't sure what Dolci had in mind. We asked Coach Lee to play along."

Troy looked at Lee. The coach nodded and puffed on his pipe. Teague watched the exchange, then continued.

"Dolci is a very clever and cautious man. Every meeting he planned with Coach Lee was so secluded it was impossible to tape the conversations. He has all the latest electronic gear to detect bugs. His method of veiling what he says makes much of what we get from Coach Lee no good on the witness stand.

"We've been unable to get his partner to surface. Dolci has never introduced him to Coach Lee, and it seems that the partner prefers to stay in the background. He's smart. This is the first time Dolci has ever exposed himself personally in one of his schemes. Normally he lets the people under him front all the dangerous operations. For some reason— and we don't know why—he chose to handle this situation himself. It's given us our first clear shot at him."

Troy looked at Lee. "What kinds of things did he offer you?"

Lee answered quickly. "He gave me money for players and offered to entice several recruits to come to Charlotte by giving them slack jobs during the summer."

"How did you keep him happy? Did we have to violate any NCAA rules?" Troy asked.

Teague looked at Lee and chose to answer the question for him. "Absolutely not. Not one penny has been used. Dolci thinks it has; we've made sure of that. Coach Lee has been very helpful in providing ways to throw him off the track. He has handled recruiting and summer jobs strictly by the book. When Dolci wanted progress reports, Bill told him what he wanted to hear."

Teague drank the rest of the ice water in the clear plastic glass. Gesturing with it, he continued. "It wasn't until a month ago that your team became prominent enough to be useful to Dolci. That's when we decided we had to bring someone else into the picture."

"Donnie?" Troy looked at Powers.

Teague looked at Powers and shook his head. "No. I'll

explain his presence in a minute. Right now, I'm referring to you. Dolci wanted Coach Lee to fix a game in the future when it would be profitable for betting purposes. Lee was very cooperative, but he steered him in your direction."

"Why me?"

"Because we wanted to involve one more witness. Coach Lee explained to Dolci that it would not be prudent for a head coach to approach a player to fix a game. He told him that their relationship could be better served over a long period if he was allowed the opportunity to excel as a head coach. He suggested to Dolci that coaching the team to a loss was risking his future career. Several well-known universities were going to be looking for a new coach this year, and he told Dolci he would have a good shot at one of those positions if he was allowed to go as far as possible in the championships. That's when he suggested that you should be the one to bribe Collins to fake an injury. Dolci grabbed the bait and we were able to keep him from going directly to the player." Teague walked over and poured himself another glass of water.

Troy shook his head and said, "That's fine, but I don't understand why you didn't come to me first and warn me."

Teague said, "We had several reasons. First, we weren't completely sure you weren't already involved in some way. If Dolci had gotten to you first, then you might have been his informant. We considered that to be a remote possibility, but it did exist. Second, we have a lot of problems with questions of entrapment. If we had tipped you off first, you might have said or done something that clouded our case along those lines. That may sound stupid to you, but from a prosecutor's standpoint it could be damaging. We will look a lot better in court when the sequence of events is revealed this way. Coach Lee was sure you would either come to him first or go to the police. He was positive you wouldn't approach Collins."

"Apparently Dolci found out my plan to go to Coach Lee?" Troy asked.

Teague sat in a chair. "Yes, and he didn't want that. That would have eventually exposed the fact that he was already working with Coach Lee, because he believed Coach Lee was on his side."

"But how did Dolci find out? Did he bug my house?"

"Yes," Teague answered. "He didn't even have to have someone go inside to do it either."

Surprised, Troy looked at him. "Rifle microphones?"

"No, an infinity transmitter."

"What's that?"

Teague explained in a matter-of-fact tone. "It's a sophisticated device that enables someone to dial your phone, keep it from ringing, and automatically turn your phone's speakers into a listening device. Since you've got three, one in the den, kitchen, and bedroom, they had little trouble monitoring your conversations. Occasionally though, they stopped monitoring, so other people could get through. To keep them from learning just how serious you were about stopping him, we jammed them a couple of times when we were able to anticipate what you were getting ready to say. We patched in some innocent conversations you and your wife had that we'd taped a couple of days before Dolci approached you. That's when we were trying to determine if you might have already been in Dolci's pocket."

Troy shook his head. "All thanks to high tech."

Teague continued. "Your plan to talk to Coach Lee would have ruined a lot of things for Dolci. Coach Lee was able to convince him to talk to you again."

"What did you tell him, Bill?" Troy asked.

"I simply told him that you apparently had underestimated him and hadn't taken him seriously. He said he would remedy that and that's why his men picked you up at Greensboro before you could talk to me. I told him that you would be a good man once you were in our camp." Lee puffed on his pipe, smiling wryly.

"But how come he didn't ask you to get me to go to Collins?" Troy asked.

Lee nodded. "He did at first. But I told him that although I thought you would go along with the bribe, I didn't think you would accept the idea from me as readily as you would from him. I told him that you would see big dollar signs once you found out through the grapevine how rich he was. Plus, it would have made a big stink if you went after me. He was obviously in a better position to protect himself. He debated a while and finally accepted my reasoning."

"OK. But how does Donnie fit into all this?" Troy asked Teague. He looked at Powers. Powers winked at him and folded his arms.

"He's an undercover agent with the DEA," Teague said.

"The Drug Enforcement Agency! Are you kidding me? Him?" Burton asked, pointing.

Powers laughed and said, "That's right, and you're under arrest for possession of marijuana."

Everyone in the room burst out laughing except Troy. He was thoroughly embarrassed. Unwittingly, he had been buying small amounts of marijuana from an undercover agent. They had smoked together on numerous occasions.

"I'm kidding, Troy. You and I both know I'm after the big-time suppliers," Powers said.

Lee interrupted and said sternly, "Troy, don't take that to mean I approve of what you're doing. I don't. Frankly, I was very surprised that you, of all people, would risk your career by smoking pot. Do you realize what would happen if you were ever caught with it?"

"Lee, don't get righteous on me. Fifty million people have smoked pot in this country. Not too damn many of 'em went through the shit I did in Nam, either." Troy shook his head and glared at Powers. He felt betrayed. A friend he had totally trusted stabbed him in the back.

Bill Lee saw the look on Troy's face and apparently sensed what he was thinking. "Don't blame Donnie for telling us about your smoking habit. He has a job to do and he does it well. The fact was important for us to know when it came time to pick someone in the department to front Dolci's bribe. When I told Dolci he could use it as blackmail, he believed it would help force you into accepting the proposition. Even with that pressure, I still believed you wouldn't buckle under. You didn't and it shows my assessment was correct. Although I hate to see anyone use drugs—especially someone in your position—I'm proud of the way you handled this situation. I want you to quit though," Lee said.

"You'll have my resignation as soon as this is over."

"No, no, no," Lee said, shaking his head, adding, "I mean I want you to quit smoking. You can't resign. We need you. You're doing a fine job."

"Thanks, but what happens when this comes to trial? His lawyers are bound to try to discredit me." Burton folded his arms.

"Let's worry about that when the time comes. It's not that important. There are judges who light up," Teague said.

Troy knew that was true, but he still didn't understand Powers' involvement. "I'm confused. I don't understand how a DEA agent got involved in an illegal gambling scheme."

Teague explained. "Basically, we've been pursuing these men from several angles. Their drug smuggling mushroomed into a massive business. The DEA made a number of attempts to penetrate their ring with undercover agents. None has been successful. When Coach Lee approached us, the strike force decided on a cooperative effort."

Troy shifted in his chair. "Go on."

Teague continued. "As you know, drugs are prevalent on campuses throughout the country. Since Dolci operates out of Florida and North Carolina, the DEA decided to concentrate some of their efforts here in North Carolina to complement our work on the gambling operations. We needed to have someone close to the situation. We fronted the operation at the Hornets' Nest. Powers was a natural for the job. It gave him the opportunity to attempt to make connections and work his way up the ladder while he kept closely in touch with Coach Lee. Unfortunately, Dolci's operations are so well guarded, he has been unable to penetrate much further than a few small-time distributors. But his cover as an avid fan and an interested businessman has been helpful in keeping in close touch with the players, the coach, and lately, you."

"I didn't realize until several years ago that you people went through such elaborate schemes to trip up criminals," Troy said, recalling two such plans in 1980, Abscam and Brilab. Both had received a great deal of attention from the media.

Teague tapped his pen on the brown veneer table. "We don't set up things like this very often. They're expensive and very time-consuming. But when you have sharks to catch, you have to use a lot of bait and a big hook. There's really no other way."

"OK. What do you want me to do?" Troy asked.

"Nothing right now. When did Dolci say he planned to make the payoff?"

Troy leaned back in his chair. "He wants me to make it in New Orleans. By now I was supposed to have already talked to Ted. I've been wondering when he would contact me again, but I haven't heard from him."

"You don't suppose he's on to us, do you Bert?" Ronson asked.

"I don't think so. I hope that tail he put on you two doesn't decide to go inside to see what's taking so long," Teague said.

Powers smiled broadly. "Don't worry, I've got that covered. My manager locked the doors fifteen minutes after we left and put up a private party sign. We had a fraternity come in for free beer and the customers that were still there got the same. We called it 'Surprise Party Night.' I thought it was a pretty good promotion, myself."

"That's good. Let's hope your manager didn't screw it up. Did he have a list of fraternity members?" Teague asked.

Powers shook his head. "He's a she, and yes, she did. Come on Bert, give me a break. You guys at the Bureau seem to think you're the only ones with any brains. Just because I look dumb doesn't mean I am. Remember, it's part of my cover."

"You sure had us fooled," Ronson said. He grinned and leaned back in his chair.

Teague said, "OK, let's get back to business. It looks to me like Dolci plans to wait and make his move in New Orleans. That will give us time to see if we can drag the other partner out of his hole. I want them both."

"Who is his other partner?" Troy asked.

Teague said, "Right now, you're better off not knowing.

You could—"

"That's bullshit!" Troy said hotly. "You know my military record. I had a top-secret clearance. And since you people decided so cleverly to drag me into this, you can just count on telling me everything—or I stop cooperating right now."

Teague's look of resignation told Troy he understood. He told Troy about Mancotta and for the next fifteen minutes he sketched out preliminary plans. His direction was firm and Troy was impressed with the steps that would be taken to protect him and Jenny during the tournament. Still, there were a number of details that were not covered. Teague planned a clandestine meeting the first day they arrived in New Orleans. At that time, they would have to see how things were shaping up. Troy's future role could not be clearly defined until Dolci made his next move.

Teague stood and said, "All right. There's not much more we can do right now." He turned to Lee. "Coach, I'm really sorry this has to spoil your experience in the championships. We deeply appreciate your patience and understanding. Not many people would do what you have done for the past three years." He shook his hand firmly.

Turning to Troy, Teague said, "And I can't emphasize enough, Mr. Burton, how important it is for you to keep everything you've heard here tonight in strict confidence."

"What about Jenny? She'll have to know."

"She already does. She called the office late this afternoon and Mr. Ronson met with her briefly. We're lucky Dolci's man has not been watching her. If Dolci knew he was getting sloppy, he wouldn't last very long."

As they walked to the door, Troy asked, "What about Coach McLaughlin? Was it a setup?"

"That's certainly a possibility. But right now we really have nothing to support that theory."

Teague's thinly veiled reply confirmed what Troy had suspected: Dolci was indeed responsible.

After everyone left, Teague thought the meeting had gone

well. For the first time in his career, though, he was uncomfortable with the decisions he was making. Moving innocent citizens about like pawns on a chessboard worried him. Everything depended upon a precision plan—one which he still had not devised.

* Twenty-four *

Coach Lee's home phone still signaled busy. As Haigler sat at his desk staring blankly across the *Observer*'s sports office, he realized how tired he really was. The hours he had been keeping over the past few weeks were catching up with him. Excitement surrounding the events had overcharged his body, fraying his nerves.

His desk phone rang. He quickly recognized the voice of Joe Meeks.

"How's it going, Joe?"

"Not worth a damn."

"What's the problem?" Haigler asked.

Meeks voice came through sharply. "Shit, reporters are crawling all over the place. We all want the same thing—answers. And nobody here who knows anything is willing to talk. They've shut their doors."

Haigler felt a tinge of satisfaction. The great Joe Meeks was striking out just as he had, and Meeks had the luxury of being on location. "Who have you tried to see? Any of those people I suggested?"

"I've tried to get in touch with everybody. No luck. The cops have got their lips sewed shut. The coroner is hiding in his lab."

"What about McLaughlin's girlfriends or family?" Haigler asked.

"I've got one name, Barbara Hollingsworth, apparently a girlfriend. She won't answer her phone or her door. McLaughlin's parents died six years ago. The only relative that's here is his sister. She flew down from New York and she's not talking either."

"What about the details of the murder scene? Anything there?"

"I've got a little information, but hell, all that stuff has probably come over the wires already. Have you seen it?"

"Yes," Haigler said, reading the wire service report on his

computer terminal screen, "but it's not much more than we already knew this morning. Wouldn't they let you in for pictures?"

"No. They claim they're still investigating."

"Christ, how long do they need?"

Meeks sighed. "I don't know. I think they're just stalling and hoping we'll all get tired and go home. McLaughlin was very popular around here. Nobody believes he killed her, but it sure looks like he did."

"It doesn't make sense, though, does it?"

"I've never seen a murder that did," Meeks said. "But people do strange things. If some of these folks aren't willing to come out and talk, maybe that's a sign that he was a little kinky. He wasn't exactly your family type, you know."

Haigler laughed. "What the hell is that supposed to mean? I'm not a family type either, but I don't think that puts me in a kooky category."

"I don't know. You've always seemed a little strange to me," Meeks said wryly.

"Thanks. I'll remember that when I win the Pulitzer."

The lighthearted chatter helped Haigler. He took his job seriously and pride motivated him more than the relatively meager salary he earned. He was well aware that other men with his education, intelligence, and initiative generally fared much better financially. And even though he had to suffer criticism leveled at him from the general readership, he thrived on the recognition he received.

"Well, what are you planning to do?" Haigler asked.

"I'm going to send in the story just like I see it," Meeks said.

"In your daily column?"

"Yes. Why don't you go ahead and write your sidebar with whatever you've got. Did you get Bill Lee's reaction?"

"No. He hasn't called me back. His line's been busy all evening."

"OK. I'd better get off this phone and start writing," Meeks said. "I'll call you tomorrow if anything important develops."

After hanging up, Haigler looked over his notes. He still

needed a direct quote from Lee on McLaughlin's death.
Other than the quotes he had from UFFM's assistant coach,
he had very little to work with. He picked up the phone
and dialed again.

"Hello," Helen Lee answered.

"Helen, this is Chuck. Is Coach Lee in?"

"No, he's not. May I take a message?"

"Listen, I'm sorry to bother you, but I need to speak with
him for a few minutes. Do you know where I can reach him?"

"I think he's still at school."

"If he is, he's not in his office. I've tried his private number
and there's no answer."

"Well, I don't know. I haven't heard from him either. In
fact, his dinner is still in the oven. Give me your number
and I'll ask him to call you when he gets in."

Haigler gave her his phone number, thanked her, and
hung up. He sat for a few minutes, massaging his temples
with his fingers as if stimulation would help him draw out
ideas for the story. Nothing came.

"How in the hell did you get into the DEA?" Troy asked.

Powers looked at Troy through the rearview mirror as he
drove north on Tryon Street. "It wasn't easy. I applied in
my senior year. I doubt I would have ever gotten in if it
hadn't been for this opportunity. They were looking for
someone to fill the bill and I matched their
qualifications."

"How many people know you're an undercover agent?"
Troy asked.

"No one other than you and Coach Lee."

"Not even your wife?"

"She knows. It's one of the few secrets she has ever kept.
She knows better than to talk about it. I could get my head
blown off if the wrong people found out."

Bill Lee sat quietly in the front seat. Although he heard
the conversation between Burton and Powers, it did not
register. He was concerned about all the problems that had
now fallen upon his shoulders. What had started out as an

effort to put Dolci behind bars three years ago had dragged on and on. It was like wrestling with a giant squid. If Lee had been able to foresee all the problems that had kicked up since the beginning of his cooperative effort, he probably would not have approached the FBI. Instead, he would have quit coaching and gotten into a more sane profession.

Coaching major college basketball produced internal conflicts that churned inside the man's stomach. A coach's life was like being on a roller coaster with no brakes.

Everything revolved around living up to expectations. That was what made different coaching positions so tricky. The men who followed giants like Adolph Rupp and John Wooden took huge risks to coach at Kentucky and UCLA. Following the footsteps of a legend bordered on sheer insanity, despite the fact that the overall financial packages were generally top notch. But in some cases, even that didn't hold true. If the head coach of a major university retired in glory, he sometimes stayed in town and controlled the lucrative basketball camp during the summer months—basketball camps mean big money.

Kids swarm into campus gyms hoping to sharpen their skills. With dreams of becoming the next great player to glide on the hardwood and soar like an eagle a mile above the rim, young players were naturally attracted to the camps where head coaches had big names and winning teams.

Winning was the key to survival, Lee knew. Fans came for the vicarious elation that added to the bottom line, the final score. During the season, it was a relentless nightmare of pressure on the man in charge.

What made it even more absurd, Lee thought, was how little control coaches really have over the final outcome. When it gets right down to it, 85 to 90 percent of a coach's job involves recruiting. No matter how well he understands the game or how perfect a teacher he is, it all comes down to raw talent. And talent includes a lot more than just physical ability. What is between a kid's ears was equally important. A coach lives and dies with his players. And as the popularity of the sport increases, so do the pressures. Win and they love you. Lose and they come to get you.

Lee hated it at times. He thought the system had rolled over the values that could only be learned and not taught. The competitive experience had become lopsided. Too much emphasis was placed on the final outcome. Losers suffered far beyond their limits. The game was no longer pleasurable. Like a tidal wave, it was drowning unsuspecting victims in its path.

As if all those problems were not enough, Lee mused, Dolci had sliced into his life. Anything or anyone that obstructed Dolci's insatiable desire for power and money was put to the blade. Lee's utter disgust with men like Dolci and what they stood for had smoldered and finally turned into a raging fire. The added task of handling Dolci coupled with all of the pressures of coaching had taken its toll.

"Coach. Coach Lee," Powers said.

"What? I'm sorry. What did you say?"

"I was saying that I think I should let you off in the back of the Hornets' Nest in the woods. There is a small road that winds in behind the place. Dolci's man won't see you. I'll go in the back door and check things out first. Then, I can drive back through the road and come in the front way so he can see me returning alone in the van. What do you think?"

"Fine."

When Powers drove down the dirt road behind the Hornets' Nest, he turned off the van's lights and proceeded cautiously. As an extra precaution, he stopped before he came to a wooded bend in the road and got out of the vehicle. He walked down the road in the cool night air. Outside lights from the building provided diffused light.

He unlocked the back door, went in, and talked to his manager. The fraternity members were making a lot of noise. Many were staggering back and forth to the bar to refill their mugs with free beer. The jukebox played loud strains of a new tune that had risen to the top of the charts. Students were busy playing pool.

Powers asked Beth Selvey, manager of the Hornets' Nest,

if there had been any problems. She said a few people attempted to crash the party, but were unsuccessful. While he was talking to her, he glanced out of the window. The car was still parked across the highway. It was too dark to see the figure inside.

Powers had not told her where they were going before they had sneaked out of the back door, and she was mildly curious. He avoided her questions by simply saying they were working on plans for a future party for the team. When she asked where Burton and Lee were, he explained they were out back discussing the tournament and would be coming in soon. He advised her he had to leave for a few minutes.

He walked back to the van and said, "OK. Looks like our friend is still across the street. Go in and have a few beers if you like. Keep in touch." Powers started the van and backed down the road.

Troy said nothing to Coach Lee as they walked down the heavily wooded road to the back door of the Hornets' Nest and went inside. The room was filled with smoke that burned his eyes.

"Let's not stay long," Lee said.

"I'm with you," Troy replied.

Heads turned in their direction as they walked to the bar. Several fraternity brothers walked up to the coach and engaged him in conversation. One member stood on top of a table with a beer mug in his hand and yelled above the music, "A toast! A toast! To the greatest coach in the nation."

People raised their glasses and downed their beers in one gulp. The crowd began chanting, "WE'RE NUMBER ONE! WE'RE NUMBER ONE!"

In five minutes Troy saw Powers come inside the front door. That was their cue to leave. He nudged Coach Lee.

They left conspicuously—out the front door. Troy saw the car that had followed them still parked across the street. Powers' plan to elude the tail had worked perfectly.

* Twenty-five *

Chuck Haigler picked up the phone on the first ring. "Sports, Chuck Haigler."

"What do you need, Chuck?" Coach Lee asked abruptly.

Haigler had no trouble recognizing Lee's authoritative voice. "Thanks for returning my call, Coach. I just wanted to get your reaction on McLaughlin's death. I'm doing a story for tomorrow's edition."

"What can I say, Chuck? I hardly knew the man. Didn't Lindsey tell you that?"

Lee sounded irritated, but Haigler had a job to do. He plunged ahead. "What effect do you think it will have on the game?"

"How should I know? I'm not down there to judge the situation," Lee said sharply.

Haigler realized he had caught the coach in another bad mood. It didn't matter. He had a story to write. "Do you think it will help your chances for a win?" Once the question popped out, Haigler regretted how he'd worded it.

"Damnit, Chuck. What kind of question is that? A man is dead. I didn't know him, but I respected his ability as a coach. Exactly what effect his death will have on the team is hard to say. There's no way I can answer that."

Lee paused, then added in an even sharper tone, "Hell, you know enough about coaching to realize that talent has a lot more to do with whether a team wins or loses. The Chargers have abundant talent. And what about their assistant coaches? They know McLaughlin's system."

"OK, Coach, I just wanted a few comments from you," Haigler said as he finished scribbling Lee's answer. It would make a good quote.

"Anything else?"

"Yes," Haigler said. "I know you only met the man briefly, but there's usually a lot of gossip about different coaches and whether they're looking for another position. Did you ever hear anything about McLaughlin? It would seem to me he would have been a prime candidate to move up after last year's performance."

"I never heard a thing about the man," Lee said.

"OK. Thanks again for calling me back. I'll see you Thursday—" Interrupted in mid-sentence by a click, then a dial tone, Haigler held the phone out in front of him and said, "at the airport, asshole." He dropped the phone back on its cradle.

He looked over his notes once again. He hadn't expected much help from Bill Lee, and that was exactly what he had gotten—practically nothing except for the quote. It was the first time Lee had ever admitted that players' abilities were more important than the coach's.

That was hardly a startling revelation. But since Lee had inherited all except one of his starters from Cliff West—the coach who preceded Lee at Charlotte—his quote would subtly point back to one area many of Lee's critics frequently mentioned. In his three years at Charlotte, Lee had yet to prove he had the ability to recruit top-notch players. With four starting seniors graduating, Lee's future team would be "also rans" if he failed to perform in the crucial recruiting function at the end of the season.

Haigler had become interested in recruiting practices over the past two years. A number of major colleges had been slapped with long probationary sentences by the NCAA for recruiting violations. That action banned them from televised games and post-season appearances.

The biggest scandal happened when the University of New Mexico's coach and assistant coach were discovered fixing transcripts. They had recruited a number of players right out of the ghetto and brought them in as junior college transfers. The facts proved that several of the young athletes had not even graduated from high school.

The FBI had played a major role in uncovering the illegal practices. Since the transcripts had been mailed, the Bureau leveled charges against the perpetrators for mail fraud. In addition, the law enforcement agency had discovered that the coaches were also involved with organized crime figures. Players admitted receiving cash incentives for playing. Although nothing had been proven, many people suspected gambling had been involved. The University of New Mexico was subsequently put on probation by the NCAA from November 20, 1980 to November 28, 1983.

Haigler thought about the trip he had taken earlier in the year with the Hornets' assistant coach, Bo Evans. They had traveled south through Georgia and Florida to watch several high school prospects in action. The story Haigler was working on had not yet been written. It was due as a feature article on or shortly after the first official NCAA signing date for recruits in the middle of April.

This would be a telling season for the whole coaching staff. He wondered how some of those "kids," as Bo and Lee called them, would react now that the Hornets were on their way to the championships. Obviously, they would prick up their ears quite a bit more.

Many college prospects were spoiled by all the attention they received in high school. College recruiters would stream into a gymnasium to see a "blue chipper." As they did so, the kid received more and more attention from his peers, relatives, and friends. That tended to turn his head, and often he found himself dreaming of being the next Michael Jordan or whatever favorite player came to mind.

Naturally, the more well known the college team, the easier it is for that school to recruit. Haigler remembered Evans' words: "If you were a high school star, which school would you rather play for: Kentucky, Notre Dame, North Carolina or the University of Whatchacallit? No question, right? That's exactly why we can't get the triple-A or blue-chip players to come to Charlotte. Perennial powers generally pick and choose. Sure they have a few battles among themselves, but they don't even worry about little guys like us. Once in a while we manage to get a blue chipper, but you can bet that when we do it's because of an unusual set of circumstances."

Recruiting philosophy at Charlotte would probably change now, Haigler thought. Evans had made it clear to him that because of the disadvantages of being unknown, they were going for players a shade below blue-chip status. "Franchises"—those once-in-every-ten-years players like Abdul Jabbar, Larry Bird, or Michael Jordan—were simply out of the question. Everybody in the country tried to recruit a franchise. And that was generally what those players turned out to be. They could do it all.

But even the most promising player could fall flat on his face. Although they would generally perform well, they sometimes simply failed to live up to expectations. Bo Evans had commented on that aspect to Haigler. It was precisely why the Charlotte coaches never sounded the trumpets when they signed a promising recruit.

Such had been the case when they had signed Thad Davis last year. He had been the first prize Bill Lee and company had inked at Charlotte, yet the head coach played down Davis's ability.

After he had gone through the scouting services reports, Haigler questioned why Thad Davis was considered a hair below blue-chip status. The only reason for the lowered assessment was his injured ankle. In an important summer basketball camp, he had been labeled as a "head case" because of his constant complaining. Only later was a bone spur discovered after an exhaustive examination. By that time a number of recruiters had walked away. Davis liked the Charlotte coaching staff and decided to leave home in Indiana and head south to attend college.

Davis had proven to be an excellent swingman. While he played a fairly strong point guard, he tended to excel when he did not have the pressure of bringing the ball downcourt. He had a superb outside shot and, at 6'4", few opposing guards had enough height to obscure his vision, much less block his shots. He had a standing vertical jump of over forty inches. Davis was quick. He could penetrate from the top or side of the key with catlike speed, leap at the foul line, and crush the ball through.

Haigler gave Lee a good rating for the recruitment. However, other than Davis, the coach had not added significantly to the Hornet roster. Replacing Collins after this year would be nearly impossible, Haigler thought. And unless Evans had hidden the names of the truly talented big men they were going after, Charlotte's program would be exactly what critics claimed it would be: "A flash in the pan." No matter how worn out that cliche was, Haigler thought, it accurately described what happened to so many unknown college teams that experienced a sudden rise to national prominence.

He vacillated about Bill Lee. The man struck him as totally unpredictable. He had an ambiguous personality—sometimes charming, sometimes bitter, often incisive. Was it the constant insecurity that the coach experienced? Other coaches seemed to handle pressure better than Lee. He was a hard-driving man and seemed to be constantly obsessed with perfection.

Yet he tended to shy away from recruiting. Evans had hinted about the difficulties he faced recruiting as an assistant coach against head coaches. Most recruits want to meet with the head man, as do their parents. When Haigler asked why Lee did not go out and recruit more than he did, Evans commented that Lee was obviously a family man. He liked to stay at home. After seventeen years of coaching, the drag of beating down doors in strange towns throughout the country had apparently gotten the best of him.

Haigler thought there must be more to it than that. He knew Lee had a big ego. The toughest job for the coach had to be facing a player who was young, immature, and in the driver's seat.

No doubt Lee wasn't especially fond of sitting and listening to the recruit play cat and mouse like a rich, spoiled child with a toy salesman. If a prospect didn't hear what he wanted to hear, then he would bestow his fabulous wealth of talent on someone more willing to pamper him.

That was not always the case and Haigler knew it. Some recruits had a level head and were honestly interested in making the best of the six expense-paid visits they were allowed by the NCAA to make to different campuses. The particularly good players sometimes had over a hundred

such red carpets rolled out. Just narrowing the choice as to
which colleges they would visit was extremely difficult.
Often their parents showed respect for their offspring's
ability to make a sound decision with regard to his future.
Those were the type of players that most recruiters enjoyed
working with.

High school coaches frequently helped in the process,
guiding the player along the way, assisting in dealing with
college recruiters. While most were dedicated to their profession, occasionally recruiters bumped into unscrupulous
coaches who wanted something in return for "guiding the
kid to the 'right school.' "

During his trip with Evans, Haigler had witnessed
another side of the story. There were some unscrupulous
recruiters hiding nets behind their backs, looking to snare
the elusive butterfly. They would use every trick in the book
to add one to their collection: cash inducements, cars,
clothes, promises of big-paying summer jobs, assurances of
a shot at pro basketball. Anything that they felt would
entice a player to attend the university they represented
would be waved in front of the recruit's nose. Frequently
their offers turned out to be empty promises. Although few
recruiters in major college basketball went to such extremes,
such practices existed. It gave recruiters a bad reputation.
Many parents had the distinct impression their sons were
going to be prostituting themselves. In some cases they were
right.

Haigler finally decided on how he would write his sidebar
about the possible effects of Coach McLaughlin's death.
He would use the quote from the assistant coach at UFFM
and the quote from Bill Lee. Due more to the psychology
of the situation than anything else, facts would point out
that Charlotte had a better shot at winning now. That was
fairly obvious.

But his story would also imply that talent, not coaching,
was the primary reason for a team's success. Haigler was
convinced Bill Lee had made it to the championships
because of his predecessor's ability to recruit. Fans put too
much emphasis on floor coaching and sometimes not

enough on recruiting.

Even in the face of a great season, Bill Lee would have to seize the opportunity to strengthen his position as a first-class coach. If he couldn't recruit soundly this year, Charlotte would likely be a flash in the pan. So might Bill Lee.

There was more to Bill Lee than met the eye—a reason behind the coach's me-against-the-world attitude. Haigler wondered what it was.

* Twenty-six *

"Ready to go?" Bo Evans asked. He stood on Bill Lee's front porch in the cool, late, evening air.

"Let me get my coat," Lee replied. "Come on in."

The tall, handsome assistant coach stepped in and shut the door. Lee walked to the hall closet to find his coat.

"Hello, Bo," Helen Lee said as she walked into the foyer.

"Are you keeping him straight?" Evans asked.

She smiled broadly. "I'm trying to. Lately I haven't seen enough of him to keep track."

Turning to her husband as he put on his coat, she said, "You just got home and you hardly touched your supper. Now, here you are going out again. You'd better slow down or you'll never make it to New Orleans."

As he walked to the door, Lee said, "I'll be all right. We've got to review a film we received late this afternoon on UFFM. I'll be home right after that."

"Can't this wait until tomorrow morning?" Helen asked.

"No, it can't. That place has been a madhouse. There's no way we could concentrate." Lee stepped outside. Bo followed him.

Before shutting the door, she called out as they were walking toward Evans' courtesy car, "Bo, bring him back early. He needs rest and I'm beginning to feel like a widow."

Evans turned, smiled, and waved his hand.

"Earl's going to meet us at the office," Evans said as he started the car.

"Good. Did he hear anything more from that kid, Bobby Furlough?" Lee asked.

"Not since the last time he and I talked. He was going to call him early this evening."

"What do you suppose the problem is?"

"I don't know. That's Earl's recruit—you'll have to ask him," Evans said, lying. He and Earl Ward knew exactly what the problem was. Bill Lee was not doing his duty as a head coach when it came to recruiting. Bobby Furlough was a seven-foot center who was ranked as one of the fifty best high school players in the country. Everybody wanted him. Head coaches were knocking on Furlough's door and assistant coaches did not carry enough prestige to stay in the running. With a player like Furlough, about all an assistant coach could do would be to break the ice. The ultimate sales job had to be performed by the man in charge, the main personality—the head coach.

Why had Lee only visited Furlough once? Evans wondered. That was simply not enough. Evans hoped Ward would advise Lee that his presence was needed again.

When they arrived at the gym, they walked up the steps to the athletic offices. Bill Lee was relieved to see that he was no longer being followed. He assumed the man Dolci was having watched closely was Burton. Lee was determined to immerse himself completely in his work in hopes that he could get the Dolci problem off his mind. So far, he had been unable to bury it, except when he was on the practice floor.

Lee stopped briefly by Ward's small office. "Come on in when you can, Earl." He continued walking back toward his much more spacious office. Evans followed him.

After a few minutes Ward walked in and sat down. Evans loaded the VCR with the UFFM versus Michigan film. They had acquired the film from the Michigan coach. Lee knew him and even if he had not he probably would have received the same courtesy. Most coaches cooperated with one another in such situations, and the rules allowed a coach to obtain as many films as he could.

However, only one in-person scouting visit by a member of the coaching staff was allowed. Because UFFM had played the same day as the Hornets, Lee had not sent Evans or Ward to scout the game. He felt they could get more information by watching the game on television. He also had taped it on his VCR.

Lee considered films and tapes to be far more valuable

than in-person scouting. His reasons were obvious. The human eye could only detect a portion of a key pattern or play at first glance. Even the studied and trained eyes of a coach could miss important subtleties the first time around.

Earl Ward sat without speaking. Lee noticed his pensive mood. "What's the matter? Problems with one of your ladies?"

"No." Ward barely smiled. "This Furlough kid is giving me fits. Coach, I'm telling you he is one of the best looking centers I've ever seen. He can do it all. He could step right into Collins' spot and play a damn respectable game." Ward shook his head.

"Well, I thought he was going to visit. What turned him off?" Lee asked.

Ward sat silent for a moment, then spoke. "Coach, I think you've turned him off."

"Me?" Lee asked as he sat in his chair holding the small metal remote-control box that operated the film projector.

Ward nodded and said nothing.

"How could I have turned him off? I haven't seen him but once with you. Since then, I've only talked to him once on the phone. We had a pleasant conversation," Lee said.

"Yes, but because you haven't been to visit him again, I think he's feeling that you're not that interested," Ward said.

"That's a bunch of crap and you know it. I just didn't have time to visit him during the last allowable contact dates. If I didn't have all this administrative bullshit to attend to, I'd have gone. You know I'm working two positions as head coach and athletic director."

Ward crossed his long legs and folded his arms. "Coach, I understand your situation. I don't think Furlough does though."

"Have you told him what the problem is?" Lee asked.

Ward said, "I explained it to him and even told him you would be coming to visit him after the tournament. We've only got one visit left and I was saving it for you."

Lee knew he was referring to the NCAA rule that allowed only three in-person visits from the coaching staff to a player's home or anywhere off school grounds, and three in-person visits to a player's school. They were referred to as contact visits. Such visits were limited to specific dates during the year. Ward had already visited the player four times. Counting Lee's one visit last year, they had only one remaining. Ward had also scouted Furlough four times, the maximum number allowed during specific evaluation periods also outlined by the NCAA. During those times he had avoided making contact. Phone calls were unlimited, but Lee knew, as did most coaches, that too many calls could be counterproductive.

Lee stopped mentally reviewing the situation and said, "I intend to see him. I just can't right now. Would it help if I call him?"

"I think so. I just hope it's not too late. He's only got one visit left to make. And like I told you Sunday, he's real high on Notre Dame," Ward said, referring to the NCAA's rule that allowed a recruit to accept only five expense-paid visits to universities.

Lee said, "Hell, I don't blame him. We can't compete with that kind of tradition. It's hard to understand why he considered us in the top six anyway. Shit, two hundred and fifty schools are after him."

"I told you Coach, it's because his girlfriend wants to come here. She apparently has a couple of friends who are enrolling here," Ward said.

"That's right. You did tell me that," Lee said earnestly. "I'm sorry I haven't been any help to you lately. There are things that have gotten out of control, and I have to stick close to the situation here. It should all be straightened out in a few weeks. I promise I'll do everything I can to help you recruit. I know it's not fair to send you guys out there by yourselves and not follow up with some support.

"I've tried to visit all the prospects within driving distance. I know that's not enough, but it's been the best I could do. If we had a sugar daddy with a fancy private jet like some of these other coaches have at their disposal, I could have seen a lot more kids. But we don't and I guess we'll just have to make do with what we've got."

Lee felt bad about the situation, but he was caught in a double bind. Three years ago when the charade with Dolci and the FBI began, he decided to step back from recruiting. It was his decision and his alone. He thought that the less exposure he had with recruits, the tougher it would be for Dolci's lawyers to tarnish his reputation and twist things around at a trial. From what he understood, Dolci was capable of setting up just about anything. For that reason Lee worked slowly and carefully with certain blue-chip recruits. He figured his tactics would lessen Dolci's chances of smearing his name with a fabricated recruiting scandal.

Still, all things considered, he realized he needed to make some stronger efforts. He couldn't let the whole program go down the drain because of Dolci. He looked up at Ward and said, "I'll call Furlough tomorrow and see what I can do to help. OK?"

"Thanks, Coach. I hope you understand where I'm coming from."

"Of course I do, Earl," Lee said. He flipped on the projector and then flipped it back off.

"Did you get the scouting report from Bertka Views?" Lee asked. He generally liked to read the report before he viewed a film. It provided insights on an opponent's strengths and weaknesses. The information was compiled by an unbiased and knowledgeable scout. The service operated out of California.

"Yes, I've got it right here," Evans answered. He handed Lee the report.

Lee scanned it for a few minutes. "Earl, did you get a chance to read this?"

"Yes."

"It's not really earthshaking is it? After watching the game Saturday night, I didn't see too many weaknesses. About the only thing I see is they lack strength at the point. What's the height of that kid, Bo?" Lee asked.

Evans scanned his stat sheet and roster on UFFM and said, "He's listed at six-one. I'll bet he's not over six. Good foul shooter, but he doesn't put it up that much."

"He'll put it up even less with either one of our guards on him. He looked damn quick, though, didn't he?" Lee asked. It was less of a question than it was a statement. He was seldom wrong when he evaluated an opponent.

"Sure did," Evans said, adding, "But when he penetrates, he usually pulls up instead of taking it to the hole. Look at all those assists. He's good at spotting the open man."

"Let's see if we can't play the percentages. No sense in chasing ghosts. If we're in our man-to-man, let's not commit on him too soon if he penetrates. We damn sure don't want to double-up on him at any time. Davis and Thames could slough off him a little bit when we're in the zone. With their height advantage, they can recover. Did you notice that he seemed to favor moving to his left Saturday night?"

"Yes," Ward said.

Lee said, "Let's shade him left. See if we can't force him right." He clicked on the projector. "Let's make sure we're right about that."

The coaches went over the film in detail. Lee advanced, reversed, stopped, and slowed it with his remote-control device. He sometimes felt like Sherlock Holmes uncovering clues at a murder scene. He could not afford to miss anything.

He believed he deserved his reputation for his excellent technical and psychological abilities. He had an uncanny knack for picking his opposition apart piece by piece, formulating a game plan, and then imparting his knowledge to the players so they could anticipate their foes' plays and moves.

He disagreed with Chuck Haigler's theory that the primary value of a coach rested in his ability to recruit. He believed he could turn talented athletes into great players.

He had a formula that simplified what he believed in: Talent multiplied by Knowledge plus Execution equals Victory. He purposely left out an important factor in his equation: luck. He never liked to recognize elements he could not control. Even so, he knew full well that luck played an important role in the eventual outcome.

Luck. He thought about it as he continued to analyze the UFFM film. What kind of luck was he going to need to keep the Dolci affair from ruining his career? Or for that matter, his life?

* Twenty-seven *

Chewing vigorously on a fat, smoldering cigar, Frank Dolci glared at his bodyguard. He removed the cigar from his mouth with his thumb and first finger, then gestured with it. "Damnit, Joe, I don't understand how in hell the Coast Guard could seize that ship in international waters. Where did you say they boarded it?"

"Southeast of Grand Bahama Island," Buona answered as he picked up a towel and dried a chair across from Dolci. An early morning thunderstorm had wet all the pool-side furniture, pouring through the screen roof that hovered over the entire pool area at Dolci's home on Captiva Island.

"We didn't have any pickups scheduled there. How the fuck could they stop a Panamanian freighter if it wasn't violating the Hovering Vessels Act?" Dolci asked, wondering aloud. He did not expect his trusted bodyguard and communications liaison to provide an adequate answer.

Buona shook his head as he sat down. The chair creaked from the strain.

"The Panamanian government must have given them permission. Those bastards! How in the world did the Coast Guard know she was loaded with coke and grass?"

Again answering his own question, Dolci said, "They must have been spotted off the coast of El Pajaro, or else somebody tipped them off." He tapped his fingers loudly on the chrome parsons table beside his white lounge chair.

Dolci watched Buona shift uneasily in his seat. He knew what Buona must be thinking. Though Joe Buona knew he was considered close "family," he always became nervous when his boss started thinking someone might be playing both sides.

Dolci knew Buona was clean, but once Dolci started rolling heads, the organization became very unstable. That made Buona's position as bodyguard dangerous. He would certainly get hit if an attempt was made on Dolci's life.

Shaking his head, Dolci said, "I don't know, Joe. Even though they loaded from a barge at night, it's not easy to hide fifty tons of grass and two hundred kilos of pure coke. They could have been spotted by a submarine. Where did Emilio tell you they were taking the ship?"

"Miami," said Buona.

Dolci thought about how upset Mancotta was going to be. "Fucking Coast Guard! They'll parade that ship all over. It'll be all over the front pages. They stumble onto a haul worth hundreds of millions because somebody either tipped them or one damn sub happened to spot the *Don Quixote* being loaded. And we take a seven-million-dollar bath."

"Yes, sir," Buona said. "Not meaning to change the subject, sir, but I called Anthony this morning right on schedule, just before Emilio called."

"What did he say?" Dolci asked.

"He thinks Burton and the coach ducked his tail with the help of some guy who owns a place called the Hornets' Nest."

"What?" Dolci asked. He had not listened closely, his mind still ruminating on the huge loss he had just suffered.

Buona repeated his sentence and added, "Anthony said to tell you he was sorry he screwed up and didn't get to find out where they went."

"He's a good man. Not too many people admit their mistakes. Did he tell you what happened?" Dolci asked.

Buona gestured with his right hand, palm cocked at an angle. "He said he followed them to a lounge just above the school and parked across the highway. He's pretty sure they noticed him."

"That's not hard to understand with just a one-man tail," Dolci said, pausing. "How come they were together? Were they in one car?"

"Yes, that's why he ended up following both of them. He figured they were just going to grab a bite to eat and talk over business. But they were inside a long time, so he decided to check on them. He couldn't get in because there was some bullshit about a private party. That made him really wonder. He waited a few minutes after he went back to his car, and then he walked around back to look in the window. That's when he saw Burton and the coach walking to the back door from a dirt road," Buona said, leaning back in his chair, raising his eyebrows.

"Did they see him?"

"No. He said he was at the side of the building behind some trees. When they went inside, he ran down the road to see where they had come from. That's when he saw a van—the same one he had seen leave the place earlier—turning around. He's pretty sure they must have been in it. He checked the license. The van belongs to a guy named Donnie Powers, the owner of the lounge. This Powers drove in the front a few minutes later. Then the coach and Burton left."

Dolci stabbed his cigar into the ashtray. "I don't like it. Bill Lee knew we were having Burton tailed, or at least I think he knew. I'm pretty sure I mentioned something to him anyway. So why would he help Burton duck us and then not tell us what was going on? You know what I think, Joe. I think our coach has got a lot of explaining to do. Before we start asking questions, though, we need to find out more about the owner of the lounge."

"Anthony's already running a check on him," Buona said.

"Good. You call him back and tell him not to worry about screwing up the tail. There was no way he could have figured Lee would pull something like that. He did a damn good job finding out what he did. We were lucky. When are you scheduled to talk to him again?" Dolci asked, referring to a prearranged communications schedule that had been set up weeks ago when they first began having Burton watched. The calls were made from one pay phone to another; locations and times varied.

"This afternoon at two thirty," Buona said.

"Get back to me as soon as you can. Are you scheduled to talk to him later tonight?" Dolci asked. He had left the details of the communications link up to Buona.

"No, sir. Do you want me to set up another time?" Buona asked.

"Yes. Make it around nine or ten. I want to keep in close

touch until we shake out the sheets. I'm going for a walk."
Dolci rose from his chair. His large belly overhung his plaid
bathing suit.

"Would you like me to contact Mr. Mancotta's lieutenant
and let him know what's going on?"

"No, that won't be necessary right now. Let's find out
what's happening first." Dolci opened the screen door at
the side of the airy enclosure and walked toward the beach
that fronted his property. Clouds drifted lazily off to the
southeast, remnants of the early morning storm.

He stepped onto the narrow beach. The light brown sand
crunched underneath his feet. Countless seashell fragments
intermingled with finer particles like multicolored corn
flakes in a bowl of crushed oats. Small rolling waves provided
a background sound similar to an intermittent drumroll. A
gentle breeze whispered through the furry Australian pines
that fortressed the beachhead.

Thinking about the problems that lay before him, he
walked slowly in the direction of Turner Beach and began
to sort them in order of their importance. The situation
that slapped him hardest was the loss of his second largest
drug shipment ever.

What other precautions could he possibly have taken?
Only a handful of people had known about the loading off
the coast of El Pajaro, Colombia. That same group had
already handled over twenty-five shipments for him without
a hitch. Though this had been a larger operation, he could
not understand where his protection had broken down. The
authorities in Colombia were paid handsomely to look the
other way.

A ship the size of the *Don Quixote* was loaded swiftly at
night; normally such operations would never be detected.
The biggest danger always prevailed when the ship proceeded to unload at predetermined areas off the American
coast. As a "mother ship," it remained in international
waters, but it was still vulnerable to search-and-seizure
under the Hovering Vessels Act whenever it off-loaded any
portion of its cargo to an American ship.

Yet the ship was seized while still underway. That could

mean only one thing: Panamanian authorities must have given the United States permission to seize it on the high seas. That breach in Dolci's veil of bribes to selected political officials in Panama meant that he could no longer count on a vessel of Panamanian registry.

The fifteen crew members would be returned immediately to Panama, Dolci reasoned. It was unlikely that the U.S. attorney would prosecute under the circumstances. A seizure in international waters would make it near impossible to gain convictions.

He had worked hard to set up his drug chain, meticulously planning all the details. Only five people knew he stood at the organization's top, and he trusted them implicitly. They had nothing to gain by tripping the smuggling operation. If there was a loose tongue, he mused, it had to come from someone further down the line.

He decided to direct Emilio to begin an investigation. Perhaps he would uncover a traitor. Probably not, but it was worth a try, he thought as he stooped to pick up a golden olive, a round, elongated shell cast by nature in a vivid enamel-like solid yellow. It lay next to a broken, white and mottled, reddish-purple calico scallop.

He held the olive up and examined it carefully. A chip made the shell undesirable for his collection; he tossed it back into the water. Depending on the wave action, the olive would either be washed back on shore or reclaimed by the sea.

He turned his attention back to the vexing problem at hand, as he walked over to a dead tree which leaned precariously toward the edge of the water. A few of its broken limbs littered the beach. He sat on a sandy bank that blocked high tide and looked westward at the vast expanse of water that shimmered before him, lapping at the shore. A white schooner with a red and yellow jib and mainsail sailed leisurely in a northerly direction about two miles out. He stared blankly at it.

He would have Emilio dismiss any underlings whom he even slightly suspected of being disloyal and eliminate any who reacted improperly. It would take a long time to recover from the seizure. Manpower, contacts, and cash would have to be restored in an orderly fashion. As far as cash was concerned, Mancotta would be hit the hardest. He would have to draw several million from his account in Liechtenstein and arrange for it to be smuggled back into the United States.

Those were the risks of maintaining a major operation, and that was why the return on the dollar was so high. Losses had to be expected, but this one was more severe than their previous losses—a fully loaded DC-3 in 1984 and a medium-sized trawler near Wilmington in 1986—to the North Carolina State Bureau of Investigation. The loss of the trawler had set them back nearly two million dollars. The loss of the *Don Quixote* shipment represented hundreds of millions of dollars worth of high-grade marijuana and cocaine that would be incinerated and fail to reach the hands of several million East Coast users.

When a large shipment like that was lost, Dolci reflected, the cost on all the various strains of weed—both imported and domestic—would be affected. Street prices would jump even higher and some smokers would turn to other exotic drugs. Some dealers would sit on their "stash" and wait for prices to increase due to the shortage. Other dealers would doctor weaker varieties of grass with chemicals like PCP or "angel dust." That annoyed Dolci. The use of those mind-bending drugs gave marijuana an undeserved bad reputation. They were dangerous substitutes for the subduing characteristics of Colombian Red, with its heavy concentration of Tetrahydrocannabinol, commonly known as THC. People seldom became violent on it.

Such was not the case with PCP. Often, with its use, moods shifted quickly and smokers became enraged and dissociative. After spraying it on "home grown," pushers tended to claim their wares to be "dynamite weed," and unsuspecting buyers became guinea pigs. Though the chemical aftertaste was detectable by most knowledgeable users, it often went unnoticed by the less experienced.

Invariably, Dolci thought, a few people went off the deep end, and authorities came under increased pressure to stop the drug trade. Word that bad dope was circulating also tended to frighten borderline users. Smuggling was never easy, and during times of heightened public awareness it was much more risky.

To Dolci the capture of his ship was paradoxical law enforcement. It took good-grade marijuana temporarily out of circulation and forced users to turn to other drugs that had far more damaging effects. Like cocaine.

The shipment of coke was big. But in the economic scheme of things, it wouldn't really be missed. Not like the pot. Imported pot had been drastically reduced.

He wondered if government officials would ever realize that legalization and control of marijuana were far better answers to the drug problem. Slowing the supply of marijuana had been the biggest reason for cocaine's rise in popularity in the '80s. It was an easier drug to smuggle and a lot more profitable. Marijuana prices had tripled in the past six years, while cocaine prices had actually decreased because of the plentiful supply.

Another case of bureaucratic idiocy. Stop pot; force coke. Dolci wondered why the government had failed to see the other benefit marijuana could bestow if legalized. It was less dangerous than alcohol. Why not control, package, and tax it just like liquor? The revenues would be astronomical, not to mention the gains the Treasury Department would realize by stopping the flow of billions of untaxed dollars. He had once seen a computer model that demonstrated how the national debt could be erased in nine years if the government legalized pot, raised marijuana, and sold a pack of twenty joints at twenty dollars.

He wasn't complaining about the situation. He profited from it. But he considered the useless enterprise of waging a drug war to be just another example of man's stupidity when it came to legislating morals. Drugs were just like gambling. They were a source of entertainment, and as long as man lived they would always be used. With that type of demand, someone would take the necessary risks to see that the supply lines remained open. He had no intention of passing up the opportunity.

He turned his attention to the questionable trip Lee and Burton had made. Where had they gone with the owner of the lounge? Obviously, it had to have been someplace they wanted to keep secret. He didn't like the possibilities.

Was Lee up to something? He intended to find out. He would know more after Anthony Giannini finished the investigation of Powers. Then it would be time to probe for answers.

If the answers weren't satisfactory, he would take Lee and Burton out.

* Twenty-eight *

In the game room of his New Orleans home, Francesco Mancotta sat in an antique rocker some twenty feet from his large-screen television. The newsman had just launched into another story. Mancotta had already mentally tuned it out.

Holding a small, black, remote-control unit in his left hand, he pointed it at the television and pressed the off button. The large screen went blank. He shook his head, then rubbed his graying temples with both hands. The noonday newscaster had led with the report that the *Don Quixote* had been seized. He wondered why his partner had not contacted him. Surely, Dolci had known what happened hours ago.

Coupled with the problems that had arisen as a result of McLaughlin's lack of cooperation and resulting death, the loss of the ship was troubling. Things were not going well at all.

He was generally stoic when serious problems arose. This was different. Harmful as it was, the *Quixote's* loss could be overcome. Yet something else gnawed at the back of his mind. It would not go away, and what made it worse was he couldn't put his finger on it.

Mentally searching for an answer, he looked out the huge plate-glass window in his New Orleans home which overlooked Lake Pontchartrain. He and Dolci had been through dangerous situations before.

Then why did he feel so uncomfortable with the impending fix? Was it Dolci's obsession with this or was it due to the fact that he was having to depend upon "peckerwoods" to carry the plan to a successful conclusion? There was a word he hadn't used in a long time. It was his father's favorite slang term which referred to anyone of non-Italian descent. His father had always blamed peckerwoods for any mistakes or problems.

The man Mancotta awaited for lunch was non-Italian. Bobby Nevada had never given any reason to be distrusted, but he was still a peckerwood. Nevada was a New Yorker who moved west, following his wanderlust to be forever close to the bookmaking business.

Known as "The Oddsmaker" because of his uncanny ability to predict the outcome of almost any type of sports event, Nevada had become friendly with many underworld figures. Their operations in the "open territory" of Las Vegas profited consistently from his advice. Mancotta struck up a friendship with the short, stocky, brown-haired man in 1973. That was before Nevada's fame spread beyond the borders of the state he chose to call home, and shortly after he changed his last name to match it. His former name was Michael Robert Thomas: much too plain for a stage name, the gambler had obviously concluded.

"Sir, your guest has arrived," Mancotta's slender male servant announced.

"Thank you." Mancotta rose from his chair and walked through the long hallway that led to the foyer. He always felt it was more polite to meet his invited guests at the door, rather than allow a servant to do the task. He believed the security fence and bodyguard on the premises were ample screening for protection.

He opened the door as Nevada stepped up the last two white-marble steps. "Hello, Bobby. How was your trip?"

"Fine, but those assholes at the airlines lost my bags. Must've happened when I changed planes in that monster airport at Dallas/Ft. Worth," Nevada said sharply.

Mancotta put his arm around the shorter man's shoulders and walked him back to the game room. "Sorry to hear that. I'll have my driver follow up on it. We'll get them here as soon as possible."

"Thanks, but that won't be necessary. I told them to deliver the bags to my hotel when they come in."

"Hotel? I was expecting you to stay with me. Cancel those reservations and stay here where you can be among friends." Mancotta walked over to the sliding glass door and pointed at the view. "Where can you stay in New Orleans that has a more beautiful view and all the comforts of home?"

"There's nothing I would like better. But I've got to stay downtown where I can be close to the action. Remember, I've got a column to write on those basketball teams and how they stack up. I've had reservations at the Hyatt Regency for months. Thanks for the offer, though. I'll take you up on it next time I'm in town." Nevada walked over to the pocket billiard table made of solid mahogany and pushed the cue ball across the length of the deep green felt. It rebounded with a soft thud. The roll was straight and true.

Mancotta was not disappointed by Nevada's desire to stay at the hotel. His offer had been made more as a gesture of courtesy than a sincere desire to have the sometimes obnoxious Oddsmaker as a house guest for the next six days. "I understand. But I insist that you join Frank and me one night for dinner before you leave."

Nevada looked up from the pool table. Thick glasses made his eyes look like large black eggs. "Frank's in town?" he asked.

"He's not here yet. He'll be in tomorrow."

"That's good to hear. I haven't seen him in ages. Where will he be staying?"

"With me, of course," Mancotta answered. The servant appeared at the door. He waited until Mancotta acknowledged him with a nod, entered, asked for their cocktail orders, and left.

"We're having your favorite New Orleans specialty for lunch, Oysters Rockefeller. I'm looking forward to it. Haven't had them in a while. Marcello has the best recipe in town." Mancotta smiled and gestured for Nevada to sit down.

"Your chef is the best in town." Nevada sat down. "You know, Francesco, I don't think I have ever known a more gracious host. I still owe you one for that help you provided on the fight. You honor me too much."

Nevada's voice sounded like the gracious tone of a political candidate before an election. Nevada obviously knew it was likely that the favor he owed was about to be cashed in.

Mancotta smiled warmly. "You owe me nothing, Bobby.

Favors from one friend to another are not to be used like markers in a casino. That cheapens the relationship."

"I agree. When will you be coming back to Vegas to visit us?" Nevada turned and saw the servant enter the room carrying a silver tray with their cocktails. When he picked up his drink, Mancotta noticed Nevada's hands were shaking.

"Bobby, is there something wrong?"

Nevada gulped down half of his drink and waited for the servant to leave. "Yes, but I can't trouble you with my problems."

"What are friends for? If not to help, then there is no friendship. What is troubling you? Perhaps I can be of assistance."

Nevada hesitated. "It's my lost baggage."

Mancotta arched his eyebrows quizzically.

Nevada decided to explain. "I never do the stuff. It's too risky for me."

"Coke?" Mancotta said.

"No, worse than that."

"Heroin?"

Nevada nodded and began to pace along the length of the pool table. "I know it was stupid. Like I said, it wasn't for me. It was for a friend. If the authorities should open that bag, I'm ruined . . . hell, who knows, maybe they already have. Maybe it's not lost. Someone might have tipped 'em."

"Relax. You can always claim you were set up. Where did you have it?"

"That's the problem. It was in a false-bottomed shaving can in my medicine kit. My prints are all over it. I should've wiped it down, but I didn't think about it."

"Bags get lost all the time. And if the feds got tipped, you can bet they'd already be talking to you." Mancotta smiled and walked over to Nevada. He put his arm around him and said, "I've got connections at the airport. I'll make a few calls. Everything will be taken care of. You've got nothing to worry about. Buy yourself new clothes, the airline insurance will pay off."

Nevada seemed to relax some. "Thanks. I owe you again."

Mancotta decided to change the subject. He raised his glass and sipped a Manhattan cocktail. "I'm planning to fly to Vegas next week to tidy up some business matters."

Both men continued to discuss various friends and mutual acquaintances they had in Vegas. Mancotta inquired about Joe Mangano, a Vegas casino executive who worked secretly to protect the organization's hidden and illegal casino interests.

Mangano had been very successful at skimming from casino funds, an operation that took guile and a lot of savvy to avoid detection by the gambling commission. The owners—Mancotta and Dolci in reality, but not on paper— approved of the practice and encouraged it. Most of it was funneled back into their pockets with Mangano taking a 20 percent cut for his services. Skimming provided a handsome tax-free profit.

Nevada said, "I think Joe needs to take a long vacation. The last time I saw him he looked tired and haggard. His heart may be giving him trouble."

Mancotta knew Nevada was unaware of the exact relationship he had with Mangano and he wanted to keep it that way. "I told him the last time I saw him that he wasn't long for this world if he didn't slow down. Casino nightlife seems to pump through his veins. I remember one time when a good-looking broad told me that when Joe came, it was in black hundred-dollar chips."

Nevada laughed and said, "I bet she swallows it all and picks it out of her shit the next day."

Mancotta shook his head and chuckled once to be polite. That was the kind of "I'll go you one better" crude statement that made him think Nevada had an obnoxious streak in him. He decided it was time to ply him with fine food and get on with the business at hand. The lost heroin had been a stroke of luck. Nevada was even more indebted to him now.

Mancotta's dining room was decorated impeccably in French Provincial motif, soft whites with deep blue curtains that framed a picture window adorned with wrought iron and intricate filigree. Through it, his finely manicured lawn—which ended at the concrete staircase seawall built to restrain Lake Pontchartrain—was clearly visible. Beyond that the lake stretched past the horizon. The scene was like looking through an elaborate spiderweb to view a fluid background of blue-green.

They began their meal with a tangy shrimp remoulade and a bowl of spicy seafood gumbo. Following that, each man was served a dozen Oysters Rockefeller. Mancotta was proud of his chef's ability to prepare the well-known appetizer to perfection and was certain that the taste could not be matched by any restaurant in the city except Antoine's.

His reasoning was simple: his chef used slightly less than two ounces of real absinthe in the Rockefeller sauce. True absinthe, an illegal liqueur with a licorice flavor, was available only on the black market. Restaurants were forced to use an absinthe substitute, Herbsaint or Pernod. Mancotta could taste the difference.

The rich, highly seasoned spinach and mixed green sauce that covered raw oysters on-the-half-shell was baked with heat, above and below, on a bed of ice-cream salt. He was convinced that Jules Alciatoire—son of Antoine Alciatoire, who founded New Orleans' most famous restaurant in 1840—would have been pleased by the reproduction of his gastronomic creation.

By the time Nevada was finished with the tasty appetizer and the servant entered with the entree, Crabmeat Lafitte, Mancotta decided to launch into discussion about the fix. He felt certain that the columnist had temporarily forgotten the mishap with his luggage. "Who are you picking to win the championships?"

"North Carolina."

"Who will they be playing?"

"Up until two days ago, I would have thought they'd be playing UFFM. But in light of recent events, I think Charlotte will beat the Chargers by five." Nevada swept a portion of the crabmeat through the delicate Hollandaise sauce that draped the main course, raised it to his mouth, and added, "You never know, though. Those kids in Florida are talented. They might rise to the occasion."

Mancotta arched his eyebrows and sipped wine, signaling that he was ready to listen, not talk.

Nevada sipped the light-bodied chablis and said, "Basketball is a tough sport to predict. There are so many variables: nuances in the game and differences in individual players. Fewer parts to the whole than football. In football you've got eleven guys on the field against eleven others.

"Say you've got a car that's got four cylinders and one of them goes out. It won't go very damn far. But you can keep on getting it with an eight-cylinder that is missing on one. Matter of numbers. And really, when you get down to it, you've got so many other players who are trained to play defense, offense, or special teams in football. They aren't having to go up and down the court and play it both ways."

"I should think that with more match-ups to worry about it would be more difficult to predict football," Mancotta said.

Nevada shook his head. "Not if you have a good system. I merely break the whole down into parts. The variables in football—nerves, psychology, and all that shit—just don't bother me as much as they do in college basketball. Every player doesn't handle the ball in football, and those who do certainly don't touch it as often as a basketball player."

"I'm not sure I follow you," Mancotta said.

"Well, let me put it to you this way: I'm right about 67 percent of the time in calling the outcome of football games, but I'm only batting about 58 percent in basketball. I'm convinced that it's not because I understand the game any less, but because there are fewer parts to the whole, and therefore more opportunities for a single player's poor showing to affect the outcome. And there are so damn many circumstances that can cause one player to fuck up, not to mention injury." Nevada sat back in his chair.

Mancotta had listened intently. Dolci had previously convinced him that the exact opposite was true. But since his partner seemed to have a better average in predicting the outcome of college basketball games than did the renowned Oddsmaker, he decided not to let the two opposing theses worry him. Instead, he decided to maneuver Nevada into position.

"Bobby, what would you say if I told you that we have first-hand information that Charlotte will throw the championship game far enough to beat the point spread?" Mancotta wiped his mustache with his linen napkin.

"I'd say that was pretty interesting and hope that nobody was pulling your leg. How's it going to be accomplished?"

"Let's just say the information is from a reliable source," Mancotta answered, "and that it involves an injury to Ted Collins."

"That would certainly kill Charlotte's chances all right. What's your angle?"

"We figure there is a golden opportunity if the oddsmakers make Charlotte the favorite. People are suckers for Cinderella teams. We'll exploit that."

"That's great, but I don't think Charlotte is going to be favored. Like I told you I think—" Nevada stopped in mid-sentence.

Mancotta smiled. "Go on. What was it you were saying?"

Nevada laughed loudly, raised his glass in a toasting gesture. "My friend, you have a brilliant idea. The only problem that I can see is that I'm going to fall another percentage point in my prediction rate, but who could ever expect me to anticipate that Charlotte's big gun would get injured. Here's to you." He grinned, then sipped his wine.

"How much effect do you think you'll have on public opinion?" Mancotta asked.

"The weekend bettor tends to watch my spread pretty closely. That, coupled with the fact that we can pull a few strings on the line coming out of Vegas, and I think we are going to have some heavy betting. How many points were you thinking? It can't be much or people will never swallow it."

"Five to seven," said Mancotta.

Nevada whistled and shook his head. "No way—not in a national championship—three to four is max."

Mancotta thought for a moment. "I can see your point. But don't you think you're going to have to make it five to convince people to go with the Hornets?"

Nevada shrugged. "What difference does it make, four or

five? Four should be enough for our bookies to offer some easy even action. Just my touting Charlotte to win by four should lure enough bettors to jump on Cinderella and start humping, particularly if they're not having to give up any points. We'll have to watch it closely to make sure the majority of the bets are swinging in our favor. There's obviously going to be a fair number of intelligent gamblers that will go with Carolina unless Charlotte blows away UFFM."

Mancotta smiled broadly.

"That's another thing. How can you be so sure they'll beat the boys from Florida? Even without their head coach there are no guarantees, but maybe you know something I don't."

Mancotta pulled his chair away from the table enough to cross his legs. "No, we don't have anything going down there. But Frank is convinced that without McLaughlin, Charlotte is sure to win."

"That's exactly what a lot of folks are going to think. It'll take some of the sizzle out of Charlotte's victory—which will make it just that much harder for you to get people betting your way," Nevada said as the servant cleared his plate, replaced it with a bowl of bread pudding, and refilled his wine glass.

Mancotta held up his hand, declining the desert. His servant nodded and left the room. "Any ideas how we can counter that?"

Nevada savored his first bite of pure butter and brandy-flavored pudding as he reasoned out his answer. "Maybe I can push that situation along a bit—write about McLaughlin's replacement and how his team system has been ingrained. I'll call the game a two point pick-em. Damn, I'm going to get two black eyes this weekend. You know that, don't you?"

"Yes, but we'll have a little something for you to buy some liver with," Mancotta said wryly.

Nevada chuckled. "Thanks. You know we might be writing UCLA off a little prematurely. They could take Carolina."

Mancotta shrugged. "So, we've still got a giant going up against a new kid on the block. Won't it work about the same?"

"Um hmm," Nevada muttered, his mouth full. He swallowed, held his spoon up, and said, "Jesus, your chef can cook. Can I take him back to Vegas with me?"

"He's been. He doesn't like the climate."

"It wouldn't be quite the same," Nevada said, switching back to their primary discussion.

"What do you mean?"

"Well, the media—myself included—is going to play up the fact that Charlotte has never been able to get a game with Carolina, and yet, they're only a couple of hours away from each other. You know, the old David finally gets Goliath to come out and take him on routine, that sort of thing. We had that when Louisville finally got to take on Kentucky. The whole country got interested, even though it was a regional-type affair."

Mancotta liked hearing the angle from somebody other than Dolci and Charlotte reporters. It was good to know that the rest of the country was tuning in to that fact, too.

Nevada leaned forward in his chair and dropped his napkin beside his empty bowl. "I'll play that angle up a bit in my column and use it as one of the reasons I think Charlotte will have an emotional edge. Another fact I can use is that Dean Smith has been a bridesmaid many times, but a bride only once. Only I won't quite put it that way—that cliche is overworked. So's that Cinderella shit, but the fans love to hear it."

Mancotta smiled. Nevada was being far more cooperative than he had anticipated. The Oddsmaker was also demonstrating a loyalty Mancotta never expected from a peckerwood. It was the added favor, of course—the baggage problem—that was it. He made a mental note to make sure Nevada's bag would only fall into the right hands—or disappear altogether.

* Twenty-nine *

Dolci looked at Buona in the fading daylight. "What did Anthony find out?"

"Powers is a small-time drug dealer who has been looking for some bigger action," Buona answered. "One of our coordinators got the word from his runner. The runner met Powers through a fellow named Russ Stinson, who owns a convenience store and head shop in Charlotte."

"What's Powers' connection with Burton and Lee?" Dolci asked.

Buona looked down at his left arm and swatted a mosquito with his thick right hand. He scratched the bloody spot as he said, "He went to school at Charlotte and is an avid basketball fan. So's his friend, Stinson. Powers bought the Hornets' Nest a couple of years ago and pals around with a lot of the players. Burton has been seen with him a number of times. Anthony says the word is Burton gets his grass from Powers and Stinson."

"What about Coach Lee?"

"He's been seen up at the Hornets' Nest, but that's about it."

Seated on the observation deck atop Dolci's island retreat, both men watched the sky slowly darken. Puffy pink clouds changed to dark gray as the sun—which had disappeared over the horizon minutes ago—became blocked by the earth's rotation.

Buona sat patiently waiting for Dolci to speak.

"I never asked Lee how he knew that Burton was a smoker. It didn't occur to me that he might be a user himself. He just never struck me as the type." Dolci paused. "He still doesn't. I wonder what he was doing with them?"

Buona shrugged.

"It's a well-known fact that many basketball players are users. Maybe there is a connection there," Dolci said, leaning back, looking up at the darkening sky.

"Anthony thinks there might be," Buona said. "The guy he talked to said that his runner was sure some of the players were users."

"Maybe Powers is their supplier or Lee was checking out what was going on. Did he indicate how hard Powers has been pushing to get into our organization?" Dolci asked.

"It really hasn't been him as much as it has been his friend, Stinson. The runner said Stinson hinted he and Powers were forming a partnership and wanted to see if they could start moving more dope. They're looking to move about fifty pounds a week." Buona could only see Dolci's silhouette: darkness had enveloped them.

"Fifty pounds is a pretty big step up. They must have some big buyers in mind. What did the runner tell Stinson? I mean how did he leave it with him?" Dolci asked.

"Just as he was supposed to—said he didn't think he could handle it, but if anything came available, he would let him know."

"Good."

"Anthony had an idea about what they may have been doing together if it wasn't drugs. He didn't know if I should bring it up," Buona said tentatively.

"Let's hear it."

"Tickets are in real big demand up there because two teams from the same state are going. Scalpers are getting as much as eight or nine hundred bucks for one lousy ticket. Anthony wondered if Burton and Lee might be making a little money on the side by letting Powers scalp a few tickets."

Dolci thought for a moment. "Could be. We don't know for sure though, do we? I don't like the coach working behind my back. There might not be anything to it, but we need to know more."

Buona nodded.

Dolci said firmly, "When you talk to Anthony again later tonight, here's what I want you to tell him. Have him get the runner and the coordinator to make contact with Stinson and offer to supply fifty pounds a week. After that, I want both men tailed. And no fuck-ups this time. Tell Anthony to use as many different cars and people as he has to. I don't want either guy to have any idea he's being followed. And I don't care where they go, stay on top of them."

"What about Burton and the coach?" Buona asked.

Dolci rose from his chair. "Don't worry about them for right now. They'll be leaving for New Orleans sometime tomorrow. Francesco and I will take care of that. Do you have your bags packed?"

"Yes, sir."

"See you in the morning," Dolci said, pressing the button on his digital watch: 7:09. He hurried downstairs to see the CBS evening news. He wanted to see the segment on the seizure of the *Don Quixote*.

He still hadn't contacted Mancotta about the loss; however by now he figured his partner had seen it on the news. It was a subject Dolci figured would best be discussed in person.

The motor home rolled smoothly down I-85 headed south toward Atlanta. The four occupants, Russ and Shelly Stinson and Donnie and Linda Powers, were singing the Hornets' fight song. They had left Charlotte at 6:00 p.m.. After nearly four hours and a fifth of Crown Royal, they were nearing Atlanta.

Powers was behind the wheel, feeling relaxed despite the fact he had allowed himself only one drink. The tensions of his undercover assignment had worn off. He was happy to be free from the burden. With the team, coaches, and Burton on their way to New Orleans tomorrow morning, he thought, the responsibility for handling the problem was shifting to the FBI in New Orleans. He would be available only if needed. Otherwise, he was to remain in the background as simply another Charlotte fan.

"That's your last drink," Powers said, glancing at his friend mixing Sprite with the blended whisky. Stinson was seated next to him in the captain's chair on the passenger's side.

"What do you mean my last drink? I'm just getting

cranked up." Stinson smiled and crossed his eyes.

"Yeah, well that's great, but don't forget you start driving in another four hours," Powers said. "Then, it's my turn to do the drinking. Why don't you climb in the back and get some sleep? No sense in us both staying awake."

Stinson arched his eyebrows and scratched his head. "Bullshit. Who wants to sleep? The party's just starting. We're going to go for it for the next five days. Don't worry about me. I could drive to New Orleans blindfolded. My radar is already locked in on Bourbon Street and my horns are up." He raised his glass and emptied it in one long swallow.

From the back seat his wife, Shelly, looked at her sister and said, "What horns? As far as I know, he's only got one and it's barely big enough to notice."

Powers roared. Stinson was constantly teasing his wife and the barb was made even funnier by the surprise turnabout.

Stinson recovered quickly, swiveled his chair to face her, and asked, "Are you complaining or bragging? A Texas longhorn wouldn't have one big enough for you." He slapped Powers on the shoulder, pointed at Shelly, and held his hands three feet apart.

Shelly blushed.

Linda intervened. "OK, you two are even."

Powers smiled, looked in the rearview mirror, and said, "Quit refereeing. It was just starting to get good."

The laughter and barbs continued as Powers drove down the road. The miles melted away as they passed through the heart of Atlanta on the interstate highway.

He knew he had been stereotyped as an avid fan. He was safe and looking forward to New Orleans.

* Thirty *

Troy Burton drove to the airport at a leisurely pace, winding through a maze of back streets to avoid the heavy morning traffic and, more importantly, to see if he and Jenny were being followed. As far as he could tell, they weren't.

Jenny sat quietly in the passenger's seat. Occasionally, she pointed at yards and city-maintained medians where early spring daffodils, crocuses, forsythia, and pansies had popped into full bloom, unaffected by the late cold snap four days ago.

He thought about the city he loved and spring. Warm weather had apparently pushed the last vestige of winter out of Charlotte. The vernal equinox had officially marked the beginning of spring on March 20, at 7:48 p.m. EST, nearly five days ago.

Charlotteans relished the seasonal change. It was evident in the early-morning downtown bustle of people walking sprightly to work from the overcrowded parking lots. It seemed as if the whole city had snapped out of the winter doldrums at once. In a couple of weeks, blossoming white, red, and pink azaleas, fruit trees, and dogwoods would burst like silent fireworks along the city's heavily tree-lined streets. Few areas in the country could boast having more blossoming trees, shrubs, flowers and well-groomed grounds than the "Queen City." Spring in Charlotte was nature's annual showcase.

The excitement of the upcoming national basketball championships added to the residents' ebullient spirits. Nearly everyone, including people who normally paid little attention to the college basketball scene, talked about the Hornets and the Tar Heels. Speculation that the two teams might meet in a national showdown churned at a fever pitch. Some Tar Heel fans who lived in the city found their heartstrings playing dissonant chords.

"Do you think we'll have to move from Charlotte right

away?" Jenny asked. She looked at Troy as he stopped at a red light.

He looked at her. Her eyes had misted. "I don't know."

"I don't want to move. I love it here," she said.

"I do too, honey. Let's not worry about that now. Why don't we cross that bridge when we come to it?"

"OK," she said softly, biting her lower lip.

Making a conscious effort to change the subject, he asked, "Where's the itinerary?"

Jenny searched in her purse for the mimeographed, type-written schedule that Bill Lee instructed Lindsey Ellis to have printed and circulated. Lee was a stickler for detailed communication. Every member of the traveling party and office personnel who remained in Charlotte received a copy.

"Here it is."

"What time does the plane leave?"

"Nine thirty-five."

"Good. We'll be there in plenty of time."

"It says here to arrive one hour before scheduled departure."

"I know. We'll make it. What time does it say the team will leave the dorms?"

"Seven fifty-five."

"It only takes about fifteen minutes for them to get there. Lee likes to roll them out early."

After parking in a long-term lot and riding to the terminal in a shuttle bus, they checked in at the Piedmont airline ticket counter. The players and coaches had already arrived. As they walked back to the Piedmont's Presidential Suite, they watched local television news teams corner Coach Lee for an impromptu last-minute interview outside of the room. A number of fans stood talking to some of the players who had not yet gone inside.

An ABC news team collared Ted Collins and began to question him. Troy figured that the crew was the same one that had been in Charlotte for the past two days. The *Observer* had reported that ABC planned to air a special ten-minute segment on the Friday night evening news to feature the "Queen City" and its Cinderella team. The news team had frequented pubs, stores, downtown streets, and even talked to bus drivers to capture the overall flavor of the Hornets' meteoric rise to stardom.

Stories coming out of Florida on the death of Coach McLaughlin had begun to dwindle. The FBI had effectively put a lid on information leaking to the press from sources close to the investigation. Many had concluded that McLaughlin's death was simply a sordid affair ending in two tragic murders. Some believed the whole tournament should be canceled, but the NCAA did not agree. The games would be played.

The Burtons walked into the private room which had been reserved by the travel agency for members of the Hornets' traveling party. A hostess served coffee, fruit juice and sweet rolls to players seated in chairs. Their long legs stretched out, consuming an abnormal amount of floor space. Some talked quietly; others read newspapers, invariably the sports pages.

Troy and Jenny walked over and sat next to Lane Gilliam on a couch.

The assistant athletic director smiled. "Morning, Troy, Jenny. Looks like we've picked a great day to fly."

"Is Edna coming?" Jenny asked.

"No. We couldn't find anybody brave enough to take on the job of baby-sitting our four little darlings," Gilliam said wryly.

After chatting casually with the players seated around them, Troy and Gilliam commented on how relieved they were to have completed their ticket duties. Gilliam's audit had balanced perfectly. Considering the scalper's market, he was pleased that he could account for every ticket.

A list of seat assignments was available. Troy had carefully worked out the seating pattern. Attention to personalities, status, and political factions had affected his computerized priority listing in several instances. Some fans simply could not be seated close to one another.

There was one problem Troy could not control, however, and he mentioned it to Gilliam. "You know the only thing that worries me is how some of our Foundation members who are Tar Heel graduates are going to handle it if we meet in the finals. Do you suppose they'll wear blue coats and cheer for the Tar Heels?"

"I'm not sure about the coats, but I'd imagine they're going to pull for their alma mater. Wouldn't you?" Gilliam asked.

Troy nodded. "It sure won't sit well with some of our more loyal fans. Blue coats in a sea of black and gold will stand out like tits on a bull." He laughed and added, "That's all we need is for some of our supporters to start slugging it out in the stands. Talk about 'color and pageantry!'"

Gilliam chuckled under his breath and rose from his chair as he heard the travel agent tell the players it was time to walk to the boarding gate.

The ABC camera crew filmed the entire traveling party as they walked down the carpeted concourse to the gate. Troy made a mental note to watch the Friday evening news. He doubted he would be recognized by anyone other than those who already knew him, but it would be interesting to see himself on the national news—a brief flash of glory on video tape. Provided, of course, that he did not end up on the cutting-room floor.

Their arrival in New Orleans went practically unnoticed at the airport. Other than a few heads turning to stare at the tall group of players, they might as well have been arriving to attend a business convention. New Orleans was a great deal more accustomed to having stars bounce in and out. Television stations would begin coverage at the times prescribed by the NCAA.

A host from Tulane University awaited the Hornets' official party, and he quickly huddled with Bill Lee and Lindsey Ellis as they gathered at the baggage claim area. Lee signaled Burton, Gilliam, Evans and Ward to join the discussion. Jenny Burton joined Julia Evans and Helen Lee at the baggage conveyor.

Lee introduced his staff to the host and said, "OK, we'll go into town on the charter bus. When we get to the

Fairmont, the NCAA has five courtesy cars waiting for us.
Troy and Lane can share one. Lindsey, you'll be staying at
the Hyatt Regency with the press, so you'll need one." Lee
looked around for Chuck Haigler, spotted him, and said,
"If Chuck needs to go someplace and you can work it out,
let him use it." He turned to his assistant coaches. "Each
of you take one."

No one in the Hornet party noticed the two figures
standing in the crowd watching carefully, but the two other
men who stood not more than twenty feet from them did.
They also had a keen interest in watching Burton, Lee, and
Collins. Dressed as taxi cab drivers, the FBI agents blended
into the airport crowd.

One of them, Don Hardin, had immediately recognized
Dolci and Mancotta's first move. He tipped his partner and
they watched closely. Apparently Dolci and Mancotta's
men were there to follow and find out exactly what rooms
Burton, Lee, and Collins would occupy.

In case of trouble, Hardin wasn't worried about backup.
The FBI's plan was solid. Twenty-six law enforcement
agents had been assembled in a strike-force team. The
special prosecutor planned to conclude the investigation on
the DOLMAN Project and begin making arrests.

The series of federal statutes under which the Dolci/
Mancotta investigation was being conducted were cap-
tioned under the acronym RICO, Racketeering Influence
Corrupt Organizations. Bert Teague was directing the primary movements of all men. Special care had been taken
to provide varying types of disguises for each team. The
cost of the intensive surveillance required for the next five
days had been estimated at $300,000.

Hardin knew the next five days were going to be tough.
It was now or never.

* Thirty-one *

Francesco Mancotta walked around his pocket billiard table looking for his best shot and said, "I hope you're right, but I don't like the sound of that."

As Dolci watched his host survey the table, he stood holding a drink in one hand and a cue stick in the other. "I don't either, but the more I thought about what Powers might have been doing with them, the more I realized that it had to have something to do with the players, drugs, or tickets."

Mancotta stopped and lined up his shot on the five ball. He stroked the cue ball into the object ball, which quickly disappeared into the side pocket. The cue ball caromed and stopped in perfect position for a shot on the seven ball. He was an excellent player, and "eight ball" was his favorite game.

Before taking his shot, he said, "It's not going to be easy to find Powers and Stinson. This is a damn big town. There are a lot of motor homes passing through, you know. It's too bad Anthony missed them."

"If this guy Powers was some sort of undercover agent, don't you think he would be sticking a little closer to Burton and Lee?" Dolci asked.

Mancotta directed his cue stick at the lower third of the cue ball and struck it smartly to impart heavy backspin after it hit the seven ball. A loud click and the target ball dove into the middle of the leather pocket. The cue ball reversed direction quickly, bounced off one cushion at an angle, and rolled to a stop less than a foot from the black eight ball. He stroked it into the side pocket. The game ended. He was still thinking about Dolci's last statement.

"You're probably right. I'd just like to make damn sure that we're not being set up. We can't afford to take any chances."

Dolci watched Mancotta begin picking the balls out of

the pockets and placing them inside a mahogany rack. He sipped his drink, then said, "I've had enough. You're five for seven and I'm ready to relax for awhile."

They sat down close to the huge sliding glass doors that spanned the back wall of the room. Mancotta looked toward Lake Pontchartrain and said, "I don't know too many people who get winded playing pool. You really are out of shape. If you don't do something about that, you'll die way before your time."

Dolci lit a cigar. "Yes, but look at all the fun I've had. I do the things I enjoy. You deny yourself some of the finer pleasures in life because you're so goddamned worried that they're going to kill you. What's going on up here can kill you." Dolci pointed at his head. "You worry too much, and lately, you seem overly concerned about the deals. We've been together a long time and never gotten in too far over our heads."

Mancotta laughed. "What do you call that deal with the *Don Quixote*. On my end it looked like about three and a half million dollars worth of deep shit."

Dolci frowned and chewed on his cigar. "Now you know that wasn't my fault. I took it on the chin just like you did. You knew the risks."

"All I'm trying to say is that we're not perfect," Mancotta said. "We have made our share of mistakes. And so far we've been lucky enough not to have gotten our balls hung on some of the fences we've been over.

"Christ, look at us. We've got more than enough to retire comfortably, yet we're still sticking our necks out. Don't you think it's time we slowed down?"

"There you go starting that retirement shit again. I don't understand it," Dolci said. "I work because I enjoy it. After this is over, if you want out, then that's your decision. I won't stand in your way. It won't be quite the same without you, though."

"It's not the businesses we own that I want to retire from," Mancotta said, standing, looking out of the glass doors with his back to Dolci. "It's these elaborate schemes, Frank. They worry me. Sooner or later we're going to get caught.

I don't really care to spend the rest of my life in prison."

"We're in too deep," Dolci said, adding, "You and I will never be able to walk away from it all. Surely, you know that."

Mancotta decided to drop the subject. His partner would never see it his way and compromise would be impossible. He realized full retirement would not be possible. With his hundreds of connections and business holdings, he could never step away entirely from organized crime. Retirement was simply a word he used to describe easing back on the illegitimate affairs. Since he had no son to leave his controlling interests to, he intended to allow his nephew to step in while he remained available for influence and advice.

He realized he was going to be forced into making the decision he had long dreaded. Choosing his words carefully, he said, "I'm not suggesting we stop all of our activities. Perhaps semi-retirement is a better word. I don't intend to abandon our partnership. Everything is tied too closely together. Our whole relationship has been built on trust, right?" Mancotta turned and looked at his partner.

Dolci nodded.

"Good. Now let's get back to the business at hand."

Dolci stared at Mancotta. He paused, as if he were trying to take in the full meaning of Mancotta's words, then he asked, "Have you gotten most of your contacts alerted about Powers?"

"Yes."

Dolci relit his smoldering cigar. "All right. If he's as big a fan as Anthony says he is, my guess is he will be hanging around the team. From the description, he won't be hard to pick out of a crowd. Anthony brought two other men down from Charlotte with him. We lost Powers, so it's our job to find him. If your contacts happen to spot him, that will just make our job a little bit easier."

"What about Burton? We've got to make sure the payoff goes down. This is your show, Frank. My men will assist yours if you feel you need them."

Dolci answered quickly. "I brought two from Florida, counting Joe. With Anthony and his two, that gives me a total of five. That should be enough. I told you I'd try to keep you out of this."

He paused briefly, then added. "In light of the situation with Powers and your apparent nervousness, I think we can squeeze this down to the bottom line quickly. We need to question Powers and his friend, Stinson, right after we contact Burton. I'm not ready to talk with Bill Lee, yet. And if it will make you any more comfortable, we'll keep at arm's length until we know how this is all shaking out. No sense in sticking our heads in a noose." He rose from his chair and added, "Let's discuss the details over lunch. By then we should have heard from our people. They probably left the airport a few minutes ago. I've been thinking about those crawfish for two days."

Mancotta grinned and stood. Dolci loved to eat the small lobster-like crustaceans that were caught in Louisiana swamps, rivers, and bayous. The meat in their tails tasted like a cross between a shrimp and a lobster. When boiled in highly seasoned water—much like crab boil—the spicy delicacy tickled the palate.

Good food, Mancotta mused, did wonders for his partner's disposition. It was time for a special meal.

* Thirty-two *

The radio receiver crackled sharply. "Base One, this is Unit Seven."

Bert Teague picked up the small microphone, pressed the transmit button, and said, "Go ahead, Seven."

"Company has arrived and is checking in."

"Any more suspects, Seven?" Teague looked up to see Don Hardin—still dressed in taxi cab driver attire—step through the door, then sit on the couch in the Fairmont Hotel room.

"Affirmative, the same two that were identified at the airport just walked in."

Teague looked at his replacement. "And three already here makes five. Looks like our suspects have a big interest in making sure they know who's staying where. That's perfect."

He picked up the microphone and said, "Seven, this is Base One. Maintain contact, but stay clear as planned. Advise units Eight, Nine, and Eleven to continue surveillance."

"Affirmative, Base One."

Teague leaned back in his chair and smiled. So far, so good, he thought. The taut muscles in his neck reminded him of the past tense days and nights. He had awakened several times with a recurring dream. In it, Dolci and Mancotta failed to pursue the fix and his meticulous preparations went for naught. It was like playing chess: an opponent's moves could never be consistently guessed.

"When do you think they'll make contact?" Hardin asked.

"I don't know, but they've got to do it soon. The more important question is who's going to do the talking. If Dolci steps out of the picture and lets one of his goons take over, then we've got some shaky evidence."

"Even with Lee and Burton as witnesses?" Hardin asked.

"Dolci's lawyers would rip Burton to pieces on the stand.

After that, I don't think Bill Lee would fare much better. What little we've got on tape is open to interpretation. No, we need more, a lot more."

Hardin nodded. "Any ideas on how you can get Mancotta to stick his neck out?"

Teague shook his head. "Not a one. The only way we might be able to smoke him at this point is if we could turn Bobby Nevada around."

"You're still sure that his visit is connected to this, aren't you?"

Teague propped his feet up on the gray-marble coffee table. "Damn right. Watch what happens in his column tomorrow. And if Charlotte wins Saturday, I'll lay you odds he picks them to win the championship."

Hardin nodded. "Makes sense, but I doubt we'll ever be able to prove it. Another thing, I don't think a man in his position would ever cross the line. Too many people would be looking to shut him up permanently. He knows that. Too bad we can't get something on him in Vegas."

Teague heard voices out in the hall; he held up one finger to signal quiet. Both men stood and put on their headsets. They recognized the muffled clicking sounds of a key penetrating the lock on the door in the adjacent room.

"It's beautiful," Jenny said, admiring the soft whites and greens that graced the French antique decor of the elegant Fairmont Hotel room.

"I knew you'd like it," Troy said as he set his briefcase on a side table. "I think it's French Provincial." He turned to the bellboy and started to hand him a two dollar tip.

"No thank you, sir. It's on the house," the bellboy said.

Surprised, but not about to argue, Troy watched curiously as the bellboy left the room. Turning to Jenny, he said, "Looks like we're getting the red carpet treatment. But I've never heard of a bellboy refusing a tip before."

They heard a knock on the door inside their suite which connected the adjoining room. He walked toward it and asked, "Who is it?"

"Bert Teague."

Troy unlocked the door. "We're sure glad to see you." He shook Teague's hand firmly.

"And this must be Mrs. Burton," Teague said, shaking her hand. "Please excuse me for not introducing my other partner. He's in there monitoring our operation. You'll meet him later. Did you notice anyone following you?"

Troy looked at Jenny. She shrugged her shoulders and shook her head. He looked back at Teague. "Neither did I."

"I didn't think you would, but you drew an awful lot of attention," Teague said.

"Your people?" Troy asked.

"Not all of them."

"Then they've already started watching us," Troy said as he sat on the side of the bed. Jenny sat beside him and he sensed her nervousness. Teague's words shocked them both back to reality.

Seeing their concern, Teague said, "Don't worry. We've got everything under control. Since you arrived here this morning, you two haven't been out of our sight. You know the fellow that just refused to accept the tip, the bellboy?"

Jenny nodded.

Teague said, "He's one of our men. That's why he refused your money."

Jenny looked surprised; Troy shook his head. The surreptitious operation was alien to anything they had ever experienced. Troy was impressed that Teague was taking extraordinary measures to make good on his promise to provide extensive protection.

"What happens next?" Troy asked.

"We wait. One of their men is bound to get in touch with you soon." Teague walked toward the door that led to the adjoining room, turned, and added, "You two can relax for awhile. I expect they'll make contact before long."

He started to shut the door, then said, "If you need anything, remember we're right here. Oh, and just so you two won't get embarrassed, I think I should warn you— we've got this room so well bugged we can hear every word that's uttered."

Troy looked at Jenny, smiled flatly, turned back to Teague, and asked, "Cameras, too?"

"No. That would have involved too much redecorating. I don't expect too much discussion will take place here anyway." He shut the door.

Hardin looked up from the radio transmitter. "Everybody's in. Unit Seven said Giannini went to a pay phone."

"Here in the hotel?" Teague asked.

"No, I'm afraid not. He went down the street."

"Damn. Base Two could have picked him up on any of the phones here in the hotel," Teague said. "Maybe we can pick up his end of the conversation with the shotgun mike. Don't bet on it though. Dolci and Mancotta have their men well trained. Who'd they follow?"

"Exactly who you said they would: Collins, Lee, and Burton."

"Giannini went for instructions. No doubt he called a communicator at another pay phone. That's routine for them."

"Are you going to talk to the Coach?" Hardin asked.

"I'm going to buzz him right now. We need to fill him in on where we stand."

"Fairmont Hotel, may I help you?" the switchboard operator answered.

"Has the Charlotte basketball team checked in yet?" Powers asked, standing in a phone booth.

"Yes, sir, they have."

"What room is Troy Burton staying in?" Powers asked.

The operator hesitated. "I'm sorry, sir, we don't give out guest's room numbers. Those were the Coach's orders. I can ring his room if you like, though."

"Please," Powers said as he looked at the shoppers bustling past him. The phone rang.

"Hello."

"Troy, this is Donnie. How's it going?"

"As well as can be expected. When did you folks get in?"

Troy asked.

"Just a few minutes ago. That's a damn long ride."

"Where are you?" Troy asked.

"Some big shopping center on the outskirts of town. It's close to that bridge that goes over the lake."

"That must be Lakeside Shopping Center. Lot's of stores, nightclubs and places to eat all around there, right?" Troy asked.

"Yeah."

"Well, you're right at 'Fat City.' It's Metairie's miniature French Quarter. That's not far from where I was raised. What route did you come in on, anyway?"

"Damned if I know. Russ was driving. We came over that long-ass bridge. He wanted us to see the sights."

Troy laughed. "That long-ass bridge that you're referring to is the causeway. It's almost twenty-four miles long. You traveled way out of your way if you came that way instead of I-10. Where are you planning to stay?"

"Don't know yet. Is everything under control?" Powers asked. Although he was confident that Teague had taken steps to ensure phone security, he had no intention of being specific.

"We're running right on schedule," Troy replied.

"What time is practice?" Powers asked, knowing the team would get their first opportunity to warm up in the Superdome shortly.

"Hold on. Let me get the itinerary from Jenny," Troy said. "Honey, hand me that, would you please. Thanks."

Powers could hear Burton unfolding some paper.

"We're scheduled to practice at four o'clock. It's closed to the public, but I'll make arrangements to get all of you in."

"Thanks. I'll see you then. What's the best way to get into town from here?"

After Troy gave directions to Powers and hung up, he heard a knock on the adjoining door.

"Come in," Troy said. They had purposely left the door unlocked.

Teague entered. "We heard the conversation. Powers has instructions to stick close, but to keep a low profile. Would you come in here for a minute, please. Coach Lee has joined us."

"OK," Troy said, following Teague, asking, "Is that phone safe?"

"As far as we know it is," Teague answered over his shoulder.

Curious, Troy inquired further. "How can you tell?"

"We have electronic devices that can detect a tap within ten miles. Even at that, I'd be careful of what you say."

Teague introduced agent Hardin to Troy. Coach Lee was seated on the couch. Troy looked around the room at the wide array of electronic equipment. He recognized the radio transmitter and tape recorder. He was unfamiliar with the other equipment.

Teague said, "Coach, I just wanted to touch base with you and give you information about our planned surveillance. After that, we'll try to stay out of your hair so you can concentrate on coaching."

"Thank you." Lee puffed calmly on his pipe.

Troy knew why Lee was calm. The ball had been nicely handed off to him. It was all beginning to fit. How else could Lee have any chance at continuing in a public job? Troy was the point man now.

Teague interrupted Troy's thoughts when he addressed Coach Lee. "Our only major worry at this point is Ted Collins. I wish you would allow us to make him aware of what is going on here. It would make things a great deal easier."

"I'm sorry, Bert, but I think we'd be making a serious mistake by telling him. You want us to get to the championship game so those people will stick with their plan, don't you?" Lee asked.

Teague exhaled and nodded. "We've got all three rooms bugged, Coach: yours, the Burtons', and Collins'. I'm glad he's rooming with another player," Teague said, adding, "I doubt the bugs will do much good, though. I hardly think Dolci, let alone Mancotta, will show their faces here."

Lee nodded.

Teague continued, "I don't know whether they'll touch base with you first or Mr. Burton. We'll have to wait and see. We're going to do our best not to let any of you out of our sight. The tricky part is going to be to get Dolci on tape making the offer."

Hardin interrupted, holding up his hand, cocking his head to the side, and listening carefully. Teague stopped talking and walked to the door that connected Troy's room. Jenny nearly bumped into him.

"Someone's on the phone asking for Troy," she said in a low voice.

Turning to Troy, Teague said, "OK, go answer it. If that's them, try to engage in as much conversation as possible. You want to meet with Dolci, but don't press the issue. We don't want to arouse their suspicions."

Troy hurried into the room as Teague slipped on the headset. The tape recorder, rigged to begin automatically recording when the phone rang, had already started. Hardin slipped on his headset. The law required that two witnesses hear any taped conversations in order for the evidence to be admissible. Bill Lee sat forward observing the flurry of activity as Jenny sat beside him.

"Hello."

"Is this Troy Burton?" the caller asked.

"Yes, it is."

"I'm calling for a friend of a friend. He would like to meet with you this evening for dinner."

"I have a lot of friends that have come down for the game. Who is it you're referring to?" Troy asked. He turned and saw Teague, headset draped over his ears, standing at the door. The agent signaled his approval of the question.

There was a pause on the other end of the line and finally an answer. "He said you would remember your last meeting with him after the game in Greensboro."

"Yes, now I remember that was—" Troy stopped in mid-sentence. Teague was shaking his head. Troy understood the meaning and quickly changed his sentence. "That was an interesting evening. What time would your friend like to meet with me?"

"Be in your hotel room after eight o'clock. We'll have a driver come by to pick you and Mrs. Burton up."

Troy looked at Teague. Both of them were surprised. The agent shook his head and pulled a pen and pad out of his coat pocket.

"I'm sorry. My wife has other plans for this evening. Tell your friend she won't be able to join us."

Another pause and the reply came back sternly. "Mr. Burton, I strongly advise you not to disappoint your host. He wishes the pleasure of your wife's company. Don't make the evening unpleasant for him or yourself."

Teague walked close to Troy holding the notepad up. On it he had scribbled the word, "Where?"

Troy nodded. "Where will we be dining?"

"Your host wishes to make it a pleasant surprise. We suggest coat and tie and appropriate attire for your wife."

Staring hard at Teague, Troy could feel perspiration beading on his forehead. No one had anticipated that Dolci would include Jenny. Teague nodded. Troy was not surprised by the agent's decision. They had little choice.

"OK, we'll be waiting. Tell him I'm looking forward to seeing him."

A click, a dial tone, and Troy stood glaring at the phone. The last thing he had wanted to do was involve Jenny. Shaking his head, he hung up.

Teague rubbed his eyes and removed the headset. Walking toward Troy, he said, "I'm sorry, I certainly didn't expect him to invite your wife. We had to accept."

Jenny heard Teague as she walked back into the room. She had a startled look on her face. "Me! You mean he wants me to come with Troy. Where? To do what? No way. If I see the man that had my dog killed, I'll—" Her voice trailed off and she began sobbing.

Troy walked over, sat down, and put his arms around her. Looking at Teague, he said, "She's right. There's no god-damn way. It's too dangerous. I'm not letting her go any-where with that bastard." Out of the corner of his eye, Troy saw Lee and Hardin step into the room.

Teague said slowly, empathetically, "Look, Mr. Burton, I understand exactly how you feel. This is a new development and we need to examine it closely in order to provide some added safeguards. Trust me, please. I'm not going to let you or your wife get hurt."

"Why does he want Jenny? Just answer me that, will you?" Troy asked loudly.

"I can only guess at that," Teague said. "He's a very clever man. By involving your wife, you'll be more likely to submit to his demands. This man is an expert at psychological pressure."

"You mean fear! Let's not use fancy terms for it. Listen, Teague, it's not your wife he's asking out, you know. How the hell would you feel if our positions were reversed?" Troy asked. Face flushed, he stood and began pacing the floor.

Bill Lee spoke softly. "Calm down, Troy. This man is here to help you."

Troy spun around and scowled. "I'm not so sure about that. I told you people before that I didn't think you handled this thing right by letting me walk into the whole damn deal blindfolded."

"There was no other way. We had no guarantees he wasn't setting us up through you. Think about it," Lee said, pausing. "You could have been on his side all along. You've seen how he operates. The s.o.b. plays a hell of a game of chess."

"Well, I don't care to play anymore. Not with my wife's life hanging in the balance."

"Mr. Burton, don't you understand that that would be the worst thing you could possibly do," Teague said. "You can't just throw in the towel and say you've had enough. You're in too deep. The only chance you have is to help us bring Dolci down."

"What about the other guy, his partner, Mancotta? If you don't take care of him, I doubt he'll stand by and watch his friend go to jail. These people play for keeps, don't they? So, what are Jenny and I going to do? Hide under some rock for the rest of our lives?" Troy asked, arms akimbo.

"The U.S. Marshall will see to it that you're guarded under the Protective Services program," Hardin said, add-

ing, "After the trial you'll be given new identities, a place
to live, and money. You'll be well provided for."

"Thanks a bunch, partner. It's not your life we're talking
about changing forever, is it?"

"Now listen to me, Troy," Lee said, raising his voice. "You
act like you're the only one involved here. I've spent close
to three years of my life fighting this thing. Do you think
I've gotten some sort of pleasure out of it?"

Troy stared at Lee and said nothing.

"Well, I damn sure haven't," Lee said, pausing, adding,
"But that's the way it is. Things don't always go our way
and sometimes life's a real bitch. It's animals like Dolci
who prey on our weaknesses, and the only way they can be
stopped is if ordinary people like you and me will stand up
and fight."

"He's right, Troy," Jenny said, wiping her eyes with a
handkerchief. "I can't let you go alone and take a bigger
risk because you're afraid of what might happen to me. I
don't think I could live without you, so whatever happens
might just as well happen to both of us. Besides, we promised
each other we would get even with him, remember?"

Troy knew he was in a box. He had realized that fact
when he began arguing. The temptation to take the offensive
had overpowered him. Nothing frustrated him more than
to be pushed into making a decision. An internal siren went
off in his mind, screaming at the thought of having only
one acceptable choice.

He leaned against the wall and folded his arms. "This is
the most absurd thing I've ever been through in my life.
Here we are discussing strategy on how to put two known
killers behind bars for fixing a college basketball game. And
you know what? We aren't even sure that when this thing
goes to trial we'll be able to get them convicted. So, instead
of them being punished, Jenny and I—and maybe even you
and your wife, Bill—will be sentenced to our own prison.
We'll have to uproot and change our whole style of living—
forced into exile, no contact with our friends or relatives."

Lee shook his head and started to speak, but Troy cut
him off.

"Why?" Troy asked loudly. "That's all I want to know is why? Is it because our whole damn system of justice has become so caught up in trying to protect the rights of the accused it forgot about the victims? Shit! This society has gotten perverted because its libertarian philosophy some- how got sidetracked into believing the criminal should have rights.

"None of this makes an impression until it touches you personally. And until an element like this smacks you right between the eyes, you believe it doesn't really exist. Nothing exists for us until it penetrates up here, right?" Troy said, pointing at his temple.

Hardin nodded.

Troy gave up. He knew when he was licked. "OK," he sighed, "that's the way it's got to be. What do you want us to do?" He sat in a soft, white chair and crossed his legs.

Teague rubbed his chin, then answered. "Mr. Burton, I simply want you to continue to cooperate. I know it's not easy, but let's look at the positive side of this. We'll have one more strong witness in Mrs. Burton. Plus, we may have a better opportunity to eavesdrop on the conversation at dinner tonight. That's something I've been worried about."

"What do you mean?" Troy asked.

"It would be too risky to wire you. I don't think he trusts you enough at this point not to have you searched," said Teague.

Troy interrupted. "I thought those things were so small they were hard to find."

"Not really. The microphone is small, but the transmitter is battery powered. It's about one eighth the size and thickness of a cigarette pack. The wire to the antenna is about two feet long and very thin. But if they search you carefully, they'll find it for sure. We've got a much safer alternative if your wife is with you. There are purses avail- able that have already been wired. The strap has the antenna woven inside. They will transmit almost twice as far as the other unit, and they can pick up just about anything said in the room," said Teague.

"You said 'much safer,' didn't you?"

Teague nodded.

"So, I take it that what you just described could be detected."

"That's true. But unless they tear the purse completely apart with a knife, they won't find it by hand search. I've got to tell you, though, that's not the only way they could uncover it. There are electronic devices—some of them very small—that are capable of detecting a transmitter when it's in operation."

Troy grimaced. "Then, we can't run that risk. Don't you think he'll be taking every precaution?"

Teague rubbed his eyes with both of his hands, then the bridge of his nose and blew air out of his mouth in a long sigh. "We've got two things to consider. As far as we know, he never used such a device when he was dealing with Coach Lee. That's why we were able to get what we did these last few months. Even though it was a lot of double talk, it'll help. Hopefully, he's going to get more specific when he's dealing with you. The real problem is that he hasn't known you as long as he has Coach Lee. So, they may be checking everything."

"Terrific," Troy said sarcastically.

"However, we can avoid detection by having the transmitter turned off," said Teague. "Any check they run is likely to be done in the beginning of your conversation, except if they have one of those constant monitors that I told you about before. One of them is a pen. A light comes on in the top of it if a transmitter is turned on. I'll show you and your wife what to look for. If she sees something that looks like a monitoring device, then she just doesn't turn on the transmitter."

"How does she do that in front of them?" Troy asked.

"The transmitter has an on/off switch built right into the latch that closes the flap. It will only come on when the switch is turned in a certain direction."

"Christ! Now you're expecting my wife to play Mata Hari. Do any cyanide capsules or exploding lighters come along with the purse?" Troy rose from his chair, looked toward the ceiling, and shook his head.

Lee chuckled. "Keep it up, Troy. He'll make sure you get the first one."

Teague ignored the exchange, turned to Jenny, and asked, "Are you sure you want to try this, Mrs. Burton?"

She nodded her head firmly.

"Good. We'll have the purse sent over as soon as possible along with some of the monitoring devices you'll need to recognize. In the meantime, I need to get our people together and plan our protection strategy." Teague stepped back into his room; Hardin followed.

Coach Lee remained for a moment. "You're doing the right thing." He walked back to Teague's room and closed the door behind him.

* Thirty-three *

Lindsey Ellis knocked on Chuck Haigler's hotel room door. When Haigler opened it, Ellis asked, "Ready?" It was time for them to walk over for the team's first Superdome practice session, which was closed to the general public.

"In a minute," Haigler said as he stepped back into his hotel room. "I was just getting some of my notes together. Let me grab my briefcase."

Ellis walked in behind him. Bold colors, flashy metal sculptures, and acres of smoked glass embellished the soaring space-age architecture of the Hyatt Regency. "Nice hotel, eh?"

"Yeah. It sure couldn't be any closer to the 'Dome," Haigler said over his shoulder.

Ellis walked to the window and looked at the Superdome. "That's a hell of an impressive structure."

"You don't realize how big it is until you get this close. Incidentally, if I haven't told you already, you did a super job on this basketball wrap-up." Haigler shoved the twenty-two page handbook that Ellis had prepared into his briefcase.

Ellis reflected on all the work that had gone into its preparation. He had labored diligently on it five days and nights, compiling and writing statistics, past records, and player profiles. Boxes of the handbook lay in a designated press room in the hotel, available like a textbook for journalists to take a quick self-study course in the Hornets' brief history.

"Thanks," Ellis said, flashing a toothy grin. "I never thought I would get finished with it."

Haigler glanced at his watch, then snapped the latches closed on his briefcase. "Let's go."

Riding down the glass-walled elevator, they scanned the events schedule that detailed practice times and press conferences. They turned and looked out every time the elevator stopped to pick up or unload passengers. The long ride down provided a top to bottom perspective of the massive structure that loomed several hundred yards away.

Haigler lowered his voice to a whisper in the crowded elevator. "Tomorrow, practice is open to the public starting at one o'clock. After each team finishes, the coach and a few of the players are supposed to come into the press room for an informal chat. I'm looking forward to hearing from some of the players from UFFM. I wonder how they're going to handle questions about McLaughlin's death."

The elevator stopped at the upper level lobby and they stepped out with most of the other passengers.

As they walked toward the wide concrete walkway that linked the hotel to the Superdome, Ellis said, "I really feel for those guys. You know the whole thing must have been a nightmare."

"It still doesn't make sense to me. There has to be more to it than meets the eye."

Ellis did not comment. He thought about the inherently suspicious nature of reporters. They loved to open closets and check for skeletons. And it never surprised them when bones crashed to the floor helter-skelter.

"Base One, this is Unit Five."

"Go ahead, Five," Teague replied.

"We've got three suspects under surveillance here at the arena."

"Has our party arrived, yet?"

"Negative."

"Where are the suspects stationed, Unit Five, inside or out?" Teague glanced at Hardin.

"One is inside. Two are standing outside at the main entrance."

"How did one of them get inside?"

"We can't find that out without risking our cover, Base One. We assume he had a pass of some sort."

Teague lowered the microphone and said to Hardin, "He must have. They've got security guards on duty; it'd be tough for him to slip past them."

"I think you mentioned in the file that Mancotta owns a private suite there," Hardin said.

"That's right. It probably wasn't too hard for him to come up with a visitor's pass." Teague raised the microphone. "Unit Five, maintain close surveillance. Are units Six and Seven close by?"

"Affirmative."

"OK, Unit Five, since they are maintaining radio silence at present, get a message to them; make sure they stick close to our party when it arrives. Don't let them out of sight."

"Roger, Base One."

Teague replaced the microphone on the radio transmitter. "Why do you suppose Dolci's men are standing by at the arena? The dinner is already on for tonight, and they couldn't have followed Burton, Lee, or Collins there. They just left the hotel five minutes ago."

"They must have known that was where they were headed," Hardin speculated.

"Yes, but that's not what bothers me. There's got to be more to it than that. Why would Dolci want them watched at practice?" Teague asked.

"Maybe he smells a setup," Hardin said.

"I don't see how. We couldn't have been spotted. I'd stake my life on that. No, I'll bet you his men are fishing for something. We can't very well ask them, though, can we?" Teague stood and walked to the bathroom.

"Tell Anthony not to let them out of his sight once he finds them," Dolci said.

Buona turned and left the room. Dolci sat back in a leather reclining chair and relit his cigar.

Mancotta glared at Dolci. "I hate the smell of those cigars. After you leave, I can smell those damn things for days."

Raising his thick, black eyebrows, Dolci swiveled in the chair. He gazed out of the window, focusing on a small fishing boat plying Lake Pontchartrain's choppy waters.

The growing discord between his partner and himself had worsened. Mancotta seemed unsettled, nervous, and unwilling to make any decisions as to how they were to proceed. Dolci didn't like the aloofness.

"What if they don't find Powers? What do you intend to do?" Mancotta asked.

"They'll find him. Wait and see. He'll be at that practice. I can feel it in my gut."

"I'm going to exercise. The run should do me good," Mancotta said. "By then maybe we'll know if your stomach knows more than your head." He turned and left the room.

Dolci puffed a thick cloud of smoke toward the window. He had two problems now. Mancotta's growing distrust and criticism indicated a need for action. Perhaps, he thought, the time for the partnership to be dissolved was at hand. It was a problem he had hoped he would never have to face. Dissolution would be a nasty affair.

"Park in that lot," Stinson directed.

Powers stopped the motor home abruptly and Stinson's beer tipped over on the console.

Stinson grabbed the beer can after it belched half of its foamy contents on the floor. "What are you trying to do, kill us?"

"In there?" Powers said, pointing at the tiered Superdome parking structure. "What are you planning to do with the top half? There's not enough clearance, asshole."

"So, we'll make this a convertible. We'll have the only one in the neighborhood." Stinson laughed and downed the remaining half of his beer in one gulp.

Powers continued driving. "What time is it?"

"Four fifteen," Shelly Stinson answered from the back.

"If you girls hadn't taken off shopping, we'd have been on time. They started practice fifteen minutes ago," Powers said.

"What's so important about a practice?" Linda Powell asked.

"It's not just a practice. It's their first practice in the

Superdome, and I need to talk to Troy about something," Powers said.

"Whoa! Park there." Stinson pointed to his right.

"Where?"

"There, in that liquor store parking lot."

"Are you crazy? They'll tow it away," Powers said.

"Would you have your best customer's motor home towed away?" Stinson swiveled in his captain's chair and grinned.

Powers leaned on the steering wheel and looked at him. "Go in and ask them. You'd better put on your shades. Your eyes look like road maps."

Stinson donned mirrored sunglasses and stepped out.

"Donnie, we must be five blocks away. Why didn't you park in that big open lot that we passed or some of those other parking lots? There was plenty of space," Linda said.

"Did you see what it cost for just one hour? You know they're not going to charge us for just one space, probably more like two or three. When we've got more time to look, and I know a little bit more about where I'm going, we'll find a better spot," Powers said.

Stinson walked out of the liquor store smiling broadly and carrying two large brown bags. Opening the motor home door, he almost dropped one of them. "Whoops! Here, take these."

"What in the hell did you buy?" Powers said.

"Two half-gallons of Crown Royal and a parking place. Back that son of a bitch in here and pull in tight into that corner."

"No way. This is your damn chariot. If anybody's going to do any backing up, it's going to be you," Powers said as he slipped out of the driver's seat.

"No problem. I'll show you how to handle this mother." Stinson plopped behind the wheel.

"I'm not watching," Shelly said. She covered her eyes with a pillow.

Stinson pulled past the entrance, waited for traffic to clear, and then began backing briskly.

Powers weaved past Shelly and Linda, making his way

to the back of the vehicle. He began storing the liquor in a bin under the bed. Judging by the supply they had accumulated, he estimated they had enough to keep the entire two-thousand strong Hornet contingent happy for an evening.

Suddenly, the motor home crunched to a halt and Powers was thrown to the floor, liquor bottles clanking together. None broke; they were jammed together too tightly.

"What happened?" Powers asked picking himself up off the floor.

"That damn wall ran into us," Stinson replied, adding, "Somebody get out and get its license number before it leaves the scene."

Looking out of the curtained back window, Powers said, "You pulled it in tight all right. You know that ladder you had on the back of this thing? You won't be climbing up on the roof anymore."

Stinson scratched his beard. "I've always been scared of heights. Now, I won't be tempted to climb up there. Toss me another beer. It's hot and we've got a long walk."

At four forty-five they walked into the main entrance of the Superdome. After giving their names to a security guard, they were allowed to pass through the gate. Each was required to wear a royal blue and white visitor's pass. Walking onto the floor of the arena through a tunneled entrance, they saw the players, scattered members of the official party, a few friends, and arena employees. It was like stepping inside a gigantic saucer-like space ship, nearly void of passengers and crew.

Powers spotted Troy Burton. "You guys grab a seat. I'll be back in a minute." He threaded his way through several empty rows.

"Sorry I'm late, Troy. We couldn't find our wives. They took off and went shopping while I was talking to you on the phone," Powers said, sitting next to Burton in the lower third of the twenty-five row segment of the movable stands.

Powers had once read an article on the Superdome's construction in an airline magazine. He remembered how the Superdome is transformed into a huge arena for basketball games.

Unique in design, the center segment of the east side
Plaza level football stands travel 248 feet across the field.
Powered by a cable drive system, the stands move at nearly
five feet per minute in ten-inch deep and fifteen-inch wide
trenches on special steel roller units to form the east side
of the arena configuration.

Powers turned his attention to the court, where the
players practiced at a relaxed, easygoing pace, taking shots
from all angles. The hollow sound of bouncing basketballs
striking the sectioned, portable court failed to reverberate,
dampened by superior acoustics.

Powers glanced quickly over his shoulder at a man seated
several rows up and to the side of them. "Who's that?"

"Take a guess," Burton said softly.

"Goon squad?"

"I think so," Burton answered. "I'm not worried. There
are plenty of friends in the building."

Under his breath, Powers said, "He's not exactly making
an attempt to stay in the shadows. What's in the works?"

"After you phoned, one of them asked us out to dinner.
Said he was calling for a 'friend of a friend.'"

"Wait a minute. You said 'us.' Not Jenny?"

"I'm afraid so."

Powers thought for a minute and shook his head. "Is she
going?"

Burton nodded.

"Damn. Since that's already set up, I wonder why they're
keeping such a close eye on you? Where's Jenny?" asked
Powers.

"Over there." Burton pointed toward the fixed seating
across the floor: tiered, multi-colored, plastic back seats
that rose toward the top, broken at several levels by walkways
that encircled the dome. "She's talking with Helen and
Julia."

Powers spotted her. "How's she feel about going
tonight?"

"It's not how she feels that I'm worried about. It's how I
feel. I don't like it one damn bit, but we really haven't got

a lot of choice."

"I wish there was something I could do to help. My orders are to stand by, but essentially stay in the background. They're trying to put pressure on you by dragging Jenny into it."

"I know. They're doing a pretty good job of it, too. Let's hope Teague knows what the hell he's doing."

They looked up when Bill Lee blew his whistle and casually walked toward center court. "OK, let's bring it in," Lee said loudly.

The players jogged in and huddled around Lee, Evans, and Ward. Burton and Powers strained to hear Lee's instructions, but his words were lost in the distance between them. When the team huddle broke and the players began walking toward the locker rooms, Burton and Powers stood.

"Where are you planning to eat tonight?" Burton asked as they walked down the stands to the floor. Both of them noticed the man following Burton had gotten closer as they began to depart.

"I don't know, yet. You confused me with all those names you gave me. They all sound good. I'll take your advice and order seafood." Powers spoke louder purposely. "I'm sorry you can't make it tonight. But I know how it is: you've got to take care of those muckety-mucks that contribute the big dollars. Your poor friends get shoved aside."

Burton role-played with him. "You know damn well that's not true. It's just that these foundation members asked me out first. Let's plan on getting together tomorrow night, OK?"

"Are you sure you won't have to be kissing somebody else's ass?" Powers asked.

"Promise." Burton held up his right hand, pledging.

"All right, but I'm going to hold you to it." He put his arm around Burton's shoulders.

Powers rejoined his group as Burton found Jenny. The three couples met briefly and exchanged pleasantries. Powers watched Dolci's man walk slowly toward the exit and disappear into the tunnel.

* Thirty-four *

"Suspects are leaving the arena, Base One. Please advise if you require us to maintain surveillance."

"Has our party left, Unit Seven?"

"Negative."

Teague turned to Hardin. "I wonder why they are breaking off contact now? That doesn't make much sense."

Hardin shrugged.

Teague paused, then pressed the microphone button. "Unit Five, do not maintain surveillance. Stay with the party."

"Affirmative, Base One."

Replacing the microphone, Teague said, "We can't take the risk of being spotted following Dolci's goons. That could blow the whole thing."

"What about tonight?" Hardin asked.

Teague stood and walked to the window. "With the transmitter and the homing signal in Mrs. Burton's purse, we won't have to stay right on top of them. Every team's available. It'll be tough for them to spot a tail when we change faces and cars that often."

"Maybe we'll get lucky and Mancotta will come out of hiding," Hardin said.

"I don't think there is much chance of that. What do they gain by bringing him into the picture? Absolutely nothing. No, I think he'll stay in the background." Teague turned from the window and sat down. "Our only clear shot at him is if we can prove to Bobby Nevada that we know what his visit was all about. Which reminds me, we haven't heard from Unit Twelve."

Teague picked up the microphone. "Unit Twelve, this is Base One." A long pause, then he repeated his attempt to make contact.

"Hold, please Base One. We have a conversation in progress."

Teague looked at Hardin and raised his eyebrows. "About all I expected to get out of that is a lot of circumstantial garbage. But Nevada might just slip up. Bugging his room might pay off."

In Nevada's suite at the Hyatt Regency, Pete Bordelon was mixing another drink. "They'll find it. If they don't, you've got a brand new wardrobe."

"If they don't, then there goes your birthday present," Nevada said.

Bordelon sipped on a scotch and soda. "Put in a claim for it."

"I don't think you understand. It's not the kind of gift an insurance company pays off on."

"Oh, I see. Well, don't give up on it, yet. Hell, you had a name tag on your bag, didn't you?" Bordelon asked.

"Of course, but that doesn't mean a damn thing. The way they handle baggage, it could have been torn off," said Nevada.

"Did you have it locked?" Bordelon asked.

"Certainly. Listen, Pete, I've got to go make a few phone calls. Why don't you make yourself at home, and I'll be back in an hour. We can go grab a bite to eat then."

"Why don't you call from here?"

Nevada walked to the door and said over his shoulder, "Hotel accounting departments maintain detailed phone records, and these aren't the kind of numbers I would ever care to be associated with."

"Take your time. I'll be good and hungry when you get back. I thought we'd go to K-Paul's for dinner."

Nevada shut the door.

Powers squatted to watch Stinson on his back underneath the motor home. They had barely made it into the hotel parking lot after noticing smoke seeping through the engine cover located inside the motor home between the captain's chairs. "The manager said it would be all right if we parked here. I think he realized we didn't have much choice. Did you figure out what happened?"

"The air conditioning fan belt broke and tore through the transmission fluid line. It's a good thing we stopped when we did."

"That's just great. Who do we call to get it fixed?" Powers asked.

Stinson squirmed out from under the vehicle and saw the towering Hyatt Regency framed by clear blue sky. "It's too late to get anybody over here today. Besides, what's the hurry? As long as it's broken, we can stay here. We couldn't have found a better parking spot."

"That leaves us without any wheels," Powers said.

Stinson wiped grease off his hands with a towel. "Let's rent a car."

"You sure like to spend money. Look, I've got a better idea. I know a couple of people here. Maybe, I can get them to loan us one."

"You never told me you had friends here."

Powers put his first finger to his lips and said, "Be quiet—the girls will hear you. My friends are females. I don't think Linda would appreciate their generosity."

Stinson laughed. "You dog, you."

Powers was lying, but he could not think of a better story. He planned to get the DEA or the FBI to spring for a car. Even if he had been shuffled to the back of the deck, the least they could do would be to provide transportation. What if there was some sort of emergency and they needed him?

Linda Powers stuck her head out of the door. "Have you got it fixed, yet?"

Powers shook his head. "No. We'll have to stay here for tonight. We're going to try to round up a car, maybe rent one. There's a mall connected to the hotel. Why don't you and Shelly go shopping while we check around."

"OK. Where do you want to meet us?" Linda asked.

"We'll meet you back here in one hour," Powers replied.

They walked inside the hotel ground floor together. Linda and Shelly separated from their husbands as they rode the escalator to the third floor of the twenty-two-story-tall, indoor garden lobby. The area was lavishly appointed with plants, fountains, metal sculptures, and an open-air lounge.

Powers and Stinson walked toward the pay phones in the lower lobby.

"Excuse me, Mr. Powers."

Powers turned to see three men. A mental alarm sounded in Powers' head. He recognized one of the men to be the same one who had been seated behind Burton at the Superdome. "Yes, what can I do for you?" Powers asked.

"Is this Mr. Stinson?"

Powers nodded.

"Good. A friend of mine would like to meet with both of you."

"About what?" Powers asked.

"You've been making some inquiries in Charlotte about expanding a little business you're in. We're here to help you meet the man that can make it all possible."

"I haven't made any inquiries. Besides, the Hornets' Nest is as big as it's ever going to be."

"Mr. Stinson made the inquiries. We're not referring to the restaurant business. It's more like having your own pharmacy."

Stinson looked at Powers uneasily. Powers knew what his friend must be thinking. New Orleans was the last place he expected to make contact with a heavyweight drug supplier who operated in North Carolina. Stinson had not liked the idea from the beginning and had argued with Powers that getting involved in smuggling could get them arrested or killed. Now he was totally in the dark and equally surprised that his efforts had come to fruition.

Powers wanted to make the contact. It would be his first major breakthrough as an undercover agent and would provide a two-pronged approach to the DOLMAN Project. But his mind raced; he sensed that the timing of this meeting was more than coincidental.

He decided to stall. "Look, we're interested in meeting your friend, but our wives are shopping up there in that plaza. We're supposed to meet them in a few minutes. We have another problem, too. Our motor home has broken down, and we need to arrange for it to be fixed."

The man smiled. "Take us to it. Write your wife a note and tell her you've got a mechanic on his way to fix it. I'll contact somebody who will repair it as a favor to my friend."

"I appreciate that, but we had plans for dinner," Powers said.

"I'm sure you won't mind changing them to keep from inconveniencing my friend." The man reached inside his coat pocket for his wallet. Removing four fifty dollar bills, he said, "Leave this with a note to your wives. Tell them to enjoy shopping some more and to have dinner at the top of this hotel in the Vendome. It has a beautiful view of the city."

Powers did not like the proposal at all. Whoever this guy was, along with the other two goons, it spelled trouble. "Listen, we really appreciate your hospitality, but let's make it tomorrow. If we leave our wives with just a note and some money, they're not going to understand."

The man opened his coat wide enough to reveal his shoulder-holstered pistol, leaving little doubt he would use force—even in the crowded ground-floor lobby—if necessary. "I want you to understand that my friend gets very upset when someone refuses to meet with him on his terms. You would be making a serious mistake to refuse his invitation."

Stinson's eyes widened.

Despite the inherent dangers, Powers knew he would have to risk going with them. Failing to do so would be a dead giveaway, and the entire project would go up in smoke. "OK, let's go write that note. We want to do business, and if it has to be now, then that's the way it's going to be. Your friend is the man, so he calls the shots."

They walked to the motor home and Powers wrote a note. "Dear Linda and Shelly: Have gone to pick up a car. We called a mechanic to come check on repairs. Here is some money for you to go shopping with. Don't forget to buy Dee a souvenir. If we aren't back in an hour, go eat in the hotel.

Love you both, Donnie and Russ."

The man picked it up and read it. "Fine. Let's go."

"I don't care what it takes or how many people you shake up at the airlines. Find out what flight Nevada came in on," Teague said, pausing. "Get the supervisor of baggage services to put a hold on that bag. Make sure they don't call Nevada when they find it. It's been lost long enough to have been entered into the EASY TRAC computer system. It could pop up before we have a chance to examine the contents."

"Right," Hardin said, walking toward the door.

Teague stopped him by adding, "Be sure you make it clear to the supervisor that we don't want that bag opened by anyone other than a special agent. Let's hope they find the damn thing before it gets opened for content identification match up."

"Sounds like you've been through this before," said Hardin.

"Several times. They have a very sophisticated system for locating bags and identifying who the owner is. I'll bet you'll find that Nevada not only changed planes in Dallas/Ft. Worth, but also connected to a different airline. That's where a foul-up usually happens."

Hardin nodded and shut the door.

Teague picked up the microphone. "Unit Five, this is Base One."

"Go ahead, Base One."

"My other agent had to leave. Join me here for backup."

"Be there in ten minutes."

Teague replaced the microphone, stood, and stretched. The break he had been looking for quickened his pulse. The taped conversation between Nevada and Bordelon had stimulated speculation. What was in the suitcase that Nevada was worrying over?

The "birthday present" to Bordelon was something that an insurance company would not pay off on. Narcotics, Teague reasoned. That had to be it. If it was, he'd have the ammunition he was looking for.

* Thirty-five *

Greg Garner, one of two FBI agents in Unit Eleven, was parked in a van packed with electronic gear two and a half blocks from Mancotta's lakefront home. Parked in the driveway of a home whose owner was on vacation, the van was unobtrusive. His partner was asleep. Soon it would be his turn to continue surveillance.

Though the day had gone slowly, it hadn't been entirely uneventful. Earlier, he had witnessed Bobby Nevada's visit to Mancotta's home and had videotaped him entering and leaving the premises. Plans to wire Mancotta's residence had been vetoed by Teague for fear that one of Mancotta's men might electronically sweep the home.

Garner looked at his watch: 6:47 p.m. When he looked up, he saw a truck backing into Mancotta's driveway. He began videotaping. The truck was marked "Cresci Brothers Catering Service."

The mob bosses were apparently planning a large dinner party. When the truck disappeared into the garage, Garner stopped filming. He made an entry in the day log.

Seated in the back of the catering truck, Dolci looked at Buona. He called up front to the driver as it left Mancotta's home. "Make a few turns. Be damn sure we're not being followed to the airport."

"Yes, sir." Mancotta's driver turned off of Lake Shore Drive and wound through several back streets.

"You said your sweep was clean?"

Buona nodded.

"I think Francesco is worrying needlessly." Dolci looked at his watch. "I wonder if he would have thought of sending the plane to another airport? What time did you tell Anthony we would meet him?"

"Seven fifteen."

Dolci smiled. "When you talked to Mark, did you ask him to rig the P.S.E.?"

"Yes, sir."

Dolci was satisfied with his plan. The weather looked perfect. His plane's flight from Baton Rouge to New Orleans wasn't going to take his pilot more than fifteen minutes as long as he didn't get caught in a traffic pattern. He was glad he'd sent the plane to the Baton Rouge airport. It had given him an extra measure of security.

He looked at his watch. He wasn't concerned about how long the plane would be on the ground in New Orleans, though it would likely be less than twenty minutes. He just didn't want a census taken. But if anybody were counting, they'd see five passengers, a pilot and a copilot board. Plus a little food.

He felt alive again. He loved interrogations. He looked up front as the driver turned left into Lakefront Airport, a private and charter plane haven with three runways. The longest runway extended north like a tiny peninsula on Lake Pontchartrain.

The driver closed the curtain that divided the front compartment of the van. When he stopped at a gate, Dolci heard him explain to airport security that he was delivering food to N5857W: the Jet Commander that had just landed.

The driver then drove to the southwest corner of the airport. The sleek, white aircraft, with a wide, red, accent stripe extending the length of the fuselage, was parked facing south. He backed directly to the boarding hatch on the port side. The tan leather and suede-padded door had already been opened by the copilot.

As daylight faded, Dolci and Buona boarded directly from the rear of the truck onto the aircraft. If the plane was being observed from the tower, no one would realize that two people, not food, were delivered.

Three minutes after the catering truck pulled away, a limousine took its place at the forward section of the plane. Inside the plane, Dolci parted the port window curtains and peeked out.

Giannini and his two men hustled Powers and Stinson

aboard under concealed gun point. The hatch was closed immediately and secured. The pilot and copilot started the twin jet engines in sequence and wordlessly completed their pre-flight check.

Seated next to Stinson, Donnie Powers leaned back uneasily in plush leather seats in the aft section. The man who had "invited them" and Dolci sat in seats directly facing them. Two other men, and a man Powers recognized from mug shots as Joe Buona, Dolci's bodyguard, relaxed on the divan that ran the length of the starboard side nearest the cockpit.

The aircraft was well-appointed with a full galley, dark-stained tables that folded flat against the bulkheads between the facing seats, two telephones, deep-pile brown carpet, and autumn-colored patterned curtains.

As a DEA agent, Powers knew a lot about Dolci's private jet. They had long suspected that it was used occasionally to transport cocaine once it arrived in the United States. But they'd never been able to gather enough evidence to support that theory.

The mob boss's private jet was impressive. Technical equipment included two instrument-control flight computers, two flight directors capable of bringing the aircraft to a hands-off touchdown, two VORs and one ADF for navigation, and three 720-channel transceivers for communication. Superbly maintained, the million-dollar Jet Commander looked as if it had just come off the North American Rockwell assembly line. But that was impossible, Powers reflected, since the company had long ago sold its patents for the plane to Israeli Aircraft. The design was currently being marketed as the Israel Westwind 1124 with fan jets.

No one spoke, and Powers hid the fact that he recognized Dolci and Buona from photos he had studied. The pilot requested clearance for takeoff. "Lakefront Tower, this is 5857-Whiskey requesting clearance for a VFR departure southbound."

"Roger, 57-Whiskey, you're cleared for takeoff on Runway

36. After departure, maintain runway heading. Contact New Orleans on one-two-six-point-five."

As the high pitched whine of the twin, tail-mounted, 2,850-pound thrust, turbojet engines increased, Powers could feel the plane begin to taxi. He reached up to part the curtains.

"Keep the curtains closed. We'll open them as soon as we're in the air," Dolci said.

"Would you mind telling us where we are going?" Powers asked.

"Some nighttime sightseeing over the Gulf of Mexico to talk over some business. Do you enjoy flying?" Dolci asked, looking to either man for an answer.

"Only when we're in a plane," Stinson replied.

Dolci smiled. As the jets powered up for takeoff, the loud increase in engine noise suppressed further conversation. Powers felt the quick acceleration and was pressed into his seat.

Dolci's pilot calmly eased back on the yoke. The normal rolling and bumping sensations ceased when the aircraft lifted off two-thirds of the way down the 5,889 foot runway at 132 knots. He banked slowly and turned south as his copilot "squawked" 1200 on his transponder to indicate to radar control that they would be flying VFR below 18,000 feet. No flight plan had been filed. Clear skies permitted them to fly visually instead of IFR. He climbed to 16,500 feet and leveled out at a cruising speed of approximately 400 knots.

Dolci opened the curtains on the windows. "Beautiful view, eh?"

Powers looked out briefly. Seeing the darkening sky, he shrugged his shoulders. "Do you mind if I ask who you are?"

"Not at all. My name is Frank Dolci. I understand that you want to increase your business substantially and have been making inquiries about how to go about it. I always like to meet the people who want to join my organization."

Powers pointed at the man holding a pistol. "Do you always greet your guests like this?"

"Only when I have doubts."

"About what?"

"Loyalty."

"What's he talking about? I've never met this man before in my life. Have you?" Stinson asked.

Powers shook his head. "You must be confusing us with two other guys. How could you be questioning loyalty? We've never seen or heard of you before in our lives, much less worked for you."

"I'm well aware of that. This is an interview. I decide whether or not you're capable business partners. We want people we can depend on. In this type of business, trust is a very important thing."

Powers did not like the direction the conversation was moving in. Dolci obviously suspected something was amiss. "Who told you we were interested in doing business?"

"One of my coordinators mentioned you were looking for about fifty pounds of high-grade Colombian a week. True or false?" Dolci asked.

Powers and Stinson exchanged glances. "I'm the one who made the inquiry," Stinson said.

"True, but I was given the impression that you two worked together." Dolci offered both men cigars from his coat pocket. Stinson took one. "Was I misinformed?"

Powers declined the offer of a cigar with the wave of his hand. "No, you weren't misinformed. Russ and I work together. I felt we were capable of handling more business."

A mental hypothesis flashed through Powers' mind. The whole meeting was illogical. Why would Dolci risk exposing himself or the organization? Could it be that Dolci had discovered that he was a narc, or was he just suspicious? More importantly, why had he chosen to address the problem here and now? Maybe Dolci was somehow aware of his involvement with Burton and Lee. If that were true, Powers knew he would never leave the plane alive.

"I'm always happy to expand my operations with capable people," Dolci said. "But in my position, I like to know who I'm dealing with from top to bottom. As you can well imagine, there are a lot of government agencies that would love to shut my business down. It's amazing how much time and effort they put in. Are you a narc, Mr. Stinson?"

"Me? No way. That's a dangerous way to make a living."

Dolci looked directly into Powers' eyes. "Are you a narc?"

Powers knew better than to look away first. Staring directly at Dolci, he said, "Of course not."

Dolci nodded slowly and puffed on his cigar. "And who do you plan to sell these drugs to?"

"Friends, other small time dealers that handle three to five pounds a week when they can get it," Powers said.

"Who's their contact now?" Dolci asked.

The foul smelling smoke from the cigars made Powers nauseous. "Different people. That's the problem. They can't depend on a regular supplier. We wanted to give them a source they could rely on."

"Would any of those people happen to be on the campus of the University of Charlotte?" Dolci asked.

"Certainly. You know as well as I do that students use drugs pretty heavily."

"How about the basketball team? Do you supply any players drugs?" Dolci asked.

Powers thought quickly. It would be better for Dolci to believe that his involvement with Lee and Burton—if suspected—was drug-related. "Yes, a few of them do dope. In fact, some of the members of the staff smoke occasionally. I take care of them, too. So, what's the big deal? A better question is who hasn't tried the stuff these days?"

The mob boss chewed on his cigar. "I'm curious. Does the coach use drugs?"

Powers was sure of one thing now: Dolci was obviously aware that Powers had some type of personal relationship with the coach. That put him in a double bind. Dolci had known Bill Lee for nearly three years and probably knew the answer to his question before he asked it. Lee had no drug habit whatsoever. At the same time, why would Lee associate with Powers for any reason other than the fact that he was a big fan? Powers conjured a more plausible answer.

Powers leaned forward slightly. "No, as far as I know Coach Lee doesn't smoke, but he checks with me every once in a while to see if I know what players are doing what. It can damn sure affect their play."

"And do you give him the information he's looking for?" Dolci asked.

Powers stiffened. "Listen, what the hell has this got to do with our doing business? I thought we came up here to talk about establishing a relationship, not gossip about who's doing what."

Dolci's face reddened. He tensed momentarily, then seemed to force himself to relax. "I have my reasons. I'm in New Orleans to watch the Final Four. Information on what the players and coaches' drug habits are can be very useful. I like to make a bet here and there, and I'm not real fond of losing on a bunch of junkies."

Powers thought Dolci possibly believed his story.

"I've got to talk to the pilot." Dolci rose from his seat. Even though he was short, he was still unable to stand up straight in the low-ceiling aircraft. He stepped past the outstretched legs of Buona. As he slid past him, Buona moved from the sofa to Dolci's empty seat. He folded his arms and stared at Powers. The two other men slid down the sofa to allow Dolci legroom to stand at the cockpit entrance.

Addressing the copilot, Dolci said, "Turn up the music. I don't want them to overhear our conversation. I've got enough to make a decision. Did you get it on tape?"

"Yes, sir, every word of it," the copilot said, pointing at the recorder.

"Good. Rewind and run it in the P.S.E. It's time we evaluated their answers," Dolci said, peering down at the square briefcase.

The copilot picked up the black leather case that encased the Psychological Stress Evaluator, more commonly known as a voice-stress analyzer. He placed the tape inside and began replaying it. The machine produced a paper tape that the copilot started analyzing. Dolci knew that the results were not considered to be as reliable as the polygraph, but as far as he was concerned, the P.S.E. produced the final verdict.

Teague recognized the man standing at the door as Harold Ofstrum, head of the DEA in New Orleans. "Come in. What's up?"

Ofstrum stepped in and Teague shut the door behind him. "We have reason to believe that our Charlotte undercover man, Donnie Powers, is in some sort of trouble."

Teague pulled a chair up, and the two other agents who had joined him over an hour ago did the same. Ofstrum sat on the sofa.

"What sort of trouble? He's not supposed to be working on this project now. He was simply supposed to be a spectator," Teague said, sitting.

"I know that, but his wife called. She's very upset."

"Give me the details."

Ofstrum hammered out the sequence of events. Teague listened intently, mulling over the possibilities simultaneously.

Powers had a standard code word worked out with his wife. He had written her a note referencing "Dee," a name which he vowed never to use in any messages or conversations with her unless he was in trouble. She had the number of the "cool phone" at the Charlotte DEA office. She called them and they contacted Ofstrum immediately. Knowing Teague had a strike force working on this project, Ofstrum responded in person. When Ofstrum finished, Teague looked as if a two-ton weight had been dropped on his shoulders.

Rubbing his eyes, Teague said, "So, that's all she knows. She has no idea where they went or who, if anybody, they might have been with."

Ofstrum nodded. "You think there is a connection?"

"You're goddamned right I do. Now I know why Dolci's men were at the arena. They were trying to find Powers and Stinson. They must know something or they are fishing for answers." Teague slapped his hand on the table and stood up. "How could I be so damn stupid to have believed that Powers couldn't have been discovered?"

He walked over to the transceiver, thinking through his response to the new development. Picking up the microphone, he broadcast instructions to all units to begin an intensive search for Powers and Stinson.

* Thirty-six *

Dolci stared at the P.S.E. paper tape, glanced at his pilot, arched one eyebrow, and said, "Start a slow descent after we serve the drinks. How far out over the Gulf are we? Are we past the oil rigs?"

"Over two hundred miles, sir. We're not close to any rigs," the pilot said, exchanging glances with his copilot.

Dolci eased back in the cabin and said, "Gentlemen, I don't know about you, but I would like to have a drink. What's your pleasure?"

"Have you got any beer?" Stinson asked.

"Did you bring any beer aboard?" Dolci asked Buona, motioning for him to move out of his seat and back to his original position on the sofa behind Dolci. Having the maximum number of passengers on board made movement seem like juxtaposing sardines in an unopened can.

"No, sir." Buona bent his large frame to squeeze past Dolci.

Dolci plopped into his seat and addressed both men. "Joe makes excellent margaritas. That's what I'm having. Why don't you join me and we'll get down to business?"

Powers and Stinson nodded and glanced at Giannini, who was still holding the pistol.

"Tony, you can put that gun up," Dolci said.

Giannini smiled as he holstered his pistol and buttoned his coat. "If the boss thinks you're OK, then so do I. No hard feelings." He shook both men's hands firmly.

While Buona sat on the edge of the sofa, he raised the hinged, rosewood bar cover to a vertical position against the back of Giannini's seat. He pulled a disappearing tray out from inside the bar until it locked in place and lay in a flat horizontal position. Eight large holes had been bored into it to keep glasses from sliding while the drinks were being prepared.

* * *

Powers' view was blocked almost completely by Giannini's and Dolci's high-backed seats. Looking between them, he could only see two of the seven drinks being prepared. Buona deftly rubbed a lemon rind around the rims of the glasses and rolled the moist edges lightly in a cup of salt. Watching the procedure suspiciously, Powers was relieved to see him crack the seals on a bottle of tequila and a bottle of Margarita mixer.

"Here you are, gentlemen," Buona said as he passed the first two drinks—the ones Powers observed being prepared—to Dolci, who in turn handed them to Powers and Stinson.

When everyone had been served, Dolci raised his glass and proposed a toast. "To our new business partners!"

Powers was a bit hesitant at first; he sipped lightly. Taste and odor were normal for the somewhat bitter, salty, alcoholic beverage. He passed his caution off to paranoid behavior.

"Tell you what I'm going to do," Dolci said, lowering his glass as Giannini relit his cigar for him. "Thanks, Anthony. I'm going to see to it that you get your fifty pounds a week and if you handle it right, I'll move you up the ladder. How about coke? That's where the big money is, you know." He puffed a large cloud of smoke in their direction.

Powers sipped his margarita as Stinson began a long-winded answer to the question in a confident, matter-of-fact tone. In spite of Dolci's friendly demeanor, Powers still had trouble understanding why the mob boss was bothering to personally handle two small-time drug dealers far below him in the natural chain of command. Compared to the tons he was shipping, fifty pounds was minuscule.

Maybe he was looking for correlating information on the basketball team. If the DOLMAN Project failed to gather sufficient evidence for conviction, then this new twist in events would be a lucky break, eventually ensuring a strong case for the prosecution. Powers could not arrest him for talking about making a deal, but he could gather solid evidence over a period of time. Deep in thought, he barely heard Stinson's reply as he finished nearly all of his drink.

Looking at Dolci, then at his friend, Powers felt a wave of nausea and dizziness. Stinson's face flushed; he breathed rapidly as he attempted to speak. With the rapid onset of asphyxia, Powers' pulse quickened; his heart began to pound. Although his senses were deteriorating rapidly and the cigar smoke confused his olfactory system, he detected the faint odor of bitter almonds. Poisoned, he thought, as he looked at Stinson.

His vision blurred momentarily. He dropped his glass and watched his friend slump forward, frothing at the corners of his mouth and twitching. The helpless thought that he was powerless to save himself gripped him at first in terror, then loosened with resignation. He was dying. Intuitive acceptance of that fact smothered all but one thought—his love for his wife, Linda.

Dolci smiled as he watched both men convulsing. His studied method was unique, and he had taken time long ago to develop his method of killing in-flight interrogation victims. He remembered what the book said about cyanide: it poisons its victim by starving the cytochrome oxidase system for oxygen utilization in cells. Having received six times the minimum lethal dose, Powers and Stinson died swiftly, albeit painfully.

Giannini turned his head after both men began gasping for air and convulsing. Dolci found his hired gunman's response ironic. The sight of blood never bothered Giannini, but the frothy sputum oozing from the victim's mouths and accompanying harsh gagging sounds apparently made him ill. He leaned behind Dolci's seat, quickly removed the upholstered cover, and vomited in the trash can.

Dolci laughed, never taking his eyes off the jerking bodies that had pitched forward, held only by loosened seat belts. "What's the matter? You've got no stomach for poison, eh?" He then turned and read the auxiliary altimeter on the small closet wall across from the sofa: sixty-five hundred feet. "Let's do it gentlemen. Make sure you pick up anything that's loose."

Hearing those instructions, the pilot moved the engine pressurization selector switch to the ram position. A loud rush of air ensued and the passengers felt their ears pop as they continued to store articles that might be swept out of the plane.

As the cabin depressurized, the pilot glanced back in the cabin. Buona removed all items from the bodies that might be blown into the jets by the sheer force of the wind: rings, watches, pocket change, wallets, shoes, and a gold neck chain from Russ Stinson. He placed everything in a weighted metal box.

The pilot retarded the engines to idle and extended the speed brakes, causing the aircraft to vibrate. The plane pitched up slightly, noticeable only to the pilots. When they had decelerated to approximately 160 knots, flap extension range, the speed brakes were retracted. The pilots began extending the flaps after trimming the Jet Commander in a nose-down attitude. They began to bring the angle-of-attack indicator into their scan—the pattern in which pilots observe the instruments while controlling the aircraft. The plane began to approach the stall speed of 100 knots.

Dolci watched Buona loosen Powers' and Stinson's seat belts. The bodies slumped to the floor in a heap. With some difficulty, he sat in Stinson's rear port side seat, shuffling his feet under the body.

Ashen, but apparently feeling better, Giannini sat in the seat facing Buona. Both men buckled their seat belts. Buona reached up and jerked off the plastic cover for the emergency exit.

"Are you ready for them to open the hatch?" Dolci asked. He remained seated in the starboard side, aft-facing seat, Powers' corpse under his feet.

"Yes, sir—one hundred and fifteen knots."

Dolci nodded at Buona, who immediately pulled on the emergency exit window. Straining hard, he finally overcame the slip stream effect from the rushing wind, and the window seal cracked. Whooshing air swirled violently inside the cabin. The wind and turbojet noise was nearly deafening.

Buona placed the rectangular shaped, metal-window plug on Powers' empty seat. He reached down at his feet, raised Stinson's corpse, and passed it to Giannini. "Make sure you get his head under that damn wing," Buona yelled.

Dolci's heart pounded. The maneuver was delicate. Feeding a body outside of the mid-winged aircraft required strength and precision. A mistake would send the body hurdling over the wing approximately two feet behind the emergency exit. It would immediately be sucked into the jet intake. A hand, a foot, or even a shoe would knock the engine completely out. Objects as small as a dime had been known to devastate jet fan blades. Although the plane could fly on the other rear jet, it would be a risky and expensive loss.

Stinson's arms flailed violently in the wind as Giannini stuffed the first half of the torso out of the window. Its aerodynamic shape temporarily altered, the aircraft yawed and pitched slightly. Gripping both feet tightly, Giannini saw that the body would slip under the wing; he let go. Stinson's corpse tumbled out of sight into the darkness and six thousand feet to the water below. They successfully repeated the difficult process with Powers' cadaver.

"Wait a minute," Dolci yelled. He reached into his coat pocket and removed the voice-stress recording along with the resulting paper tape from the P.S.E. "Stick these in that box."

With the wind swirling about violently, Buona lifted the metal lid just enough to stuff the damning evidence inside. After shutting the box, he handed it to Giannini, who shoved it out, making sure it dropped clear of the wing.

Both men struggled to replace the hatch. As they neared completion, the wind howled shrilly through the remaining opening. After shutting it as tightly as possible, a whistling noise remained.

"We'll have to get that seal replaced as soon as possible. I hate that damn noise," Dolci said, turning to Buona, "What about that ice? Be sure and flush that shit in the toilet."

Buona rose and stepped to the bar as the Jet Commander's flaps were retracted and the cabin was repressurized, the small leak minimally disturbing the process. Their ears popped again as the cabin pressurization simulated dropping to near sea level. The aircraft gained altitude and speed. Buona lifted the melting ice in its sealed stainless-steel container as one of the other men removed the front sofa cushion to expose the self-contained toilet. He dumped the contents in and closed the lid.

"They never think about the fucking ice, do they?" Dolci said, referring to his idea of freezing the liquid form of cyanide and then flash-freezing it again with an outer third of pure water. Invariably, his victims came to trust the drink and overlooked the changing characteristics in taste as they continued to ingest the melting poison. With two canisters of ice, one with poison, one without, the execution was surreptitiously secure.

"How soon until touchdown?" Dolci asked loudly.

"Approximately forty-three minutes to block, sir," the copilot answered, sticking his head out of the cockpit.

"Good. Telephone ahead and have Mr. Mancotta's chauffeur pick us up at the airport." Dolci leaned back in his seat and looked out of the window.

He began carefully assessing his situation. It was too bad he could not have interrogated Powers, but that would have been messy and quite possibly fruitless. No doubt the undercover agent would have refused to talk. Had they been able to isolate him, perhaps they could have found out exactly what his role with Burton and Lee was. Nevertheless, he had to assume the worst: Burton and Lee were informants. The fix would be off. How much did the authorities know? What was on tape, if anything? Probably not enough or they would have already made arrests.

* * *

"Base One, this is Unit Nine."

Teague walked to the transceiver and picked up the microphone. "Go ahead, Nine."

"Suspect's aircraft should be on the ground shortly."

"Maintain surveillance, Unit Nine, but do not, repeat, do not make contact. Identify party deplaning," Teague said.

Teague replaced the microphone, turned to Hardin, and said, "Want to make any bets on who gets off that plane?"

"No thanks. I've had my share of surprises already today. What makes you so sure Dolci got on it to begin with?" Hardin asked.

"That catering truck."

"What catering truck?"

Teague rose from his chair and walked to the window. "You were out at the airport trying to run down Nevada's baggage when this popped. Garner taped what he thought was a delivery being made by a catering truck. Unit Nine later found out that same truck made a delivery to the plane. I'll bet Dolci was on that truck."

"Where do you think they went?" Hardin asked.

Teague leaned against the wall. "There's no way of knowing. By the time Unit Nine got to Lakefront Airport and discovered Dolci's plane had flown in and out, we were unable to establish radar surveillance. They didn't file a flight plan. They went out VFR, headed southbound. My best guess is they went for a little ride over the Gulf of Mexico."

"And you think Powers and Stinson were on that plane?" Hardin asked.

"Maybe. If so, let's pray they get off it," Teague said.

"Did anyone see who or how many got on?"

"No. The plane was parked briefly and didn't refuel. I don't think they wanted anybody to know how many actually boarded."

"Where do you think they flew in from?"

Teague scratched his head. "Since they didn't have to refuel, it had to be some airport that was fairly close by.

Fuel consumption is poor on a turbojet flying at low altitude."

The transceiver crackled. "Base One, suspects are on the ground. Aircraft is currently taxiing down Runway One-Eight. Limousine is awaiting their arrival."

Teague picked up the microphone. "Get some good pictures."

Although it was dark, Teague knew Unit Nine was equipped with a STAR-TRON MK 426 passive night-vision system with a 230mm f/2.8 telephoto lens, manufactured by STAR-TRON Technology Corporation. By amplifying available light sources and providing a minimum light gain of sixty-thousand times, the system enabled them to video-tape subjects in the lowest possible light.

The agents had configured the STAR-TRON with a camera recorder made by Panasonic. They would tape the deplaning 115 yards away while hidden in a parked twin-engine Beechcraft.

"Base One, suspects have deplaned and we have tape," Unit Nine said.

"Were our missing persons on board?" Teague asked.

"Negative."

"What about D or M?" Teague asked, spelling the first three letters of each man's last name. Although the radio frequency would be difficult for anyone to locate and monitor, Teague did not want to risk using names.

"Negative on M, affirmative on D."

"How many people deplaned?" Teague asked.

"Including D, there were five and a pilot and copilot. Units Four and Five are following suspects as requested."

"Please remain on station until Ten and Six relieve you to conduct on-board search. Have that tape delivered at once and return to Base One," Teague said.

"Roger, Base One. Unit Nine out."

Hardin raised his eyebrows and said, "Looks like you were right. He was on board."

"After working on a case for six years, you begin to think like they do. Problem is, I'm one step behind the son of a bitch right now. I covered every possibility except this one.

I never dreamed they would link Powers to Burton and Lee. That was damn stupid on my part." Teague shook his head and looked at the floor.

"There was no way you could have anticipated this situation. I would have done exactly the same thing. If they had known about Powers, it seems to me they would have grabbed him before he got out of Charlotte. And they continued right on making contact with Burton. It didn't look like they were worried about anything. You still don't know for sure what happened. They may be holding them somewhere."

Teague stared at Hardin. "Bullshit. We'll never see them again."

* Thirty-seven *

"How can you be so damn sure we won't be linked with their disappearance?" Mancotta asked as he walked with Dolci to the dining room.

"You have nothing to worry about."

"That's what you've been saying all along. If I hadn't been so suspicious, you might not have taken these steps, and we would have walked further into their trap."

"Did you notice that van parked a couple of blocks away from here? One of my men has been keeping an eye on it since you left. He's positive feds are in it spying on us," Mancotta said.

Dolci shrugged his shoulders and sat in his normal place at Mancotta's dining room table. He was famished. "Let's relax for a few minutes and enjoy the meal. If we get upset, we won't be able to do justice to your chef's superb cooking."

Mancotta nodded. As far as he was concerned, the whole scheme had been reckless from the beginning.

Mancotta's servant entered the room and asked Dolci, "May I get you another drink, sir?"

"No thanks. The wine's enough."

Turning to the servant, Mancotta said, "Go ahead and serve the oysters."

The servant nodded and left the room.

Looking at his plump partner across the table, Mancotta imagined Dolci was already salivating like Pavlov's dog at the sound of the bell. "OK, I don't want to ruin our meal either, but I want to talk this thing over and come to some sort of understanding as to where we go from here."

"Fine. I'm sure we'll be able to arrive at an agreeable solution. We always have in the past." Dolci smiled easily.

"You agree then, that we should call the whole thing off?" Mancotta asked.

"Definitely."

"I think you should leave for Captiva tonight."

"What's the rush?"

"It'll take some heat off of me. I've still got to get a message to Bobby Nevada and tell him the fix is off. I imagine he's already contacted some people in Vegas. He'll be in hot water if he doesn't get back to them immediately."

The servant walked in carrying a silver tray and a bottle of chenin blanc. He served each man a dozen raw oysters on the half shell.

"Have Mr. Buona step in here for a moment," Dolci instructed.

The servant responded immediately and left the room.

Dolci speared another oyster and dipped it in the cocktail sauce. "OK, I'll leave tonight. I'd be careful how you get any messages to Nevada. If they saw him visit you, they are probably watching him, too."

Mancotta toyed with an oyster. "I don't care if they are staked out in Nevada's room, we'll make sure he gets the word."

Buona walked into the room. "Yes, sir."

Dolci looked up. "Get the pilots out of the hotel room. Tell them we'll be leaving around midnight for Captiva. The other men are with you, right?"

Buona nodded.

"Tell them to stay in town for a couple of days and catch a flight back later. I don't want us all going back like we're running with our tails between our legs."

Buona left the room as the spinach salads were being served. Lightly garnished with raw mushrooms, shredded carrots, and onions, the salad's flavor was enhanced with a light oil and vinegar dressing seasoned with parmesan cheese and a hint of fresh squeezed garlic.

"Did you leave anybody at the airport to watch your plane?" Mancotta asked.

Dolci speared a mushroom and lettuce with his fork and held it up over the plate, gesturing. "No, let those bastards search it. They're not going to find anything. They'll probably hide a second transponder somewhere. We'll find it. We may even have some fun with them and stick the bug on somebody else's plane."

Both men ate quietly for several minutes. Mancotta picked at his food pensively while Dolci finished the oysters and salad.

Mancotta broke the silence. "You really enjoy all this cloak and dagger, don't you?"

"Wouldn't trade it for anything. Hell, I'm smarter than they are. Got to hand it to them, though, they came close this time."

"I don't think we're out of the woods, yet." Mancotta raised his wine glass and eyed Dolci over the brim. "They've obviously had this set up for a long time. You don't know what kind of case they have developed so far."

The servant entered, cleared the empty plates, and served the main course: lobster tails stuffed with crabmeat parmesan.

Dolci spoke between bites. "What have they got? A lot of talk is about all. Remember, we haven't made the payoff. So, I gave Bill Lee a few lousy bucks and arranged a summer job or two. Are they going to lock me up for that? I think not. Our lawyers would make mincemeat of the whole idea. As for the murders, they've got to prove we killed somebody. That's not going to be possible."

Mancotta sipped his wine. "I admire your confidence. I will admit, though, that I have a lot less to worry about than you. I don't see how they can tie me into this."

"Exactly," Dolci smiled. "Watch out, though. I may be tempted to blackmail you. Guess what I'd ask for?" He pointed toward the kitchen.

"My chef."

"Yes, and judging by the way you pick at his food, I bet he would enjoy working for somebody that truly appreciated his culinary talents."

"You're probably right," Mancotta said, pausing. "What about Burton and Lee?"

"Let them stew for a year or so. By that time, things will have died down, and I'll arrange for them to have some unfortunate accidents."

Mancotta nodded. Revenge was a poor motive for killing; protection was not. Dolci's thirst for intrigue had gone too far. He had thrown caution to the wind.

Troy glared at Teague. "You really take me for some sort of fool, don't you?"

"Speculation that they are dead is unfounded at this point."

Troy turned and stared out of his hotel window. "Then why has our meeting with Dolci been canceled? The weather is nice. I don't see any rain out there. Or is it that things have gotten just a little too hot for him?"

"There's no need for sarcasm, Mr. Burton. We're both intelligent men and can level with each other."

"Really! That would be unique at this point. You've fed me a line loaded with hooks all through this whole deal. I'm tired of it. What else are you hiding from me? I get the feeling that you know a great deal more than you're telling me."

"We're still searching for your friends. At this point we have no proof that they are dead. All we know for sure is that Powers used his code word in a message to his wife signifying that he was in trouble. We can't even be sure what kind of trouble they're in," Teague said.

"You wouldn't be telling me this if you weren't sure there was some kind of connection. You're trying to keep me from getting too much information at one time. You don't want me to choke on it, right?"

"What I don't want you to do is to go off half-cocked. I'll admit that I'm inclined to believe Powers and Stinson are in serious trouble. The fact that Dolci has apparently broken contact with you looks bad. We've got to show patience and exercise some restraint at this point."

"Why don't you arrest them?" Jenny Burton asked.

"Mrs. Burton, any move we make right now might jeopardize the lives of your friends. We can't arrest either Dolci or Mancotta just because we suspect they are kidnappers. We've got to keep waiting for them to make a mistake or uncover information that can link them to the crime."

"What about arresting them with what you've already

got?" Burton asked.

Teague glanced at Hardin. "We really need more corroborating evidence. Anything we do at this point that's based on conjecture is dangerous. What we need is more time and more proof."

"Fine, what you need is more time and what we need is to get the hell out of this hotel room for a little while," Burton said as he put his arm around Jenny.

"That's too dangerous," Teague said.

"Bullshit! We're a couple of clay pigeons here. At least out there we're a moving target. Not only that, I think you and I both know that Dolci's probably going to keep a low profile. Like you say, you need more evidence. He realizes that, so he's decided to cool his heels for a while. Send a couple of agents with us. They might enjoy Bourbon Street as much as we do." Burton loosened his tie.

Teague shook his head. "That's very risky. There are a lot of people down there even this late at night."

"Which is precisely why I want to go. I'm tired of looking at these four walls. They aren't going to be able to pick us out of a crowd. If your people make sure we're not followed, don't you think Bourbon Street is the last place they'll be expecting us to go?"

Teague paused. He sat in a chair and scratched his head. "I'm going to send four agents with you."

"Great, the more the merrier."

"What makes you think I want to go?" Jenny grabbed her husband's hand and squeezed it tightly.

"With four bodyguards! You're crazy. Change out of that dress and put on some jeans. We're going." Burton glanced at his watch as he turned to Teague and Hardin. "Gentlemen, if you'll excuse us while we get dressed, please. We'll be ready to go in twenty minutes."

Troy and Jenny sat at a brass-top table in the medium lit, wood-rafter bar. Heavy German steins adorned the superstructure. Large pictures of old New Orleans covered a wall.

Troy ordered two Hurricanes: fruity drinks for which Pat O'Brien's had become famous, served in tall souvenir glasses. He doubted Jenny would finish hers.

Nothing had changed, he thought, only aged a bit. The same two women still entertained at twin pianos, cracking jokes between songs, playing and singing a mixed set of familiar tunes—some Irish, some jazz. A black man in dark glasses provided a one man percussion section by tapping the underside of a silver serving tray with thimbles on his fingers. The audience sang along.

Intermittently sipping their drinks through straws, the Burtons watched the reverie. When the music stopped and the entertainers left the small stage for a brief intermission, Troy felt someone tap him on his shoulder. Turning to see who it was, he recognized Chuck Haigler immediately.

"Chuck, what brings you here? Women, liquor, or song?" Troy asked loudly to be heard above the crowd noise. He held his palm up briefly to wave off an agent who had swept in and was about to collar Haigler from behind.

The quick gesture went unnoticed by Haigler, who answered, "All of the above and precisely in that order. Mind if I join you?"

"Not at all. Pull up a chair if you can find one."

Haigler picked his way through the crowded tables searching for an empty chair. When he finally found one, he lifted it over his head and carried it back to the table. "I always wanted to visit here. Looks like I'm not the only one," he said, sitting down, looking around the crowded room. "You used to live in New Orleans, didn't you?"

"Yeah. After my mother and father divorced, my mother brought me and my brother down here from Charlotte. My mother's folks lived here and were fairly well off financially, so they helped my mother raise us. We both went to a private military day school in Metairie.

"The first time I came in here I was under age, but I had a phony draft card, and I looked eighteen. A friend and I got so drunk we almost didn't make it home. He had to shinny up one of the street signs to read it so we could figure out where we were. God truly watches fools and drunks. We were both."

"Sounds like you were pretty wild and woolly then."

Troy laughed. "A lot of kids who grow up in New Orleans learn to suck on a liquor bottle very early."

A waiter stopped and Haigler ordered a Hurricane.

Troy ordered another drink, then turned to Haigler, "So, how's the newspaper business?"

"Busy."

"Got any juicy stories for the readers back home?" Troy asked.

"Not really. That story about the Chargers' coach seems to have died a little, no pun intended. Nobody seems to want to talk about it."

"That's because you don't know the right people," Troy said, winking at Jenny.

She glared at him with warning eyes. She was not yet that drunk.

"Do you know something I don't?" Haigler asked.

"A lot."

Jenny kicked her husband under the table.

He ignored her. "It's real simple, Chuck. You see McLaughlin was on the take from a mob guy who wanted him to fix the game and lose to us. He refused, so the mob had him greased," Troy said nonchalantly.

Haigler raised his eyebrows. "Sure and the fairy godmother waved her magic wand and the prince became a frog."

Troy smiled. "Right. How's the song go, Chuck, 'Fairy tales can come true, it can happen to you.' Something like that."

"I thought you were going to give me some hot tip. You've got a hell of an imagination. Does he always like to put people on, Jenny?"

"Only when he's drinking," Jenny replied.

Troy watched her scan the room looking for the agents. None was close enough to have overheard their conversation above the crowd chatter and the juke box.

Finally, they all rose from the table and bade each other good night. Jenny felt no pain. Troy guided her outside into the cool, fresh air.

The sober, weary agents walked with them down darkened streets. Troy was deep in thought as he held his arm around Jenny, steadying her. Passing into the stillness of the night away from the humming nightlife, he first heard, then spotted, the silhouette of a solo saxophonist leaning against a building, playing a lonely melody.

* Thirty-eight *

For the third time in less than an hour, Frank Dolci stumbled from his bedroom to the bathroom and vomited violently. He could hardly stand; his chest ached. He leaned on the marble sink as wave after wave of heaving sapped his strength. When at last he stopped and his eyes began to clear, he saw blood in the bile-like vomit.

As he tried to return to bed, he lost his balance and slumped against the door. The room spun and he collapsed on the floor. He had to get help. His heart pounded. Gathering as much strength as possible, he cried out, "Joe! Come help me."

Waves of nausea returned. He could not move. As he heard footsteps, he turned his head and retched on the floor, losing control of his bowels simultaneously.

"Oh, my God! Hang on, sir. I'm taking you to the hospital." Buona snatched a blanket from the bed, wrapped it around Dolci, lifted him, and carried him down the hall. He called to the chauffeur, "Get the car started! We've got to get him to the hospital!"

Francesco Mancotta was still winded from his mid-afternoon workout when his servant stepped into the exercise room and told him Joe Buona was calling from Florida.

"Hello, Joe. What can I do for you?" Mancotta asked as he sat naked on the massage table.

"I'm afraid I have some bad news. We had to rush Mr. Dolci to the hospital this afternoon."

"What's the problem? Is he going to be all right?" Mancotta sounded sincerely concerned.

Buona stood at a pay phone in the hospital corridor. "We don't know. He got up feeling fine, took a dip in the pool, and ate a big breakfast. Shortly after that, he began feeling sick to his stomach and started puking real bad. It looked bloody. He could hardly move, so we rushed him to the hospital. By the time we got him here, he was acting real confused, like he didn't know where he was."

"Do the doctors have any idea what the problem is?" Mancotta asked.

"No, sir. They think it might be food poisoning. They're just guessing, though."

"What did he eat for breakfast?"

"He got up late—had eggs and pompano. That's his favorite, you know. The doctor says the pompano could have made him sick."

"Pompano? I didn't know it could make you sick." Mancotta motioned with his free hand for his short, stout masseur—who had halted abruptly at the door when he saw Mancotta was on the phone—to enter the room.

"The doc called it cigutu . . . ciguturea . . . "

"I think that's ciguatera," Mancotta said, correcting Buona's mispronunciation. "I've heard of it before, but I didn't know you could get it from pompano."

"The doc says it's rare, but it has been reported in about 300 different kinds of fish," Buona said. "He's not sure that's what it is, though. He said that usually the fish poison causes a numbness or tingling in the face and lips. Mr. Dolci isn't having any of those problems."

"How long after he ate did he get sick?" Mancotta asked. The masseur began rubbing his shoulders.

"It wasn't even an hour. The doc is worried. When it happens that quick, it is a pretty bad sign that the fish was real poisonous."

"I see."

"They asked me what he had to eat last night. I told them I'd call you and make a list. Could you give it to me?"

"Sure, but I ate the same thing he did and I'm feeling fine. Then again, we had raw oysters. Maybe he got a bad one. Have you got a pen?"

"Yeah."

"We had oysters on the half shell, a spinach salad, and lobster stuffed with crabmeat. Is Frank so sick he can't remember?"

Buona finished scribbling the information. "He's real confused. They're running a bunch of tests on him. It may be a real bad stomach virus. They just don't know."

"Do you think I need to come? I can be on the next plane."

"The doc says it's serious, but they haven't listed him as critical. I don't think there's anything you could do if you came. If he gets worse, I'll call you," Buona said.

"By all means. What hospital is he in?"

"Cape Coral Hospital. He likes the doctor that works here. They've got him in intensive care. I think they're worried that his heart might go from the strain of all this vomiting and diarrhea."

"I'm concerned about that, too. Frank's overweight and he's getting up in years. About the only exercise he gets is that little bit of swimming. Keep me posted. And tell Frank I send my best. I'll have some flowers delivered to brighten his room."

After Mancotta hung up, he rose from the table and said, "Excuse me for a minute please." He slipped a towel around his waist and walked to the kitchen.

The chef looked up as Mancotta walked in. "I just got a call from them. He's in the hospital and we've had a real stroke of luck. They think he's got ciguatera. He ate pompano for breakfast."

The chef smiled. "Then they don't suspect mushroom poisoning?"

"No. He's too confused to remember what he ate last night."

"I want you to take a couple of weeks off and enjoy your bonus. I'm sure I don't need to remind you that you and I are the only ones who know what's killing him. Keep your mouth shut and you'll be set for life. Understand?" Mancotta asked.

"You have my word," the chef replied.

Mancotta turned and walked back to his exercise room where his masseur was waiting patiently. He climbed back up on the table and laid flat on his stomach.

He was pleased with the results. Dolci had simply gotten too reckless. In time their partnership would have been dissolved one way or the other. He couldn't afford to wait. Dolci always had a tendency to make the first move. The deceptive murder would avoid the inevitable repercussions of an open hit. The other mob bosses across the country would never be the wiser.

The irony was that Dolci's own library on poison had taught Mancotta all he needed to know: Amanita Phalloides or the Death Cap, as the fungus is more commonly known. It looks, smells, and tastes like its edible cousins. There are no known antidotes. Even when treated shortly after consumption, 50 percent of its victims perish.

The Death Cap kills slowly. The first symptoms generally appear between twelve and twenty-four hours. By that time the use of a stomach pump is ineffective. The toxin becomes attached to the liver cells within minutes after ingestion, then begins attacking cells throughout the body. The heart is heavily affected. Cooking weakens the toxin's potency, but when the fungus is eaten raw, the victim nearly always expires. Death occurs in five to ten days, sooner with those whose vital organs have suffered disease or trauma.

Mancotta knew Dolci had previously had a heart attack, was overweight and aging quickly. He was pleased he had considered all these circumstances.

Now, he thought, what should be done about Burton?

* Thirty-nine *

By late Friday afternoon, Troy Burton and everyone involved in the DOLMAN Project realized the fix was off. The mob had apparently killed Powers and Stinson. Troy was more aware of that fact than were Powers and Stinson's wives, who still clung to a modicum of hope. A missing persons report had been filed with the New Orleans Police Department.

Seated with Jenny in the Superdome stands to watch public practice of all four teams, Troy reflected on the entire situation. Many of the people in the crowd were getting their first in-person look at the nation's four best teams. The sports pages of papers around the country and in New Orleans were brimming with articles on the NCAA championships. The Charlotte Hornets gained recognition throughout the nation and TC continued to receive top billing.

Stories on McLaughlin continued. The most widely accepted theory on the twin murder was that the hooker apparently threatened blackmail. But at three o'clock on Friday afternoon, the medical examiner in Florida exploded that hypothesis with a bombshell for the media. At the request of the FBI, Dr. Vaughn held a press conference and read a carefully worded statement that suggested the whole scene might have been staged. Teague hoped the smoke would force Dolci to give orders from his hospital bed. They had bugged the intensive care unit.

Intrigue sprang from the shadows into the spotlight. The jealous lover theory was considered most frequently. Some reporters suggested mob connections, but McLaughlin's death was not linked with a fix attempt. Since no one could substantiate the claims, most editors felt that was crossing the line toward rampant and unfair speculation. Unknown to the press, the NCAA had quietly begun an investigation of the Chargers' basketball program.

Since 1939, when the NCAA began the tournament and Howard Hobson coached Oregon to the first national title by defeating Ohio State, no championship team had ever been stripped of its first place title.

But several had come close. The first scandal to rock the Final Four occurred in 1961. St. Joseph's of Pennsylvania had its third place finish vacated in the final standings because players were later declared ineligible. That same year, three of St. Joe's top players were implicated in an alleged point shaving scandal and were expelled from school.

Exactly ten years later in 1971, the Final Four was tainted with not one, but two teams who were deleted from the record books. Second-place Villanova, which lost to John Wooden's UCLA in the finals, 68-62, and third-place Western Kentucky, which defeated Kansas 77-75 in the consolation game, were found to have been in violation of NCAA rules.

After lengthy investigations, Long Beach State's 1971, '72, and '73 appearances were deleted from the record books. In none of those years had they made it to the Final Four. Other teams later blacklisted were Southwestern Louisiana in '72 and '73 and Austin Peay in '73. Neither team had advanced past the second round of play.

The Hornets were the last to take the court. Troy studied the history of the championships briefly as his team took the court in front of a medium-sized crowd. A loud cheer from most of the fans demonstrated that the public had indeed embraced the role of the Hornets as the Cinderella darling of the Final Four. Troy looked up from his program occasionally to watch his team work out in the spotlight.

"What's the matter?" Jenny asked.

He stopped reading. "Did you say something?"

"Where is your mind? I've never seen you this quiet before."

Troy leaned over and whispered, "I'm sorry. I guess I'm just losing interest. It's funny. We dreamed about making it all the way to the top. Now here we are and look what kind of a mess we're in. Our fans are flying here to cheer the team on to victory. I'll bet not one of them would ever suspect that a basketball game could bring so much grief. It's amazing what greed can cause people to do." He shook his head as he watched the Hornets leave the court and head for the locker room. Many were stopped by autograph seekers.

Still under heavy FBI guard, Troy and Jenny returned to the Fairmont. Teague was waiting for them in their room.

Teague rose from the sofa and walked to the window. "I've debated about whether to give you this news or not, especially this early. But I promised I would keep you informed, and perhaps you'll feel better when you hear this."

Troy shoved his right hand into his pocket and leaned against the wall. "We could use some good news right now. What is it?"

"After you left for practice, our agents in Ft. Myers contacted us. We've been maintaining close surveillance on Frank Dolci since he returned to Florida late last night. We hoped he might still make another move. We don't think that is a possibility now. He's in the hospital dying." He did not mention Dr. Vaughn's press conference. Going into detail about that aspect of the case would serve little purpose. When Burton read the papers, he would probably assume that the medical examiner had called the press conference on his own.

"What happened?" Jenny asked before Troy could speak.

"We don't know for sure. I received a phone call half an hour ago from our agent at the hospital in Cape Coral. Dolci entered the hospital several hours ago with apparent food poisoning. The doctors aren't sure, but they think it came from some fish he ate. It made him violently ill. He never has been in good health. He's suffered a massive heart attack and is listed in critical condition," Teague said, wanting Dolci to die, but feeling cheated.

"Where does that leave us?" Troy asked.

"If he dies, it obviously means that we haven't got a case. You can't try a dead man. And at this point, we've got nothing on Francesco Mancotta as far as a fix is concerned."

Teague had decided not to mention the slender thread which still existed that could conceivably compel Nevada to implicate Mancotta—the lost suitcase. It had not yet been found.

"But what about Mancotta? Won't he have us eliminated? Isn't that the way the mob works?" Burton asked in rapid succession.

Teague sat in a high backed chair and crossed his legs. "Sometimes, but I don't think you have anything to worry about in this case. I've known Mancotta a long time. He's not the type that kills for revenge. You and Coach Lee pose absolutely no threat to him. You've never even met the man. Murder is risky; that's a fact Mancotta respected far more than Dolci."

"But what about Dolci's organization? Surely whoever takes over will try to seek revenge. We spoiled their plan," said Burton.

"True. There's one thing you have to understand, though. Dolci has left no heir apparent to assume clear command. That's going to cause a power struggle. His organization will probably fragment. It's hard to understand why a man as thorough as he is never made provisions for his eventual death. It's almost like he thought he was immortal."

"Maybe he is."

Teague looked at Troy quizzically and rose from his chair. "All I can tell you is that he's a very sick man right now. The doctors say they have done all they can."

"It's in the Lord's hands," Jenny said quietly.

Troy stared at her. "The Lord? Someday you'll have to explain that to me."

Teague ignored the private exchange. "I'd better get back with Hardin. I'll keep you posted."

Before Teague disappeared behind the door, Burton stopped him with a question. "Mind if we go out to dinner?"

"I'd prefer that you stay in the hotel to eat. We're stretched pretty thin right now. There's some good entertainment in the Blue Room tonight."

"All right. If we're just staying in the Fairmont, will you be sending anybody with us?"

"Certainly. Don't get the wrong impression. We're not

abandoning protection. We have no idea what kind of orders
Dolci left with some of his men who stayed on here in town."
Teague shut the door.

Hardin replaced the microphone on the transceiver and
looked up at Teague. "I just heard from our people at the
Hyatt. Bobby Nevada checked out of the hotel and is on
his way to the airport. They taped a call to the airlines
when he made his reservations. He's headed back to Vegas."

"Figures. Mancotta probably got a message to him that
the heat was on. There was no way to stop that. Any word
on the suitcase?"

"No."

"Damnit, I'll bet it was off-loaded at Dallas/Ft. Worth
and somebody grabbed it." Teague took off his coat and
tossed it on the chair. He felt like a fisherman who labored
skillfully as he reeled a trophy catch close to the boat and
watched in dismay as his prize slipped the hook and swam
into the depths of translucent blue, leaving behind a melting
cascade of bubbles and a memory of what might have been.

And the big problem was Teague had no idea if his theory
about Mancotta leaving the Burtons alone was correct. If
Mancotta didn't, Teague was not going to lose his last
chance at the prize. Troy Burton might still be tempting
bait.

* Forty *

The words kept echoing inside Troy Burton's mind: Dolci is dead! Dolci is dead! Music to his ears! Like a catchy phrase in a song, it reverberated repeatedly. Shutting out the entire crowd around him, he looked at Jenny and smiled wryly.

He could not even remember walking into the Superdome or finding their seats, close to the court, in line with the top of the key at the north end. Dazed, he had walked past scalpers, program hawkers, and souvenir stands filled with memorabilia dedicated to all four teams.

"Can you feel the excitement?" Jenny asked him.

He stared at her blankly, then looked at the cavernous manmade structure as it filled with a gathering of expectations. The four college pep bands alternately played their fight songs, each of them sparking their fans into a raucous frenzy. As the competition for noisemaking stiffened, all four played simultaneously.

The distinct fan sections were clearly evident, like four different kinds of fruit neatly placed in equal quadrants of a bowl of cereal. Some students, a sprinkling of faculty, politicians, and middle to upper-class avid alumni, all became the supporting cast to the sports spectacular that would have the undivided attention of over thirty million television viewers nationwide.

At one end of the hardwood court, trimmed in royal blue, the words "Final Four/New Orleans" were painted white in a type style reminiscent of the fleur-de-lis; at the other end the words, "Louisiana Superdome"; the royal-blue jump circle was lettered "NCAA." A white banner adorned the scorer's/press table with the words NCAA FINAL FOUR, NEW ORLEANS, LOUISIANA. Behind that table, additional press row tables were tiered into two more rows. Troy spotted Haigler on the first row.

Colorful banners—hung over the terrace level by zealous,

artistic fans—fluttered crisply. Troy read the Louisiana Superdome's statistics in his program. Steady blasts from the Superdome's nine-thousand-ton air-conditioning system pumped nearly three million cubic feet of air per minute inside the main arena and five hundred thousand to the support areas.

He lacked the normal ebullient spirit befitting the occasion and knew he appeared distant to the partisans who stopped by to shake his hand, briefly speculate on the outcome of the games, and thank him for their tickets. For once, nobody complained about his or her seating location. They were just happy to be present at one of the premier annual sporting events in the country. The Final Four now ranked with them all: the college football bowl game most-likely to produce the national champions, the Super Bowl, the World Series, or the Masters golf tournament. If you were fortunate enough to attend any one of those events, Troy thought, you'd remember it for a lifetime.

But he felt drained, lifeless, like a marionette whose strings had been cut. His emotions rested in limbo. Only two hours ago, Teague brought word that Frank Dolci had died from a heart attack. Teague decided that all concerned would remain under protection until they left New Orleans. Beyond that, he was convinced they were no longer in danger.

Bill Lee received the news stoically. Troy had been unable to detect any emotion whatsoever. Lee's mind was obviously on the game and nothing else. The coach had immersed himself in a sea of work to keep his mind off the tense behind-the-scenes events.

On Friday night Chuck Haigler had left numerous messages with the desk for Troy to call him. The news of the medical examiner's press conference in Florida apparently gave him second thoughts about Troy's flippant remark that McLaughlin was killed by the mob.

After discussing it with Teague, Troy called Haigler back early Saturday morning and laughed it off as idle chatter, the product of a good imagination. The reporter readily accepted Troy's answer, explaining that he figured the remark had been in jest, but felt compelled to confirm that fact.

The public address announcement jogged Burton. "LADIES AND GENTLEMEN: IN ONE MINUTE CBS WILL BE ON THE AIR. LET'S GIVE A ROUSING WELCOME TO THE MILLIONS OF VIEWERS JOINING US NATIONWIDE." Troy looked at the teams warming up on the court and wondered how that would affect their nerves.

Bands played forcefully and cheerleaders motioned for the crowd to crescendo to forte. Few needed coaxing. Fans quickly became extras without pay, a film producer's dream. The largest crowd ever on hand to witness a college basketball game roared in unison.

Troy looked toward the court. Four CBS commentators were prepared to go on the air. Jim Nantz stood on the hardwood at the north end of the court in front of a CBS camera. James Brown stood at the south end of the court in front of another camera. Brent Musburger and Billy Packer huddled together at center court. Nantz's camera blinked on. The games were on the air.

Troy had no trouble imagining what angles commentators would discuss. The first match between UCLA and UNC was a contest between perennial powers, giants of college basketball.

Dean Smith was making his eighth coaching appearance in the Final Four. In his previous seven, Smith's team finished fourth twice, third once, second three times, and won the championship in 1982 when the Tar Heels defeated Georgetown here in the Superdome. Now a second NCAA title was possible after a long drought. UNC had not made it to the Final Four since 1982. A second championship would assure him a ranking with greats like Wooden and Rupp.

Troy had great respect for Dean Smith. He had guided the 1976 Olympic basketball team to gold. Smith had developed the famous "four corners" offense, a slow-down offense that was no longer a big gun in his arsenal because of the forty-five second clock.

Walt Hazzard was at the helm for UCLA and had obviously gotten off to a superb start. Coaching at UCLA was like walking on hallowed ground, the ghost of John Wooden-past, twenty-seven years of basketball supremacy. Wooden's career record of 620 wins against 147 losses included ten national championships, seven of which were earned consecutively from '67 through '73. Even the legendary Adolph Rupp, the "Baron" of Kentucky basketball, did not match that record, but his four national titles put him in an unchallenged second place.

After Wooden retired, two talented coaches at UCLA, Gene Bartow and Gary Cunningham, crossed Wooden's happy hunting grounds two seasons each. Despite 85 and 86 percent winning records respectively, they resigned. With UCLA's glorious history, anything less than a Final Four appearance was unacceptable for most Bruin fans. After Bartow and Cunningham, Larry Brown had delivered in 1980 by coaching UCLA to a second place finish. When Brown resigned to accept another coaching post, Larry Farmer, one of Brown's assistant coaches and himself a player on three NCAA championships under Wooden, took the reins. Again, no repeat performance to even closely approximate the glory years under Wooden. After a number of seasons, he was replaced by Walt Hazzard, the former UCLA player and NBA pro.

Until tip-off, the CBS analysts would obviously focus on the coaches' techniques, as well as the two teams' styles of play and player match-ups. Brief highlights of their tournament victories—four straight each to reach this point—were highlighted to demonstrate the caliber of precision play that could be expected.

Sitting in the stands, viewing the pre-game activities on the seventy-five-ton gondola suspended high above the Superdome floor, Burton imagined what the commentators were saying. The six huge television screens, each measuring 22 by 26 feet, provided the only close-up view for the fans who were sitting as far away from the court as 375 feet on the north end terrace level. But with seventeen-TV camera locations, instant replay, and slow motion, everyone present would have an excellent view of the games on the closed-circuit system. Some fans would have difficulty deciding whether to watch the court or television.

Watching the skirmish on television had its advantages. Through the technical artistry of the medium, the finer points of a single play could be appraised: soaring dunks, pirouetting jump shots, and choreographed play patterns.

Troy and Jenny stood with the rest of the crowd as the national anthem was performed by the Air Force Band. Lyrics flashed on the scoreboards, prompting many to sing along.

Troy's thoughts drifted. The stunning experiences of the past few days were still with him. He just couldn't shake the effects. He felt cheated. For years he had longed for this very moment, yet he stood unfulfilled in the midst of an eye-popping sports drama. The Dolci proposition had knifed his perspective. The wound festered.

Two years ago he was certain he had found his niche in life. Working with Charlotte's young and vibrant sports program made him feel important, useful, and needed. To Troy, sports were an essential part of life, a model for learning what it means to compete and strive for a goal while working hard and having fun.

He had helped build the university's sports future to one of national prominence. But in the long run was that accomplishment or ill-fate? Preeminence was supposed to bring dividends: pride to the community, the students, the faculty, and the alumni; increased student enrollment; more donations for scholarships, both athletic and non-athletic. Those were the positive aspects he had accepted and preached to numerous civic clubs and organizations throughout Charlotte and the outlying areas.

But what about the negatives? Big time competition—as he had already witnessed—provided a catalyst for corruption. Was that the fault of basketball, the people who ran it, or the outsiders who tried to take advantage of the system? As he heard the teams' starting fives being alternately introduced, he groped for an answer. College basketball was big business, clear and simple. Its objective: grind

out ever-increasing profits. A college coach's objective was
much the same: chalk up wins.

Ultimately, everything came down to the bottom line.
Frequently, both the coach and the businessman had to
steamroll anything or anyone who got in the way. College
sports were breeding corruption. Perhaps they needed to
be totally revamped, even reduced to intramurals. Troy
checked his thoughts. He realized he was swinging the
pendulum too far by suggesting that the child needed to be
dumped down the drain along with the dirty water.

No, he thought, you couldn't condemn the sports institu-
tion because greed latched on like a leech and began sucking
its lifeblood. That was hardly fair. True, many student-
athletes were being prostituted, but many were also receiving the intended benefits. One thing he knew now was that
his early belief that big-time college sports fostered ama-
teurism was ridiculous.

He had walked into the sports pasture with eyes open
wide and found himself stepping in shit every few feet.
Scholarships were a form of pay. Judging from what he'd
seen in his brief two year service, that was merely the tip
of the iceberg. The NCAA tried to police its member
institutions, but as the spectacles grew in popularity, so did
cheating and greed. He had heard enough stories beyond
his own experience to know that there were far too many
colleges whose coaches and players were rife with corruption. Organized crime had obviously begun to recognize
that the fatted calf was ready for the altar.

"Troy, who are you going to pull for?" Jenny asked as the
teams squared off at the jump circle. She waited for a reply,
then finally gained his attention with a nudge.

"What?"

"I want to know who you're going to pull for."

"It doesn't matter," he answered, shrugging his
shoulders.

She stared at him. "You're really not into this, are you?"

The Bruins gained possession on the tip-off and the crowd
roared. Jenny's question was nearly drowned by the din.

Troy looked at his wife. "I guess not."

Jenny needed no further explanation. She shared some of his same feelings. Her emotions had been battered. The resultant bruise was obscured only by her strong faith.

UCLA lost possession and the Tar Heels scored. Carolina blue coats in the Hornet section stood and cheered. On the opposite side of the court the entire Tar Heel section waved a sea of blue and white shakers.

"Look at all the Tar Heel fans sitting in our section," Jenny said.

"I know. It's to their credit that they're here. Remember how many times Bill and I went out and preached the two-allegiance theory to get them to donate to us, too? It obviously worked. They'll pull for us when we get ready to play. Some of them told me they brought their gold jackets along and would change between games. The rub comes if we meet in the championship." Burton looked at one of the scoreboards as a Bruin guard hit a twelve-foot jump shot. The score was tied, 8 to 8.

Francesco Mancotta sat in his private box suite, one of sixty-four in the stadium. Since there were exactly sixty-four parishes in the state of Louisiana, each suite had been named for one. The decision to name them accordingly came when someone realized the number of suites equaled the number of parishes.

Mancotta's suite, number 53, the Tangipahoa, was situated on the west side and provided him an excellent view of the court. Located just 73 feet above the hardwood on the 400 level, the suite had closed-circuit television, a bar, a phone, comfortable seating in a modern decor, room service, and a $30,000 price tag, not including tickets to events and a yearly fee of $11,500.

As the game progressed, he watched the crowd rather than the action on the court. He was looking for Troy Burton, but since the Hornet contingent was right below him, he could only see the backs of their heads. He had yet to spot Burton.

Mancotta's young, shapely, female companion, Sophia,

sat watching the game, unaware of his reason for interest in the Hornet contingent. She was a sports enthusiast. Her favorite form of recreation was a romp in bed. Mancotta believed a round with her was like running a six-mile obstacle course.

"Did you find him yet, sir?" one of his men asked.

"No."

"Would you like me to go down and see if I can spot him?"

"No." Mancotta picked up his binoculars and looked at courtside, sweeping back to where he had located Bill Lee. The coach also had his back to him, but was turning to talk to his assistant coaches. They were apparently discussing the progress of the game and looking for chinks in either team's offense or defense.

Mancotta thought about the successful disposal of his partner. No one had suspected mushroom poisoning. Even if they did, nothing could be proven. Dolci's wife was back from Europe and she was insisting that no autopsy be performed. That had been her husband's wish. With her money and standing in the community, she might win her argument, as long as the doctors could be persuaded that there was no reason to suspect foul play.

The funeral was scheduled for Monday. Mancotta and many of the other mob bosses from around the country would be in attendance. He would keep up appearances and play the role of the bereaved partner, carefully avoiding the power struggle that would result within Dolci's organization. The partnership would be totally dissolved.

He felt brief remorse when he learned of Frank's ultimate demise. Buona had called and said that Dolci had never regained consciousness after his heart attack. Mancotta remembered how he felt at that moment, relieved but empty.

The scheme to fix the games came close, Mancotta reflected, but not close enough. It was reckless, involving too many people. The best way to fix a game was to approach the players directly. Since many of them enjoyed drugs, cars, and women, a bribe could always be pulled off. Some coaches were susceptible like McLaughlin, but they had to be picked with the utmost care. The most important thing was to never let them know what cards you were holding. Keep them off balance and you could manipulate them.

He had no intention of getting further involved, though. It was time to retire and let his nephew run the business. He would be available for advice, and occasionally to exert some influence, nothing more.

Mildly interested, he looked at the scoreboard. His deceased partner had predicted a UNC win over a week ago. They would have to make some adjustments. With only ten seconds to go in the first half, the Tar Heels had fallen behind by ten points.

Bill Lee, Bo Evans, and Earl Ward rose from their courtside seats at halftime. It was time to join the Hornet players in the locker room. Only Evans would return to finish watching the game. Nobody really expected to see any surprises. The Bruins and the Tar Heels were simply matching talent against talent. A new defense or offense would probably not be a part of either team's repertoire after they had come this far.

"Anybody get sick after they ate, Earl?" Lee asked as they neared the locker room door.

"Not that I know of," Ward replied. He was dressed in a dapper, black, pinstripe suit.

Earlier Ward had told Lee that Ebony magazine had approached him for a feature article. He had been chosen one of the ten most eligible black bachelors in the nation. Knowing that the personal publicity would add names, addresses, and phone numbers to the pages of his second date book, he had readily agreed.

"What about Collins? Where'd he eat?" Lee asked.

"MacDonald's," Ward replied.

Evans laughed and Lee shook his head as they stepped into the locker room. It was like walking into a tomb. The players were changing into their uniforms quietly.

Lee surveyed the scene. Most looked alert and intense. He watched Bowman, one of the starting forwards, and wondered why a player with his talent had ever sniffed cocaine. He didn't anymore. The new mandatory drug-testing rule the NCAA had enacted at the tournament had already proven that Bowman was drug-free.

But Lee had been certain that Bowman was involved in the drug early last season. After Lee had benched him for two games, upon confronting him on the subject, he had noticed some improvement in performance consistency.

Since Lee began coaching seventeen years ago, drugs had become a serious problem in college basketball. The death of Len Bias had really emphasized that fact.

Up until the time drug testing began, Lee had known that most of the players occasionally smoked marijuana. There had been little he could do to stop them, although he did his best to discourage it.

Over the past three years, Donnie Powers had given him much of his inside information. The thought brought anguish. It was hard to believe Powers was gone.

He addressed the team. "All right now, listen up. We've come a hell of a long way. You've proven that you can play with anybody in the country. You beat the number-one team in the nation to get here. Don't forget that."

He walked to the chalkboard and began diagramming a triangle-and-two zone defense. "Let's go over this one more time. If their guards get hot with the three-pointer, we'll switch to the tri-two and try to shut them down. Mac, you take Wells. Thad, you've got Harrel. TC, shut off that middle and keep movement in there."

Coach Lee did not like gimmick zones, but in the right situation they could stifle an opponent's momentum. UFFM's guards had incredible range and could bomb a team out of a standard zone in a heartbeat. He would try to stop that with his combination man-to-man/zone. But if the Charger forwards or center started filling the bucket, it would be totally ineffective.

"We'll start with our 2-3 zone. Let's press them early, trap, and see if we can force some turnovers. They're quick, so watch the back-door. They'll probably press us, too. When they do, I want Mac and Thad to work the ball into TC. I don't think they can take it away from us. Be patient.

"Thad, run our regular. We'll switch to the 'L.A. inside' every few possessions. We'll run the 'Philly stack' occasionally. Watch for my signal. Let's try and save the 'L.A. outside' for the second half," Lee instructed.

He pocketed the chalk. It wasn't necessary to go any further. They had already been over the game plan countless times in practice and while watching Chargers' game films. His last-minute instructions were designed to get the players concentrating on their assignments and to loosen them up.

They were tight. He recognized that fact and hoped they would settle down when they got into the flow of the game. If not, and UFFM grabbed an early lead, they could be blown off the court. The Chargers had more tournament experience and more depth. Even minus McLaughlin, they would be tough.

He knew he was gambling by pressing early in the first half. But his team's defense was very quick, and he hoped to capitalize by forcing mistakes before the Chargers could settle into a rhythm. He would have to watch the foul situation closely. The Hornets' bench strength was their Achilles heel.

"OK, everybody relax. They're probably about ready to start the second half," Lee said, glancing at his watch. "If you have any questions, bring 'em up now."

"How's it going, Chuck?" Ellis asked.

Sitting at press row, Haigler looked up from his notes and saw the Hornets' sports information director standing behind him. "Not so good for the Tar Heels. That big kid Hazzard recruited is killing them on the boards."

Ellis nodded and put his hands in his pockets.

Haigler said, "Smith will have to make some changes. I don't think he can go man-to-man with them. One thing's for sure, this cavernous cavern is hurting everybody's depth perception. I think that is definitely screwing up the Tar Heels' three-point shooting. They've only hit two for ten thus far."

"I'm on my way back to the press room. Can I get you

anything?" Ellis asked.

"Yeah, how about finding out who killed the Chargers' coach?" Haigler said.

"Anything else?" Ellis asked, smiling.

"Nope. But if you find out, share it with me, OK? I'll credit you with half of the byline."

"You're all heart, Chuck. See you after our game." Ellis walked off toward the pressroom.

Haigler turned his attention back to the court. The buzzer sounded and the two teams walked to the jump circle. The Tar Heels' guard, Worley, stole the ball on the tip-off and threw a perfect strike to a breaking forward for a high-flying slam dunk. Carolina was fired up for the second half.

Midway through the second half, UCLA found itself in a tie ball game. That was precisely what Walt Hazzard had hoped to avoid. Smith's team was hitting a scorching 65 percent from the floor, 52 percent from three-point range. They had found the mark.

Several times the Bruins forced the ball inside and lost it to the sticky-fingered Tar Heels. A boisterous crowd surged with the fierce competition. The tug-of-war provided ten lead changes. With less than four minutes to go, the Tar Heels capitalized on a back-door play set up by a thinned man-to-man UCLA defense that had been deployed to stop the three-pointers. The Tar Heels' forward, Bissel, banked in a reverse lay-up and was fouled by UCLA's center, his fourth. When the foul shot swished through the cords, Carolina gained a four-point lead, 86-82, with 1:40 to go.

UCLA missed on its next attempt, a partially blocked jump shot from the top of the key. The Tar Heels spread out, passing and dribbling to run time off the clock. They held the ball successfully for thirty seconds, when an errant pass from a forward in the frontcourt soared over a guard's head in the backcourt. The Bruins' fleet-footed guard, Kochek, raced the ball downcourt and jammed in a punctuated two-pointer. UCLA was only two down with fifty-one seconds to go: 86-84.

* * *

Smith called a time-out. In his well-known nasal tone, he calmly instructed his players to settle down. He still wanted them in the four corners, but emphasized that they were failing to go for the basket and were overcontrolling the ball.

When play resumed, Carolina dribbled up the court and ran into a tough Bruin defense, a sagging man-to-man. UCLA attempted several double-team traps in the backcourt. With less than thirty seconds to go—on one of the double teams—Worley broke for the basket. The double-teamed swingman looped a pass to him. A Bruin forward moved in to cut him off a half step too late. He was whistled for blocking.

Hazzard signaled for a time-out. It served two purposes: he wanted Worley to think about his foul shots, and it gave him time to diagram a play, optioning Terrel, the power forward, or Wessley, the center.

At the other bench, Dean Smith cautioned his players not to foul and instructed them to play a tight man-to-man. He said nothing to Worley about the critical free throws.

When the buzzer sounded, both teams broke from their huddles and returned to the court. Worley stepped to the charity stripe and coolly sank both shots: UNC-88, UCLA-84.

The Bruins in-bounded the ball quickly. Kochek, their point guard, zipped the ball to the power forward off a pick-and-roll. He swished a three-point jump shot from above the top of the key with nineteen seconds remaining in the game: UNC-88, UCLA-87. The crowd noise was ear-splitting.

UCLA pressed as the Tar Heels started to in-bound the ball. Bissel had trouble spotting the open man. A split second before he would have been whistled on a five-second violation, he spotted Chaney, the other forward, breaking three-quarters down the hardwood. He heaved a long pass over Chaney's head, who caught the ball on the first bounce and scored on a twisting lay-up: UNC-90, UCLA-87.

The Bruins called their last time-out with fourteen seconds to go. Troy knew their only hope was a possible three-pointer to tie and a quick steal to win, or two quick unanswered buckets. He watched as Hazzard diagrammed another play on a chalkboard.

As play resumed, the Bruins successfully completed an in-bounds pass to Kochek. He raced across the timeline and lofted a long pass to Terrel in the corner. The Tar Heels had him covered, but he fired up the three-point shot anyway. It missed by inches and caromed off to Wessley in the middle of the lane, not more than seven feet from the basket. He lofted a sky-hook that banked in. Six seconds remained on the clock: UNC-90, UCLA-89.

The Tar Heels quickly in-bounded the ball to their guard, Worley. The Bruins promptly fouled him on an attempted steal. Four seconds remained. Worley stepped to the line and canned the front end of a one-and-one opportunity. When he hit the bonus shot, UCLA still had a chance with a quick three-pointer: UNC-92, UCLA-89.

As Terrel released a desperation Bruin shot from thirty-five feet out, the buzzer sounded and the red light behind the basket blinked on simultaneously. The ball caromed hard off the glass. North Carolina won 92-89.

* Forty-one *

Between games, Troy Burton walked up to the Plaza level
to buy two beers and Nachos Grande. The aroma of fresh
popcorn, beer, and steaming Superdogs wafted through the
noisy, crowded corridors. Troy had read some Superdome
statistics in the program. It had numerous and varied outlets
for merchandising food and drink: forty-four concession
stands, five cocktail lounges, eight bars, portable cocktail
and beer bars, rolling food stands, a cafeteria, and a gourmet
restaurant just below the Stadium Club.

He stepped up to one of the bars. After purchasing two
cups of beer, he walked toward a Nachos Grande stand and
felt a tap on his shoulder.

"Mr. Burton, I need to speak with you for a moment,"
Teague said.

Troy turned, nearly spilling the beer. "Anything
wrong?"

"No, I just wish you wouldn't wander off from your seat
without making sure our agents are still behind you. We
nearly lost sight of you."

"Watching the cheerleaders?"

Teague looked around. No one seemed to be paying any
attention to them. "Actually, they're scanning the crowd."

"Do you think somebody is going to gun us down in front
of all these witnesses?" Troy asked, lowering his voice in
the crowded corridor.

Teague shook his head. "Not really. It pays to be careful,
though."

"Is he here?" Troy asked.

Teague nodded. "Right above you in his private suite."

"Which one?"

Teague hesitated.

"For Christ's sake, I'm just curious. Don't you think I —"

"Number 53," Teague said, interrupting Troy.

"What about Dolci's men?" Troy asked under his breath.

"We haven't spotted any. Frankly, I think the whole thing is over. The man wouldn't have come here if he planned any violence. He'd want to be as far away as possible."

"Here comes John Windsor, the president of the Foundation. I'd better speak to him," Troy said, looking over Teague's shoulder.

"I'll see you back at the hotel." Teague walked away.

"A new member?" Windsor asked, pointing toward Teague.

"No, just a friend from New Orleans. Enjoy the game?"

"Yes, but I'm afraid Dr. Thorpe didn't," said Windsor, frowning.

"Why? He's a graduate of Chapel Hill. He should be ecstatic."

"He's a little steamed over the way one of your Stinger Club members treated him."

Windsor looked concerned. Dr. Thorpe—a wealthy, retired heart surgeon capable of leaving thousands to the Hornets' Athletic Foundation—was a personal friend of his. He had joined the gold Hornet Club two years ago and was also a big supporter of UNC's Rams Club. Troy wanted to know the particulars. "What happened? Do you know who it was?"

"I can't recall his name," Windsor said. "I believe he's one of the Stinger officers. He's sitting right behind the doctor. Apparently, he said something to the effect that blue coats shouldn't be sitting in the Hornet section. Dr. Thorpe knew the remark was directed at him."

Although the Stinger Club operated under the umbrella of the Athletic Foundation, it met independently. Only one of its members served on the Foundation's Board of Directors, Mike Collier, last year's Stinger president. John Windsor did not have time to keep up with the Stinger Club's activities. That was Troy's duty as executive director.

Troy recalled the V.I.P. seating chart. He knew the important patrons and memorized their seating location. This made it easy for him to bring forth a mental picture. He remembered whom he had placed behind Dr. Thorpe. "Is he medium height with thin, light hair?"

Windsor nodded.

"Damn, that's Frank Jeffers, the president of the Stinger club. Of all the people, I figured he'd have better manners. That's why I put him in that area. He's letting his emotions carry him away. If we piss-off our Chapel Hill friends, we can kiss a hell of a lot of money good-bye." Troy suddenly realized his mind was back on his job.

"How well I know. That's why I wanted to let you know about it. Maybe you can speak to him," Windsor suggested.

"I will. If we are having that kind of problem with the president of our working club, I wonder what's happening with some of the rest of them that came here. If we win, they'll be punching it out during the championship. Jesus!"

Windsor laughed. The crowd began cheering loudly. The starting five were being announced. "Well, this is it—the one we've been waiting for."

"I'll pull Frank off to the side at the half," Troy said as Windsor turned to go inside the arena.

Troy walked over to a fan standing in the corridor, who had a small-screen television in his hand. The CBS analysts had already given a thorough rundown on coaches, players, and style of play. The Hornets were patient and employed pressure defense. The Chargers were a run-and-gun team. Both would attempt to dictate the tempo.

Musburger cast the Hornets in the role of the Cinderella team. Packer disagreed, commenting that no team that had come this far could be considered a Cinderella.

The effects of McLaughlin's death on the teams was discussed. Tim Sherwood, acting head coach of the Chargers, was labeled as a competent replacement. He knew McLaughlin's system as well as anybody and changes in style were not expected. Certainly, there would be a great deal of pressure on him and the team.

The fan started walking back to his seat. Troy could no longer hear the commentary. It didn't matter. He would see and hear the pre-game festivities when he returned to Charlotte. Before he left, he had given the technicians at the Learning Resources Center instructions to tape everything. He had also asked his neighbor to tape the games.

On his way back to his seat, numerous supporters stopped him. He was gratified by the recognition, but he did not delude himself—his position provided automatic social acceptance. The fund-raiser was the "insider" who sat in the stands like an associate pastor with his congregation. That was what gave him the celebrity status he enjoyed.

The teams came to center court for the tip-off. The crowd stood and the Hornet contingent chanted in unison: "GO, HORNETS, GO!"

Jenny covered her eyes. "I don't want to look. I'm too nervous."

Troy laughed. "The only thing covering your eyes will do is keep you from knowing when to cheer."

Collins won the tap and Thad Davis, the muscular 6'4" Hornet guard, controlled the ball. Dribbling across the timeline, he held up two fingers with his left hand. The Hornets settled into their patterned offense.

After working the ball around, Kevin Taylor, the power forward, had an open shot in the right corner, fifteen feet away from the basket. He fired up a brick: the ball hit nothing but air.

The Chargers' center, Jeffries, grabbed the errant shot. He zipped a quick outlet pass to his forward, Hall, who relayed the ball downcourt to Sims for an easy lay-up and the opening lead.

The Hornets missed their first seven shots, and the Chargers capitalized by jumping out to a 11-0 lead. Troy had never seen the team that cold. It was their worst start of the season. They were choking on the big apple.

Coach Lee was waiting for a television time-out. He didn't want to waste one early in the game unless absolutely necessary. As Davis dribbled across the timeline, he looked over at Lee, expecting a signal for a time-out. Instead, Lee put his hands out, palms down, a gesture signaling the astute guard to set the offense and settle the team down. Finally, the Hornets scored on a put-back shot by Collins that broke the ice.

The referee called for a TV time-out. Commercials paid the bills and fattened NCAA coffers. Lee didn't care about that. The time-out was what he needed, and time-outs were jewels to be saved.

At the Hornet bench, Coach Lee squatted and looked at his players who sat before him, toweling off. The subs and assistant coaches crowded around. On the perimeter the team physician and team manager craned their necks to see and hear.

Lee's penetrating eyes made sharp contact, and his tone—like that of a drill sergeant—boomed with resolve and confidence. "You're working the ball fine. The shots aren't falling. Don't worry, they will. Relax. Defense looks good. Keep the pressure on and they'll throw it away some more. They're missing shots, too. Thad, next time down, run the L.A. inside. Keep hustling."

Lee watched as the first half pressed on as a defensive battle, a low-scoring affair. Neither team sparkled on the offensive. Both had difficulty finding the range. The cavernous Superdome was obviously affecting depth perception. Nerves were a factor, too. Had either team managed to hit their shots, it would have been a lopsided game.

The Hornets managed to dictate the rhythm, yet their shots rimmed out, agonizingly close. The Chargers hung onto their eight-point lead until the last minute of the first half, when the Hornets hit two quick unanswered field goals and connected on the front end of a one-and-one. The halftime score: UFFM-35, UC-32.

Troy looked at the halftime statistics on the large-screen TV overhead. He imagined what was going on in the locker room.

Both coaches would obviously complain about shot selection. Neither team looked impressive statistically. The Chargers had shot a poor 40 percent, the Hornets a dismal 33. The Chargers had turned the ball over eleven times, the Hornets only five. The Hornets held a slight edge in rebounding. Normally, such lackluster performances would take a team out of the game in the first half.

That was an encouraging point for both teams, Troy mused. The Chargers held a three-point lead despite their below par shooting and ball handling. The Hornets could look at the score and see that they were within easy reach. Troy left his seat and headed for the men's room.

"Frank, may I speak with you a second?" Troy asked, trailing Jeffers to the bathroom line.

Turning around, Jeffers said, "You sure can. You're just the fellow I've been looking for. Who's the turkey that's sitting in front of me?"

Troy saw a tactful opening. "I'll have to think for a minute. Why? What's the problem?"

Jeffers flushed and raised his voice. "The old bastard keeps turning around complaining that Janet and I are yelling too loud, and it's hurting his wife's ears. He's a damn Tar Heel. Got his Carolina blue coat on. A lot of the Stinger Club members are upset. Look at all the damn blue coats that are sitting in our section. How'd they get tickets? Makes me think about all our people who had to stay home."

Troy looked around to make sure no one in the Hornet contingent was within earshot. He spoke in a conciliating tone. "You know the score. We've been able to persuade a number of Carolina supporters who live around Charlotte to support the local team. Can they help it if both their teams made it? You can't blame them for supporting their alma mater."

"Bullshit! If they're going to sit with us, they ought to wear black and gold." Jeffers stepped inside the bathroom and Troy followed.

Troy stood in a urinal line next to Jeffers and said, "I looked around. A lot of them changed coats at intermission. I think that's Dr. Thorpe sitting in front of you. He's very wealthy and could leave the university a hell of a lot of money. He's one of our Gold Hornets."

Jeffers reached the urinal, began relieving himself, and

spoke while looking at the wall. "Yeah, well he's not wearing it. He's still got that damn blue coat on."

Troy stepped to the urinal beside Jeffers and unzipped. "Did you say anything to piss him off?"

Jeffers shrugged. "He might have heard me remark about the coat."

"Maybe that's why he's still got it on. He's got as much right to be here as you do. He's contributing big bucks."

Nothing further was said until they walked outside. Troy put his arm around Jeffers' shoulders. "Look, Frank, please don't get into it with Dr. Thorpe, and try to calm down some of your other members. It will help the athletic program, and it'll help you."

"Me?"

"Dr. Thorpe's got a lot of friends on the board. You asked me to try to get you on this year. I can swing it, but not if you make a lot of waves."

"All right, I'll bite my tongue. Are you still not planning to have any Foundation cocktail parties while we're down here?"

Troy realized that Jeffers and a number of other members could not understand why the executive director had failed to plan at least one social in New Orleans. "No, I'm afraid not. We'll just have to let smaller groups make their own plans. I imagine a lot of them would rather go out on the town, anyway."

They walked back to their seats as the second half was about to start. Jenny stood with the rest of the contingent and clapped time to the Hornets' fight song. Troy joined her.

He wondered whether Jeffers had believed him. He disliked the Tar Heels as much as Jeffers, maybe more. Charlotte had languished in their shadow much too long for there not to be envy. Yet, he had a job to do, and he knew his fund-raising efforts had to wrench dollars loose from Chapel Hill's older and more established alumni.

As the teams were about to square off at center court, the childishness of the situation slapped him hard. Here adults were squabbling over what colors they were wearing. It was like allies in war failing to attack at dawn because they were too busy arguing over the uniform of the day. That was almost as absurd as killing people to fix a game.

For Troy, the start of the second half was a surreal meshing of bodies flowing, colors swirling, and objects moving. His responses were mere automatic gestures, like a lemming following its species to the sea. He was out of touch, drifting alone in a sea of humanity. During the first twelve minutes of play, the score did not register with him.

A break in the action—a UFFM time-out with 8:54 remaining—brought his thoughts back to the game. He glanced at the scoreboard: UC-65, UFFM-62. He stood and turned, peering over his shoulder at the private suites.

"Where are you going?" Jenny asked.

"To the men's room."

"Now? Can't it wait?"

"Not hardly. Want a coke or something?"

Jenny frowned. "No, thanks."

Troy walked briskly up the steps toward the exit. When he reached it, he spotted Teague standing just inside the open corridor.

"Where are you headed?"

"You know, Teague, you're really getting to be a pain in the ass. I'm going to the head to take a crap." Troy sensed that Teague was tired of maintaining surveillance.

Teague shrugged and turned his attention back to the game as play resumed.

Troy stayed in the bathroom no more than fifteen seconds. He walked to the exit, stopped, and peered around the corner to his right. Teague had turned his attention back to the court.

Troy quickly stepped out of the bathroom and turned left in the direction opposite from Teague, toward the nearest tunnel that would gain him access to other areas of the Superdome. The crowd's noise echoed inside the huge carpeted tunnel: the game was apparently intensifying.

After several minutes and two wrong turns, Troy reached the 400 level. Signs indicated which direction he needed to walk to reach suite number 53. The halls were empty. Crowd noise—muffled by the enclosed private suites that circled the arena—faded noticeably. Troy nodded at a security guard engaged in conversation with a concessionaire.

Continuing down the long, circular hallway, he finally reached suite number 53, the Tangipahoa, and stood at the door. Moist palms, heart pounding, he knocked. No answer. He pounded harder.

It opened. The large frame of a man filled the entrance. "Can I help you?"

"Yes, I need to speak with Francesco Mancotta."

"He's busy."

Troy glared at the man. He could see others in Mancotta's party staring at him, holding drinks in their hands, occasionally glancing back at the action on the court. "I don't care what he's doing. Just tell him Troy Burton wants to talk, now! I'm alone. You can search me if you like."

"Wait a minute," the man said, closing the door in Troy's face.

Standing, waiting, glancing around the empty hall, Troy shoved his right hand in his pocket. Finally, the door opened.

"I understand you want to talk to me? What can I do for you?" Mancotta asked, staring at Troy.

"Nothing, now. But there was a hell of a lot you could've done a long time ago," Troy said, recognizing Mancotta from pictures the FBI had shown him.

"What are you talking about? I don't even know who you are."

"You know damn well who I am or you wouldn't have come to this door. But what the hell, go ahead and play your silly game. You people seem to be especially good at that."

Mancotta said nothing.

"Never mind, I can see I'm wasting my time," Burton said, shaking his head, turning away. Suddenly, impulsively, he spun around, swinging a hard right-hand punch that landed solidly on Mancotta's left cheek. The mob boss reeled backward into his bodyguard's arms.

Troy stood glaring at Mancotta, who almost fell to the floor before he was caught. Several of the women in the room gasped as the bodyguard lifted Mancotta to his feet, then lunged at Troy.

"No!" Mancotta yelled. "Leave him alone."

Fists clenched, the guard stepped aside as Mancotta regained his composure and moved toward Troy. Standing face to face, they glared at each other. Mancotta removed a handkerchief from his breast coat pocket and dabbed his bleeding lip. "I don't ever want to see your fucking face again," Mancotta said. "If I do, you're a dead man."

Troy felt Mancotta's warm breath and smelled a twinge of alcohol. In that moment, there was total understanding: Mancotta would not pursue him. Troy turned and walked down the hall, hearing the door slam behind him.

He found his way back to the Plaza level, passing Teague in the hall. The agent was apparently relieved to see him, but said nothing.

"Where have you been?" Jenny asked as Troy sat down.

He ignored the question, looked at the court, and asked in rapid succession, "Who called the time-out? Who's got the ball?"

"The Chargers called the time-out and it's their ball," Jenny responded, clapping time to the Hornets' fight song.

Troy nodded, then watched the teams break from their huddles. The Hornets led 79-76 with forty-eight seconds remaining.

As the teams took their positions on the floor, Troy sat quietly in a crowd that was caught like a fly in a web of tension. The Chargers' point guard, Ennis, received the inbounds pass and promptly lofted the ball to Jeffries standing near the basket. Collins guarded him. They leaped together. The ball went off Collins' fingertips. Jeffries caught it in midair, twisted, and jammed it through: UC-79, UFFM-78. The referee whistled a foul on Collins. Jeffries stepped to the charity stripe, and Coach Lee signaled Davis to call time-out.

At the Hornets' bench, Lee exhorted, "Let's not give them the game. Make them work for the shot, but don't foul." Lee looked at the clock. "There's only forty-four seconds left. The shot clock's off. If he hits his free throw, I want you to hold it for the last shot. Thad, run the motion offense and call time-out with about ten seconds to go. Spread it high. TC, you post low. If we get to a situation where we need to foul and you get my signal, make it Hall or Jeffries."

The buzzer sounded and Jeffries stepped to the line. His free throw hit the front of the rim, the glass, and banked in. The score was tied: UFFM-79, UC-79.

As the Chargers pressed, the Hornets inbounded the ball. Thames passed it to Collins. Unorthodox as it was to have a center bring the ball upcourt, the tactic worked smoothly. Collins was a superb dribbler. Jeffries was unable to stop him. Even in a double-team situation, Collins' height and long arms enabled him to quickly find the open man.

He worked the ball across the timeline. As he dished off to Davis, twenty-three seconds remained. The Hornets worked the ball high in the frontcourt to free a player off a screen, pull back out, and penetrate past the hash mark once again. With eleven seconds remaining, they called time-out.

Coach Sherwood instructed his Chargers to go to a man-to-man on the inbounds play and shift immediately to a 2-3 zone. He decided to gamble by instructing his players not to call a time-out if they rebounded the ball. Instead, when the Hornets put up the shot, Ennis was to slip downcourt and look for a long pass.

Coach Lee diagrammed an out-of-bounds play, and then an option to either Collins cutting across the top of the lane or to Taylor in the corner. "Don't put it up too soon—we've got eleven seconds. Crash the boards and get the tip-in, but don't go over anybody's back." He looked at the players as they all stacked hands and broke from the huddle.

Lee watched as the inbounds play went to Mac Thames, who quickly tossed it back to Thad Davis. Davis spotted Collins coming toward the foul line from low post and bounced a pass to him. The crowd roared as Collins dribbled once, cut toward the basket, and flipped up a scoop shot. The ball hit the iron, rolled around the rim, and off into the waiting hands of Jeffries.

The Charger center promptly lofted a two-handed pass over his head. It sailed over Ennis' head, who caught up with the ball, racing downcourt three steps ahead of Davis. He dribbled twice and leaped, soaring, suspended in air, and crushed the ball through. A split second later the final buzzer sounded and the red basket light blinked on. UFFM had won. Jubilant UFFM players and staff poured onto the court, celebrating. Lee rose from the bench to find the UFFM coach and congratulate him.

Troy looked at the scoreboard and watched it change: UFFM-81, UC-79. The crowd divided: some sat mute; others screamed wildly. He looked at Jenny as she lowered her head dejectedly. Tears streamed down her cheeks.

His eyes moistened. It all flashed back through his mind: the death of Drop; the murder of McLaughlin; the loss of Donnie and Russ; the confrontation with Mancotta.

All for nothing? No. He knew he could get the story out. He would give Chuck Haigler the scoop of his career.

Then he would go out and buy a puppy.

ABOUT THE AUTHOR

Roy H. Parker graduated <u>cum laude</u> from the University of North Carolina at Charlotte (UNCC), where he later served as executive director of the Athletic Foundation. During his tenure, UNCC streaked to the Final Four in Cinderella fashion. "Fortunately, nothing like what I created in this book ever happened," Mr. Parker states firmly.

In 1986 Mr. Parker founded Parker Communications, an advertising, marketing, and public relations firm. He lives in Charlotte with his wife, Libby, and is at work on his next novel.

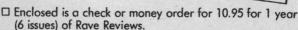